ALICE THE TORCH

THE WONDERLAND COURT SERIES

A MAGIC OF ARCANA UNIVERSE SERIES

ASHLEY MCLEO

MERAKI PRESS

ISBN e-book: 978-1-947245-67-9

ISBN paperback: 978-1-947245-74-7

Cover by: Get Covers

Editing by: Jen McDonnel of Bird's Eye Books

Proofing by: Kurt Leopoldt

CHAPTER I

Despite how odd Wonderland was, how it made me question basically *everything*, I knew three things with absolute certainty:

1) Hatter was supposed to be playing chess with Alran, but I could feel his eyes on me, watching.

2) I hated that being queen meant talking to so many people on the daily.

3) A group of gryphons were approaching the castle from the sea—a new development if there ever was one. Since my aunt's imprisonment, fae had been *leaving* Wonderland.

The last point was the most concerning. Not the leaving part; if I'd been trapped on an island for decades, I'd want to leave too.

But who did the gryphons belong to?

I leaned out the window of the North Tower suite, where the guys were staying. It was actually the same grouping of rooms that the Red Queen had given me and my friends upon our arrival, but after the Aether Trials, when I asked if they wanted to move, the males declined. In Hatter's words, 'the tower was large enough for the massive elf Alran, the blue-haired dwarf Sansu, and him'.

I noted he didn't include me.

Apparently, now that I was seen as a real royal, now that more eyes were upon me, I could not stay in the same room as the guys. But I did get to hang out here, when we had a rare free moment.

Squinting into the breeze rushing off the sea, I tried to figure out who was stopping by. Was that a green flag on one of the creatures? What did that mean?

"Alice?" Henri asked. "Are you well?"

"Yeah," I replied. "Someone is coming for a visit. Does a green flag mean anything to you two?"

Chairs scraped the stone floor, and the next thing I knew, the elf and faerie were squishing me between their broad shoulders to peer outside.

"That's a royal escort," Alran breathed. "It has to be."

"Agreed. Rather small, isn't it?" Still, Hatter looked awed.

It hit me that they were going off what they'd learned in history books, or what their parents had told them. Both men were a little older than me, and though they potentially could have seen a royal escort when they were children, they might not remember it well. Wonderland had been isolated for so long.

"Green indicates the Riverlands," Alran added. "They must have heard of the Red Queen's imprisonment."

My eyes widened. "The Riverlands . . . wasn't my father from there?"

Was I about to meet distant family? Were they here to help?

"Indeed. He was a Torna," Alran replied. "If this is Queen Aquatia, she is a relative of yours."

"Who else could it be?"

"Messengers," Hatter answered. "Or perhaps the king, Elan Geysis. He's of the Cove Court, though, so not a direct relation to the White line. The prince could come alone too."

"Where will they land?"

Hatter and Alran exchanged an amused look before Henri turned his full attention to me.

As often happened when he looked at me with those intense, evergreen eyes, my breath hitched.

"We don't know," he admitted. "We're about as knowledgeable of the castle as you."

Well, duh. Until days ago, my companions were underground rebels. Neither had stepped foot on these grounds for years.

"Let's find someone who can show us to the landing pad."

I whirled, barely hearing Henri mutter "Landing pad?" and Alran reply, "No idea where she gets these terms from" before darting out the door.

We only had to make it down the tower stairwell to find a castle guard—a tall, gangly man dressed in light leather and metal armor. At the sight of me, he fell into a deep bow.

"Princess Alice."

"You don't have to do that." I cringed at the title, though I supposed it was better than 'Queen,' which many people still used. It was like no one could believe that I didn't want the crown.

I gestured to the guys trailing me. "We don't know our way around Heart Castle yet. Can you show us where people from the Riverlands would arrive?"

"We have . . . guests?" The soldier blinked.

"Seems so." I shrugged. "I'm as surprised as you, but I'd prefer not to keep them waiting."

"But of course. This way."

We trailed the guard through the castle, passing others as we went. Each person stopped and bowed to me, and every time, my discomfort grew. As with using the title, I told them the gesture wasn't necessary, but they insisted.

Evidently, a few days wasn't enough time to change the fabric of a kingdom.

Stepping outside into the salty sea air was such a relief. Fewer people were present, and those who were had their eyes focused on the visitors dismounting their gryphons.

I scanned the newcomers too, noting that most were dressed in armor heavier than that of the guards in my castle, clearly here for protection. Only two wore normal clothing.

Well, sorta normal.

The woman donned a lovely green dress that seemed a touch too nice for riding. One of those simple and elegant pieces that probably cost far more than it looked like it should. Despite the long skirt, she somehow dismounted with grace and poise, and once on the ground, she pulled back her wind-swept, bright red hair, revealing pointed ears, and extended her silver-veined wings, stretching.

Wings and pointed ears meant they were faeries, rather than elves. The latter did not have wings.

The male fae was younger and dressed in pants, a tunic, and a jacket, also green, and lined with gold. His boots shone to high heaven, and I got the sense that, though he was dressed for travel, given the chance, he'd be much more fashionable.

"Welcome." I approached the pair. "I'm Alice White. And you are . . . ?"

Behind me, Hatter sputtered, and I instantly realized my error. Clearly, these two were royals.

Would they expect me to bow, like all the guards we'd passed had done for me? But I was a royal too. What should I do?

"Uh, sorry," I added, feeling like I should fess up. "I'm new here and don't know all the courtly stuff."

The young man's eyes twinkled with amusement. "That's refreshing. I recently had the pleasure of meeting people from your world. They struck me as being that way too." He paused and bowed. "I'm Prince Halad Vapos of the Riverlands. And please allow me to introduce my mother, Queen Aquatia Vapos."

The queen inclined her head, and, feeling on display, I performed a curtsy that must have looked beyond awkward, because Aquatia did not acknowledge it, but rather turned to her escort and began giving orders.

Cringing, I twisted back to the prince. "Your last name isn't Torna?"

I'd been told my father's people ruled the Riverlands.

"No," Halad replied. "They are close relatives, but the royal line is actually House Vapos."

"I see." So many intricacies of this realm still caught me by surprise. "Well, it's good to meet you, and please, call me Alice."

"Halad will do for me too." He leaned closer and winked. "But don't get so friendly with my mother. Not right away, anyhow."

"Wouldn't dream of it. So, what brought you here?"

"We heard of the recent overthrow of Sela White." Her business with the guards done, Queen Aquatia came forward and answered me. "And we had to see that the rebellion had truly happened. Given we were even permitted in Wonderland's airspace, I presume it had. No one has been allowed this close to the island for years. Do we have you to thank for that development? You said your name was Alice White?"

"It is," I said. "I'm the daughter of Isobel White and

Frederic Torna. And yes, my aunt is in the dungeons. She's been sentenced to death. The execution will take place tomorrow, actually—for both my aunt and her king consort."

I didn't know what Queen Aquatia would say next, but the brilliant smile she gave me certainly was not what I'd expected. "It's about time."

I snorted. "I take it you weren't part of her fan club?"

The queen laughed delicately. "She was horrible, even as a child. Sela and I never saw eye-to-eye. Your mother, however, was a dear childhood friend."

A pregnant pause followed, in which I debated asking my question before I could hold it back no longer. "Did you try to help my mother? When the Red Queen took over."

Aquatia's poise faltered, but only briefly. The moment she regained her composure, she nodded. "I did. As did the Crown of the Snowcap Court . . . but we failed and lost many lives. Your aunt had this kingdom firmly in her thrall. And many creatures at her disposal. Dangerous ones." Her lips thinned. "Beasts that the rest of Faerie is not adept at fighting, because they're native to this area only. Eventually, we had to leave the island to her, for the good of our own people."

The part about the creatures of this island tracked. My aunt was a strong, aether-blessed fae, capable of controlling herds of bandersnatch, queen krakens, and even a jabberwocky—which, thank the old gods, I had not seen. If those beasts converged to fight fae armies, that would be a hurdle indeed.

"I do hope you won't hold that against us," the queen added, her tone genuine.

I realized I was staring at her, probably making her feel awful. "I don't."

It wasn't their fault that my crazy aunt had taken over the kingdom. Could they have done more? Maybe. But maybe not. I'd never be able to change the past, but I did want to help create a new, brighter future for the land of my birth.

"I hope you've come as allies?" I asked.

The queen smiled. "We have."

"Then, how about a tour?" With a flourish of my hand, I welcomed them into the castle.

"You'll have to excuse me." I gave a sheepish smile as we went inside and I realized this 'tour' would be like the blind leading the blind. "I don't know my way around the place, but I do know where the throne room is. We can start there and hopefully find someone more qualified to continue our tour."

Walking between the royals, I led the way through the halls, relieved the guys had followed us whenever the queen or Halad remarked on a painting or a tapestry, and one of my friends was able to add more context. Henri and Alran had more general information about the king-dom's history and art scene.

Although the other royals were no doubt only trying to make small talk, my lack of knowledge only amplified the sense that I didn't belong here. That I was not the person to lead this land, despite what the people said.

"And here we are." I turned into the throne room. "I—"

Oh, my hell.

The pixie twins, Dee and Dum, were dancing their asses off in the center of the room as a group of male fae appreciatively took in the show.

I closed my eyes, unable to believe the timing. What the heck were these tiny tarts even doing in here?!

"They seem like they're having fun," Halad remarked with an amused smile.

His mother, on the other hand, simply watched.

Is she scandalized? Does she find humor in this?

As her face was a mask, I had no idea.

"They must be drunk," I lied. The girls would totally do this sober. They were boy-crazy and always doing comical, sometimes absurd, things for attention.

I cleared my throat. "Hi there, Dee and Dum! What's going on?"

The twins whirled in unison, wide smiles falling from their faces. The men just stood stiff as boards. The servants were meant to be redecorating the throne room, disposing of the horrible hearts that Sela White loved to adorn every surface of the kingdom with.

My aunt probably would lop off their heads for standing around.

"Alice!" Dum's cheeks pinked. "Hatter and Alran! What are you doing here?"

"Showing Queen Aquatia and Prince Halad of the Riverlands the throne room." I crossed my arms over my chest. Usually, I didn't care what these two did, but damn, this was embarrassing!

"A prince, you say?" Dee stepped forward, wide eyes blinking.

A snort of a laugh rolled out of Halad. "She did. A single one too!"

"Oooooh!" Dum piped up. "Then allow me to introduce myself. I'm Lady Dumtalora."

Lady?! Since when?!

Unable to believe the gall of the pint-sized fae darting toward us, I twisted and caught Hatter's eye. In an effort to keep in his laughter, his fist was pressed to his mouth. I supposed he was used to this kind of crazy—the girls used to flirt with him all the time.

You have competition, I mouthed.

"Why are they walking?" the queen asked suddenly.

"Excuse me?" I gave the ruler of the Riverland Court my full attention.

"They're walking. Pixies often fly because it's faster." She examined the sisters shrewdly. "They could have already been to us by now, and as such, are wasting precious seconds that could have been used to steal my son's heart."

I exhaled at the joke, but the reason for the pixies' method of movement kind of sobered the humor. "My aunt's witches sealed their wings together. They can't use them."

Queen Aquatia's eyebrows knitted together. "And you did not undo the spell? You are aether-blessed, correct? Aether magic should be able to reverse that."

"I am," I said, scanning the room and noticing that the male fae who'd been watching the pixies were gone. Apparently, they'd seized the chance to run off. "But I didn't know about my aether magic until recently. The twins are my friends—which, maybe given what you saw, I shouldn't admit to—but I didn't want to ruin their wings in my inexperienced attempt to fix them."

"I see," Aquatia replied as the twins reached us and fell into perfect curtsies.

"Good day, Your Grace and Prince Halad." They spoke as one, as though they'd rehearsed this moment.

"Good day," the queen replied. "Your names?"

"Lady Dumtalora," Dum repeated, her attention only briefly flickering to the prince, who stood regally at his mother's side.

"Lady Tweedle Dee. Two words," Dee said, beaming.

"Lovely names," Aquatia replied.

"A pleasure, ladies." Now that his mother had been properly respected, Halad knelt and extended his hand, palm up.

Together, the pixies rushed him, placing their palms on his in a sort of handshake. As they did so, Dee closed her eyes, as if in ecstasy.

The girl was going to pass out from touching a living, breathing prince.

However, their fawning was short-lived, as Queen Aquatia redirected their attention.

"Alice here tells me that your wings are bound by a witch's spell. Would you like me to attempt to undo it?"

Tiny gasps pierced the air.

"Could you?" Dum asked, eyes shining up at the queen.

"We would *so* love to fly again," Dee added, her hand still comically placed on the prince's.

"I will do my best," the queen said, and turned to me. "You should watch. Perhaps rest your hand on my forearm so you can feel the aether flow. Learn how it's done."

"I-I'd love that," I stammered, taken aback by her offer.

I hadn't had a mentor since learning about my aether magic, and now, here one was, offering her wisdom.

"Do you think you could help me in other areas too?" I asked, hoping I wasn't pushing my luck. "I have questions, but my aunt is the only other aether-blessed fae on the island."

"She'll be of little help," the queen scoffed. "Of course, I'll teach you what I'm able. I can stay a day or two, if you wish?"

"That'd be great. We're even having a feast tonight, if you'd like to join."

The prince arched his eyebrows. "A feast to celebrate an execution? That's rather gauche."

"Not for that," I assured him. "It's more so I can meet

the high-born fae of the city. They groveled before my aunt, but I suspect—or maybe I should say I hope—it was more out of fear than respect. I figure they deserve a chance to meet me, and I'll assess from there."

Really, I wanted to meet them all before the execution so I knew who to keep my eye on. The event would be public—as the fae of Wonderland requested—so knowing who my aunt had considered an ally, and therefore, who might pose a problem, would allow me to breathe easier.

"That's fair. Halad and I would love to meet them too. My son here has a sort of sixth sense about people."

"Great." Tension that I hadn't realized I'd been carrying seeped from my shoulders. "I'll make sure you're at my table."

The ruler of the Riverlands smiled kindly and turned back to the pixies. "Do you mind being lifted?"

The twins shook their heads.

"Halad?" Aquatia nodded for her son to assist the pixies, who shared an excited look before carefully climbing into his open palms.

The prince lifted the pair so that his mother did not have to kneel. Once they were in position, the queen silently extended her arm in my direction. I took it, in awe of how classy and graceful she was.

Had I been her, I would have crouched on the floor to work my magic, but not Queen Aquatia. She didn't stoop. She recognized that if she extended a helping hand, others would take it, without question.

This is why I'm not cut out to be a queen.

"I do not mean for it to hurt, but this might sting," Aquatia murmured to the pixies. "Brace yourselves."

Dum rolled her shoulders back as Dee clenched her fists and gritted her teeth.

Aquatia nodded her approval, and suddenly, white light trickled from her fingers toward the girls.

Because I was touching her, I could feel the jolt of magic as it started flowing.

"Pay attention to when it unzips the wings," Aquatia murmured.

I did as she said, studying the way her magic swept over them, caressing the edges. How it flowed, and its precise temperature and vibration.

Though, I didn't know *how* I was noticing these things —Aquatia herself likely had a lot to do with it.

The moment the twins' wings separated and unfurled to their natural position, green smoke seeped from the membranes, disappearing into the air.

"The spell is undone," the queen announced.

The pixies began to cry in elation, their wings back to normal and fluttering as they lifted themselves into the air.

"That's what the smoke meant?" I asked.

"It was. And now that you've felt how my magic moved through me, you should be able to replicate it, if the need arises."

I gave a hollow laugh. "Let's hope it doesn't."

Still smiling, I looked on as the twins hugged each

other. Since the witches had spelled them, they'd put on a brave show, but I was sure they'd been miserable.

"Shall we get started on other lessons?" Aquatia asked. "Perhaps Halad and I can teach you a few more tricks and skills before the feast."

"I'd love that," I said, excitement bursting through me.

Before their unanticipated arrival, I'd resigned myself to learning about aether magic through trial and error. This was much more preferable. Everyone needed a teacher.

"But let's move to the gardens for a bit more space," I suggested, well aware that once we left the servants would feel more inclined to continue ridding the palace of the many decorative hearts that plagued it.

"Indeed," the queen replied with a smile. "Lead the way, my dear."

CHAPTER 2

"It was so amazing watching your lessons today, Alice!" Dee flew in through my room's open window like this was her private quarters too. She wore a crimson gown, and her red hair gleamed in its curled, half-up, half-down 'do.

As I was still in my robe, I felt underdressed.

"Queen Aquatia is wonderful, isn't she?" Dee added when I didn't reply right away.

"The best," Dum agreed, following close behind. Matching her own hair, she wore blue, but unlike her sister, had opted for a full updo.

I smirked. Though I had to agree with them, the pixies were over-the-top with their praise. For hours, they'd doted on the queen, complimenting her, exclaiming when she worked her aether magic. No one could say that they weren't grateful that she'd unstuck their wings, that was for sure.

Hell, I was grateful too. Queen Aquatia had taught me many new ways to use my own aether magic. Though it would take a lot of practice to become super powerful with it, I was prepared to stretch myself and find my potential.

"Halad too." Dee sighed and came to stand on the vanity I'd been sitting in front of. "I can't believe you're not done with your makeup, Alice."

"I'm in the middle of it."

Fae cosmetics were spread out before me in a kaleido-scope of colors. I'd already done my eyes, opting for a more natural shade of gold that complemented my wings, though I had been tempted to try a lilac-teal shimmer.

Here, they favored outlandish hairstyles and color palettes. In the human world, they'd be deemed gaudy, but for fae, there was no such thing. I supposed that when your hair, skin, and eyes could be any color of the rain-bow, it made sense. This realm was simply more vibrant.

I fingered the pot of lilac-teal powder. One day, I'd try it, but not today. It would be too much with my dress.

"Do you think he'd be open to dating across king-doms?" Dum asked.

"What? Who?" Had they been talking and I spaced?

"Halad, of course!" Dum frowned at me. "Honestly, Alice. Don't you *ever* listen to me?"

My lips pressed together as I held in my laugh.

"What's so funny?" Dum demanded, stomping her tiny foot.

"Nothing," I assured her, face straightening a touch.

"I just . . . didn't think you were so serious about Halad."
I paused. "Shouldn't he marry a princess or something?"

"Dee and I have royal ties." Dum lifted her chin and turned to the mirror, tilting her head from side to side, assessing her look for this evening. "Haven't we mentioned that?"

"You haven't," I said, glad to be off the topic of Halad for a bit. The man was charming as hell, and I loved the girls, but size mattered.

In a lot of things, actually.

I snorted at my joke, earning me a glare from Dum in the mirror.

"Tell me about your family," I said instead, pretty sure she wouldn't appreciate my humor.

"Well, the Pixie Court is really old," Dum started, selecting a palette of blue eye shadow from among my cosmetics. Apparently, they were getting ready here, too. "But we don't maintain a castle like Wonderland. We're travelers."

"But our kind *do* claim large territories in the woods," Dee added. "We don't bum around other kingdoms."

"Of course not!" Dum looked scandalized. "We have class!"

"Anyone can see that," I assured her, picking up a neutral lip rouge and painting my lips carefully. "So, your family was royal? What happened?"

"It was a long, long, *long* time ago, but one of our ancestors was overthrown," Dee explained as she painted her own lips crimson. "Our bloodline is originally from the Summer Court, you see."

"Is that far away?"

"Quite. We relocated here because the king at that time was welcoming newcomers to Wonderland Island. Our ancestor even lived in the castle on the far side of the island for a while. Like we are now!" Dee looked around the room.

"Don't tell me that my aunt kicked you out of your palace?" I dusted my cheeks with blush.

"Oh, no. Our family set out on their own before that. Like I said, we're travelers."

"Well, now this is your home, if you want."

The pair beamed at me, any earlier annoyance gone from their faces.

Since I was done with my makeup, I rose. Across the room, my dress hung on a screen. Like the other times I'd gazed upon it, the sight made my heart beat faster.

The gown was sleek and silk, just how I preferred, but while black was my color of choice, this one was a glorious shade of teal, and the off-the-shoulder neckline was decorated with gold silk roses.

The colors and symbol of House White. My family.

I sucked in a breath. It had been so long since I'd had a family—people who cared for me. Before Wonderland, Jax, the ex-boyfriend I'd given everything to, my first—and so far, my only—love, was the sole person I could count on. We'd always said that, after I aged out of Xavier Doru's contract, we would travel the world.

Once upon a time, I was certain that we'd always be together. That he was the only person who'd ever understand me, because we'd grown up the same way: under the thumb of a vampire lord. Killers.

That was no longer the case.

Now I had Hatter and the pixies in my corner. Alran and Sansu were becoming my friends too.

And soon, I'd find my sister. After the execution, I'd set out.

My heart clenched at the idea of seeing Elise— meeting her, really—again. Though I had no intention of remaining in Faerie, I had to admit that Elise would make departing more difficult.

Maybe she'd want to go to the human world with me? After all, what had Faerie given her? She'd been kidnapped as a child and led to believe her family was dead.

Perhaps, once we got to know one another a bit, I could convince her to leave.

"It really is beautiful, isn't it?" Dum cooed from behind me as I glided to a stop before the gown.

"Gorgeous," I murmured, fingers trailing over the smooth silk. "To be honest, I'm shocked that it exists."

Had my aunt heard of a gown with these colors, the creator would have lost his or her head. But to think that someone could have made such a glorious garment in the few days my aunt had been imprisoned was preposterous.

"Isadora started working on it the moment she met you," Dee said.

I whirled about. "Isadora made this?!"

Damn! Color me officially impressed.

"Of course. She's a talented seamstress, but even she just finished it yesterday," Dee said.

"I'll have to thank her when I see her," I replied, pulling the dress down and rounding the screen.

Luckily, I didn't need assistance changing—a fact that many in this world seemed to think was absurd. The dress slipped on like it was made of water, caressing my skin.

Once everything was in place, I stepped out from behind the screen. The pixies gasped, and when I saw myself in the mirror, I understood the reaction . . . and had to agree.

The gown fit me perfectly, and was stunning. Easily the most beautiful thing I'd ever worn.

"The color looks so good with your hair!" Dee soared over to land on my shoulder. Smiling, she pushed a lock of white-blonde hair behind my ear. "You look beautiful."

"Henri won't be able to take his eyes off you!" Dum added saucily.

Heat crept into my cheeks.

A few days ago, I would have denied anything was blossoming between Henri and me, but that was impossible now. We flirted too openly, and every time I turned, he was watching me.

"Thanks, girls," I said. "Help me choose earrings, will you?"

My pulse raced as the pixies and I neared the Grand Hall.

Already, music—the lyrical notes of a harp and other stringed instruments—and voices, poured down the corridor. It sounded fun in there, boisterous even, but all I could think was that fae of all kinds were in that hall, waiting for me. Waiting to see me. To judge whether I was worthy of the crown. I suspected that only a minority were waiting to prove themselves *to me*.

In my opinion, most should grovel, but I wasn't so optimistic to think they would. In the face of my aunt, the nobles of this land may have been as powerless to change Wonderland as the poor fae, but they'd still kissed her ass. They'd laughed at her jokes, gone to her croquet matches. They had attended the Red Queen's feasts and let their brothers and sisters on the less affluent side of town starve.

My lips tightened as I recalled the neighborhood rebel headquarters was located in. Those fae had been all skin and bones.

No matter how little the nobles thought it necessary, no matter that they could claim they were enchanted, they would need to apologize. Good people like Hatter and Alran and Sansu had stepped up to the plate to free

Wonderland. People who had almost nothing to give. The nobles? They'd done nothing. So now they'd acknowledge those faults, and step it up to make the court a better place.

Two dozen or so paces away, guards stood at the opening of the Grand Hall, and between them waited Hatter.

"Dashing," Dee whispered.

"I'll say," I agreed.

He wore a jacket, black, with gold buttons and embroidery around the wrists, and black trousers. His long, black hair was pulled back so his pointed ears appeared more pronounced than normal. It was only when I got closer that the finishing detail of his outfit became plain. Tucked in his front jacket pocket was a teal square of silk, a tribute to my family.

Simple. Classic. Not too extravagant. Loyal.

Perfectly Hatter.

"Dee and I will fly in before you." Dum fluttered her wings faster so she soared in front of me. Her hand went to her hair, then her dress, making sure she still looked impeccable. "We don't want to steal the spotlight."

"Gee, thanks, girls," I said, caught between amusement at the pixies' supreme confidence and a desperate urge to beg them to stay.

"Hatter will be with you," Dee said, as if sensing some of my reservations. "So at least half the room will be looking at him."

"One can hope," I muttered, stomach twisting.

I was somewhat surprised at the nerves popping up. Normally, I didn't care what others thought.

Truth be told, I still didn't, but I did want to make people proud, to represent my family, and to set the kingdom to rights.

"You'll do great, Alice," Dum assured me, holding her fist out. Dee joined in, and I fist-bumped them both.

"See you!" Dee said, and the pair zoomed toward the door, pausing only to fist-bump Henri too.

"I should never have taught them that," I sighed when I reached him, standing to the side of the wide door. "Half of the time, they don't even use it correctly."

"I like it." He held out his arm for me to take. "It reminds me of you."

His green eyes locked with mine, and I swallowed, not sure what to say.

"Shall we go in?" I took his arm, trying to ignore the muscles bulging there as I gestured to the door with my free hand.

"We shall, Princess." Hatter turned to the guards. "No announcement."

Oh, thank the old gods he was here. I hadn't even thought of that.

Not that arriving unannounced changed much. The instant we entered the room, all eyes were upon us. Even more unnerving, conversations stopped mid-word. The musicians, shunted in the corner of the Grand Hall, continued playing, though more softly. The scent of roses permeated the air, and I noticed the white blooms. Not red. White. My confidence boosted a touch.

Shoulders back. Chin high. Wings out.

"Did I mention you look stunning?" Henri breathed.

"Thank you." My nerves dissolving a bit at the compliment, I gave him a once-over that had a number of young fae twittering. "You don't look so bad yourself."

One corner of his lips lifted, and in sync, we swept into the center of the room.

As Hatter did a slow turn, probably to show me off, a nearby male and female fae, dressed in matching gold brocade, pressed their hands to their hearts. The female had dyed her beehive updo teal and adorned it with golden roses—a gesture that no one could miss.

I smiled at them, but not too wide, not too friendly.

I didn't want anyone here getting the idea that we were automatically good. A tribute to my family was one thing, but I'd need to speak to the couple personally, and hear an apology for their part in what had been allowed to happen.

Finally, Henri stopped our movement, and at that same moment, the music did too.

Slowly, he slipped his arm out from mine. Raising his voice so all could hear, he said, "May I present to you, Princess Alice White of Wonderland."

A wave of bows and curtsies rippled through the room, presenting me with a topside view of hats and elaborate hairstyles in every color of the rainbow.

Only Aquatia did not extend the courtesy. I did not

expect her to. I was a princess by birth, but Aquatia was a queen. Despite this not being her kingdom, she ranked highest here.

Once everyone stood upright again, I clapped my hands delicately. "Please, drink and dance. Dinner will be served shortly."

"I'll get you a fae wine, so you have something to do with your hands," Hatter said, showing how well he knew me.

"Thanks," I said gratefully. "Be quick."

"Of course."

He left my side, and the fae of Wonderland resumed their dancing and drinking. Most looked away, still gathering their courage to speak with me.

With their attention elsewhere, I took in the room more readily.

The Riverlands royals sat at the head table where I would eventually settle. At my request, Henri, Sansu, Alran, and the pixies would too. Both Halad and his mother looked resplendent in finery of green and gold, their court's colors.

A few rebels I recognized were present as well, but for the most part, I did not know the faces around me.

Beyond the attendees, the decor was vastly different from the first feast I'd attended at the castle. No red lined the walls. No hearts. Since the Trial by Aether, castle servants, and even some soldiers, had been busy removing every speck of evidence of the Red Queen they could find.

Now teal tapestries softened the room, and white roses provided elegance. It wasn't much, but there'd be more later. And when combined with the crystal chandeliers, the soft light from the candles enchanted to float in the air, and the fae themselves—a colorful bunch if there ever was one—the room was absolutely gorgeous.

Their efforts warmed me. I suspected the servants had to search Heartstown to find this much teal to honor my family.

"Good evening, Princess."

A soft voice interrupted my musings, and I steeled myself for my first awkward interaction of the evening. But when I turned and found Isadora, clad in a gorgeous purple dress, with white roses wreathing the long bell-sleeves, I grinned.

She looked amazing, her voluminous, dark hair tamed into a sleek style that suited her round face, her eyes bright.

"Hey there." I held out my arms for her.

I wasn't normally much of a hugger, but the brownie was like a second mother to me. A rebel who'd lost her daughter to the cause, she could have hated me . . . and yet, she didn't. She grieved, but didn't blame me for the loss she suffered. Didn't stop caring about or supporting Wonderland.

That took a really big person.

Isadora returned my embrace, pulling away with a smile. "You look lovely, Princess Alice."

"As do you. Thank you so much for coming. And for the dress. Your work is stunning!"

"I'm so happy you like it." Conspiratorially, Isadora raised a bushy black eyebrow and scanned the crowd—most of whom were stealing glances at us. "I see that no one who needs your approval has gotten the courage to request it yet."

"Not yet. I'm okay with it, though. Hatter is getting me a drink, and—"

"Dear Princess Alice, a word?" A male fae swept in from the side, cutting me off.

He was older, looking to be about forty in human years, which meant he was easily over a hundred. Likely over two hundred.

"Of course." I shot Isadora an expectant look that said *'Here we go'*.

"I'm Lord Ezekel, and . . ." He trailed off, his gaze shifting to Isadora for a moment. "You may leave."

I stiffened at the condescension in his tone. "What did you say to her?"

"The brownie may leave. I have matters to discuss with you, Princess. Discussions of the sort that commoners should not be privy to."

My mouth fell open, but Isadora looked to the floor and took a step back, clearly about to do as this asshat asked.

"Where are you going?" I gripped her hand.

"To give you privacy," she replied, her tone smaller than before.

Among the rebels, she was warm, kind, and outspoken, but one word from this male, and she'd shrunk.

Isadora could stand against the queen. Being bold in the face of pure evil was difficult, but the brownie was brave. However, when confronted with the rest in the city? Those whom she lived among? I got the sense that she felt they were still above her.

This was the world my aunt had created.

"Stay. I value your opinion above most," I said firmly. "And I believe that *you*, Lord Ezekel, would do well to remember that things are changing here. Speaking to others like that will no longer be tolerated."

The fae lord gaped. "Apologies, Princess, but I must disagree. A brownie's place is beneath higher fae—particularly elves such as myself, and faeries like you."

I was dumbstruck, but thankfully, Hatter appeared, wine in hand, giving me the perfect retort. I took the wine from Henri with a sweet smile, and then threw the entire glass of liquid in Ezekel's face.

"I—how—what is the meaning of this?!" Ezekel roared, stepping back a few paces as he wiped at his drenched face.

"I do not appreciate how you speak to my friends, my people," I growled. "So I'm showing you as much respect as you're showing them."

"Princess!" the lord sputtered. "This is not how things are done!"

"You're right. It's not." I took a step closer. "As I said, things are changing in the Wonderland Court, Lord

Ezekel. If you don't like it, you can leave, but don't you ever dare insinuate that because you have a fancy title, you're better than those here. *Particularly* those who risked it all to rid this island of evil."

"As if they had anything to risk," the man seethed back. "I can see I'll have to reconsider my relationship with the Crown." He whirled and marched off.

I snorted. "We have no relationship."

"Uh, what was that about?" Hatter asked, his eyes wide.

"Douchebaggery."

His brows crinkled.

"He was being vile to Isadora," I clarified.

The brownie sniggered. "And our princess told him that would no longer be tolerated."

Hatter cleared his throat. "As proud as that makes me, perhaps we can do without the drink-throwing next time?" He glanced about. "You want people to approach you tonight, to talk about how you intend to change Wonderland? If they're worried they're going to end up soaked in wine, those conversations are unlikely to happen."

He was right.

My sense of righteous justification deflated. I'd acted from anger, and Lord Ezekel *was* in the wrong, but . . .

Had I screwed up my efforts to shift the nobles to our side?

"Oh, stop it, Henri," Isadora said. "Ezekel might badmouth our princess, but the other lords and ladies will want to be in her graces. Might take a bit more time, but," her chin tilted up in pride, "she did what was right."

Henri exhaled. "Of course, she did. I didn't mean to say otherwise."

"Might I add something?" a voice spoke to my right.

When I twisted and found no one there, I gasped, but quickly put two and two together.

"Cheshire Cat," I hissed. "You scared me!"

"Apologies. I wish not to attract attention." He allowed his eyes to appear, perhaps in a sort of compromise, though I wasn't sure if that was better or worse than seeing no one.

"Yeah, okay, fine."

I could understand that desire. He was a Cheshire cat, a rare creature even in Wonderland, and bound to me. Many would want to speak with him.

Actually, *I* was one of those people. I hadn't seen the cat since the day of the Trial by Aether.

"Hey, you got a name I should call you?" I asked. "I wondered before, but we were kinda . . . busy for formalities."

"A kraken trying to kill you does tend to take precedence," the cat replied dreamily. "No one has asked me my name in a long time. Not since your mother."

A lump lodged itself in my throat. My mother had been dead for over a decade.

"Well, I'd love to know your name. If you want to give it, that is?"

"Chester."

A laugh bubbled up my throat, but I held it back. *Chester the Cheshire cat.* I wasn't sure what I'd been expecting but it wasn't that.

"Good to officially meet you," I said with a straight-ish face. Then, ready to bring the conversation back to where it had started, I inquired. "Did you want to add something to our discussion on Lord Ezekel?"

"Not him," Chester replied. "I merely wish to warn you—"

"Is my aunt trying to break out?" I asked, heart rate spiking.

Sela White, the now dethroned Red Queen, was being held in the dungeons, bound by iron shackles and aether shields, and watched over by no less than a dozen guards. Still, I wouldn't put it past her to use the feast as a distraction to escape.

"Not that I'm aware of," Chester said. "I merely wish to inform you that I sense a new . . . presence . . . in Wonderland."

A presence?

"Like Queen Aquatia and Prince Halad? They arrived earlier today." I gestured to the head table. "They'd probably love to speak with you."

"Not them. Someone not of this world, though they are masking that quite well. Someone—"

"Someone who has traveled a long way to get to you, Al," a male voice drawled from behind me.

Cold dread washed over me.

CHAPTER 3

I stood frozen in place, unable to move or breathe or even blink.

That voice. I knew it intimately, had heard it scream, whisper, moan.

But how?

Was this real?

"Al? You okay?" the man asked, and though I still had not turned around, footsteps came closer as he rounded me, smelled the woody scent I'd once loved.

My eyes squeezed shut. *No. Just no, no, no.*

"Alice? What's wrong?" Hatter spoke now, his tone gentle, and a hand fluttered to my shoulder, landing lightly.

"Who are you?" Isadora demanded of our intruder.

"We haven't seen one another in a while," the man said. "Clearly, she's overcome with joy."

Joy? JOY?!

The presumption!

"Who. Are. You?" Hatter repeated the brownie's question.

"I'm Al's boyfriend."

Isadora gasped softly, and my eyes flew open. I spun on the man—Jax—who just stood grinning at me with the same confidence that had once drawn me to him.

"Hey, sweetheart." A blond curl lazily fell into his face.

"What the hell are you doing here?!" I hissed.

I couldn't believe Jax Altru stood in Faerie. He had the same molten amber eyes. The same dimple in his chin. The same scent and black leather jacket.

"Looking for you, of course." Jax motioned to where a number of fae were waltzing. "Wanna dance?"

"You've got to be joking!" I roared so loudly the music faltered. If people weren't already watching me, they definitely were now.

"I realize I'm underdressed," Jax gestured to his dark jeans and tight, black t-shirt. "But it was murder getting in here, so take pity on a guy."

"Take pity on you?" My fists clenched, and only vaguely did I notice Hatter, who still hadn't taken his hand off of me, squeezed my shoulder. "Jax, what the heck are you doing here?"

"I came to see you," he repeated. "You aged out of your contract, so it was safe for me to come back, to find you."

"You—what do you mean safe?!"

Jax's steady stare took me in with curiosity. "Al, Doru told me he'd kill me if I didn't get the hell out of town. Get away from *you*. The moment I no longer belonged to him, I had to leave. He didn't want me distracting you—his prize assassin."

It was like someone had stuck a knife through my heart.

Jax, my first love, had left me without a word, and I'd always thought it was because he was . . . over us. That he no longer loved me.

But was Doru really to blame? The same damn vampire who'd stood by and just watched me break down when Jax left? The overlord who had told me Jax wasn't worth my time?

When I got back to the human world, I was so staking that vampire.

"Did you think I left because I wanted to?" Jax's tone was light, almost joking, but this wasn't a joke to me. Nothing about this situation was funny.

"I-I—need to dance." I said the first thing that came to my mind—and immediately regretted it. If there was one way to put even more attention on myself when I was inches from losing it, dancing was it.

"Allow me." Henri's hand slipped down my arm to grasp my hand, and he pulled me away.

Only then did I realize I was trembling.

I sucked in a breath, determined to make sure no one else noticed.

Dancing fae parted as Hatter led me into their midst.

Across the way, Halad was gliding gracefully on the floor, his arms around a female fae with antlers that appeared to be dipped in gold.

I scanned the side of the room for the Riverlands Queen, feeling like a sub-par host. I hadn't even gotten to say hi to them yet, and now I wasn't sure I wanted to. I felt too raw, as if someone had rubbed sandpaper over my heart. Like I'd snap at any second.

Thankfully, the queen had remained at the head table, and people surrounded her. No doubt, she'd noticed my outburst—*how could she not?*—but she didn't appear to be dwelling on it.

That was fine, I'd obsess enough for the both of us, thank you very much.

Henri stopped us in the middle of the crowded floor and extended his hand. I took it, and we were off, spinning through the sea of dancers.

"Who is he?" Henri asked quietly so only I could hear.

His eyes weren't even on me, and now that I'd been pulled from my inner turmoil, I noticed that he was stiff. Angry.

"An ex-boyfriend."

My dance partner cleared his throat. "That much is obvious. Are you sure he is in your past? He seems to have traveled far to find you."

"He—" I swallowed down the pain that always came with remembering the day I'd awoken in my apartment to find Jax's side of the bed empty. His clothes, stripped from the closet. He'd cast a silencing spell over my room before he left, ensuring I didn't wake to stop him. "We aren't together. Haven't been for months."

I couldn't even say we'd broken up, because that hadn't happened. I'd simply woken one day to find the best part of my life, the most important part, gone. And I'd never heard from him again.

Until today.

The music shifted, and flowing with the tide of dancers, Hatter spun me. When I came back to face him, our noses inches from one another, he looked different from the proud man who'd presented me to those attending the feast. Almost like he was crumbling from within.

"Do you love him?" Henri asked suddenly, as if the words were being ripped from him.

I pressed my lips together. I wanted to deny it, wanted to scream that I hated Jax . . . but did I?

The blond wizard had been my first love, and though I'd thought little about him since arriving in Faerie, he'd always been on my mind in the human world. I'd see reminders of him constantly, and every time, it would hurt.

"It's okay if you do, Alice," Henri added, his voice cracking slightly as the music slowed to a stop.

I'd taken too long to reply and now . . .

Oh god. "I—"

"Can I cut in?"

Again, the sound of his voice made me stiffen. How dare he?!

I turned to find Jax grinning. As if he hadn't just shattered my entire world.

"Hey, Al. I don't know the moves, but can I take you for a spin? I wanna talk."

I pulled away from Henri, fists balling at my sides. "You do, do you? Funny how *now* you want to talk!"

Oh god, there I went, yelling again, but I couldn't help it. Even if Doru was to blame, which I wasn't sure I believed yet, Jax could have tried to contact me. He could have done something, *anything*. We were trained assassins! We literally got away with murder, so it wasn't like we were idiots.

"I've wanted to speak to you for months," Jax replied. "But you know how Doru is, Al. Please, let me explain."

"No." I waved a hand, gesturing broadly to the Grand Hall. "Can't you see this is the worst possible time for this?! How did you even get here, anyway?!"

"Excellent question," Henri growled, his tone so low and dangerous that it tore my attention from Jax.

I sucked in a breath. Hatter's face was stone, his jaw so tight a muscle ticked in it. I'd never seen him so pissed. He looked like he wanted to throw down.

"Fae from Wonderland are trickling into the human world." Jax shrugged. "News is spreading through the magical community that the queen was overthrown by a girl who called herself the Dagger. Once I heard, I knew it had to be you." He studied the room. "Didn't expect this princess stuff, but can't say I'm that surprised. You've always had that sort of command."

"You didn't answer her question," Henri pressed. "Did you break through a portal into this kingdom?"

In keeping with her other isolation tactics, my aunt had sealed the portals between Wonderland and the human world. I'd only gotten through with the joint efforts of a witch from the human world and a fae on this side who was willing to break the rules. At the behest of the rebels, they'd worked together to keep the doorway open while Herald came to get me.

"Nah. Just paid to get to the Snowcap Court and then bought a pegasus from there. I had a guide, of course. He's sightseeing in the city."

"And no one thought to inform me that more *guests* arrived?" I couldn't believe it. I'd been so fast to spot the Riverland queen that others hadn't had a chance to tell me, but the guards should be better at sending up the alarm.

"I made sure we arrived undetected."

Jax smirked, and I wanted to slap that smug smile off his face.

Ugh, jackass. He must have used an invisibility potion. Or maybe a spell.

When we were together, Jax hadn't mastered that spell yet, but things had changed. He was free now. Able to travel the world and learn from whomever he chose. Surely, he could have learned a trick or two in our time apart.

Hell, in just a couple of weeks, I had rid a kingdom of an evil queen. By comparison, learning a freaking spell was nothing.

"So you snuck into my kingdom and crashed a party to ambush me?" I snorted derisively. "What makes you think I want to *see* you, let alone dance with you?"

"You know you can't say no to me. I'm too charming." The cocky asshat winked and placed a hand on my arm. "I messed up, but I was scared of Doru. We all were. Give me a chance, Al. I'll make it up to you."

"You're probably only here because I'm a princess," I muttered, pulling my arm back.

"Why the hell would I care about you being a princess!" Jax growled so loudly that around the room, people began murmuring.

Oh no. I'd been so focused on Jax, I'd pretty much forgotten I had an audience.

Jax's eyebrows knitted together as he came closer, his tone dipping lower. "I know you, Al. Where you've been. Who you are. What you've done. I don't care if you're a princess or not. Now come on, dance with me. Please?"

As much as I hated this situation, Jax was right about a couple of things. He *did* know who I was, what I'd done, where I'd had to go to do those horrible things. People here didn't know me as Alice the Dagger. They'd heard the name, but they didn't know my past. Here, I was Princess Alice, a warrior—or liberator, to some—but really, I wasn't that at all.

I was a trained killer. A person who'd taken on a

queen. And with the skillset I'd had since I was young, aided by my new aether magic, I was unbeatable.

But noble? Regal? Maybe by blood, but in reality, I was a street kid.

Though, sometimes, when I saw the way Hatter or the pixies looked at me, a small part of me thought maybe I could be those other things.

"Al?" Jax held out his hand.

For a moment, I stared down at it. For a moment, I almost took it. But Hatter shifted next to me, pulling me from the trauma of my past life, and I shook my head.

"Nah. I'm good. Feel free to help yourself to some food before you leave."

A shadow crossed Jax's face, but he dropped his hand. "Fine. No dance. But I'm not leaving, I—"

"The princess told you that you're not welcome in her kingdom," Hatter interjected, his voice a growl.

"Unless it's a murderous vampire lord doing the commanding, I'm not famous for doing what I'm told," Jax shot back. "Besides, if I leave, will that change her mind?"

"You won't," I declared.

"That's what I thought. So, I think I'll stay rig—"

Hatter lunged and threw a punch. A crack rang out as his fist connected with Jax's jaw.

I stepped back, hands flying to my mouth. What the hell had just happened!?

"Hatter!" I yelled. "Stop! *Henri!*"

But he had apparently had enough of the wizard.

A circle of onlookers formed around the two men, stopping a healthy distance away and greedily watching the events unfold. Jax punched back, and Hatter retaliated with wind, blowing his opponent backward.

Jax righted himself, not missing a beat as sage-green magic sprayed from my ex's fingers, slamming into Henri. The fae fell to the ground, toppling over a nearby lord and lady. Before he could rise, Jax was already winding up again.

"No! Stop!" I shouted, vaguely aware of the pixies yelling for someone to put an end to this. "This is absurd!"

Gathering up my skirt, I made to intercede, but Prince Halad burst from the crowd, running toward me, the pixies flying at his side.

"Don't hurt Henri!" Dum shouted as aether magic shimmered from Halad, creating a wall between Jax and Hatter.

The men stopped going at each other, but their eyes were still narrowed and burning with anger, their chests heaving.

"I think that's quite enough for tonight, gentlemen." The Prince of the Riverlands locked eyes with me. "Perhaps these two should be shown to their rooms, Princess Alice?"

"I'll show myself out," Hatter grunted, turning and marching from the room.

I wanted to follow, but Jax reached out and touched my arm.

"Yeah, Al. I'll stay quiet in my room. Maybe someone —*you*, perhaps—can show me the way?"

The balls on this guy!

I glared at him. "Fine. You can stay. But don't return to the celebration tonight."

"You got it, babe."

"Improper! She's a princess! Not a babe!" Dee hissed, as the rest of the crowd murmured.

Very few were so casual with me here.

"Don't call me that," I said. "It's 'Princess Alice.'"

The hypocrisy in that statement stunned even me, but I had to distance myself from him in any way that I could.

"Guards," I snapped before Jax could give me another one of his smart-alec remarks. "Show this man to the South Tower."

A guard I didn't know approached. "Are you sure, Princess? Usually guests are kept in the North Tower. Or the West."

I was absolutely sure. I wanted him far from me.

"There are bedchambers in the South, no?" I asked.

"There are."

"Then that will suit him."

The armored man motioned for Jax to go with him.

My ex understood he would get no more from me, because he moseyed toward the soldier. "Night, Al. See you tomorrow." He winked at me and blew an air kiss— gestures that sent even more murmurs through our audience.

"We'll see." I turned my back on him to face the crowd.

As if getting the lords and ladies to want to win my affections tonight hadn't already been difficult, that scene would make it all but impossible. All night long people would talk about Jax. Or maybe how Hatter had lost his cool.

Well, screw them.

I wasn't here to kiss their asses. Or answer their questions about Jax or Henri. And I certainly wasn't going to take the blame for my ex showing up and ruining the night.

So, well aware that they were already watching me, I pointed to the musicians. "Play."

They did so, and before I could decide what to do next, Prince Halad swept in.

"Would you like to dance?" He leaned closer. "Just act like nothing happened and that we're having fun. That will shift their focus. No one can resist a prince wooing a princess."

Although I still wanted to race after Hatter, to soothe the anger in him, I couldn't. Duty kept me rooted. I was here to meet the nobles. It was the first step in bringing change to Wonderland. They might want to gossip about Hatter and Jax, but I'd do my best to dissuade them.

So, I took Halad's hand. "You're a lifesaver."

He kissed my knuckles, a gesture that sent a wave of gossip rushing through the crowd. "I've been in the spotlight when I didn't want to be."

Though people were still watching us, as Halad and I began to dance a slow, easy waltz, others either followed suit, joining us on the dancefloor, or returned to their table.

"I take it that wizard was interested in courting you?"

I couldn't stop the snort of laughter that escaped me. "You could say that. We were together for a long time, but not anymore."

"Why not? Because you're here?"

"No. We broke up long before I learned about Wonderland." A sigh parted my lips. "It was complicated then, and it's even more so now. He told me something about our history that I didn't know."

Not that Doru's interference changed anything, but it did make me soften toward Jax. I blamed my new, gentler nature on the pixies. Maybe on Hatter too.

"I see. If it's any consolation, your people seem to have moved on." Halad gestured behind me.

I twisted to find the pixies putting on an outlandish performance that had captured the attention of half those present at the feast.

Dee caught my eye and winked, making my heart clench.

"They're good friends," I said, all too sure the twins were making fools of themselves for me.

"Agreed. They're also quite persuasive. Did you know that Dee has already invited herself to my court's next ball?"

A laugh burst from me. "She didn't."

"Oh, she did. I suspect I should be relieved she hasn't persuaded me to propose—not that she isn't lovely, but I'm not prepared for that sort of commitment." He paused. "Yet."

I swallowed. Had Halad and his mother come here to do more than check on the fate of the rebellion?

CHAPTER 4

The back of my neck prickled as my steps rang down the corridor. Early morning sunlight flooded in through the windows, illuminating my pants and tunic as I passed through it. I huffed out a heated breath. Though nothing of note had happened yet that day, I was sure it would soon. I was in the process of tracking down Henri, Alran, and Sansu to make them listen to me.

Much to the servants' confusion, my friends and I preferred to take our meals in a small dining room, rather than the monstrosity of a space my aunt had used, which was nearly the size of the Grand Hall.

I knew that Hatter, Alran, and Sansu were already eating, because I'd sent the pixies down to check. When the girls reported back to me, they swore they'd remained unseen and that Hatter would have no idea I was coming.

Though I didn't enjoy the idea of ambushing him or having an awkward meal, I needed to clear the air about Jax.

Taking a deep breath, I closed my eyes. Why had he come back? Why was my past here to haunt me? I just wanted to do right by the people in this kingdom and move on—start my own life. One that I could finally be proud of.

Opening my eyes and shaking off my insecurities, I approached the dining room door and barged through before anyone within could hear me coming.

The men looked up, Hatter's lips compressing at the sight of me, and my stomach pitted.

Yup, he was still pissed.

I was so unused to that expression being pointed at me.

"Hey, guys." I pulled up a chair and took a seat opposite Henri. "I need to talk to you about last night. I—"

Servants chose that moment to swoop in, offering water and tea. I took them up on the latter. Between Hatter's annoyance, Jax's arrival, and Halad's insinuation that he might be here to court me, I hadn't slept well at all and needed caffeine.

All these problems from men. They're the bane of my existence. I sipped from a teacup rimmed with gold.

"So, what do you want to talk about, Alice?" Alran asked, his tone softer than normal.

"Jax," I said simply. "You met—or saw—him last

night. He's an ex-boyfriend of mine that really knows how to make an entrance."

Hatter snorted his contempt, but said nothing. He merely continued to eat his porridge; each bite more aggressive than the last.

"I want you guys to know that I didn't invite him here. He's from my past, but we haven't spoken in *months*. I didn't expect him to come back into my life, and I certainly did not expect that fiasco last night."

"He seemed sure that you'd want him in your life." Henri ripped his eyes from his food to scowl up at me. It was then I noticed the shadow on his square jawline, the bruise where Jax had landed a punch.

"Are you alright?" I traced my own jawline with my finger. I'd been punched a couple of times—it was unavoidable, growing up doing what I did—and it sucked.

"Fine. I'll see a healer later."

"Okay. Good."

A pregnant pause followed, the silence swelling by the second. In that echo of nothingness, I swore I was breathing louder than normal, but I was determined to get through the awkwardness.

When it became clear Henri wasn't going to say anything else, I broke the silence.

"So, yeah, Jax was important in my life. Probably the *most* important person—"

"As you were to me, Al."

My heart rate spiked and, unable to believe how

godawful his timing was—had it always been like this?!—I spun to find Jax standing in the doorway, arms folded over his chest.

Behind him, a soldier stood, looking apologetic. "He insisted I bring him to speak with you, Princess Alice."

"I did," Jax boomed, totally *un*apologetic. "I didn't get to finish what I came to say last night."

"Oh, I think you did." I pushed my chair back. "In fact, I think it's time we get you back to the mainland."

"Not until you hear me out." He swaggered into the dining room, blond curls waving in the crisp sea breeze coming in through the window.

I hated how confident he was, how good he looked. Then I hated that I'd acknowledged he looked good, if only to myself.

"I've literally crossed into a new realm for you," he continued. "I was Faerie-drunk for two days, and paid out the ass to get to this island, *Princess*, so I think the least you can do is hear me out."

Not a word was spoken. It was so silent; I wouldn't have doubted that the men had stopped breathing.

"Fine," I grumbled. "If I listen to you, will you leave?"

"If that's what you really want, I will." Jax pulled up the chair next to mine.

This close, I was shocked to find he wasn't bruised. Hatter had gotten in a good slug, and bore the signs of their fight. Why didn't Jax?

"Healing potion." He winked.

He'd always been good at reading me. I used to find it charming.

Not anymore.

"Did you forget that all good assassins keep one on them?" he teased. "We can't go around all busted up like this guy." He gestured to Hatter.

The sound of wood scraping against stone ground through the dining room as Henri shot out of his chair, looking like he was going to murder someone. "I'll take my leave."

"Hatter, you don't have to go."

My words were of no use. He was already rounding the table.

"I think it's best that I do," he called without looking at me. "I'll see you at the execution, Princess Alice."

The moment Henri was out the door, the other two males stood too, though they looked a bit sheepish about it.

"We have much to prepare for today," Alran said. If he wasn't a fae, and therefore incapable of telling an untruth, I'd have called him a liar. "Until this afternoon, Princess Alice."

Sansu looked even more guilty as he retreated with his friend.

Like last night, I wanted to follow, but refrained. Maybe, if I really did hear him out, Jax would leave, and I could get on with my life.

Once we were alone, Jax chuckled. "Is it me, or *you*, who scares them?"

"They're not scared," I grumbled. "You're that annoying."

"I beg to differ, though if I make them quiver in their boots, I'm pretty damn sure I'm not the only one. An execution, Al?"

"My aunt."

He didn't look surprised by that, which made me raise an eyebrow. "I see you have already learned of her fate."

"I do my research."

This was something I knew about him, and it was a useful habit. He researched. I thought fast on my feet. We worked well together on missions. It had always been me and him, ruling the underground world.

Until it wasn't.

I pursed my lips. "What else did you hear about me?"

"That you now control the aether." The wizard rocked his chair back and put his feet on the table. "I guess you're not demi-fae, but full? Never heard of anyone less than full fae controlling aether."

"That's right," I muttered.

"Which means . . . If you're not already, you'll be limited by fae weaknesses." He smirked. "That healing potion isn't the only elixir I brought with me to this realm."

I sucked in a breath. "Are you saying . . .?"

I could hardly utter the words out loud. After all, if I did, it was basically saying that I wanted to lie—which wasn't the case.

But my past was shameful. More than that, I had a secret . . . one I wasn't keen to have spread.

The prophecy my aunt told me about still haunted me.

Apparently, on the day of my birth, an oracle proclaimed that I would pull those of Wonderland into darkness. That I would end the kingdom.

It was vague, so my parents ignored it, but that was the justification my aunt used to murder them and take over the kingdom.

I hadn't told anyone about it yet. Not even Henri. It was never the right moment. And now, he was so angry . . . Would that moment ever come? Did I *want* to tell him?

Was it even real?

Where I came from, prophecies were flimsy. Notoriously unreliable. But was that the case here? Faerie was so different from the human world.

Still, I had to know I could keep that information safe.

So, finally, I asked, "Did you bring the potion that Xavier made me take every moon cycle?"

"Yup. I have one in the very same. The potion that will allow you to lie," Jax said. "But I'm not just going to hand it over."

My fists balled up before I caught myself, and Jax noticed the reaction.

"And I see you want what I have." He pulled his feet from the table and grinned. "I already told you my truth. That Xavier made me leave, but I was gonna come back for you. And I know you're pissed—"

"You don't say!" I scoffed. "Maybe leave a note or something?!"

"Couldn't. You know how the vamp is, Al." Jax's tone dipped. "But I can see that you're still peeved about it, so I'll make you a deal."

Here we go. "What?"

"I stay here. We spend time together daily, and you give me a real chance. Give me a week, tops. If at the end of that week, you still want me to go . . . fine. I will. But you'll get the potion, allowing you one more month to hide whatever it is you want to." He snorted. "Like we don't have a lifetime's worth of horrors to keep hidden."

I swallowed. He wasn't wrong.

"*But*," he continued, "if you find, at the end of the week, that you want me to stay, I will do that too." Jax's molten amber eyes stared into mine in a way that made my insides warm. I hated that I was so attracted to him. "I want a chance, a *real* chance, to reconnect. To make it up to you."

"Why?"

"Isn't it obvious? I still love you, Al." For the first time, every inch of smugness was gone from his face. His sincerity made it hard to breathe. "I was an idiot for obeying Doru, and I've regretted it every day since. I want to be the man you deserve."

I didn't respond . . . I couldn't. Months ago, this would have been exactly what I wanted—no, *needed*—to hear. But I was different now. I'd grown up. I was free.

Plus, I had met Hatter. There was something real there. Maybe not love quite yet, but it wasn't far off.

Then again, I still planned to leave Wonderland.

I hoped Elise would come with me, but if not, I figured I'd make due with frequent trips to Faerie. Now that my aunt was gone, there was nothing stopping me from stepping through a portal and coming here.

And there was no denying that I *had* loved Jax fiercely, and when we were together, he'd returned that love. I'd given everything to him.

My first love . . . everyone said that was a special thing.

I blew out a breath, unsure I wanted Jax to stay, but sure I wanted that potion—needed it, to hide the details of the prophecy and other stuff about myself. I'd never be comfortable sharing my whole life, and the prophecy . . .

My stomach twisted.

"Fine. I get the potion either way?"

"No matter what you choose, I'll give you the potion. Then you can get it analyzed here." Jax looked around the dining area, wrinkling his nose at the Old-World appearance. "Actually, maybe not here. Perhaps a more modern Court that's heard of science. There's one of those, right?"

If there was, I didn't know of it. But I'd take the vial and figure out its components, even if I had to make the damn brew myself.

"One week is all you get," I told him firmly.

"One week is all I'll need, Princess." With the smoothness of a jaguar, Jax rose and bowed. "I'll see you at the execution."

***

The morning passed by quickly. Though I wasn't involved with the logistics and planning of the execution, I had plenty on my mind to keep myself occupied.

Jax, and the deal I'd struck with him.

Hatter, who had totally been avoiding me since breakfast.

A freaking *execution*.

Finding Elise.

How the hell was I going to get into the Dark Court? Though I'd never seen it, I knew it was surrounded by an impenetrable force I didn't understand called the Rift.

I strolled the garden, enjoying the sun, and the faint breeze made my wide-legged, linen pants flow around me. For once, I was alone, and I seized that time to think and take in the new topiaries. It felt weird, taking a second to literally smell the rose-perfumed air of the garden.

Any ode to my aunt had already been vanquished, hacked off with the leaves, and gardeners were at work reshaping the greenery. Many shrubs and hedges were shapeless with no direction, but as I rounded the corner, I found one that was fully formed, and it made my breath hitch.

Herald, the crier of Wonderland. The fae who'd

informed the Red Queen that she could not, in fact, deny a Trial by Aether once challenged. The creature who'd taken the godsflame into him, assuring that the trial went on—even at the cost of his own life. The pooka who'd approached me as a white rabbit in my world, had been immortalized in this garden.

"Looks exactly like him," I whispered, approaching the topiary.

It even had the waistcoat and pocket watch that the pooka favored. I could almost hear Herald fretting that we were late.

Unbidden, tears flooded my eyes. He'd been remembered with a small funeral, but he deserved more. Whoever had given the instruction for this to be created was a genius.

"It's lovely," a feminine voice said softly.

Quickly, I wiped my eyes and twisted to find the queen of the Riverlands. She stood some twenty paces away, two soldiers accompanying her. That I hadn't heard their approach spoke to how deeply I'd been in my own head.

"He's something of a hero," I said.

"Since being here, I've been told the tales of the Trial by Aether and become aware of his sacrifice," the queen replied. "Brave of him, to stand up to such a crazed woman."

"Absolutely." I faced her properly. I was certain that she hadn't found me by chance. The queen had something to say. "What can I do for you, Queen Aquatia?"

She smiled. "Shall we walk?"

"Sure."

The queen motioned for her soldiers to follow at a distance. Whatever she had to say, she didn't want to be overheard.

We'd gone only a few paces when Queen Aquatia spoke. "There's no good way to bring this up, it's always awkward, so I'll be out with it. I wanted to broach the subject of your ascension to the throne." She looked at me, intelligence brimming in her eyes. "And if you have considered a royal pairing?"

I stopped in my tracks—which the queen seemed to anticipate, because she halted too, and far more smoothly than me.

"I understand that in your world, young people often wait to wed," Aquatia added, "but you're of royal blood. And in Faerie, marriages are used to cement alliances. I would be interested in creating one with the Wonderland Court."

I wanted to yell that I'd barely turned eighteen, but the queen was watching me expectantly, regally, so instead of indignation, a question bubbled up my throat.

"I, uh, with Halad?"

"Precisely," Aquatia replied. "You're close to the same age, and though your interactions have been few, you seem to get along."

That was true. Halad was a good guy—and hot to boot. I was sure he had a number of princesses nipping at his heels. But whether I was among them . . .

I cleared my throat. "If I'm being honest, I hadn't considered it."

"Nor would anyone have expected you to. Even if you agreed to a marriage bond today, you would be within your rights to request a year or two of true courtship."

Aquatia began walking again, and I fell into step with her. "Are you aware that I met your mother before Frederic did? He was my cousin. A close one. I knew they'd pair well. But Sela was the eldest princess of Wonderland, and he was betrothed to her. That didn't last long, though."

I inhaled sharply. "Did you know my mother and father when they were together though? Did you see them together?"

"I attended their wedding," Aquatia's face softened with the memory. "It was a binding of two kingdoms and two hearts. Quite a beautiful day."

I wished there were photos, but the closest thing this realm had were paintings. None portraying my mother and father had survived the rule of the Red Queen.

"My aunt was pissed."

"She was. From that day on, word spread of the elder princess. The Scorned One, many called her. As royal duties prevented me from flying to visit Frederic, I never witnessed her anger firsthand, but others said fury consumed Sela, and she became dark."

The queen pressed her lips together until they became white. "When I heard what Sela had done to take the crown, I was enraged. But not surprised. She'd always had a hint of madness to her . . . Frederic had noticed it too.”

Yes, my aunt was crazy. Cruel and manipulative too.

“I’m hoping this proposal of courtship between you and Halad can bring our kingdoms together again,” the queen admitted.

I swallowed thickly. “I might not stay here.”

She twisted, gazing upon me incredulously.

“I will for a while,” I amended. “To find my sister. But I’ll be leaving shortly after we bond.”

“Curious,” Aquatia replied. “I’d gotten the sense that you were comfortable here. You have friends.” A pause. “Perhaps more? That gentleman from last night seemed quite upset that you had a caller.”

“Henri Hatter,” I breathed.

“The way you speak his name is telling, Alice.”

“I have a bit of a crush.”

“Nothing more?”

Yes, but it felt like too much to say that to a stranger. Hatter and I had only known one another for weeks.

I feigned nonchalance. “Like I said, I plan on giving up the crown and leaving, so it doesn’t matter, does it?”

The queen had mastered the art of lengthy pauses, and she enlisted one now. Only the sound of our footsteps on the garden path and the chirping of birds filled the air.

“I suppose not,” she replied finally. “Halad will be sorry to hear it. He, too, noticed that you had . . . a suitor, perhaps two, but he took a liking to you.”

"Sorry to disappoint."

"We ladies do what we must. I have to say, I'm envious of your position. That you truly have a choice." She gave me a small smile that indicated she really did understand. "My own marriage is wonderful, but I did not have that."

Now that we were through that minefield, I sought a change of subject. "The Riverland Court is by the Dark Court, right?"

"Neighbors."

"You've seen the Rift?"

"It is a blight on the countryside of the Riverlands."

"We plan to go through it to get to the Dark Court."

Aquatia inhaled. "I had wondered . . . You know that's quite dangerous, correct?"

"Yes," I chewed on the inside of my cheek. "Has anyone done it?"

"Those who do are altered."

"What do you mean by altered?"

"The Dark Court has soldiers, called Shadows. They were once fae, and now are something different. Something evil. They may pass through the Rift, and have. They often take prisoners too."

The queen assessed me. "I know your sister is there, but are you sure you can do this?"

I wasn't sure of anything.

"I have to try," I replied instead. "Do you think, when we make the journey, we can go through your border?"

She looked conflicted. "If that's what you truly wish."

I exhaled. That, at least, would be easier than approaching from the sea.

"Might I offer a bit of unsolicited advice, Princess?"

"Of course."

"I have not met a normal fae who crossed the Rift, but there is a rumor that someone has done so."

"Really?"

I couldn't help feeling somewhat annoyed that she hadn't come out with that information before. Still, I didn't press. She looked uncomfortable just talking about the place.

"Yes." Her cheeks colored. "I do not wish for you to learn of the stain on my land, but if you're insistent, it might be worth investigating. The fae who allegedly crossed the Rift was from the Crystal Court."

"Crystal Court. That sounds nice."

"They are a land of mystics. Oracles. And snobs."

I laughed at the unexpected description. "What makes you say that?"

"Their court is an island, like this one, but even further flung from the mainland. As such, they're isolationists and do not participate in gatherings. They even had the nerve to throw an invitation from my own parents back in their faces."

Her lips twisted. "I am not sure I trust them, but for you, paying a visit there could be beneficial."

As in, it might keep me alive.

"The fae returned there?" I asked.

"He was on the brink of death when he emerged

from the Rift. Stories tell he'd been trapped in the Dark Court for years, but really, it was the Rift that nearly killed him. He did go home, though I know little of that, as my court did not assist."

"Who did?" I asked, trying to draw a mental map of that area of Faerie in my mind.

"That would be the Snowcap Court. They are quite trustworthy."

"Then this fae seems like a lead I should keep in mind."

CHAPTER 5

The hour I'd been both awaiting and dreading had finally come.

Bells tolled outside, and, though there was no way such sounds could penetrate the thick stone walls, I imagined I heard the whispers of fae as they streamed toward the castle.

Alran had told me to prepare for how many people would show, how many people would want to see my aunt die. I hadn't doubted him, but when I peered out the window of my tower room, I still gasped.

Thousands of fae waited on the lawn near the execution site.

"She had a knack for making enemies," I murmured, slipping a dagger into a sheath hanging on my hip and pulling my hair back.

Alran had also mentioned that I should probably wear a dress, but screw that. I liked pretty things, but I was tired of playing dress-up. If I couldn't wear my comfy leggings, then black trousers and a gold tunic with a hood would do for the day. Plus, the sun had been overtaken by clouds, and it looked like it might rain at any moment. For that kind of weather, I wanted pants and a hood.

Not to mention, pants were better for situations when I had to be on my toes. My aunt was set to die, but I didn't think for a second that meant she'd go easily. That word wasn't in her arsenal. I was ready for anything.

A knock came at the door, and I steeled myself. All day long, Hatter had avoided me, sending Alran to give messages regarding the execution. But surely, he wouldn't leave me high and dry right now, right?

I hoped not. I'd done nothing wrong—it wasn't like I'd invited Jax here!—though, somehow, I still felt like I was in the wrong. I wanted to speak with Henri alone, to clear the air.

So when I opened the door and found not Henri but Prince Halad, I frowned.

"I'll admit, women don't usually look at me that way," he said, a playful smile on his lips.

"Sorry, I was expecting someone else. We have . . . things to discuss."

He extended his arm for me to take. "I was sent because others seem to think that you arriving with another royal will quell any lingering Red Queen support-ers. How they could be so blind as to support that woman still, I don't know, but the idea had merit. To the execution?"

I closed the door behind me and took his arm. "Sure."

We'd only made it a few steps down the stairs when Halad cleared his throat. "My mother tells me she spoke with you today of a marriage alliance."

"Uh, yeah." Unease trickled through me. I didn't really want to get into this before an *execution*.

"I wanted to let you know that I'm not disappointed by your choice. And I still want to be friends."

Oh, well . . . that was better than I'd anticipated. Though there was definitely some ambiguity in his words.

"Is that what we are?" I pressed. "Friends?"

"We could be."

"Did the queen tell you that I won't be here much longer?" I asked softly.

"She did. But I have friends in your realm. What's a portal hop?"

I smiled at that. "How often do you see them?"

"Not often. So far, they have only come here. My court gave them refuge before the demon war. However, one day, I hope to visit the human world, if only briefly."

I stopped and stared at him. "I was in the demon war."

"The Riverlands Court was proud to harbor key players," Halad said. "I was caught unawares, and injured by Dark Court Shadows, right near the Rift. It was shortly before the Battle of Spellcasters." He pulled aside his shirt to reveal a scar on his shoulder. "I could not help during the fight at the academy. Not that my mother would have allowed it anyhow. I am the heir."

My heart rate increased. "I was at that battle! Who was at your court?" This conversation was getting more interesting by the second.

"Odette Dane, her paramour Alexander Wardwell, and many of their friends. I believe they are something of celebrities in parts of your world."

I gaped. "I fought alongside her!" I paused. "Did you hear what happened to her?"

Halad swallowed. "I did. Strange things are happening in both worlds."

They were. Odette was proof of a new magical age. Now that I thought about it, the Rift was too—even if it had been around for years, it was evidence that things were changing. Or had been for a while.

Did anyone really know where it came from? How had it formed?

"A lost princess returning to their homeland happens to be one of those strange affairs," Halad added with an easy grin.

I hadn't thought to include myself on that list, but perhaps he was right. It seemed much more normal than ancient magic resurfacing, like Odette and her friends believed.

We turned into a wider corridor, and fell in with a stream of people all heading the same way we were. When they noticed a princess and a prince were in their midst, they gave us more space, though we didn't require it for long. Halad and I arrived at the door to the outside quickly and stepped through.

A salty breeze teased my skin, flowing in off the ocean below the steep cliffs. Before us, a crowd spread far and wide, and at our appearance, many bowed or curtsied.

I scanned the people and finally found Hatter. Alongside Alran, Sansu, and the pixies, he'd positioned himself at the front of the crowd, near the guillotine—apparently a favorite tool of my aunt's.

Our eyes met, and he nodded.

It wasn't a smile, but he was here and acknowledging me. It was a start.

"Clear the way!" a soldier shouted, and with another armed fae, barreled through the crowd, making an aisle in which Halad and I could pass.

"Shall we?" the prince asked.

"Time to get this over with," I said.

As we walked through the masses of fae, many inclined their heads with respect or smiled. Only a few wore unpleasant expressions on their faces, their lips pursed, their brows pinched, and eyes narrowed.

Were they Red Queen sympathizers? If so, would they hurt others for the queen they loved? The dagger hung heavier on my hip. Perhaps once the execution was done, I'd bring them in for questioning. Just to be safe. Though I did not want to claim any title, I felt a responsibility for these fae's safety.

After what felt like years of being stared at, Halad and I reached the front. Hatter stepped forward, and I caught

Dee and Dum, perched atop Sansu's shoulders, craning their necks so they could listen to our conversation.

Nosies.

"Hey," I said, not sure what else to say. I didn't want to get into what happened last night or this morning. Not here. Not with so many people around.

"Your aunt wishes to speak with you," Henri replied.

"Oh. I—"

"Al!" Jax pushed his way through the crowd, his timing as fantastic as ever. "Where should I stand?"

Henri's jaw worked from side to side, but always the bigger man, he inclined his head. "I'll be over here if you need me."

"If I do, will you *actually* be there?" I asked, unable to help myself. I believed that he cared, but this morning had been rough.

For a moment, his face crumpled. "Alice, I know things have been strained, but I'm here for you." He exhaled loudly through his nose. "Can we talk after this?"

"I'd like that." Hell, I was about to see a family member beheaded; I'd *need* someone to talk to after this, 'cause even for an ex-assassin, that was next-level.

"Al—"

"*Shut up*, Jax!" I yelled, not bothering to look back at the wizard. "I don't care where you stand. Keep out of the way."

A few fae sniggered, and though it was petty, I took pleasure in that. Jax shouldn't be here. And he was making my life much more difficult right now.

I climbed the stairs leading to the platform that the guillotine was on. Though I'd been unsure about this whole setup, thought it a bit much, honestly, the others who'd passed judgment on my aunt had insisted upon it.

An ax would have worked fine to achieve justice, but the guillotine made a statement. My aunt had always relished saying 'Off with her head!'. Now she'd get to live it in the most flagrant fashion.

Sela White stood at the back of the raised wooden platform, her hands bound behind her in enchanted iron manacles, preventing her from using her magic and, from the looks of it, giving her one hell of a rash.

Behind her, down the steep cliffside, an empty beach crawled into a sprawling sea. It was the same beach where Chester had fought a kraken for me in the Calling of Creatures Trial. Somewhere beyond the water was the mainland of Faerie. We'd be there soon, infiltrating the Dark Court.

Beside Sela was her King consort. He'd been sentenced to die too. After all, he might not have partaken in every horrific act Sela had, but he'd stood by and watched it happen. If anyone had the power to stop her, it was him, but after a trial of his own, it was determined that he hadn't made a single move against her. He'd been happy to stay quiet and allow himself to benefit from my aunt's wicked streak. He was as guilty as her.

I walked up to the former queen, chin lifted. "You requested to speak with me?"

"You're really going through with this? Killing off your blood?"

"I don't see why you think it's appropriate to ask me that," I said. "You killed my parents. Would have killed me, had I not overpowered you."

She snarled at that, but regained her composure quickly. "I . . . have anger issues, but you're better than me, Alice. We're blood, and if you give me the chance, I can do better."

"You're no blood of mine," I said. "You gave up that right long ago."

"If you get rid of me, Alice, then the prophecy is yours to bear alone. But I can guide you back to the light. I could watch out for you." She quirked a dark eyebrow, and I hated that, even now, after she'd been imprisoned for days and dirt smeared her face, the Red Queen was still beautiful. "I assume you have told no one of your fate? What it is I'd tried to avoid?"

"I will not pull the kingdom into darkness. Nor 'kill many,'" I hissed. "My parents didn't believe in that, and I don't either."

Liar.

Despite my inner voice's accusation, I wasn't sure is I believed in the prophecy or not, but it did make me think my plan was smart. If I wasn't in this realm, I couldn't pull Wonderland into darkness. If I wasn't here, I would have no hand in its course.

"Your sister knows of the prophecy. She believes it."

I snorted. "Why am I even talking to you? You're a

psychopath. A liar. You're the one who was dragging the kingdom into darkness, not me."

"Perhaps. But perhaps not. Are you willing to take that chance?"

I scowled. *No more of this.* "I'm going to give you one more chance to earn a shred of my respect. Tell me exactly where Elise is."

Sela smirked. "You know where she is, Alice. The only place she could be." Her red lips pursed. "The Dark Court."

I stared at her, unable to believe that she'd actually said it. She'd hinted before, given me enough to be 99% certain, but she'd not actually spoken the name. The fact she'd actually given me something to go on was shocking.

"You'll never see her," Sela added. "She's there forever."

"We'll see about that." I waved at the soldiers standing a respectful distance away. "Off with her head."

As I descended the stairs, heavy footsteps assured me that the soldiers were doing as I requested, and by the time I reached the ground, Sela was standing before the guillotine.

I nodded to Alran, who, after the death of Herald, would play the part of crier.

The tall elf marched to stand in front of the platform, and the crowd silenced. Only the faint sounds of the ocean filled my ears.

"We stand here today to witness the execution of the once-queen, Sela White," Alran boomed. "She was found guilty of many crimes, the most severe of which were against the fae of Wonderland, the very people she was sworn to protect."

Jeers came from the crowd, but we weren't having that. I wanted this over with fast, wanted others to witness it and leave. Wanted to get on with saving my sister.

I blasted aether into the air, creating a *boom*, and every single trap shut.

"Go on, Alran," I ordered in the restored silence.

He cleared his throat. "For that, Sela White, you are to meet your end by beheading. Any last words?"

I'd rather not have given her any, but apparently, it was tradition. So I just crossed my arms over my chest as Alran joined me, Hatter, Sansu, and the pixies, and waited.

The once-queen was still standing between two soldiers, her hands clasped in front of her. The executioner, who had only one job, waited behind the fallen monarch.

My aunt sneered down at the people of her kingdom. "You lot will rue the day you turned your backs on me."

"Is that all?" I yelled.

She sneered, but said nothing more.

"Proceed," I commanded the guards.

The pair of soldiers shoved my aunt to her knees, and the executioner approached. One pull of the string that held the blade, and it would fall, severing her neck.

That gruesome effect wasn't something I ever thought I'd want to see, but I did want vengeance for my family, so

I remained rooted in place, determined to witness every second.

The executioner got into position, and murmurs rippled through the crowd. My aunt lifted her chin. She looked supremely confident.

Part of me respected her for that, but a much larger part hated her ass.

She has no right to be—

A growl rumbled through the air, turning into a roar, and I stiffened.

What the hell was that?

The question had barely formed when a frigid breeze blew over the cliffside, so cold that I wrapped my arms around myself.

Something was wrong . . . off. And I wasn't the only one who sensed it. On the platform, the soldiers had frozen—the executioner too.

Sela, on the other hand, was laughing. And as a dragon—the fabled jabberwocky—blasted out of the clouds, understanding dawned.

"Now!" I screamed. "*Now!*"

But it was too late. The moment the jabberwocky appeared, dark figures climbed up and over the cliff. They were black as night, moved like smoke, and had eyes that gleamed like garnets.

Fae screamed. Some pushed at others and began to run.

"What the—"

"Dark Court Shadows! The civilians need to run!"

Halad shouted as the jabberwocky's two tails pierced through the hearts of the soldiers on the platform.

They fell, their eyes vacant. The beast then wasted no time spearing the executioner.

"Soldiers, attack!" Halad yelled, taking control of the situation like a trained soldier would.

My aunt rose to her feet as four Shadows approached her. One placed its hands on her manacles. The iron dissolved as if it *weren't* metal designed specifically to keep fae trapped.

How did it do that? Aren't they fae?

Then another detail struck me.

"Is that demon magic?!"

The red color was so similar, but I couldn't be certain. Some witches had red colored magic too.

I squinted, trying to determine how to best this new opponent, as my aunt used her aether magic, not to attack, but to free the king consort.

"Al!" Jax yelled, and suddenly, I was tossed to the ground and sent rolling.

Fae cried and screamed and trampled all around us now, desperate to leave, to save their own skin.

I pushed at the person who'd flung themselves at me. "Get off!"

"Al, I saved your ass." Jax shot back, pulling me up. "Look!" He pointed to where I'd just stood, and I gaped.

The ground was scorched. I hadn't seen the attack coming, but it had very nearly killed me.

Wait . . . I hadn't been standing there alone. Where was Hatter?! The pixies? Alran and Sansu?

The answer came a moment later as Hatter pushed his way through the crowd. The others were right behind him.

His emerald gaze cut to Jax, and he nodded.

"We need to stop her!" I yelled.

"Too late." Hatter pointed toward the sea.

All my breath left me. My aunt was on the dragon's back, and the creature was flying away. Right behind Sela, the king sat, stealing terrified glances back at the crowd. The Shadows were riding the jabberwocky too, red eyes gleaming our direction, as if anticipating an attack.

"Let's follow her," I pressed. "Let's—"

"Bad idea," Halad barked from behind me.

I spun to find the Prince of the Riverlands speckled with blood, his sword drenched. My heart leapt into my throat. Where was his mother? Was she unharmed? The prince carried weapons, but the queen . . .

"Your mother?"

"She's fine. Her soldiers shielded her, but it was a close one."

I exhaled. Only one queen was meant to meet her end today, and it was not Aquatia. "Good. Then to the stables. If we get the gryphons ready, we can catch up."

"No," Halad said, his tone an order that froze me before I'd even taken a step. "Alice, remember the scar I showed you?"

"Yeah."

"A Shadow gave me that. On the other side of the Rift there are armies of them. You're not prepared to face them; their magic is different. She's going to the Dark Court, right?"

"I'm aether-blessed." I challenged, not answering his question.

"As am I. But they're faster and stronger than normal fae."

"You told me you were caught unawares before."

Halad scowled. "True, but you wouldn't catch her anyway. The jabberwocky is fast."

I wanted to retort, but a glance at the sky told me he was right. The dragon had already disappeared into the clouds.

CHAPTER 6

My friends and I marched through the castle corridors, seeking a place to speak plainly and, hopefully, solve the catastrophe I now found myself in.

In a mere hour, the city had gone from celebration to uproar. Fae who'd been present during the botched execution had dispersed into Heartstown, taking with them the tale of my aunt's escape.

I suspected that her few supporters would spin this in a way to validate her claim to the throne. And while I might not want to wear the crown myself, we certainly couldn't have *her* back in power, so I sent squadrons of soldiers out into the city to squash any uprisings before they began.

A general had warned me against sending armed fae away from the palace, arguing that the Red Queen might return at any moment, but that would not be the case. Sela was long gone. She'd seek refuge in the Dark Court.

When she gets there, what will happen to Elise?

My pulse quickened, and as if he could hear it, Hatter eyed me sidelong. I swallowed and looked away.

My aunt knew I intended to save my sister. Would she move her? *Could* she? How was Sela White even going to get into the Dark Court? Aquatia had said only one person had crossed the Rift and he hadn't been well afterward. Could Sela get through unscathed?

But then again, the Shadows had gone through the Rift too. Would their magic help someone cross the Rift?

My fists clenched so tightly that my fingernails cut into my palms. I'd been so close to getting vengeance for my family, and then *poof!* . . . my victory vanished.

"In here," Sansu said.

He'd been leading those closest to me, plus Halad and —of course—nosy Jax, through the castle, to a quiet place to talk. How he'd become so familiar with the fortress, I didn't know, and didn't care. Right now, I only wanted to find my aunt.

The blue-haired dwarf opened a door decorated with two crossed, steel swords, and we marched inside to find a space dominated by a wooden, circular table. Etched into its surface was a map of Faerie.

"Is this a . . . war room?" I asked.

"It was. Your grandfather was the last to use it, according to one of the older guardsmen," Sansu informed me. "During his rule, Faerie was in a time of great tumult."

I turned, taking in all the details.

Most of the castle had been transformed in Sela's rule to reflect her warped sense of herself. Hearts adorned nearly every surface and wall, even lining the steps down to the dungeons. Here, however, there was none of that. Taken by itself, I would have thought this space belonged to another castle.

"Did they redecorate already?" The thin layer of dust on the table made it seem unlikely.

Sansu shook his head. "The Red Queen never used it. By her design, Wonderland was isolated, so there was no need for a war room." He brushed off a few chairs, and dust filled the air. "Actually, the guard I spoke with said she avoided this place."

Interesting . . .

"How did the old king die?" I asked.

"Rumor has it, he passed in his sleep," Alran replied, though he sounded skeptical.

Fae lived much longer than humans. Since learning I was full fae, I hadn't considered my grandparents much, but now it struck me as odd that they'd perished. Even human grandparents often lived to see their grandchildren well into adulthood.

But perhaps my grandparents were super old when they had Sela and my mother?

Or . . .

"Did Sela get along with her father?" The question was out of my mouth before I could guard it.

The others exchanged unsure glances, and Henri shrugged. "There's no way for us to know, but there are older fae working in the castle. Perhaps ask them?"

I nodded and made a mental note to put Chester on that task. Fae loved Cheshire cats and rarely spoke with one. So when fae could speak to one they really seemed to open up to the cat. Plus, I didn't have the time to conduct those interviews myself. If the others agreed with my plan, I wouldn't be staying here much longer and would need to rely on my friends to help in my absence.

Figuring we should get on with it, I waved my hand, calling my air magic. Wind gusted over the table, sending the dust soaring out an open window. "Should we begin?"

Everyone sat, and as I did so, I took in the map.

Wonderland Island was obvious—it was the largest landmass off of the mainland, but not the only one. There were actually many islands, most of them small, but that didn't mean fae did not live there.

"Where is the Crystal Court?" I asked.

"Why?" Alran's eyebrows knitted together.

"Because I spoke with Queen Aquatia earlier, and she said that only one fae, other than Shadows, has passed through the Rift, and they came from there."

Eyes widened all around.

Dee recovered first, fluttering from where she'd sat cross-legged on the table to a spot on the map. She landed and spun, which made Jax nod like an old, gross lecher.

Appropriately, Dee scowled at him before directing her attention to me. "Right here."

I squinted, taking in the island named, simply, Crystal Island. "That's small."

The landmass had to be at least a fifth the size of Wonderland Island. It was also very far away, as if it had been flung into the middle of the sea by a giant.

"How many people reside there? And in the Crystal Court specifically? How long will it take to fly there?"

"A day," Halad replied. "As for the population, no one knows for sure. Not a soul has spoken to a fae from that court in . . . decades. Maybe longer."

"Why not?"

"They do not leave the island, and only accept certain visitors," Halad explained. "Royal ones. For marriage."

"But in a pinch, it's rumored they marry brother to sister," Sansu inserted, nose wrinkling. "That's what they do if no other court wishes to wed off an heir. Which is common. After all, the other court will never see their family member again, unless they're permitted to visit the Crystal Court."

"Okay, one—gross. Two . . . I thought royal marriages in this realm were for alliances? If they never leave the island, then what good is their allyship? Aren't allies for . . . war?"

"They are," the prince agreed. "But the Crystal Court

does not battle. Instead, they offer up their resources to those in their good graces."

"What resources?" I asked.

"Crystals. Magical ones."

"What do they do?"

"Many things. Though, most who own them keep them secret. They're valuable."

The more I learned about this court, the sketchier it felt.

"Okay, well, I think I need to go there and learn how one of their citizens crossed the Rift, because I'm one hundred percent sure the Red Queen is heading to the Dark Court, and the only way there is through the Rift." I leaned back in my chair. "I need to get to her before she moves Elise somewhere."

Silence shrouded the table, only to be broken by Jax.

"I'm new here and all, but isn't the Rift a cloud of deadly, all-consuming darkness that surrounds two kingdoms?"

"It is," Henri gritted out, pointedly not looking at the wizard.

"It surrounds both the Dark Court and the Cove Court," Sansu elaborated. "The Cove Court is basically a hostage of the Dark Court."

"Then how the hell do you think you're going to get through it, Al?" Jax looked at me, a million questions in his eyes.

"Oh, not just me," I said. "I'll be taking an army. Elise is a princess, and my aunt is still wanted for her crimes. I need to figure out how to get through—which is where the Crystal Court comes in."

"You do know that they won't give you something for nothing, right?" Halad spoke up. "If you truly wish to bargain with the Crystal Court, you best have something they want."

"I have gold."

The coffers of Wonderland were, apparently, full of it. Though I had meant to spend most of it on renovating the city, I was willing to set aside a sizable portion for this.

Elise mattered. Catching a tyrant mattered.

"That might be enough," Halad considered, though he didn't look convinced. "They also might request a favor."

My face fell. A favor? I wasn't sure what Halad knew about my past, but I excelled at one thing: killing. And with the exception of Sela White—who was being executed by committee—I didn't want to do that again. Thought I'd walked away from it.

"I guess I have to be prepared for what they may want, and willing to negotiate. But that brings me to my next point." I stood and leaned over the map, pointing to the Riverlands. "I spoke with Queen Aquatia. She is allowing us to enter the Rift through her territory. But, since not all of us can go to the Crystal Court, I need some to stay behind and ready an army."

"I'm with you," Henri said, and my insides warmed.

"Us too!" Dee and Dum shouted.

As I couldn't see how they'd be any help in organizing an army but knew them to be charming buggers, I wanted them with me. "For sure."

"If you wish," Halad began, "I will assist your army and bring my own. You will be traveling through my lands, after all."

My heart warmed. Halad was really staying true to his offer of friendship. I wouldn't forget it.

"I'll assist with the army too," Sansu said.

"Wherever you think I'll be best, that's where I'll go," Alran put in.

So far, it was me, Henri, and the pixies journeying to the Crystal Court. Alran was a burly elf, and having a bit more muscle as backup never hurt, but I had a feeling that coming with a smaller entourage would be better. Less threatening. Plus, Sansu and Halad would need assistance to prepare an army so quickly. Especially one that had not had to leave Wonderland for years.

"Help Sansu move the army to the Riverlands," I told Alran. "We'll meet you there once we're done at the Crystal Court. A week at most."

"As you wish, Princess Alice."

"And of course, I'm with you too, Al."

How Jax even thought this had anything to do with him was a testament to how self-centered he could be.

"Yeah, no. You're staying here."

"Remember our deal? Plus, I saved your tits." He winked. "Out of everyone here, I'm clearly the best bodyguard."

"And someone who does not belong in this world," Hatter growled.

I chewed on my bottom lip. Jax annoyed me because we had a past, but while I could understand Henri feeling uneasy over the wizard, he seemed to dislike him more than I thought was reasonable.

We'd need to talk about that.

"Which, to be fair, might work to your benefit," Halad said of Hatter's point. "The Crystal Court likes novelty—or so I hear. I suppose it makes sense. None of the royals have ever left the island. Bringing a sort of . . . show horse in the form of a wizard could work in your favor."

"I'm no show horse," Jax shot back. "But I'm willing to *act* as a distraction. For Alice."

"Okay," I sighed. "You can come."

If Halad thought it was smart, I'd put aside my reservations. Plus, I didn't want Jax hanging around even longer because I'd gone back on my word.

"Sansu, can you get working on the army stuff? Ask any soldiers—or rebels—if they want to join the cause. Alran, can you get me gold and gems before helping Sansu? And take Halad."

The prince arched an eyebrow. "Is this because of how I dress?"

He did resemble a peacock a bit, but in a surprisingly manly way. I liked it. Though, that wasn't why I'd chosen him.

"You're more likely to know what sort of priceless

baubles a royal would want. How many people are in the royal family anyway?"

"Last I heard, there was the king and queen, and their adult children, three princesses and one prince." He shrugged. "That could have changed. The queen and king still live, so there might be younger children now."

"And who rules? Have the king and queen handed over the crown?"

"I can't say for certain."

This is going to be interesting.

I considered our options, and one more name came to mind.

"Do you think we should bring Chester? My Cheshire cat?"

Henri's eyebrows pulled together. "You can't. Cheshire cats are bound to Wonderland Island. It's why they exist here, but nowhere else in Faerie."

"Oh." My stomach sank. I'd been hoping to bring Chester along. No doubt, he would have been handy.

Then again, he could be an asset here too. After all, when I returned, I'd need a trusted source to tell me what had happened in my absence.

"That settles that, then. The rest of us . . . " I straightened my shoulders. "Let's get changed and pack whatever we might need for a few days. Once I get that gold, and the gryphons have been readied, we're leaving."

I stepped into the musty-smelling stables to find I'd beaten Henri, Jax, and the pixies there, but Halad had arrived before me. He stood next to a winged unicorn so white and glittering, it looked like it had rolled around in freshly fallen snow.

"Aren't you supposed to be helping Alran? You trying to sneak into our group?" I teased, approaching the prince and the mythical creature slowly.

If there was anything I'd learned so far in Wonderland, it was that no matter how beautiful or serene in appearance, anything could be deadly.

"The elf has it handled. He'll be here shortly with bags of gold and gems for you to take to your negotiations —but there is another matter I consider important to your mission."

"What's that?"

"Ensuring your stable hands know what to have you ride. You mentioned gryphons, and that won't do."

"Why not?" I'd reached them now, and set down my bag filled with clothes and a few choice daggers.

"As I suspected," Halad laughed, "you need royal etiquette lessons."

"Probably for years," I snorted. "But seriously, why not gryphons?"

He and his mother had ridden a gryphon here. The creatures were dependable and built for flying long distances.

"The Court you're arriving at is quite stuck in the past —which is saying a lot, because we're here and not in the human world. Things move slowly in Faerie. I can't be certain, but I believe they'll see it as an affront. If a royal arrives on a gryphon, it's as though your visit is not worth the best Wonderland can offer their court. So you will be riding this beauty."

A thrill ran through me as I looked over the winged unicorn. "What's her name?"

"Valia."

"Lovely. Can I pet her?"

Halad laughed. "She's yours."

Oh, right.

Technically, everything in this castle was, and that still weirded me out.

Slowly, I extended my hand, and Valia didn't balk when my palm landed on her neck. Beneath my fingers her coat was pure velvet, so soft and warm.

"Hey there, pretty," I whispered. "I guess you and I are in for a long journey."

"Thankfully, she will keep up easily with the gryphons your friends will be riding. And that's another thing." Halad cleared his throat. "You'll all have to take a rest tonight."

"But I want to be there in the morning."

"I figured as much, but that would be poor form too. Try to arrive around midday. It's traditional."

I huffed. "Fine."

"There are smaller, uninhabited islands on the way. You can camp on one of those. By my calculations, you should fly over a grouping of them before the sun sets."

I'd noticed them on the map, and had procured a paper copy for the journey, so I nodded.

I had a good sense of direction, and Jax was actually amazing at that too. At least, he had been in our world. I hoped the skill would translate to another realm, because I couldn't count on anyone here to know the way. They'd been kept locked up for far too long.

"Valia seems to be taking well to you," Halad said with a smile, stepping back. "I suppose I should get on with my duties. Raising an army takes time. We'll see you in the Riverlands within the week." He waved, and had gone no more than three steps when I twisted.

"Hey, Halad?"

"Yes?"

"Thanks for this. I know this isn't your fight, but I appreciate the help."

"The Rift is on my court's land. And we are allies. I will do what I can to assist." He cocked his head, and the sound of high-pitched voices met my ears. The pixies were on their way. "I believe you will be leaving soon. Fly safe, Alice."

I had only a minute of peace before the pixies zoomed in with Henri.

"We're all packed!" Dum singsonged, pulling a small, blue trunk behind her. How it was even aloft was beyond me. The thing had to be nearly as large as Dum herself.

"Do we each get one of those to ride?" Dee beamed, leading her own trunk, which was similar to her sister's but red.

"Uh, I doubt you'll be riding alone," I said. Then, because I couldn't resist, I added, "Unless there's a large fly around here somewhere?"

Predictably, the girls scowled at my joke, but Hatter's lips pulled up in a smile.

My heart warmed. Things had been so strained with us since Jax's arrival. I wanted it to be back to normal.

But is that smart? You're leaving, the voice in my head reminded me, and not for the first time, I questioned myself. Could I really do this? Leave my friends, and soon, my sister?

All I knew was I didn't want the crown and everything that came with it. I wasn't built for caring for so many. For leading others.

"We're going to see if there's something for us to ride," Dee said haughtily. "I don't know if I want to sit with such a sarcastic person for such a long flight. Even if you do get the most beautiful creature."

They flew off, and I snorted a laugh. I hadn't known my comment would put them in such a tizzy.

"They're definitely riding with one of us," Hatter said as he approached, staring at the winged-unicorn. "Halad told us you'd be on an alicorn."

"Her name is Valia." Slowly, I stroked her neck. "I didn't know that was what her kind was called. She's beautiful."

"Not as beautiful as you."

I broke from worshiping Valia and suddenly, nothing else in the world existed. Only Henri, his emerald eyes, his beautiful soul. That smile that had so often captivated my attention. The air even changed, became charged and certainly warmer.

Boy, do I have it bad.

"Alice," Henri cleared his throat. "I want to say that I'm so—"

"We ready to get this show on the road?!" Jax's voice cut through the tender, soft moment, setting my teeth on edge.

How does he do it!?

Ignoring Jax, I grabbed Henri's hand. I wanted a little healing between us.

"Don't worry about it. I—he's a lot."

"You don't say," Hatter grunted as, at that exact moment, an arm flung over my shoulder, causing Valia to shuffle back a few paces.

Henri looked like he wanted to punch Jax's lights out, but the wizard leaned into me, like we were the best of friends, like he belonged.

"You scared my ride," I chastised my ex, shimmying out of his grasp.

"Yeah, that's a sweet horse. Pretty . . ."

Valia stomped on the ground violently, and because he wasn't a total idiot, Jax backed up.

I thanked the gods I hadn't called her a pegasus or a unicorn. Clearly, Valia understood English and wanted to be recognized for what she was.

"She's obviously not a horse. She's an alicorn," I scoffed, as if I'd known the term all along.

Hatter's lips pulled up, and I winked at him, acknowledging our inside joke.

"What are we riding?" Jax asked.

"We're taking gryphons," Dum piped up, soaring back our way, her arms crossed over her chest. "Jax and Hatter are, that is. The stable master is sizeist! He won't give Dee and me our own."

"Uh." Whether from the pixies' dilemma or the idea of riding a gryphon, for once, Jax was speechless.

As it turned out, he didn't have to worry about responding, because at that moment, Alran strode into the stables with two soldiers, each carrying two bags weighed down with treasure.

"This should be enough," Alran said. "There are some very valuable gemstones in there, and enough gold to set up numerous families for life. We'll have to tie three bags to a separate gryphon, though. They're heavy."

"Will the one without a rider fly with the rest of the flock? It won't veer off?" I asked.

The stable master appeared a short distance away. I wasn't sure how long he'd been there, nor did I really care. We hadn't said anything that the fae of Wonderland shouldn't know.

"It's called a drift, Princess Alice, not a flock," he corrected. "And the royal gryphons are trained to remain together during flight."

"Perfect. Let's get the pack-gryphon weighed down with gold and gems," I said, ready to move, "then we can saddle up and hit the skies."

CHAPTER 7

My inner thighs ached, and my cheeks stung from the ever-present wind whipping across my face. Hoping to spot land soon, I craned around Valia's thick neck.

We'd been flying for hours, and the sun was officially setting. Prince Halad had mentioned we'd reach a smattering of small islands to camp on by sunset, and before leaving Wonderland, I'd calculated the same. In flight I'd checked the map too. Twice. We should be coming across them at any moment.

So where the hell were they?

The ocean stretched on and on and on, blue and vast, as if nothing else existed this far away from Wonderland Island.

"We should be seeing land, no?" Jax yelled from the back of his gryphon, his blond curls flying every which way.

"Any moment now," Henri yelled back. Dee craned her head over his thigh and shot me a gleeful thumbs up. "Alice has led us true. Something is off, though."

"Any ideas?" I called out, eyes stinging from another strong, salty gale.

From where she perched in front of me, Dum tipped her head back to get my attention.

"What's up?" I asked.

"I think they're hidden by magic!"

My lips parted with surprise. "But why?"

"The Crystal Court doesn't want visitors, and they know most people who come anyway will have to stop. At least to let their mounts rest." Dum patted Valia's heaving neck.

She was right. For the last hour or so, my alicorn had become increasingly tired. We really needed to land so she and the gryphons could take a breather.

"That's devious of them," I muttered.

"It's something your aunt would have done," Dum replied.

But the fact was, she hadn't—and Sela was aether-blessed, capable of performing pretty amazing feats of magic. That led me to believe she couldn't hide an island as big as Wonderland.

Which meant the Crystal Court not only had magic gemstones, but powers the likes of which I had not yet seen.

Will Crystal Island be hidden too?

I groaned but didn't want to get off-track, so instead

of wallowing, I called to the others. "Dum thinks the island might be hidden with magic!"

"That—that's a valid idea!" Hatter agreed with the pixie, sounding surprised he hadn't considered it.

"How will we find it, then?" Jax asked. "Is it hidden by aether?"

"Let me try with my earth magic," Henri replied.

He slowed to hover in the air, and Jax and I followed suit. Magic sprayed from Hatter's palms and floated down to the water. It struck the surface and spun lower, green swirls in the blue-gray of the water, radiating outward.

Hatter's best elements were earth and water, directly in opposition to my fire and air. If anyone could find solid ground, it was Henri.

An instant later, he had an answer for us. "I sense land below. It can't be too far, if I can feel it, but someone has hidden the islands we're seeking."

"Maybe I can use my aether to find it," I said. "Dum, take the reins." I handed her the straps, then rubbed my freezing hands together to warm them before pressing them out in front of me.

Reveal what's hidden from sight, I willed, hoping that would be enough.

I had learned to wield aether with instinct, and after my lesson with Queen Aquatia, was feeling more confident with my relatively new magic, but there was still a lot I didn't know, and many feats that seemed too big for me. Would this be one of them?

My shimmering white magic soared downward in a

beam of light, toward the churning waters. My magic raced over the sea, clinging to the waves and the spray. I held my breath, watching, waiting.

Will it know which way to go?

Suddenly, the aether power stopped and began to expand, revealing land inch by inch.

In moments, an island appeared where water had just been.

"By the old gods," I murmured.

"Told you! They're crazy," Dum said, clearly proud she had been right.

Crazy and very, very powerful.

"Let's discuss this on the ground."

My aether had broken the shield of magic, and as such, the barrier was disintegrating. I'd uncovered a beach, part of a jungle, and more was coming. But I couldn't be sure how long it would last.

Additionally, I didn't want to risk whatever magic the Crystal Court had used to cover up the island overtaking my power and disappearing again. Surely, once we were on land, we'd continue to see it.

At least, I hoped so.

Together, our group directed our mounts toward the land. With each beat of their wings, and push of magic, more geography was uncovered, another curve of the island.

We touched down on sand, bones jostling with the impact.

"I need to use the woods!" Dum leapt off the saddle, soaring away on buzzing wings.

"Don't go too far!" I yelled as Dee leapt from Hatter's mount and followed her sister into the jungle off the beach.

At first glance, this island appeared tropical, so unlike Wonderland's temperate climate. It was definitely warmer, too, by at least ten degrees.

"I think my legs are actually asleep," I moaned as I slipped off of Valia's back to stand on wet sand.

"Same, Al. That was rough." Jax rubbed at his thighs, and I had to admit that he'd probably had it worse. The gryphons were wider than Valia.

Hatter was the only one who looked unaffected by the ride. As if he realized the same thing, he waved to Jax and me. "Walk a little. I'll take care of the supplies."

"You sure?"

"Absolutely."

"Thanks, Henri." I smiled and began to walk down the beach.

"That was wild, wasn't it, Al?" Jax ran up to me, his gait awkward after our journey. "Hiding a whole island is some serious magic."

"Yeah, but I don't think it's too large." I stared down the beach, both trying to get a sense of the size and to avoid looking at him.

"Still. I couldn't do it."

"Aether-blessed fae are a different breed." I was fully aware I was talking about myself now, though I didn't feel that way. "Honestly, I think this Court will be stronger than other fae know."

Jax turned to me. "How does it feel? To be aether-blessed?" His tone was genuine, full of curiosity.

It must have come as a big surprise to him to learn I could wield aether. When we'd dated, I thought I was demi-fae, not a full fae of royal blood.

"It's challenging to use but also kind of natural now," I replied slowly, "but at first, I didn't believe Henri about what I could do. He knew who I was, though . . . what I was."

"How was your power hidden?"

"By trauma," I admitted. "I guess it had kind of buried itself inside me. Now, I feel more whole."

"Do you feel like you belong here?" He stopped, and I was compelled to do the same. His amber eyes studied me like he was trying to work out what I'd say. Who I was now.

I wasn't even sure I knew the answer to the latter.

Faintly, I became aware that my legs had regained full sensation. My feet too. I dug my toes into the sand and took a deep breath of Faerie air.

A week ago, I would have answered the question of belonging with a resounding *no*, but with each passing day, I became less sure of my convictions.

I didn't totally fit in here. But I also didn't feel as if I'd fit in back home, either.

"Kind of," I said instead. "I'm getting used to it, but I still plan on returning to the human world."

Jax nodded slowly. "Can I tell you something?"

"Uh, sure?"

"I think you *do* belong here, Al." He exhaled. "Not with that guy, but here, in this world."

I snorted. "'That guy'? As in Henri?"

"Obviously. I came here for you, and I'm happy I did, but it's easy to see you're super comfortable here." He paused. "So, if we can fix things, I'm down to stay."

Oh riiiiiight. I was actually supposed to be giving him a chance.

In that case . . .

"You know how shattered I was when you left, right?" A huff escaped my lips. "I felt . . . broken. But didn't even get the chance to process it in a healthy way, 'cause . . . Doru."

Jax cringed. "He didn't give you any time?"

"Not a single day. I was on a mission the afternoon after you left."

He swallowed. "I had to leave, couldn't risk staying when I hit eighteen. His threats were real."

"Still, did you have to leave in the middle of the night? You couldn't wait until morning to pay off the vampire and say something to me then?"

My ex looked away, and something in his expression made the skin on the back of my neck tighten.

"Jax? You *did* pay the rest of what you owed Doru, right?"

"How could I?!" he retorted. "He wanted me gone right away, so as not to distract you, and I wasn't messing with that. I seriously didn't have time to even gather funds, and it's not like I had credit or anything at that point. I just ran."

"Oh. My. God. You didn't pay him!?"

My heart rate accelerated at the idea, even though I'd done the exact same thing. The difference was I'd told Xavier *to his face* that he wasn't getting the money; that he owed me for keeping my past a secret. And shockingly, he'd agreed.

Jax could claim none of those things.

"He could have hunters after you right now!" I spit out.

"That's why I think staying here is a good idea," Jax admitted.

I gaped. "Are you telling me *that's* why you came? You thought you'd be safe in another realm?"

"No . . . I mean, it was part of it, but I really did come for you, Al."

His gaze met mine, revealing so many things in the depths of his eyes. Shame. Sadness. But also, truth.

We were so messed up, the pair of us. Maybe we really were meant to be together.

My stomach tightened.

Down the beach, Valia neighed, breaking my connection to Jax. I turned and saw Hatter pulling the saddle off of her, his shoulders so bunched and his attention so pointed on the alicorn that he had to be fighting his urge to watch Jax and me.

His presence washed over me, calming, though he wasn't even looking at me.

I took a deep breath and let the air clear the fog in my mind. Jax might be here, and yes, we had a past, but *Henri* was the person I wanted. I just had to come to terms with the fact that having him meant I'd have to make a choice: Faerie or my old world.

The fire crackled, and the waves crashed on the shore. We'd finished a dinner of sandwiches and apples, and darkness was beginning to settle on the island.

Though we hadn't been here long, we'd already done a sweep of the beach. The island was deserted, save for a few animals—evident by the droppings we'd found. However, no one had gone too far into the jungle. Why would we? We only needed to ensure the beach was safe and create a spot to sleep.

The latter was my job. As an aether-blessed fae, I could, theoretically, create a sort of shield around us. Between that and the blankets we'd brought, I was sure everyone would crash quickly. Then we'd be up at first light and continue flying south.

Dee lifted into the air, a yawn parting her lips as she stretched her thin arms wide. "I'm pooped!"

"Me too, sis." Dum looked at me. "Can you make the sleeping area now?"

"Sure." I rose and walked to where the jungle met the beach, as far away from the water as we could get.

In my world, the worst thing that could happen was the tide would roll in and we'd get wet.

But here . . .

Memories of the Calling of Creatures Trial came rushing back.

If a queen kraken could pull herself out of the water, I was sure any number of other dangerous beasts could do the same. Considering that possibility, we'd all rather have some space between us and the beings of the deep.

Jax used a spell to cut three enormous leaves from the jungle trees. They were so large, even Hatter, the tallest in our group, could lie down on one. It wasn't a mattress—hell, it wasn't even a sleeping pad—but it would keep the sand out of our cracks and crevices.

"Everyone good with right here?" I asked, approaching where the leaves had been set out so the remaining condensation could dry.

The guys were tending to the animals, preparing them for rest. The bags of gold and gems were set between the beasts; a deterrent if there were any fae on this island. The animals would warn us of thievery.

At my question, both men nodded gruffly.

Apparently, rather than go at each other's throats, they'd decided to ignore one another. That was better for me, though, so I turned to the girls.

"It's perfect," Dum said, pulling a smaller leaf from a

nearby tree and rolling it up into a pillow. "Can we sleep on yours with you, Alice?"

"Of course. There's room for three." *Well, when two of those people are four inches high.* "But don't hog the middle, or I'll have to wake you when I come to bed," I warned. "Got your blankets?"

Dee had been wrestling with something in her trunk. At that moment, she pulled out two wool blankets about the size of cloth napkins, and soared over with the bedding clutched in her hands. "Here!"

The pixies settled in, and I began working my protection magic, just how Aquatia had taught me.

I'd never had a need for that skill before now. My aether magic had come on so fast and mostly been used to battle my aunt. It felt good to use it for keeping those I cared for safe.

The shimmering white magic appeared as a dome, a basic shield I'd seen witches in my world make. I figured, 'if it ain't broke, don't fix it.'

The dome settled into the sand, undulating for a moment before solidifying.

"Will we be able to get out and go tinkle?" Dee asked.

"Good point. These will allow you to pass." With a flourish of my hand, aether badges in the shape of a rose appeared, pinned to their dresses.

Two others soared to the guys. I knew when they landed, because both men exclaimed their shock.

"Some notice next time, Al!"

"Oh, you're fine, Jax," I huffed, but couldn't resist a smile. "Night, girls. I'll join you soon."

"Night, Alice!" both pixies chimed.

I turned back toward the sea and found Hatter standing a few feet away, waiting.

"Care for an evening stroll?"

"Sounds great," I said, smiling.

Who could say no to some privacy on a secluded beach at night?

Well, not so secluded, I amended as Jax caught my eye.

He looked put-out, but he'd have to deal. I hadn't asked for him to return to my life, and in recent days, Hatter and I had barely had any alone time.

"We're going on a walk," I announced. "We'll be back soon."

"Stay in sight," Jax said, his lips downturned in annoyance.

If I was being charitable, I'd say the request was for safety, but I was certain that wasn't the case. Still, I'd pretend like it was.

"We'll be fine. Can you put the fire out?"

Jax snorted, but set to the task, clearly recognizing there would be no telling me what to do.

Henri did not bother to hide his smirk as we made our way down the beach, away from camp.

Once we were far enough away not to be over-heard, I turned to him. "Thanks for being so cool about everything. Jax, mostly. He's a pain in the ass, but the more I think about it, the more I have to admit he will probably be useful in the Crystal Court."

The wizard was a charmer, after all. Perhaps he could sweet-talk the royals into giving us what we needed, and in record time. If not, I hoped the gold and gems we'd brought would do the trick.

"If anything, having varied magics is useful," Hatter grumbled. "And they won't expect someone from the human realm. Honestly, I think you need him here."

"Why?"

"To make your choice."

"Which do you mean?" I kicked sand, unsure about this conversation.

"Me or him. Wonderland or your homeland."

My gut clenched. I was certain I was falling in love with Hatter, but the last question made committing scary. Like I was turning my back on my own dreams.

"You're who I want," I said. "But Jax won't let me go until I've given him a shot. Believe me, he's tenacious like that."

"I have no doubt. The man finagled his way into another realm for you."

I pursed my lips and kicked at the sand.

"Why do you want to go home so badly, anyway?" Hatter asked. "What's calling you back?"

In truth, no one and nothing. Just the world I'd grown up in, and the chance to actually *choose* who I was. Because here, I'd always be Alice White, Princess—or Queen—of Wonderland.

"I-I'm not sure you'd understand, but I've never been able to be anything but Alice the Dagger." I stared out at the waves, hating discussing my assassination days with Hatter. He was so good, so noble. "And here, I'd always be Alice White. Now that I no longer work with Doru, *if and when* I go back to my world, I can finally be whatever I want."

He stopped walking, so I did too. Slowly, we both turned to face the sea. Waves crept up the shore, coming within a few paces of our feet, and the water sparkled like diamonds in the moonlight.

"I do understand," he murmured. "Though, I admit I've never thought about it like that. Considering how you arrived in Wonderland, that was short-sighted of me. I apologize."

"There's no need." I paused. "To be honest, I wouldn't mind staying here if I had more choices. But so far, my time here has been targeted. First, my objective was to kill the Red Queen. Now, it's to *find* her and kill her —and rescue my sister, too. After that, I want to get to know Elise."

Silence wafted between us, as soft and welcoming as the sounds of the ocean. It struck me that this was one of the first times since I'd entered this realm that I felt still, calm.

With Henri next to me, it made the moment all the more special. I yearned to touch him. To lean into him and let go, just a little. To feel his skin next to mine.

As if he sensed my want, his fingers fluttered against my palm on their way to intertwining with my own.

My breath hitched, and slowly, I turned to find Henri watching me intently, his face ringed in moonlight, an entire sky of stars twinkling behind him.

I swallowed, inching closer.

"Alice," he whispered as I placed my palm on his chest.

"Yeah?"

"I want you to know, if you choose to stay, that would make me really happy."

Tears stung my eyes.

Henri was the best man I'd ever known—a fact that he'd proven time and time again. Did I want him? Hell yes. Did I deserve him? I wasn't so sure.

But I'd always been one to take what I wanted, so I leaned closer.

He didn't pull back when my lips met his, soft and warm. He didn't stiffen or say that we should stop. Instead, a large hand wound around my back, pulling me closer.

And then there was just us, Alice and Henri, our lips exploring, our hands wandering across muscle-hardened planes and soft curves, our hearts beating. For a moment, we were everything and all that there was.

Two people, finally taking what we wanted, beneath a riot of stars.

CHAPTER 8

We made our way back to camp, my cheeks flushed, and happiness gushing through me.

Not that Hatter and I had finalized anything—what I'd do later was still something I had to consider—but a kiss like the one we'd shared was enough to turn around even the worst days.

I'd treasure it forever.

What I would *not* treasure, however, was the scowl on Jax's face as we got closer. Had he been watching us? Seen us kissing?

"Took you two long enough," he grumbled.

"You didn't have to wait up," I retorted. "We're all adults here."

"Sure. Whatever, Al." Jax rose from where he sat on the beach. "I'm going to bed."

At the mention of bed, even if it was an oversized leaf, my bones melted. "Same. I'm beat."

Henri came with, all three of us slipping beneath the protection I'd created. The pixies were already fast asleep, Dee snoring loudly, and Dum muttering something about a flying tortoise.

I smirked, already planning on teasing them tomorrow. They both thought they were dainty sleepers, but they absolutely were not.

At least they left me some space. I scooted onto the leaf, careful not to jostle the twins, and got settled. Once I was comfortable, I glanced at Hatter.

He winked, and the thrill of our kiss struck me again, as if we were locking lips at that very second. Butterflies filled my stomach.

"Night," Jax said, annoyance lacing his tone.

"Night, guys," I sang to let Jax know I didn't care about his feelings on matters pertaining to Henri and me. "Whoever wakes first has to get the rest of us up."

We fell quiet, and soon, the only sounds in my ears were that of the ocean. The waves lapping the beach relaxed me, and my body grew heavy. Knowing it was coming, I anticipated sleep claiming me.

And then, a distant sound made me sit straight back up.

Is that . . . wings? But it's so loud.

I glanced up at the sky and saw nothing. Waited for a creature to appear. Perhaps the jabberwocky?

A chill gripped my spine. Would my aunt actually follow me when she could remain safe in enemy lands?

Yes, one hundred percent she would. And I didn't

think for a second the shield I'd placed over us would hold up to a dragon.

I made to stand, to try and determine what the hell was actually happening, when the trees behind us leaned —no, nearly *bent in half,* with a gust of wind.

All my breath left me in one go as what had nearly toppled the jungle trees came into sight. A bird as big as a house! And another one just behind it, smaller, likely a baby—although it was still the size of a sedan . . . not exactly tiny. Both creatures had silver feathers tipped with black. Talons that had to be at least five-feet long glinted as the older bird flexed them.

I'd studied these beasts before the Calling of Creatures Trial. They were rocs—giant birds capable of carrying large loads.

I unleashed a stream of curses as the birds soared toward the gryphons, the larger plucking up one of our sleeping rides as if he were nothing more than a piece of popcorn.

The baby went in for a kill too, but it didn't scoop up another gryphon, or my alicorn. No, it wasn't large enough to manage those creatures so the youngling went for the bags of gold we'd brought, gripping all six in its talons.

Coins spilled out, hitting the sand and glinting gold in the moonlight.

My heart began to hammer. "Wake up, guys! Wake up!"

Henri and Jax rose immediately, shooting to their feet

in time to hear the stolen gryphon's cries for help, and witness the other gryphons take flight and Valia gallop down the beach to safety.

The pixies were only a second behind the men, shouts of astonishment leaving the twins' lips as they woke from slumber.

"What the hell is that?" Jax hissed.

"Roc. A giant bird."

"*Obviously!*"

"It can lift an elephant," I elaborated. "And—"

The larger roc stole the words from my mouth as its talons squeezed its prey so hard, the gryphon stopped screaming for help, stopped living.

The bird had literally squeezed it to death.

The roc then dropped the gryphon and surged upward, preparing to hunt another one of our mounts.

"They're going for more!" I yelled. "We can't let them!"

If we didn't have enough creatures to transport us, we'd have to fly to the Crystal Court on our own steam. Considering the distance, I wasn't even sure that was possible . . . especially when we took into account that Henri and I would have to trade off carrying Jax.

"We have to stop the big one," Henri said. "The small baby won't be able to lift any of the gryphons or Valia. If it could, it would have done so already."

"Don't hurt it, though," I said. Since arriving in Faerie, I'd had to injure the bandersnatch herd and kill a queen kraken. I hated hurting animals, and still had remorse about both. "Just make them leave!"

"What can we do to help?" Dee shouted, her eyes wide.

Honestly, I wasn't sure. This bird was enormous, but the twins were so small. Would it even be able to clutch them in its talons? Could they actually do something to help?

"No. Stay here. Stay safe," I urged, not wanting to risk it. They might evade the talons but what if the rocs snapped their beaks at the twins. It would be game over. "Out of the birds' reach."

Henri, Jax, and I left the cover of our shield, and the moment we did, the birds' attention snapped to us. I hadn't made us invisible, so clearly, they simply hadn't seen us before.

Our positioning up against the trees must have worked to hide the group. Too bad I hadn't made sure our mounts were in the same area.

Racing toward the birds, the adult screeched at the baby, which lifted higher into the air to protect itself. Two of us could have flown to follow it, but really, the larger one was the bigger threat. The adult that was now launching toward us, talons extended.

"Jax! Shield us!" I yelled, knowing he was talented in this magical act.

A bubble surrounded us, and the roc crashed into it. Beneath the weight of the bird, the shield shuddered violently.

Jax grunted, strengthening it on the go, and his magic held strong.

"On my word, drop it. I have air!" I instructed Jax and informed Hatter.

"Water!" Hatter called back, and where the waves lapped the sand, I spotted tendrils of water begin to lift and swirl.

I had no idea what he planned to do with them, but knowing Henri, he had something brilliant up his sleeve.

The bird rose into the air again, clearly intending to dive at us. The moment it was high enough to achieve maximum impact, it plummeted.

"Hold strong, Jax," I urged.

"Got it," he gritted out.

The roc slammed into the shield a second time, and the barrier actually cracked, but Jax was true to his word. Green flecks of magic lit up as he worked them to make the ward stronger.

This pissed off the bird, who beat its beak against the dome of magic surrounding us, pounding into the shield again and again and again, until blood speckled both our protection and its own feathers.

Finally, it reared its head back, fury in its yellow eyes. The moment had come.

"When it leaves to dive-bomb again, that's when we'll attack. Use its momentum to send it into the water."

The smaller one was circling out over the sea, near where it had dropped our gold and gems. It occurred to me that maybe if we got the adult that far out, the baby would call its parent, and the larger one would leave us be.

As I expected, the roc beat its wings, soaring backward.

"Now!" I commanded.

"Shield down!" Jax shouted back.

Henri and I struck, me with wind, and him with water. The bird hadn't been expecting the assault, and it spun backward, toward the wide-open ocean.

With some space between us, I had another idea that would probably ensure it forgot all about us.

Conjuring. I created a spectacle once . . . I can do it again.

I called on my aether magic and visualized the jabberwocky in the air, flying toward the baby roc. Once that image was clear in my head, I pushed my magic outward.

It soared toward the young one, forming as it went. And when it coalesced into the shape I needed, and the roc took notice, I pumped my fist into the air.

The larger bird wheeled, going after the dragon with admirable bravery. But I couldn't let it get too close. If it tried to sink its talons into the dragon's hide and found only air, it would know the threat was fake. Once that happened, it would probably return for us.

I needed the adult roc to believe in the danger so thoroughly that it left the island. So I steered the conjuring toward the baby, mouth wide and teeth bared, though no sound came out. If I could create sounds with aether, I hadn't learned how to yet.

Thankfully, the small one fell for the illusion, screeching and flapping frantically farther out to sea. Its parent laid chase, but my creation was faster, and I allowed the jabberwocky to get close enough that, if it were real, it would have bitten the youngling.

At the last second, the baby swooped upward, and I didn't move as fast, continuing my jabberwocky's straight trajectory. The parent, too, veered up, loud shrieks of indignation bursting from its beak as it collected its young one, shielding it.

Knowing this was my chance, I twisted the conjuring in the air, and again bared its teeth.

The roc hovered in the air, appearing to be deciding if retaliation was worth it. A soft keening from the young one sealed its choice, and the larger bird changed direction, flying away from the dragon, away from the island.

I waited until we could no longer spot the glimmer of silver feathers in the moonlight to release my breath and the magic. Immediately, my shoulders sagged.

Fear had boosted me through that event. As a result, I hadn't realized how much effort it had taken to create such an elaborate work of magic. Now that I had a moment to relax, I gulped down air, relishing the full breaths. I felt so drained, as if I'd swam all the way back to Wonderland Island.

"Al, that was awesome," Jax whispered, his tone slightly shaky. "I've never seen you do that."

"Aether magic," I answered wearily. "I'm still learning, and that conjuring was pretty big. Now, I'm dead."

"We all could have been *really* dead, though," Henri said. "That mother was out for blood. I wonder if this is her home?"

"How do you know it was female?" I asked.

"The fathers don't stick around, but the mothers are fiercely protective of their young and their land."

I swallowed. "Do you think the threat of a jabberwocky will keep her away? At least for the night?"

Hatter let out a soft hum. "It probably will, but we should take turns keeping guard. In case she comes back."

"After we get the gryphons and Valia," I sighed, scanning the beach.

I spotted the gryphons first. They'd landed right by Valia, who gleamed white against the night. Each creature was careful to maintain a fair distance,

She'd run away at the first hint of trouble, and neither roc had chased her, so I was sure she was fine.

"We can try to coax the alicorn back for you?" Dee suggested.

"That'd be great," I said. I was still breathing so hard.

"I'll approach the gryphons, but what about the gold?" Jax frowned. "Don't you need it?"

I did. It was our best chance of bartering with the Crystal Court.

"Do you think we could find it all?" I asked, though I

was certain it had been scattered. I'd seen the coins flutter from the bag, likely ripped by the young roc's talons. "Hatter, can you use your water magic to search for the treasure?"

"I'll try," he said.

As he'd offered, Jax went to try to bring the gryphons back. I hoped they didn't take flight when he approached, 'cause if they did, he was screwed. But I decided to let him deal with that, while I stayed to watch Hatter.

Henri walked to the ocean's edge and knelt, dipping his hand in the waves. Though I couldn't see his face, I imagined he closed his eyes to sense.

I willed him to feel the money, hoping it hadn't been scattered to the corners of the sea.

But Hatter's shoulders sagged as he rose. I deflated, sure that we were well and truly screwed.

He turned back to me, shaking his head. "I can't feel any metal or gemstones. Just normal minerals in the soil and plants. Some of the gold might wash up, though?"

I sighed. Even if a few coins or gems did wash ashore by morning, it wouldn't be enough leverage.

So, what now? Did we turn around? Return to Wonderland for more treasure, then start the journey again? Was it possible to bargain with just my magic?

No one knew exactly what powers were prominent in the Crystal Court. It had been so long since someone had been there. Or maybe the promise of an alliance would do? We were, after all, the closest thing they had to neighbors.

I tilted my chin to the sky, begging it for answers to questions that would probably keep me up the rest of the night.

CHAPTER 9

After a terrible night's sleep, and some deliberation, the next morning my friends, Jax, and I searched the beach for any treasure that may have washed up in the hours since the excitement. I was surprised to find a few coins and one enormous diamond.

We pocketed them, but they wouldn't be enough to barter with. Still, no one wanted to turn around, so we continued on.

In this matter, time was of the essence. I needed to infiltrate the Dark Court before my aunt thought to move Elise elsewhere.

So we flew. And as we flew, I thought. About how to convince the royals of the Crystal Court to help us. About my kiss with Henri. About the battle to come after we secured a way through the Rift.

And I thought about how, perhaps most shockingly,

Jax, Henri, and I had worked together the night before to get the rocs to leave the island. And this morning, the men in my life had barely been at one another's throats.

Progress.

"Is that land?" Flying at my left, Jax shielded his eyes from the brilliant sun and squinting into the distance.

I leaned over Valia's neck. She'd been skittish all morning, and I was willing to bet the giant diamond in my saddlebag that she hadn't slept well either.

For my mount's sake, I hoped we were getting close to our destination. She needed a plush stable and some rest.

"That has to be it," Hatter said from his place on the right. "The large structure on the cliffside looks almost like a castle."

"That *is* a castle!" I exclaimed, taking in the man-sized crystals glinting atop the spires, and the gorgeous stained glass in the windows.

The castle was every color of the rainbow, and though that design risked looking gaudy, it did not. It was fabulous, like a basket of gems gleaming in the sun.

"Doesn't look like any palace I've seen," Jax yelled into the wind.

"Which is how many? Two?" Henri countered.

"We have castles in the human world," I snorted. "But for reals, Jax. You haven't seen that many."

"You don't know what I've been doing these last few months," he retorted.

The moment he said it, his face fell slightly, but I

didn't comment. He was right. I had no idea—because he'd up and left me.

I wasn't going to pry and make him think I cared. I had cared way too much after he left, but I'd had to move on. To save myself.

Of course, that didn't mean I had to make him feel better about his actions.

Let him stew.

"How should we approach?" Henri asked.

This was not a matter I'd considered. Having never traveled to another court, I had no personal experience of such protocol, except for Halad and his mother visiting me. And they'd just flown up, seemingly with an idea about where to land—which I didn't have.

"Are landing pads generally kept in certain areas of a castle?"

Henri shrugged, and I was reminded that this was his first trip off Wonderland Island. We were all totally clueless.

"Maybe we can spot it when we get close?" Jax suggested.

"Yeah, sounds good." Hell, it sounded like our only option. "Let's veer right."

The guys followed my lead, and soon, we were close enough to the island to make out the features of individual fae. A few spotted us and pointed, but as far as I could tell, they were civilians, dressed in loose pants, tunics, or, in the case of females, dresses. They were not soldiers.

I wanted to land quickly, before any armed fae could approach and potentially tell us to leave. Of course, I'd pull the royal card if I had to, but as I was a new princess, I didn't know how much weight that carried.

Did people in this court know about the events in others? Would they take me at my word?

Would they care about royalty that was not their own? In the human world I was an American and I never thought about monarchies. Not unless I had to attend a high-society event for a job—which was rare.

I really wished we still had our gold. That would probably make things easier.

"There's a clear spot," Hatter pointed. "Close to the palace, too."

"Perfect. Go there."

We landed as one, with me in the middle of our small cluster. As soon as we touched down, the guys dismounted and surveyed the area. When no threat leapt out at us, Henri came to me, hand extended.

"If you want them to believe us," he began, "it's time to start acting like a real princess. From now on, we're not only your friends, but your guards."

"I have to keep my hands off you?" I teased softly.

"Preferably not," he rumbled. "But in public places, perhaps that's a good idea."

"An excellent one," Jax ground out.

"Shut up, Jax," I muttered.

A chastising along the lines of *what I do with Henri is none of your business* was on the tip of my tongue, when a number of fae ran up to us, armed with staffs topped with brilliant amethyst gems.

Staring down multiple threatening crystal-tipped weapons, I eyed Hatter sidelong. "Uh, are those for magic?"

"I guess so."

"They're pretty, but *weird*," Dee added softly.

I agreed. I also didn't want to take any risks regarding unknown weapons. So we didn't get blasted back to Wonderland Island, I held my hands up. "We come in peace. I'm Princess Alice White of the Wonderland Court, here to speak with your leaders."

Murmurs flitted through the ranks of the armed fae, and for a moment, no one moved. Then one, the smallest of the lot, lowered his staff and stepped forward.

His face was mostly covered by a large, bushy beard, but his silver wings were delicate. Between the pointed ears and wings, I marked him as being of the faerie race.

His eyes took me in with undisguised interest. "A princess, you say? Firstborn? An heir, or a bastard?"

"Um, isn't there a lot in between?" I joked.

The man scowled, telling me that my attempt at humor did not land, so I cleared my throat.

"I'm the firstborn heir of Isabel White and Fredric Torna. As it stands, I'm the only princess of my court, though that should change soon."

"You're with child?" the soldier asked, his nose wrinkling.

"What?! No!" I liked kids, but couldn't think of

anything worse for me right now. "My sister was taken long ago. She's alive, just not in my court."

"How old is she?"

I swallowed. I was getting the vague feeling that this was some sort of questionnaire.

"I wish to speak to your leaders," I repeated, not answering his question. It didn't feel right.

"Prince Cirrus is unavailable."

Dum hissed softly. That someone would not make themselves available to me was, apparently, unfathomable to her.

"When will he be able to entertain visitors?" I asked, not about to take no for an answer. "We've traveled a long way."

"We're under no promises to receive you, Princess Alice," said the short, silver-winged soldier. "However, if you wish to meet the prince, you must first go through a decontamination process."

"A—what?"

Images of standing in a room butt-naked and being sprayed with water came to mind. There was no way in hell I was subjecting myself, or my friends, to that.

"You cannot walk our sacred island as you came, and you certainly cannot be in the presence of our royal family." The soldier arched an eyebrow as if I was covered in mud.

Damn. I couldn't look great—who did, after a day of flying and camping on the beach?—but I couldn't look *that* bad!

"Do you consent to being cleansed? If not, you must leave Crystal Island."

My lips pursed. "What does the process entail?"

"I cannot say, for I do not perform the cleansing." The bearded soldier tilted his chin skyward. "I was born of this island, and have never left to acquire the taint of the greater realm on my skin."

I eyed Henri sidelong. He worked his jaw, but inclined his head to me, as if saying, '*We'll do what you think is best*'.

"Does it hurt?" I asked our reluctant hosts. "I won't consent if it's going to hurt us."

Another of the soldiers, a tall female with half of her head shaved, cleared her throat.

The one we'd been speaking to turned to her. "Yes, Aza?"

"Commander," she dipped her head to the silver-winged fae, marking him as a rank above her own. "I have undergone a cleansing. It does not hurt."

The commander turned back to us. "There you have it. Now, do you agree? Or shall I be forced to evict you from our paradise?"

They really think highly of themselves, don't they?

I wanted to push back, to insist on seeing the royals first, but I could tell from the looks in our welcoming party's eyes that we weren't going to get anywhere that way.

We were in a new place, a new culture, and we had to submit.

At least for the time being.

They try any messed-up stuff, and I'll tell them to go to Hell.

"We agree," I said finally.

"Very good. Come with me."

I gripped Valia's reins and followed the soldiers, my friends just behind me.

We'd landed close to the castle, but were now rounding the structure, which gleamed like the inside of a jewelry box. I wondered if the whole thing was made of gems, or just the outside. If it was totally composed of precious stones, that was a ton of crystals.

Not only was the palace stunning, but the people on its grounds were too. By the way they carried items or gardened, I assumed we only saw normal fae going about their day, but each one wore a gem-toned robe that fluttered in the breeze coming in off the sea. And small stones glimmered in their hair, even the men's, catching the light. Perhaps they were nobles?

"I want to do that," Dum whispered in my ear from where she sat on my shoulder, as we passed one fae female with green hair that grazed her buttocks and was dotted with violet gemstones, running down her locks like a waterfall. "She's beautiful!"

"They all are," I said.

The commander stopped us in front of a nondescript door. "Hand over your mounts. They'll be taken to the stables."

"They don't need to be cleansed too?" I asked sweetly, annoyed.

"Beasts wouldn't tolerate the fae methods. They have their own process." The commander scowled at me.

Apparently, people didn't question him often.

We relinquished the reins to our rides. When I did so, Valia looked at me, betrayal plain in her eyes.

"You'll be okay, girl. I'll get you later. Promise."

Three of the soldiers led our animals down the path, and I turned to the commander.

"Where to now?"

"Here." He slammed a fist against the door we'd stopped in front of before opening it.

Inside, we were met with a stairwell descending into darkness.

I frowned. "Where does this go?"

And was that knock some kind of code? Should I trust this fae?

"To the purification chambers."

"Are those in the dungeons?"

The commander's eyes widened in pure astonishment and then, to my shock, he let out a roar of laughter. "We have no dungeons here, Princess! We're not heathens."

"So, no one misbehaves?" Jax piped up incredulously.

"I never said that, but we do not force troublemakers to live below ground. There is a small prison, but it is rarely used. We live in a land of peace and goodwill and plenty. Not barbarism."

The *'unlike you'* that he refrained from adding at the end hung in the air.

"Now, if you don't mind," he sniffed, "I did not plan

on shepherding uninvited fae around all day." He gestured to the stairs.

Henri stepped forward. "Me first."

It was my duty, being the royal and all, the one who should set an example, but this was how Hatter showed he cared. I allowed him to pass by.

"I'll take up the back guard," Jax announced, obviously trying to match Henri's chivalry.

"You're all going to the same place, and I'm coming with you to make sure you do," the commander muttered. "So just get in."

"Dee?" I patted my shoulder, and Dee perched there, content to sit with her sister and be quiet for once.

They were on guard too.

We descended the stairs, which were as dark as they'd looked at the onset. Though, when we reached the bottom, we were greeted by a female fae with a short bob cut, waiting at a desk.

"Oh, outsiders!" She leaned forward, like we were a freak show she couldn't get enough of. "And look at those auras!"

My eyebrows drew together. "Excuse me?"

"I'm an aura reader." She waved her hand in the air. On it gleamed a ring with a ruby gem that glowed brightly, as if lit from within. "It's easier to do in the dark, which is why I'm posted here and not outside."

"Oh." I paused. "What color is mine?"

"Blue—no, more of a teal."

My house color.

"And mine?!" Dee squeaked, looking thrilled.

"Yours is a lovely, warm red. Like the rest of you." The fae answered the pixie.

Dum opened her mouth, surely to ask about her aura, when the commander stepped in front of us.

"Enough niceties! As long as they're not malicious, we need a cleansing. Now."

The aura reader swallowed . . . the first hint that this place wasn't a total utopia. Still, she nodded. "They're not here for trouble. And the purifiers are in the back."

"Good," the commander grunted. "Follow me."

We walked past the desk, and Hatter shot a glance over his shoulder at me.

"Auras?" I whispered so low only he could hear.

He shrugged. "I didn't know that was a fae talent."

Nor did I. Fae were elemental, with aether being the fifth and final element. Sometimes, a mind fae appeared here and there, though usually, they had some witching blood in them that created the new type of magic.

But the girl hadn't been hesitant to tell us she read auras—like it was nothing unusual.

The hallway the commander led us down was better lit, illuminated by lanterns I could easily imagine in a Moroccan teahouse. The deeper we went, the more colorful the hallway became, until it opened into a space resembling a cavern. Or a spa going for the 'all natural' look.

The cavern was also lit with the lanterns in every color possible, and stalactites hung from the ceiling, each with multicolored gems crusting the structure. A pool, glimmering blue and beautiful, rested in the middle of the space below. The air was warm and humid, damp smelling but also faintly like mint. As if someone used essential oils in the space to keep it fresh.

I exhaled. "Do we take a dip in there?"

"I looooove it," Dum cooed from where she and Dum perched on my shoulder.

Was this purification as simple as taking a bath? If that was the case, I was down for it. I was filthy, and the pool looked delightful.

The commander snorted. "Hardly. That is for fae who wish to be closer to our island's essence. Go through here."

He led the way to a side door that I had not noticed. When we walked through, we were met with another brilliantly lit room, where more fae, two male and one female, were waiting for us.

"These are the outsiders?" One of the males looked me over in a lecherous way.

"Obviously." The commander drawled. "Do what you must. They wish to see the royals. I will go relay their presence now. Message me when you're finished."

And with that, the gruff, bearded commander was gone, leaving us alone with these new people.

One of the males stepped forward and reached out to me, but the female extended an arm, cutting them off.

"I'll take the girls. The pair of you will have one each as it is."

"Can you get through them all?" asked the male who had been about to touch me.

I got the distinct sense he shouldn't have tried to claim me. Hatter's shoulders were stiff, telling that he didn't like it either.

The female glared at him. "I'll be fine. Two of them are quite small. We'll take the center room."

She gestured for me to follow, which I did, thankful to be away from her cohort.

"He's always trying to get his hands on pretty young things," the female huffed as she closed the door behind us.

"He's gross!" Dee hissed, which actually drew a chuckle from the fae.

I smirked, glad that the female had been present, and completely agreeing with Dee. "Well, if he tries anything with my friends, they're going to give it to him."

"Good. Our island is mostly peaceful and serene, but that one could do with a *purification* session himself."

"What exactly are you going to do?" I asked.

She gestured to a five-tiered bookshelf on the side of the room. On each shelf, crystals of every color gleamed. They were cylindrical, emphasizing their resemblance to large crayons. "We need to run each type of gemwand over your body. The crystals pull out any negative or unwanted energies."

"What does that mean?"

"Melancholy, anger, fear . . . they're all unwelcome here."

I stiffened. "These regulate emotions?" My teeth dug into my bottom lip. "So, you don't experience those?"

Because that was creepy as hell.

"We do, though to a lesser extent than the other king-doms of Faerie. We get cleansed often. Not as thoroughly as I'm about to do for you, of course. This is to banish any outside negativity."

This whole concept was very weird, and I should've been more worried, but I was here to get things done. If I had to let this fae wave a gemwand over me, then so be it.

"Who wants to go first?" she asked, going over to the cabinet and grabbing a clear crystal. "This will tell me which colors you need more of, but everyone will need at least a little of each one. Particularly when they've never been purified before."

"I will," I volunteered.

The woman nodded, then stared at the twins for a second and seemed to change her mind. "Actually, the pixies are so small, I think I will try to do you all at once. If it doesn't work, I'll do three different cleansings, but I have a feeling that won't be necessary."

She smiled at the twins. "We haven't had pixies here in quite a while."

"No pixies?" Dum asked, aghast. "What kind of place is this?"

"We are . . . unusual in this court," the crystal-wielder said. "I don't know how much you know about our island."

"Basically nothing," I replied.

Without asking, she began to run the crystal over me, kind of like a miniature metal detector. I didn't feel anything strange—or anything at all—coming from the stone, which allowed me to relax.

"We were curious about the magic, though," I added.

"Hm. While no one here is aether-blessed, I hear you're a princess of another court, so I suspect you are?" She pursed her lips.

"I am."

"And where do you come from?"

"Wonderland Island."

"Our nearest neighbors. My grandfather used to tell me that we were allies with you."

It had to be true, since this woman was fae and they couldn't lie. Unless of course the fae here *could*.

It wasn't out of the question. If people here could read auras, and no one was aether-blessed, what other differences might there be?

"Are there elementals?" I asked.

"A few, but mostly, we have specialized magics, all born from the power of the crystals that you'll find around the island."

"We already know about your aura-reading," Dee mused. "What other kinds are there?"

"Oracles are common. Some can speak with animals."

She listed off a few other powers I had never heard of, like shadowwalking, cartomancy, and bone magic. With each one, my awe of this place grew.

"Moving on to the ruby," the female murmured. "This may take more time."

Apparently, she had decided she was just fine purifying all three of us at once, so we stood as still as we could as she ran the crystal over our bodies.

From time to time, it tickled, and my lips curled up. Dum straight up burst into giggles.

"Do most of them feel this way?" Dee asked, squirming.

"The crystals give different sensations. And, as you can see, there are many of them." She gestured to the cabinet. "You might as well get comfortable. It's going to be a long while until you're released."

I frowned. There had to be at least twenty more colors to go through. We were on a timeline, and I hadn't anticipated this. Yet, I suspected there was no way out but through, so I sat back and fully resigned myself to the Crystal Court's machinations.

CHAPTER 10

Two hours later, I exited the purification room, feeling lighter, happier, like I didn't have a care in the world.

Which was total B.S., because my sister was a political hostage, and the Red Queen was free. Not to mention the mess that was my personal life. I should have been on edge and alert . . . which only went to show how effective the purification process was.

Henri and Jax were waiting for me in the main lobby, chatting amicably. My eyebrows arched, and I looked at Dee and Dum, once more riding on my shoulders.

If I wasn't already feeling the direct effects of the crystalwork, seeing the guys talking like friends would have been enough to convince me that it had worked.

"Are you quite ready?" asked a voice I didn't recognize.

I twisted to find an older fae—the first of his age that

I'd seen on this island—watching me. He had a long, silver mane, wore robes of sparkling midnight blue, and his air of superiority hinted that he was in a position of importance.

"Who are you?" I asked, my tone cheery, even though normally, if someone spoke to me like that, I would have told him to shove it.

"High Counselor Larrel. I'm to show you to your apartments."

Annoyance trickled in despite the fact I'd just been thoroughly cleansed. "I was hoping to meet the royal family. I have business with them."

Never mind that I had no way to repay or thank them for the information I needed, but I was sure we would figure out how to get what we needed *and* keep the Royals of Crystal Island happy. Even if it took a few more trips back and forth between Wonderland, I'd pay them double, *triple*, the amount of gold I'd originally packed.

"Suffice it to say, our royal family does not work on your time. Prince Cirrus is quite a busy man, but you will meet him and his sisters at the feast tonight." Counselor Larrel looked me up and down. "You are about the size of one of his sisters—and a princess too, correct?"

"Princess Alice White of Wonderland," I confirmed.

"Good. Then the attire I set aside will be appropriate. As for the rest of you, servants will be by shortly to assist." His eyes raked over Henri and Jax, both filthy from our journey. "You'll surely need new clothing before you can be in the presence of our royal family. Now, follow me."

Without another word, the man twirled and left the room.

The guys exchanged a look, the usually unfriendly pair still alarmingly loose toward one another. But none of us said a word as we followed the counselor back down the hallway and stairs. He offered no information either.

We emerged into the bright sunlight and once more the breeze coming off the ocean caressed my skin. Soft and warm and salty. I breathed in deeply. After being down below ground for so long, nature and open skies were welcome.

People stared at us as the High Counselor showed us to the front of the castle and through the gates. We were now entering like actual guests.

At least, I thought we were, until Larrel veered away from the large door leading into the palace and headed instead to a narrow path running alongside it.

"Are we not staying inside the castle?" I asked.

Such hospitality was not a good way to make allies.

"We do not know you, Princess Alice. You arrived unannounced and uninvited. We have no reason to trust you—least of all because I've never heard your name in my life. As such, you will be staying in the apartments outside the palace, and you will remain there until someone comes to collect you for the feast. Is that understood?"

We didn't seem to have much choice in the matter, and I really needed information on how to get through the Rift, so I held my tongue.

"Very good. Here we are." He gestured to the two-story building we'd been approaching.

It was cute, actually . . . very English cottage-like but with crystals lining the window panes and the path up to the amethyst-colored door.

"What time should we be ready?" I asked, trying not to sound frustrated.

"At nightfall."

At that, Councilor Larrel was apparently done with us, because he turned around, leaving the five of us standing at the door.

"Shall we?" Jax asked, opening the door.

The apartments were plush and filled to the brim with crystals. Even the bookshelf was made of gleaming black stone.

Onyx perhaps?

I sniffed the air, noting how clean it smelled. Like lemon and pine. They must have recently spruced up the space for us. The separation aspect still rankled, but the comfortable luxury of the space and the clear effort to make it livable was reassurance that the royals were not being mean. They simply didn't trust me yet.

As much as that annoyed me, I understood. I didn't trust people quickly either. So it seemed that there was nothing to do but wait. In a few hours, when we got to the feast, I would broach the topic of my visit.

"Alice, which room do you want?" Henri asked.

"The biggest!" Dum hollered. "She's sharing with us."

"Are there such things as pixie rooms?" Jax asked.

"Not here. They don't even have pixies," Dee replied.

"Is that normal?"

"No!" She looked horrified. "It's quite a shame. A whole region, deprived of pixies? I can't imagine!"

"Yes, this is a strange place." Henri rubbed the back of his neck. "I didn't feel comfortable removing my clothes for the purification process, but the fae insisted. And all the crystals are . . . unique."

"Hold up!" I raised a palm. "You had to get naked?"

"I removed my shirt and pants, but kept on my undergarments."

"Me too," Jax said. "That must have been why that woman was so keen on taking you," he told me.

"Uh," I cleared my throat. "We were clothed."

The guys stiffened.

The pixies eyed me, and I rubbed my hands on my thighs uncomfortably. "I hate to say it, but I think they played you, boys."

"Th-that's wrong!" Jax hollered. "I feel so used!"

"Agreed. It was uncalled for." Henri lifted his chin, as if the offender was right in front of him and he was telling him off.

Again, the guys were agreeing, but I wasn't sure this time was from the weightlessness the purification left behind. Rather unfortunately, it was over them both having been violated.

But I couldn't change it, and for now, I'd take the development. I needed them to work together, to not fight. To be a team. Because in a few hours, we'd be meeting the royal family, and I had a feeling they would be unlike any other fae I'd ever encountered.

The hours passed slowly. Even with the plethora of new items and decor to wonder at in our surroundings, I couldn't help but glance out the windows every ten minutes, waiting for the sun to set.

When it was finally descending, I began my preparations.

I'd actually packed a gown, foreseeing that I'd have to participate in some regal event. Faerie was so steeped in tradition, it was pretty much unavoidable. But the one I'd brought was pretty wrinkled, and no one had thought to provide us with an iron.

Fortunately, there were a dozen dresses for me to choose from, hanging in the wardrobe of the upstairs bedroom. All of them were stunning.

In the end, I settled on the one that spoke to my status: an aquamarine gown with a plunging neckline and back. It had bell sleeves, and the wrists were embroidered with bronze diamonds. The colors weren't the teal and gold of my house, but they were close enough. They would do.

Dee and Dum had also been given dresses. The question of why a region with no pixies had small dresses on hand popped into my mind, but I didn't voice it.

Perhaps some of their kind had stayed here once? Or perhaps they were doll dresses?

If I ran out of things to talk about, maybe I'd bring it up at dinner.

Dum wore a dress with a silver skirt and a blue top cut in a sweetheart neckline. Dee chose a ballgown in her favorite color, red, with gold stars on the skirt.

"We look amazing," I said as I finished applying the cosmetics that had also been generously donated to our apartments. "You two done?"

"Yeah," Dum said, studying herself in the mirror. "Do you think the prince will like my outfit?"

"I bet he likes red better," Dee interjected, her tone superior.

Oh, good grief. These two could not stop themselves when it came to pining over a prince.

"We'll see soon enough," I said noncommittally, but my friends didn't reply, having fallen into bickering.

Ignoring them, I rose to go to the door. When I opened it, footsteps filtered up the stairwell. Someone was moving around in the living area.

I left the pixies to their sisterly squabble and went downstairs to find the remaining two members of our party. When I did, my heart rate kicked up.

Henri and Jax lounged in chairs, both looking stunning in black trousers and jackets worn over tunics. Henri's tunic was longer and an amethyst color that looked amazing with his green eyes. Jax's was sapphire blue. In a way, their attire reminded me almost of modern-day suits.

"Don't you two look dashing," I said, walking into the room.

"And you are beautiful," Henri breathed as he stood up.

I got the impression that he might have been holding his breath a touch too long.

"There won't be a more gorgeous girl at the feast," Jax added, rising as well and offering his arm.

I glanced at it, but sat in one of the empty armchairs.

"So," Jax said, his tone slightly irritated. He resumed his seat, while Henri remained standing. "What's the plan for tonight?"

"I don't know that there is one," I admitted. "No one knows what to expect, so I guess I'm going to play it by ear."

"But of course, your number one prerogative is to get the information about the fae who crossed the Rift," Henri said.

"Yes. Though I'm not sure they'll tell us. If they would, don't you think other courts would know how to do it by now?"

"Yes, I do," Henri agreed. "Many citizens from all over Faerie are trapped in the Dark Court and the Cove Court, since the Rift extends past their eastern boundaries, into the ocean. If people knew how to breach it, they would want to get their lost family out."

"That's what I thought too. This information will cost

me, of course. I just hope I can pay their asking price. If not . . ." I allowed my fingers to graze my thigh, where a dagger was hidden beneath my skirts.

I might be acting diplomatically tonight, but that didn't mean I'd go in without protection. And a dagger was one of my most trusted weapons.

"I might have to figure out other ways to persuade them," I finished.

Jax frowned. "I can do that for you."

He knew I'd always hated forcibly extracting information from people. Slitting throats, particularly those of the scum we usually targeted, was easier than speaking with the people attached to them. Otherwise, I learned too much personal information, allowing even the worst monsters to become too human for my tastes.

"Let's hope it doesn't come to that," I said as a knock came at the door.

Already on his feet, Henri strode across the room to answer it. "Are you our escort?"

I couldn't see our visitor beyond Hatter's broad-shouldered frame, but the wobble in the young, soft voice was undeniable.

"I am, sir, if you're ready. I'm your escort for the length of your stay. May I show you to Ruby Hall?"

"We're ready." Hatter turned to me. "The pixies?"

"Dee! Dum!" I shouted in the direction of the stairs. "Get down here!"

The fae at the door—a young male of about eight,

dressed in plain but well-made clothing—glanced away at my shouting.

Weird. I hadn't been that loud. Maybe he was extra sensitive to sounds? Fae here had very different powers to those of the rest of Faerie, so it was a possibility.

The next moment, the pixies shot downstairs and beamed at the young fae. "Sorry! We were . . . debating about eye makeup."

As they looked exactly the same as they had when I left, I knew they'd likely been arguing all that time. But I appreciated the fact they were keeping their drama under wraps. The five of us needed to appear as one united front.

"Let's go." I stood from the armchair and swept out of the apartment first. "Show us the way."

The boy began leading us down a path, toward the castle. As he went, his green wings splayed out, hinting that he might be proud to be escorting us. I took that as a favorable sign.

Despite my boosted optimism, I was still somewhat surprised when we entered through the front door. Since our arrival, we'd been so hidden away, I wouldn't have blinked an eye if he'd shuffled us in through the kitchens.

Once we were in the thick of things, walking crowded corridors that must lead to where the feast was taking place, we garnered notice. Fae donning magnificent gowns or tailored suits stared openly, waiting for the party to begin. Servants darted glances as they provided flutes of wine and aperitifs to guests. Apparently, the royals were treating the whole of their palace as some sort of reception hall. Weird, but there wasn't much about this place that wasn't.

One brave servant approached us, and the boy who was showing us to Ruby Hall paused.

"Would you like a drink?" he asked our group, his tone barely a whisper.

"What is it?" Henri wanted to know.

"Wine from the south of the island."

"Is it strong?" I interjected.

I'd heard some courts had wine that would knock you on your butt after a sip. Since I would soon be doing business, I wanted to avoid looking sloppy.

"I've never had it," the boy said, and looked at the server.

The older fae shrugged. "It's all I've ever had, but I've never felt ill from it."

Probably not that bad, then.

I took a glass, which I found to be heavier than it appeared, and the men did the same.

One sip told me I had been right about its contents. There was no burning in my throat. Rather, the drink reminded me of champagne, but with a faint berry flavor.

"Delicious. Thanks."

The server bowed shallowly and went on his way, so the boy waved once again for us to follow.

Within the castle, crystals were everywhere the eye could see, just like on the outside. Somehow, the fae of this island had figured out how to work precious stones into practically any shape. Emeralds framed paintings. Quartz had been constructed into vases. After a brief examination, I learned that even the glass I held was made of stone, a light sapphire that had been altered to look like glass.

"This place is so interesting," Dee whispered in my ear.

Neither she nor Dum were riding on my shoulders now—we were trying to appear regal, after all—but they were flying close, almost the way I imagined other royals would expect their ladies-in-waiting to.

"And you're from Wonderland, so that's saying something," I teased.

A pause followed before Dee said, "I suppose our island is a touch odd, compared to the rest of Faerie."

A touch? The girl's reference point was definitely skewed.

The young fae leading us stopped abruptly before a door. "Here's Ruby Hall. Prince Cirrus and his sisters are waiting inside to speak with you. You'll have plenty of time to yourselves before the other guests are ushered in."

"Oh, great." I'd been more than ready to battle for their attention—expected it, even, after the day we'd had —so this was a nice surprise. "Guys, flank me?"

Henri and Jax promptly took up positions on my right and left, and the pixies fluttered in the air between us. Once properly surrounded, I entered Ruby Hall.

Immediately, all the breath whooshed out of me. If I'd thought the rest of the castle was elaborate, it had nothing on this room. Rubies adorned every available surface, including the floor, which was midnight-black, so the red stones appeared to be crimson stars, dotting a night sky.

The red gems also hung from the chandeliers, and the scarlet walls had that strange reflective quality that told me they were made of crystals too.

What had these fae done to create that? Did magic coalesce the gems together? Crushed them and then painted the walls with their essence?

However, they had accomplished it, the effect was mesmerizing.

And then there were the thrones on which five people, clad in stunning attire, sat. The chairs themselves demanded attention, their backs twenty-feet tall and made of gold, crusted with crimson precious stones. But the people were even more captivating.

The prince sat in the middle. On his right, two female fae perched, their eyes wide as they took me in. On his left was another female fae, and High Councilor Larrel.

"Those must be the princesses," Dum sighed. "They're beautiful!"

I snorted. "Like that's a shock?"

Every single person we'd seen here had been attractive. Well, maybe not the High Councilor, but the odds for great beauty really seemed to be in the fae's favor on this island.

"Come forth!" the prince's voice boomed over the hall.

We did as he requested, and as we approached, I studied him carefully. The prince was probably around Hatter's age. He had long, white-blond hair, violet eyes, and earrings that ran the length of each earlobe. Most appeared to be sapphire studs, the blue standing out against his silvery-white hair. Dressed in all-black, including a cape that poured over one shoulder, he gave off a dangerous and sexy vibe.

Two of his sisters looked much like the prince, their coloring exactly the same, while the other had red hair and vibrant green eyes.

We stopped at the base of the thrones. Henri dropped into a low bow, and Jax, belatedly, followed suit. The pixies landed and curtsied.

I merely dipped my chin. Royal to royal, we were technically the same rank. Unless the prince and princesses stood, I would not curtsey.

The prince arched his eyebrows and rose, bowing shallowly. I matched him with a curtsey, and his sisters went deeper than me.

It was all posturing, and while I'd never played the game exactly this way, I understood it in my bones.

"Greetings, Princess," the prince said.

Now that we were closer, I could see the detailing of his attire better. Sapphires lined his cape and adorned his hands. The stone of one ring was nearly the size of a quail's egg.

"I'm Prince Cirrus, secondborn to King Jandar and Queen Valahal, and heir to the Crystal Court. We welcome you to Jewel of the Sea Castle."

Secondborn? I wondered what happened to the firstborn.

"And I'm Alice White, firstborn and heir to the Wonderland Court."

"So I hear." Cirrus took to his throne again, allowing his sisters to do the same, though they did not introduce themselves. "What brings you this far south?"

"We come to create an alliance," I said, which was true, if not the entire truth.

"And?"

I swallowed. This was the moment when I'd learn what the prince was really like. "I need to infiltrate the Dark Court. My sister is being held captive there. Rumor has it, someone from your island escaped through the Rift. Is that so?"

"It is." Cirrus smiled, but it didn't reach his eyes. "I take it you wish to know how so that you might replicate his success?"

"I do."

"And what did you bring as payment?"

I exhaled a long breath through my nostrils. *Here goes nothing.*

"We had bags of gold and gems, but on our way here, they were thrown into the sea by a roc."

"Pardon?" The princess with red hair leaned forward with interest. "How so?"

"Its mother attacked us and one of our gryphons. She had a youngling with her. The baby likely thought the bags were a sleeping beast and wanted to have its own kill. It scooped up all of the bags. When it figured out that the bags were just objects, it released them into the sea."

"What a story!" the red-haired princess exclaimed. She opened her mouth to speak again, but the prince held out a hand.

"It is, but your tale is also quite unfortunate. You see, we do not give away information for nothing."

"I could have more delivered," I assured him. "As much as you like. But I need the information soon. We're marching into the Dark Court within the week."

The prince leaned back in his throne, a thoughtful expression crossing his face. "Actually, I believe I have another idea of how you might pay me, Princess Alice. But first, my people are waiting."

He clapped his hands, and the guards outside the doors appeared.

"Get the guests," the prince ordered. "It is time to feast and dance."

At his word, two dozen other fae appeared out of nowhere, running in from the sides of the vast room. They held long crystals in their hands, like fat wands, and waved them in the air. Where the fae walked, circular tables appeared.

"What the hell?" Jax whispered.

"Conjuring fae," the prince said smugly. "You've never seen one?"

"Uh, no," I replied. "Although, some can conjure with aether. Just not in that manner."

"Yes, I've heard of that. Our conjuring fae are a little different. They will prepare the room with the last-minute details. It will be ready by the time my people arrive to meet you. I'm sure they'll be quite interested to hear about your methods."

Although the magic was pretty cool, annoyance built within me. I didn't want to wait to discuss the Rift. But the prince smiled indulgently as if he were doing me a great favor. Clearly, he wasn't going to budge. I'd have to roll with his whims to get what I wanted.

"Once we're fed, we will speak of business and how you might earn our secrets," Cirrus purred. "Until then, join me at the head table, will you, Princess Alice?"

CHAPTER 11

Stuck at the head table, I shifted uncomfortably in my seat. It wasn't the seat itself, or my dress, or any other physical thing that was making me feel weird. It was the fae staring at me every few seconds that made me want to crawl beneath the table and hide.

Since the moment the subjects of the Crystal Court had flooded into Ruby Hall, it had been this way. Even the appearance of all the tables, topped with stunning faux-floral centerpieces made of glittering crystals, and the welcome speech from Prince Cirrus didn't stop the curious stares. I supposed it didn't help that I was seated between Cirrus and Princess Roshia, the youngest of the Laval royal line.

Only my friends, seated at the table closest to the head table, didn't stare at me like I had three heads. They actually seemed to be trying to ingratiate themselves with the fae at their table, only occasionally glancing up to check on me.

I wished the prince hadn't separated them from me, but the only non-royal allowed up here was High Councilor Larrel. Asking to fit four more felt like pushing my luck.

"How is your soup?" the prince asked, turning from his other sister—Elisha Laval, thirdborn—to face me.

"It's good," I said, jumping at the chance to have his ear.

Elisha and Nambra, the fourth Laval sibling, had monopolized Cirrus' time since we sat down. They'd been discussing matters of the court, and since I was asking for a favor, I hadn't interrupted. Instead, I'd made small talk with Roshia. But at least twenty minutes had passed, and I was ready to be getting on with what I'd come to do.

"Might we talk about my objective now, Prince Cirrus?"

"As much as I'd love to simply give you what you wish," he replied, his tone all charm and grace and poise, "I feel like I must get to know you first, Alice White. Surely that's understandable?"

My jaw tightened. He could have been doing that instead of chatting up his sisters! Why was this guy playing with me? Did I look like someone who tolerated that?

"Ask what you want," I gritted out, fully aware that the potion Xavier had given me before I journeyed to

Wonderland was still in effect. I'd been here less than two weeks and it should last an entire moon cycle.

Thanks to the potion that enabled my missions in the human world, if I didn't want to answer truthfully, I could lie. It might be morally wrong, but if I needed to do so, I'd fib, or stretch the truth. And I did require something from the Laval family, but they did not need to know everything about me—specifically, my past as an assassin. I owed them no such insight.

"You are a royal fae," the prince stated. "Are you aether-blessed?"

"Yes," I said, and his lips curled up. "I've heard that no one here is?"

"Correct. There is not a single aether-blessed fae on this island."

"Is there a reason for that?"

"It's said that the old gods did not bless my father's line with the power of aether because the crystals found only on our island already give us unique magic." Cirrus frowned. "Apparently, they thought we had enough power to play with. I've never agreed with that sentiment."

I wasn't sure *I agreed* with Cirrus. The fae of this court seemed prosperous, and that often equaled powerful. But I wasn't about to say that.

"Speaking of your father, is he here?" I asked. "I expected the king and queen would be at the feast."

I'd expected nothing of the sort, but I wanted more information on these fae. Roshia was lovely, but she'd sidestepped every topic of real significance pertaining to the island. Perhaps her brother would be more forthcoming.

"Our mother has passed, and our father is ill. He does not leave his chambers."

"Oh, I'm sorry."

I had lost both of my parents, and though I didn't really remember them, the idea still pained me.

"He is quite old, so it does not come as a surprise," the prince replied indifferently. "We've become used to the new state of the court. For all intents and purposes, I have been ruler of the island for years now. I only need to be properly crowned, which I hope will occur soon. But thank you, your concern is warming."

Cirrus' violet eyes raked over my face. "Your hair is lovely, did you know? Quite unusual, even for fae."

"I have noticed its rarity." My white-blonde hair had been enough to give me away as being a descendant of the royal White line when I arrived. "Though, you, Princess Nambra, and Princess Elisha are similarly fair-haired. Just a little more silver," I added. "Perhaps we share a distant relation?"

Maybe if he felt more bonded to me in the familial sense, he'd be more inclined to give me what I wanted.

"Doubtful." Cirrus replied dryly.

"I thought that, in this kingdom, alliances were made by marriage?"

"They are. The last marriage that involved another court was my parents'—though, I am looking for a bride, so that might soon change." He patted my hand.

My eyes widened. *Oh no. Is he——?*

The main course arrived then, and I was spared speaking further, when Councilor Larrel appeared at the prince's side and whispered in his ear.

"I think he fancies you." Roshia leaned closer to me, her lips pulled up in a small conspiratorial smile. "He rarely gives females the time of day."

"I can see that now," I hedged.

I had no interest in the prince. Hell, with Jax trying to wedge his way between Henri and me, I had enough boy trouble as it was. But would rocking the boat be wise when we still hadn't learned the secret to passing through the Rift?

"His recent oracle reading probably doesn't hurt," Roshia mused.

"What do you mean by that?" I turned to the princess, the one who, with her red hair and green eyes, didn't really fit in with the rest of her family.

Her eyes lit up. "You know of oracles?"

"I do," I said, and then an idea struck. "One actually made a prophecy at my birth. I hadn't considered it before, but they were probably from here?"

Roshia nodded, lilac-veined wings fluttering softly behind her. "When other courts welcome new babies into the family, we send out our oracles. It is a way of maintaining ties. But none have been sent for many years. I wonder if you were the last?"

"My sister is younger."

"Oh, right. That slipped my mind. Perhaps she was the last, then."

I wasn't sure. No one had mentioned an oracle being present at Elise's birth. Would Hatter recall if there was? Probably not. At that time, he would have been, what . . . six, at the oldest?

Cirrus and the High Councilor were still occupied, so I decided to dig deeper into this topic with the princess. Perhaps I could learn something about oracles that would appease my worry over the prophecy hanging over my head.

"How common is that power?"

"Very. But the strongest seers are kept here, at Jewel of the Sea. High Councilor Larrel is among those."

"Does he read for your brother?"

"Yes, and he mentioned we'd have company that would be in our best interests to receive."

The soldiers we'd met when we landed said we came unannounced and uninvited. That did not equate unforeseen.

"The group of guards sent to retrieve my friends and I when we arrived . . ." I pondered. "That troop was smaller than usual, wasn't it?"

Roshia grinned, showing off perfectly straight, white teeth. "We've been on watch. Normally, the welcome party would have been much larger."

That only made me more annoyed that the royals insisted we wait to speak with them, but I pushed that aside. For the moment.

I took a casual bite of my meal, a delicious, roasted bird with a side of a vegetable that looked like a hybrid carrot-beet thing and tasted a lot like a radish. I never knew what I'd be served in Faerie, so I didn't ask—I just ate. "What did the oracle say to him?"

Roshia had been sipping her wine, but my question sent her into a coughing fit. Her sisters leaned forward, silently questioning if she was okay, and again, I felt the hundreds of eyes in the crowd watching us.

What I wouldn't give to be sitting down there with Henri, Jax, and the pixies, not the center of attention with the royals of this weird court.

Finally, the princess mastered herself, and raised a hand as she assured our audience, "I'm fine."

Once most of the faces had turned away and she was sure no one was listening, she leaned closer. "We do not discuss that."

A pit formed in my belly. Did she mean that even if I somehow found the oracle who had spoken at my birth, the seer wouldn't talk about it? Or did she simply mean that it wasn't polite to discuss prophecies related to other people? Or perhaps the vision regarding Cirrus was just that horrible?

She must have seen the consternation on my face, for she added, "However, I *can* tell you that I believe my brother will want to get to know you. *Quite well.*"

The pit in my stomach deepened, growing into a chasm. Did he think I'd come here to be his wife? I'd need to set the record straight.

Unfortunately, at that exact moment, Cirrus excused himself, leaving with Councilor Larrel. "Stay, Princess Alice. Enjoy the meal."

I began to protest, but there was nothing to it. Cirrus left and didn't bother to turn back around.

What was he up to?

I was left wondering that for an excruciating amount of time. The fae ate slowly and the prince didn't return until the main course had been taken away. I was practically vibrating with annoyance when he finally swept back into the room. But Cirrus didn't seem to notice. He came to me, hand extended.

"What are you doing?" I asked, but placed my palm on his because I felt put on the spot.

"I request a dance."

"Oh . . . Okay."

No one was dancing yet, and though I was taken aback by both his forwardness and the spectacle we'd make, I went along with his invitation. At least this way, I'd be able to ask him about the Rift somewhat privately.

He led me to a cleared space between the tables that I'd thought was intended to allow the servants more room as they bustled in and out of the Hall, or the people present to more easily approach the head table, but now it was a dancefloor.

"I'm not very good," I warned as Cirrus twisted to face me and placed a hand on my waist.

That was a lie. I just didn't know the moves to what I

predicted was going to be a very fancy sequence. Nor did I really want to dance. I wanted to get down to business.

But the prince was not to be dissuaded.

He smiled though it did not reach his eyes. "You do not need to be, Princess Alice. I shall lead you."

Briefly letting go of my hand, he snapped his fingers, and, as if they'd been waiting for this moment, a string quartet began to play.

"The floor is open!" a deep male voice called out, and chairs all around the room pushed back as others rushed to join us.

The prince didn't seem to notice the chaos, though. He flowed right into the dance with such grace and familiarity, I wondered how often the Crystal Court held feasts like this.

He was an even better dancer than Henri—and that was saying a lot. But seeing as I hadn't come here to marvel at Prince Cirrus' footwork, I seized the moment of our relative privacy.

"Do you know if the fae who crossed the Rift is present tonight?" I asked, feigning nonchalance.

The prince stared at me in amusement. "You are quite the tenacious creature, aren't you?"

"I am," I replied, tone even, as if waiting for hours for an answer wasn't killing me inside. "But in this case, you must understand. My sister's life depends on my learning to cross that boundary."

"Family is the most important thing to me," he

replied, though the words were oddly tight. "Do you agree?"

"Yes," I said. Before, I'd never had the chance to agree to such a statement. I hadn't known any blood family—just a couple of close friends I treated as such. Then I'd learned about Elise, and determined I would do anything to rescue her.

"I'm pleased to hear it." A gleam of interest sparked in his violet eyes. "Does your sister have the same aether magic as you?"

I tilted my head, unsure where he was going with this. In a way, I was glad we'd stayed on the topic of Elise, but why bring up her magic? Cirrus seemed too interested in aether-blessed powers.

"I'm not sure," I said honestly. "I only discovered her existence recently, as we were separated when we were young. She might have been too young to even display her powers."

"A shame. I hear aether magic runs strongly in some royal lines and less so in others."

Sure. Wasn't that the case with most things?

Brushing off his bizarre comment, I pressed on with my agenda. "I suppose I could find out about Elise's magic and get back to you once I retrieve her."

The prince chuckled. "You could, yes. Anything keeping you on my island is welcome."

My skin prickled at the comment of remaining here. It sounded possessive, but maybe I was reading too deeply into the prince. I knew so little about him. So far, Cirrus had kept his cards close to his chest.

The current song ended, and the prince guided me to a stop. I wasn't sure what the protocol for separating was, so I waited for him to lead.

He took a step back and bowed shallowly. I responded to his gesture with a curtsey. Then, thinking we were done for the moment, I made to leave the floor and regroup with Hatter and the others. If fae were dancing, maybe my friends and I could speak freely, and they would have a better idea of how to get the prince to tell me what I needed to know.

However, before I could take so much as a step, Prince Cirrus wrapped a hand around my wrist. "A moment, Princess Alice."

I turned to him, my head tilted in curiosity.

All around us, people were watching. Prince Cirrus smiled widely at them, but when he lifted our joined hands into the air, I stiffened.

What's his game?

"Fae of Crystal Island! I have a glorious announcement."

Silence fell over the hall in a rapid wave. It was so quiet, I suspected the people closest to us might be holding their breath.

"It is with great pleasure that I inform you that I am now courting Princess Alice White of Wonderland."

My mouth fell open. *What the what?!*

"After the traditional courting period, we will be wed,

right here in the palace!" He shook our hands, where he still held them aloft, still entwined.

Fae cheered loudly, but I stood in place, absolutely dumbstruck. Had I given off the vibe that I was interested in him? I was sure I hadn't. I'd smiled and played nice, but *marriage*?!

How the hell had he gotten to that?!

Done with his announcement, Prince Cirrus turned to me. "Your arrival is a true blessing. Once we wed, I will be able to fill you in on the secrets of our court."

Oh no. No, no. No.

I tore my hand out of his, and only then did I realize that I was shaking. "I never agreed to marry you!"

"You do wish to save your sister, correct?"

I clenched my jaw. Of course, I wanted to save Elise! More than anything. But should I have to marry someone I barely knew, someone I found slightly odd and off-putting, for the slightest chance to accomplish that? Absolutely not.

My defiance must have shown clearly on my face.

"This is the price for that information," Cirrus said as if he were simply telling me how much a pack of gum cost. "I have no need for gold and jewels. What I require is a bride of royal blood and an heir."

"Well, you're not getting that from me! I—"

My words died in my mouth as Henri and Jax barreled through the crowd. The pixies fluttered above, their eyes huge and questioning as they met mine.

I didn't have time to assuage their worries, though,

because Hatter rushed right up to the prince, coming so close that I feared he was going to shove him—or worse.

Apparently, several palace guards thought so too. They were there in a heartbeat, blades adorned with gems that glittered in the candlelight pointed at Hatter.

"Don't hurt them!" I commanded.

"She won't marry you," Henri growled at the prince. "She doesn't want to."

"That may be true. However, she does wish to save her sister. And no one in my court will give Princess Alice the knowledge she seeks." He turned to look down his nose at me. "That is, unless you agree to join our houses."

"You do know how disgusting this is, right?" I sneered. "Trying to force someone to marry you is the foulest of foul moves."

"Perhaps. For me, it's that, or I wed one of my sisters." Cirrus shrugged. "It's been done before, but I'd prefer not to go that route."

"Why not invite other royals to your island?" I threw up my hands. "I don't know how many other princesses there are in this realm, but they'd flock here! People are curious about this court."

"Precisely why we don't want them coming. But you are already standing upon my soil. You know of our island, and though our hair is similar, I am sure we are not related. Though, I am pleased that our progeny will likely bear the Laval coloring."

Eeew. This guy was next-level gross.

"She's not marrying you," Henri ground out, green eyes burning with fury. "No matter what you say."

"I second that," Jax added, and though he didn't sound as animalistic as Henri, I could tell he was holding back from blasting the prince with magic.

Cirrus shrugged again, unfazed by our protests. "Your options are to agree to this, or to leave my island."

His tone of finality stunned me. There had to be another way. I needed the information he possessed, but I also wasn't about to marry the man.

"Actually, brother, there is *one* other option," a high-pitched voice called out from the head table. "Have you forgotten?"

I glanced over to find Roshia standing from her seat, smiling. She seemed relaxed, her hand lazily holding a glass of wine, as though it might tip from her fingers at any second.

By contrast, her brother had stiffened at my side. I didn't need to look at him to know he was glaring daggers at his sister.

"What other option?" I asked loudly, wanting everyone to hear her answer.

I had no idea what she was playing at, or why she'd go against a brother whom, by all earlier appearances, she adored.

I also didn't care.

"A courting tournament," she replied. "Should any male or female who wishes to marry another fae be challenged for their intended's hand during the courting process, they must accept if they wish to continue wooing the one they love."

Roshia smiled sweetly as the crowd began to murmur. "It's an old law, easily overlooked, which I'm sure is what happened. Right, brother?"

Cirrus cleared his throat, but before he could speak, Henri stepped forth.

"I challenge Prince Cirrus for Alice White's hand!"

"I'll fight for her hand too," Jax raised a fist.

I groaned. Jax wouldn't let this opportunity slide.

I gave them both a look that clearly said I wasn't marrying either one of them if they won. Henri inclined his chin, understanding.

I mean, I liked the guy a lot, but . . . marriage? I was only eighteen!

Let's try going on a few normal dates first.

Jax, on the other hand, did not give any indication that he'd noticed my ire. This was likely at least partially because Prince Cirrus had thrust his hand out in front of my ex.

On the prince's hand, five rings glowed, each set with a different crystal.

Jax took a step back, wary. "What are you doing?"

"You're no fae." Cirrus wiggled his fingers as if the rings had told him as much. "As such, you cannot compete in our tradition."

"Why not? Does the law state that?" the wizard demanded.

No one spoke.

No one knew.

"Councilor Larrel and I will learn if that is true or not," Princess Roshia stated suddenly. "But clearly, the other contestant is fae. So, do you accept his challenge for the hand of the princess, brother? Or do you forfeit the female who might be your queen?"

It really sucked that, evidently, I had no say here. I was royal, and yet, at the mercy of males.

And Princess Roshia, who was definitely pulling some strings.

Why that might be could wait until later.

"I accept your challenge," Cirrus told Hatter, his tone low and dangerous. "We begin the tournament in two days' time."

Having set the terms, the prince whirled, his black cape splaying out behind him as he marched from Ruby Hall.

CHAPTER 12

I stood on the dancefloor, still in shock over what Prince Cirrus had pulled. All around, fae whispered and stole glances at me. Some even pointed.

These people lived for gossip, and we had served up a steaming vat of it.

"We need to leave," Henri stated. "I can't just stand here."

"For once, we agree," Jax grunted. "But I'm not sure I know how to get back to the cottage."

I was in the same boat—a hole-riddled canoe that felt like it was sinking. There had simply been too much to absorb on our way here for me to keep track of our path.

From the looks on their faces, neither Hatter nor the pixies had any idea where to find our temporary home either.

"I see the boy who brought us here hovering by the

door," Dee proclaimed after soaring higher to look over the heads of those in the crowd. "I'll get him."

She zoomed out of sight, but returned in no time at all, yelling for people to get out of the way and let 'little Zeb' through.

When the faerie boy appeared in front of me seconds later, I clapped him on the shoulder. "Your name is little Zeb?"

"Just Zeb, Princess Alice. I don't know why *she* called me little. I'm much bigger than her!" He eyed the pixie with annoyance, fluttered his green wings, and stood taller, almost making him four-feet tall.

"They both think they're bigger than they are," I explained, hiding a smile. "Don't take it personally."

He looked at me expectantly, waiting for a command as he'd been trained to do.

"Can you take us back to our apartment?" I asked, hating that I was running but seeing no other option. "I need a quiet place."

"Come with me," Zeb said.

No one in the crowd of fae stopped him, nor us as we followed him.

After we exited Ruby Hall, we speed-walked through the corridors. When we burst out a side door into the cool night air, I exhaled fully for the first time in what felt like hours.

"No words," Henri bit out when I turned to face him. "Not yet."

Right. It probably wouldn't do to start badmouthing a

prince in the place where he owned everything the sun shone upon.

Zeb led us straight to the cottage-apartment, even opening the door and bowing like a gentleman.

"You don't have to do that," I said.

"You're courting my prince."

"I—"

"Inside!" Henri barked, and the others filed into the apartment.

"Thanks, Zeb. We'll see you tomorrow, I guess. You're supposed to escort us, right? Do we call you?"

He shook his head. "That was for tonight so you knew how to get to the feast. Tomorrow, you can roam the palace grounds." He paused and looked nervously behind me. I didn't turn, but I felt Henri's glare. He wanted to speak to me and the poor kid thought Hatter was mad at him for keeping me. "I don't think you'll be able to get anywhere unless they want you to, so you'll know what's allowed."

"Yeah, you're probably right." I gave him a smile to ease his worries about Hatter. "Well, goodnight. Thanks for the help."

"Good evening." He motioned for me to go inside and shut the door behind me.

"Kid's chivalrous," I said, facing my friends.

The guys stared back at me, stony. The pixies perched on the settee, eyes wide because they knew as well as I did that something was about to go down.

"Why didn't you warn us, Al?" Jax said finally. "That douchebag—"

"I didn't know!" I cut him off. "How could you think I would have agreed to that?"

"You sat with him for the whole dinner!" Jax yelled back. "And it looked like you had a nice conversation."

By the old gods. I really wanted to slap him.

"For your information, we did talk. I mostly wanted to discuss the Rift, which Cirrus was not open to. He kept saying weird things, like asking—"

"If you were aether-blessed?" Henri inserted.

"How'd you know?" I asked.

"Because everyone at our table made a big deal about it. There are no aether-blessed on the island. I had a hunch then that Prince Cirrus might try to woo you. That way, maybe his children would have the power. But I hadn't expected it so soon." Henri ran his hand through his long, black hair. "Maybe we should leave."

"We can't!" I cried.

"You want to go through with this? To court him? To watch me fight in a *tournament*?"

"And me," Jax added, even though no one had told him he could actually fight yet.

"No," I assured them. "I don't want to do any of those things. But we haven't gotten what we came here for. I don't know how to get through the Rift. Without that information, I have no chance at rescuing Elise."

"I don't think we'd be able to leave anyhow," Dum

chimed in. "They took our rides. Does anyone know where they're being held?"

"No," Henri admitted. "But we can find the stables. That has to be where they are."

"I doubt that will be happening tonight," I said. "If they have the slightest hint that we're going to run, they won't let us near the stables. Cirrus wants a bride and an heir, and *soon*—I don't know why, since it doesn't seem like he has any competition, but there has to be a reason."

"Maybe Dum and I can look for our animals tomorrow," Dee suggested.

"You stand out here, though. There are no other pixies."

"We can make it work," Dee promised. "We'll find the stables so if we need to make an escape, we'll know where to go. Then we can—"

"Princess Alice!" A pounding came at the door, making all of us jump. "Are you in there?!"

The deep voice didn't sound like Cirrus, or even High Councilor Larrel. And it definitely didn't sound like Zeb. I moved to greet whoever it belonged to, wondering who else could possibly want something from me.

Standing outside the door was a group of five soldiers, all armed. The one in front stepped forward.

"Princess, you cannot stay here any longer."

"Why not?"

"Orders from Prince Cirrus. He cannot abide his intended staying in the same dwelling as two challengers."

I scoffed. "He's the one who put us here!"

For a second, the lead soldier looked almost sympathetic. "I know. However, now I must move you."

"But my friends still have to stay out here? How do I know they'll be safe?"

"Tournament laws govern the safety of challengers," the soldier said. "No fighting or violence toward them is to take place until the tournament begins. Now, we are here to gather your things and show you to your new quarters inside the palace."

I huffed out a breath. This was absurd, but I didn't think I could get out of it no matter how loud I screamed.

Not that I wanted to do that either. It looked weak, and though I was new to this world and at a disadvantage there, I wanted to appear strong so I could wrangle what I wanted from the royals.

I'd play nice. For now.

"My room is up the stairs. There's only one large bag and it's mine."

"Get ours too!" Dum shouted. "We're going with her. We're her ladies-in-waiting!"

I praised the old gods for Dum's quick thinking. Tough-girl appearance aside, I didn't want to be alone in that castle tonight.

"That's okay, isn't it?" I asked the soldiers. "They're not challengers, and I would like them with me."

"They're females and your ladies, so of course."

"Our bags are small trunks," Dee said in the tone of a highborn lady. "They're on the vanity."

"Yes, miss." A soldier detached himself from the group and charged up the stairs, returning in less than a minute with all our bags. "These them?"

"Yes," I said, and turned to the guys. "I guess we'll see you tomorrow. Try not to tear one another's heads off, will you?"

The men side-eyed one another, which wasn't promising. Since the purification, they'd been doing so well! But now that a prince had claimed I was to be married off, apparently, they'd backslid.

Maybe getting out of this room wasn't a terrible idea . . .

No matter that my relationship with Henri was none of Jax's business, I would not rub it in and kiss Henri in front of everyone. We needed to look like a team. Plus, I didn't want that information getting back to Cirrus. I didn't trust the prince. So instead, I threw them both an awkward wave before walking outside. The pixies flew up next to me and settled on my shoulders.

"This is crazy!" Dee said. "The prince is being all possessive. Which is kinda sexy, you have to admit, Alice."

"No, I don't." I didn't like Prince Cirrus much before he'd tried to force-court me, and I didn't like him any better now. "You're boy-crazy."

"True!" Dee sang and held out her fist for Dum to bump.

Her sister obliged, earning us confused looks from the soldiers escorting us.

Unlike when we arrived at the feast, we didn't enter through the front door. I was glad for it. Undoubtedly, people were still leaving the castle, and I didn't want to be a freak show any longer.

"You'll be staying in the royal's guest wing, as befits your rank," the lead soldier said as he ushered me down an empty hallway.

"The prince won't be staying near me, though, will he?"

I didn't trust that sucker as far as I could throw him. I wasn't even sure I wanted to be in the same part of the castle as him.

Then again, he has legs. He can walk to wherever I am. I'll lock the door with aether tonight. I'd love to see him get through that.

"He will not. You are in the area reserved only for guests."

We arrived at my new room shortly after, and a soldier opened the door. When I laid eyes on the inside of the chambers, I gasped.

Crystals were everywhere—mounted on the walls, hanging from the light fixtures, two even stood to the sides of the large window, as tall as my hip. The gems made the entire room glow. The dominant shades were blue, green, and a light yellow. Calming colors, and my favorites. Had the prince picked up on that? Or was it the luck of the draw?

"Are the bedposts covered in diamonds?!" Dee

squealed, soaring toward one of the poles and running her hands along it.

"Quartz. We find it more useful than diamonds, which are mostly used for jewelry," the lead soldier answered as the one who'd been carrying our bags set them on the bench at the foot of the large bed. "Will that be all, Princess?"

"Yes."

"If you need anything, two guards will be stationed outside your door at all times." The soldier gestured for the others to leave. "Good evening and rest well."

They filed out the door, and then, we were alone.

"I guess I should have expected being moved," I sighed, circling the space.

Dee and Dum didn't seem to hear me. They were too busy flying around the room and checking things out. I went to my bag.

Now that I wasn't going to be up half the night, brainstorming with the guys about what this tournament might entail, it was probably best that I got some rest. Traveling here on a few short hours of sleep had begun to take its toll, and if the feast had proven anything, it was that I needed to be alert at all times.

"Which side of the bed do you two want?" I asked as I laid my night clothes out on the quilt.

"Right!" Dee called at the same time Dum shouted, "Left!"

I snorted. "You know what, it's big enough for me to

sleep in the middle, so you can both get your wish. That sound good?"

They fist-bumped one another, which I took to mean 'Yes.'

I started to undress, groaning as I slipped off the boots I wore. Next, my fingers found the sleeves of my dress. I had begun to pull them down, when Dum let out a shriek.

"What?!" I whirled, certain she'd taken her eye out with a crystal, but found the pixie looking at me, her face pale.

"The wall!" Dum hissed, her tone tight with fear. "It moved—oh, by the aether!"

Her curse came as the wall next to my bed slid open.

In a flash, I grabbed for the dagger strapped to my thigh. I had it out and ready by the time the person hiding in the wall appeared.

"Well, aren't you a surprising sort of princess?" Roshia asked, ginger eyebrows raised. Her diaphanous, lilac wings were out and tensed, ready to take flight if she needed.

My heart was pounding hard. "What are you doing here? And why did you come in that way?"

"There are guards outside your door. I wish to speak to you, but they need not know." She held up her hands. "I have no weapon, so if you'd like to talk, might I suggest you poke your head out and explain the commotion? Otherwise, the soldiers will certainly check on you—"

A knock came at the door, and she smirked. "They're quite fast."

I was sure she wasn't there to harm us, and seeing as I wanted to find out why she *had* come, I slipped my blade back into its sheath—earning me an impressed look from Roshia—and went to respond to the guards.

"Yes?" I peered around the door as if I were indecent.

"We heard a small scream. Is everything alright?"

"Oh," I gave a dry chuckle. "One of the pixies scared the other. They love playing pranks."

The soldier studied me for a moment before shrugging. "Very well. Thank you for assuring us. Prince Cirrus would be quite displeased if something happened to his intended."

My lips tightened, but I refrained from retorting. before softly shutting the door. I turned to find the princess perched on my bed, her hands folded in her lap.

"Sit with me. We have much to discuss."

"Yeah, we do," I said, going to her side and perching on the bed too. The pixies joined us, sitting between me and Roshia with their legs straight out in front of them. "How about we start with why you reminded Cirrus about the tournament? I mean, I'm grateful, but isn't your brother furious with you?"

"He certainly is," she said as if she couldn't care less. "I'm not worried about Cirrus at the moment, though."

"What about loyalty?"

"I'm very loyal to my family. There are matters in the works here that you can't understand. Nor will I share them. They're really none of your business . . . and I say that with the most respect possible."

Roshia smoothed her dress, the same one she'd worn to the feast. "Now, do you want to speak about the tournament? And then perhaps I can more freely talk to you about your goals on the island."

My breath hitched. "You know how that fae crossed the Rift?"

"I do not. Unfortunately, only my brother and his circle of advisors know that. However, I believe it was documented in the same place we keep all of our most important information—the Hall of Prophecy."

"You have a whole space devoted to that?"

"We do. As I mentioned, we have many oracles here. Not all prophecies come true, though."

I swallowed thickly as hope overcame me, and the princess nodded her understanding. "Which I sense might be of interest to you. I assume the prophecy regarding you was unwelcome?"

"It—"

"Do not tell me!" She held up her hand. "I do not need to know, and it is bad luck to share them here. However, if you gained access to the Hall of Prophecy, you might learn the accuracy of the seer who foretold your potential future. Some are deadly accurate. Others, not so much.

"To be fair, most are on the less accurate end, but as you're royal, I can be sure our court would have sent someone who's seen at least one of their predictions come to light."

If the oracle who'd been present at my birth had a low success rate, that knowledge would help me breathe easier. And I'd be even less stressed if I could find out how to pass through the Rift.

"Can you take me there? To the Hall?"

"Alas, no. You will require permission from my brother. Either that or a very, *very* good sneak to get you inside."

I gestured to the hidden door. "You seem pretty good."

"I am," she said smugly. "But there are no secret passages that lead directly into that room. And it is always guarded by at least five lethal soldiers. Your entry would require a diversion at the very least. Something huge."

"Perhaps a tournament?"

Roshia winked. "It's a start. A good number of our palace guards will be diverted to the arena during the tournament. However, to be safe, a way for you to become invisible would be ideal as well."

I chewed on my bottom lip, not sure Jax could do that.

One thing at a time . . .

"Why are you telling me this, Princess Roshia?"

"I could see that those males truly love you. It wasn't right what my brother did."

"That's all?" It sensed that she was holding back.

"I have a vested interest in him not officially taking the throne."

"You want it yourself?"

"I don't. That is all I will say on the matter."

I studied the fae. She was offering me the information I needed to succeed here, but she wasn't exactly forthcoming on other matters. Did I trust her?

I wasn't sure. But right now, doing so seemed to be my best, my *only*, option.

CHAPTER 13

The next morning, I slid into pants I'd brought with me, since the closet was filled solely with dresses. I didn't hate the gowns, but I preferred pants. And I definitely didn't want Prince Cirrus to think that I was okay with him dressing me.

Plus, sneaking around in dresses was way more difficult.

"Are you sure about this plan, Dee?" I asked.

After Princess Roshia had left through the hidden wall passage—and I'd promptly locked it behind her with aether—the pixies and I had stayed up for hours, talking.

It was clear that I needed to find my way into the Hall of Prophecies. How exactly I would do that was uncertain, but in the end, it was decided that I'd simply ask.

Yup, I was just going to ask Prince Cirrus. Maybe because he was my 'intended,' he'd allow it.

Then again, maybe not. I was fully prepared to be denied—which was where Dee came in.

"I want to search for the stables too," she said. "I'll do that after I look for the Hall of Prophecy."

"Fine, but don't get caught."

The last time the pixies had been sent spying, two witches captured them and sealed their wings together. Though I could probably unstick them now, thanks to Queen Aquatia's teachings, I didn't want that to happen again.

"I won't. I've learned a few new tricks, Alice! You guys play it up that I'm ill from the wine."

"It was *really* strong," Dum added. "Hatter gave me a sip of his, and I nearly fell over!"

"Maybe next time, don't be such a lush," I teased, which earned me a slap on the shoulder at Dum's hand.

I snorted. "That was like a mosquito bite!"

She produced her fangs. "I could have used these."

"Uh, no thanks." I'd seen those teeth rip food to shreds. They were tiny, but sharp. And venomous. "I'd like to remain poison-free today."

"One bite wouldn't hurt you. It'd be more like a zing of energy."

"What?" I blinked. "You told me—"

"A swarm would kill you, probably ten bites would be debilitating for someone your size." Dee didn't look at all worried. "But one to three is fine. It's all about the dose!"

I arched my eyebrows, unconvinced.

"It's true," Dum said. "Some people sell our venom and put it in their tea for a jolt."

Okay, that was weird.

"I think I'd rather . . . not."

Dee settled back into the bed, as if she couldn't care less. "You two should leave so I can get started spying. Make sure to tell people I want to be alone."

"Will do." I waved to her and nodded to Dum, who soared next to me.

When I opened the door, two new guards were there, as we'd been told they'd be.

I twisted. "Feel better, Dee!"

"Don't puke all over the bed!" Dum added for good measure.

"Is there a problem?" the younger of the two guards asked.

"One of my ladies-in-waiting overindulged at the feast. She's only this tall," I demonstrated with my hands, "and someone allowed her fae wine." I shook my head. "Now, she's not feeling too hot."

The guard peeked inside, and I could only assume that he caught sight of Dee hamming up being sick, because his expression softened.

"A shame," the guard said. "The prince has requested you meet him for breakfast and was hoping to speak with those closest to you."

"I'm ready and willing to serve Princess Alice," Dum sang, playing her role of dutiful lady-in-waiting to perfection.

"Has he invited Hatter too? And Jax?"

I added my ex's name to make it appear as if my entire group was a united front. He was no longer among those I considered close, but Cirrus didn't know that.

"The prince will be entertaining only you today. You will not see the contenders for your hand until later."

That changed things. I'd been planning to tell the guys all about Princess Roshia's visit, but now . . .

Suddenly, Dee started coughing up a storm from her place in the bed.

My eyes widened, and I spun to find the pixie waving me over. "Water!" she rasped.

What had she done? Choked on her own spit?

When Dee made a weird jerking motion with her head, it clicked: she wanted to speak to me.

The guard moved as if to help her, but I stopped him. "I prefer that male fae whom I do not know not enter my chambers. I'll do it."

They didn't fight me on that, so I rushed over to Dee.

"Are you okay?" I picked up a small glass of water and held it for her.

For appearances' sake, she sipped, but then whispered, "I'll find our guys and tell them about our visitor last night."

"Thank you," I whispered back. I placed the cup back on the nightstand, and in my regular tone, said, "Call us if you need anything, but no one will disturb you otherwise."

"Thank the aether!" she wailed. "I need rest!"

This time, we really did leave the room, and the guards led me through the palace.

Last night, I'd considered that some of the artifacts might have been on display for the feast. As it turned out, I was wrong. The palace was simply decked out in crystal all the time.

"Here you are, Princess Alice." The guards stopped in front of a closed set of double doors. "The Breakfast Room."

"Is there a lunch and dinner one too?"

They stared back at me, but Dum laughed daintily. At least someone was on my level.

After an awkward beat of silence, one of the guards opened the door and announced my presence. Prince Cirrus answered with a rather formal invitation for me to enter, and when I did, I gaped.

He was seated alone at a table long enough to sit twenty and weighed down with food. The prince was at the head of the table, with only three servants at the edges of the chamber for company.

Each servant wore a beautiful robe of sapphire, hemmed with twinkling blue stones. My attention dipped to Cirrus' plate, full of food and surrounded with gemstones the same shade of blue.

I was beginning to understand that sapphire was a Laval House color, and suspected the crystals people kept closest to them might help charge their magic.

"Will your sisters join?" I asked, gesturing to the massive table.

"Just us today."

I squashed a groan. I hadn't considered that I'd be eating with him *totally* alone. But I didn't want to look weak or like a lost precious thing, so I strode toward the table.

The prince's eyebrows pinched together when I stopped at the seat next to his, and he tilted his head. "What are you doing?"

"You invited me to breakfast."

"That," he pointed down the table, "is your seat. The opposite head."

Was he freaking joking? We were going to eat with a million feet of space between us?

"A-are you serious?"

"I don't know how you do things in the Wonderland Court, Princess Alice, but here, things are done properly. Now, please. Sit. Your lady will take the spot next to you, if you wish."

It wasn't an invitation so much as it was a command.

Slowly, I walked down the table, Dum fluttering at my side. When I got to the end, a servant who had been hovering in the corner rushed over and pulled out my chair.

"Thanks." I took a seat.

Once I was situated, the servant asked, "Would you prefer juice, tea, or something else for your beverage, Princess Alice? The royal family prefers to serve themselves food from a banquet spread at breakfast, but I will bring you whatever beverage you wish."

"Water is good. For my lady-in-waiting, too. Obviously, she only requires a very small cup."

The servant rushed off, and I turned to the prince. "I'm surprised your sisters aren't here."

"Indeed, as shocked as I am to see that your other lady isn't tending to you."

"She's not feeling well."

"The same can be said for Nambra. Elisha is resting with her."

"And Roshia?" I asked when he left her name hanging between us.

"I have not seen or spoken with my youngest sister since the feast."

"Are you upset with her?"

"For interfering?"

I shrugged. "Seems to me like she was making sure the law was followed."

"Perhaps. But no, I'm not upset with her for that. Roshia has always been a stickler for the law. I'm more upset that she seems to have fled Jewel of the Sea."

I recalled that the red-haired princess came to my room, still dressed in the gown she'd worn to the feast. Had she snuck out of the palace via the secret passages right after visiting me? Why?

Something isn't right in this kingdom.

Like Wonderland had been corrupt, like the Dark Court was rumored to be a nightmare, it seemed the Crystal Court had its demons too. I was beginning to think there might not be a single place in Faerie that was totally straightforward. Or even close to perfect.

"Hopefully she turns up," I replied, because Cirrus was watching me closely.

"She will when she wants to. Roshia is talented at hiding."

A pregnant pause filled the air.

What did he want me to say? To do?

It didn't matter. A moment later, Cirrus heaved a sigh, as if I'd epically failed to meet his expectations.

"It has been brought to my attention that today would be a good day to show you my kingdom," he stated. "It will get you out of the castle and take our minds off this fussy tournament taking place tomorrow."

Translation: I wouldn't see my friends at all today. Thank goodness Dee had offered to fill them in.

I crossed my arms. "Why would I want to see your kingdom?"

"To become familiar with the fae of the Crystal Court."

"You seem very sure that you're going to win the tournament."

"I am. Your friends are an elemental fae and a wizard. They are no match for me."

Uncrossing my arms, I leaned forward. "Wait, so Jax can compete?" I didn't want him to fight—why risk it?—but no one had told me one way or another yet if a wizard was even allowed.

"It seems that our laws do not preclude other magical

races from entering the tournament. He will likely regret it, though." Cirrus looked smug. Like a man confident in his power and status.

"What kind of magic do you possess?" I asked warily.

"You'll see tomorrow." His tone was ominous, and that made me worry for the guys.

As if he could sense my thoughts drifting away, Cirrus pressed, "Is there something you would like to see while we're out, my beloved?"

My jaw tightened at the forced term of endearment. He was really laying it on thick.

"Do you enjoy gardens?" he continued. "Parks? Historical monuments?"

This was my chance to suggest the Hall of Prophecy, but how to do it? I couldn't come out and say Roshia had told me about it, could I? Not now that she'd fled . . .

"Or perhaps you'd like to see the market?" he suggested when I made no indication of preference. "Speak with the people? They'd—"

"I like libraries," I blurted out. "Especially ones with one-of-a-kind information."

"Like records," Dum added helpfully.

"Yes. Something I can't see anywhere else."

Cirrus set down his fork as a server approached with my glass of water. I grabbed it, thankful to have something to do with my hands while the prince studied me.

Did he suspect I'd already learned about the Hall of Prophecy? Or were there so many special libraries here that he was going through them in his mind?

"If the library has magical connotations, even better," I said, trying to narrow the options.

"Hmm, I shall think of places like that," he relented finally. "Perhaps we'll begin with the market, and if I've come up with a library that fits your interests, we'll go there next."

The bastard. There was no way someone could not recall an elite room filled with prophecies—and the exact information I needed to cross the Rift. He was playing dumb.

Cirrus wouldn't allow me into the Hall of Prophecy even if I came right out and asked for it—which I wouldn't do, because that would expose his sister's influence. I didn't want to do that. She'd tried to help me, so I'd protect her in return. As best I could, anyhow.

That meant I'd have to go along with Cirrus' plan to show me around the kingdom today, and hope that Dee found something useful as she scouted the area.

Hours later, I entered my room and shut the door behind me with a heavy sigh. Immediately, I turned to press my back to it and give something else the weight smothering me.

"Where have you two been all day?!" Dee demanded, soaring over to hover in front of my face.

On my shoulder, Dum yawned. "The prince wanted

to show Alice his kingdom. It was interesting, because this place is weird, but he was going overboard."

"Trying to keep me occupied," I grumbled, shuffling to the bed and flopping onto the mattress with a groan. "And a few times, I think he was trying to force a feeling of intimacy."

The memories of his hand on my back or caressing my shoulder before I pulled away still made me shudder. Clearly, my disinterest didn't matter to him at all. The prince wanted what he wanted—and that was me.

Basically, one of the guys *had* to win the tournament, or we'd have to somehow escape this kingdom before Cirrus forced my 'I do.'

However, before *that*, I had to get the information I sought, or coming here would have been a complete waste of time, on top of everything else.

"How are Henri and Jax?" I asked Dee as I propped up onto my elbows. "Prince Cirrus deliberately kept me away today."

"They realized that was happening when they were told they couldn't leave their apartment," she replied. "I had to sneak in through the window!"

"But no one else saw you, right?"

"Not a soul! I've really gotten better at spying."

"I don't know if that's a good thing. What did Hatter and Jax say about all this? I feel horrible that they're locked up. And what else did you find?"

"They're fine," Dee assured me. "Not hurt or neglected, just bored. And pissed." She glanced at me thoughtfully. "Hatter especially. He's really planning to go all-out in the tournament."

"Of course he is!" Dum scoffed. "He loves Alice!"

I swallowed thickly. "I don't know about *love* . . ."

"He does." Dum's eyes sparkled. "I see it in the way he looks at you."

Okay, Dum was over the moon about the possibility, but for me, the idea was heavy. My only other relationship had ended in disaster and, at present, there were more important matters to worry about. So much that could go wrong. Whatever was happening between Henri and me was not what I needed to think about right now.

"What about the Hall and the stables?" I changed the subject. "Did you find either?"

"Both!" Dee held out her fist for her sister to bump, and then offered it to me.

I obliged, because if this wasn't a fist-bump occasion, I didn't know what was.

"I even created a map to the Hall of Prophecy," she added, lifting a small bit of paper and giving it a wave.

"What?! How?!"

She rolled her eyes. "You guys were gone *all day*, and there are lots of tapestries to hide behind in this castle. What else was I going to do? Plus, it's not that far, really. I was thinking . . ." Her gaze slid to the opening of the tunnel that Roshia had popped out of yesterday. "This secret passage might even lead us close to it. But I couldn't be sure, since you locked it."

"Roshia said there was no passageway there."

"Yeah, but what if it's only a hallway or two away? I could sneak over! You might not be able to go invisible but you could glamour yourself. It's worth a try!"

I gaped, sensing that I was starting to have a bad influence on the twins. "I guess that's true." I paused. "To be honest, even if it doesn't go anywhere near the Hall of Prophecy, I want to see where it goes."

"Ooooh! Let's do it!" Dum squealed.

I put up a single finger. "Hold up."

I rose and went to the door. As ever, two guards stood on the other side, making sure I stayed put.

I applied aether magic to the wood, locking it from the inside. Once that was done, I went to the hidden entrance in the wall and dissolved the spell I'd placed on the tunnel yesterday. Then I opened it.

The guts of the castle were so unlike the rest: no bright colors, no crystals, no show of wealth. Here, it was simple stone, dark, and dank.

"Thank goodness fire is a specialty," I murmured, producing a ball of flame in my hands. "You girls ready?"

The pixies joined me, and with my free hand, I closed the wall softly behind us. Once I was sure that no one would be able to tell from the other side that anything was amiss—who knew if the fae here could break through my aether lock?—we proceeded.

Though I'd never been in a secret passageway before, it was pretty much what I expected. There wasn't a lot to see. As such, I soon realized we'd have to move really slowly to determine what areas of the castle we were traversing through, and adjusted my pace accordingly.

Thank the old gods I did, because at that very moment, I spotted a crack in the wall. An opening.

"Dee. Dum. Look." I pointed to it. "Where do you think we are, Dee?"

She studied the handmade map she'd brought with us. "We haven't gone far from the room. I bet this is a study I passed earlier."

"Should we find out?"

"Listen first." Dum pressed her ear to the wall.

I did the same, and after a full minute, had to admit I didn't hear a thing. Either no one was there, or they were being really quiet—which, in a study, would make sense.

"I say we risk popping in," I said. "If it's the place you saw, then we can pinpoint ourselves on the map. And if someone is there, I'll knock them out or something."

"If you're sure . . . " Dee didn't sound sure at all, but I was feeling reckless, more like my old self, and wanted some action.

Slowly, I pulled the wall to the side, allowing a crack of light to seep into the dark passageway. Again, we listened, and still, I heard nothing, so I pulled the panel open the rest of the way.

A slow smile spread across my face. Dee had been spot on, this was absolutely a study. And best of all, it was empty.

"Mark it down," I said triumphantly.

"Oh, this is helpful!" Dee notated the study on her

map. "I wonder if there are turns in this passageway, though. Because where we're going is not a straight shot from here."

"Let's find out," I replied, shutting us back into the tunnel.

I ran my hand along the walls as we proceeded at our slower pace. When we came to a bend in the tunnel, I cheered in my head. "Does this lead the right way?"

Dee looked at her map again. "It seems like we've been following the same corridor, right? The one our room is in?"

"I'd say yes. Dum?"

"That's what I think."

"Then the Hall of Prophecy would be to our right. So yes, I think this is correct."

This part of the hallway was longer, so it took a bit more time to shuffle along, but eventually, my fingers snagged on a gap in the wall, another opening.

"Guys, wait. Let's listen here."

Pressing our ears to the wall, we again found silence. This time, I didn't even check with the pixies before prying the wall open.

Once it was out of the way, it revealed that we were in a bedroom. An empty one.

"Princess Roshia's room," Dum whispered, landing on the vanity.

"How do you know?" I asked.

"There's a letter here for her."

My fingers itched to take the parchment, to read it,

but surely whatever was inside wasn't any of my business. I was simply curious about the princess, who possessed a very different agenda than her brother.

"My room was directly connected to hers? I wonder if anyone else is aware of that," I mused, looking around. "Do you know where her room is in relation to the Hall of Prophecy, Dee?"

"I do, but you're not going to like it."

My stomach sank. "Why's that?"

"The Hall of Prophecy is down the next hallway . . . but on the opposite side."

"Meaning we won't be able to travel through the walls any longer." I frowned as we ran up against the issue that Roshia had probably already considered.

"And there were guards outside the door," Dee added, as if I could forget.

Maybe I really could glamour myself and trick the guards to get close? But I couldn't do much for the twins. Altering their appearance would be easy, but enlarging them so they wouldn't be identifiable as pixies? That was far more complex than changing hair color or adding freckles.

"Okay, so . . . you two are going to hate this, but I'll just glamour myself and go alone."

"Not a chance, Alice!" Dum hissed. "We'll find a different way. We—"

Voices sounded in the hallway, loud and getting closer with each passing second. I caught the words 'my traitorous sister,' and my heart stopped.

For a moment, I was frozen in place. But when Dum leapt into the air and grabbed her own sister by the wrist, I moved too.

Wordlessly, we scurried back to the tunnel, closing ourselves in darkness as the door to Princess Roshia's room opened.

"You truly wish for us to upend it, my prince?" a familiar male voice asked.

"Do what you must to find her. As it stands, she is my biggest threat. Planting ideas in the Wonderland heir's head," he growled. "Thankfully, my bride-to-be showed her cards, and I was able to extract any information she might find useful from the Hall of Prophecy."

No! My fists balled up. Cirrus was already two steps ahead of me.

"You are brilliant, my prince."

"I prefer 'cunning,' Commander. Now, do as you will with this room. I must place these manuscripts in my chambers."

"Do you wish me to charm them with protections, Prince Cirrus?"

"I will take care of it. If Princess Alice wants answers to her questions, she will have to wait until after we are wed."

CHAPTER 14

The tournament was upon us, and I awoke feeling sick to my stomach. I couldn't shake the notion that someone would get hurt today.

"Alice?" Dum whispered as I smooshed my face deeper into the pillow. "Are you awake?"

"Unfortunately."

Though I had a lot of faith in Hatter's and Jax's magic, Prince Cirrus was proving to be a formidable foe. And confident. He didn't seem at all fazed to be facing two challengers today.

"I was thinking . . ."

Dum's continued whispering made me believe Dee was still sleeping. A second later, a loud snore ripped through the quiet morning, confirming my suspicion.

That girl snored like a trucker after a twelve-hour shift. Though annoying, I also found it sort of impressive that such a dainty creature could create such a huge sound.

"What if the prince was pretending?" Dum finally asked. "What if he never took the information you need from the Hall?"

Dum was sweet, but she was reaching on this one. "Why would he lie? They didn't know we were in the secret passage, so it's not like they were saying that to throw us off. Plus, he was pissed at his sister. And his proximity to her room meant he had recently left the Hall of Prophecy. Maybe he told the commander what he'd done because he wanted assurance that he was doing the right things."

"I guess that makes sense," Dum said, sounding defeated.

It more than made sense. I was certain I was reading things correctly. Though the prince sounded confident in his plans, he couldn't be. Not completely. His sister had left and given privileged information to the woman he was trying to force to marry him.

For some reason, Roshia didn't want Cirrus to occupy the throne. That had to make the prince question himself. So he sought reassurance, and the commander seemed like the type to tell the prince whatever he wanted to hear.

I wondered what the other two Laval sisters thought. I hadn't spoken to them much at the feast and hadn't even seen them since.

I sat up so abruptly, I jostled the bed and woke Dee.

"What's going on?!" she cried, blinking awake and looking around as though we were being attacked.

"Nothing. Sorry. I had a thought." I peered down at the girls. "You two are sisters. Would you say that you tell each other everything?"

"Close to it," Dum replied. "Like, ninety percent."

"That's about right," Dee agreed on a yawn. "But what has that got to do with anything?"

"Dee, do you know where the prince's chambers are?" I asked, already planning a break-in to get the manuscripts he'd taken.

"No, I didn't come across any fancy-pants rooms when I was looking for the Hall and the stables. Why?"

I didn't think so, which meant that Princess Nambra and Princess Elisha were even more valuable.

"I think we need to pay a visit to the other two princesses today. Maybe they can help me get into the prince's chambers. If I mention that Roshia was helping me, they might too. They're all sisters."

Dum stiffened. "That feels even more risky than sneaking into the Hall of Prophecy! Dee and I are close, but not all sisters are, Alice. And even if they *are*, Roshia might not have mentioned to them what she's up to. They're all related to the prince, you know."

I exhaled. She was right, but it was worth a shot.

"I can feel them out first," I said. "See if they're worried about Roshia's interference. Cirrus was, but if they aren't, then maybe they don't want to see him take the throne either. And if they help me get the information

I need, we can escape before this stupid tournament even starts."

I leapt out of bed, determined to find the princesses immediately. It was still early enough that they might be breakfasting.

"I don't have to play spy today, right?" Dee asked.

"It would look too suspicious if you were still ill from the wine. You're both with me."

As I got ready for the day, I made sure to wear regular clothing beneath my gown. I had to be prepared for the chance that this went my way and my group was able to avoid the tournament and leave Crystal Island.

When I opened the door to my room, the two guards on the other side turned toward us.

"I see your other lady is well again," a handsome elven guard I hadn't met yet said.

"I am. Thank you," Dee replied, her tone filled with warmth as she batted her eyelashes at the fae.

I pressed my lips together to keep from laughing. We were trying to leave this island as fast as possible, and yet, here Dee was, flirting it up.

"No one would want you to miss the tournament today." The elf's neck grew red. "It will be quite the affair."

"Speaking of the tournament," I cut in before Dee could seize the conversational reins and try to wow the male. "I was wondering if the princesses are available to speak this morning? If there's a possibility I'm to become part of the family, I'd like to know them better."

The pair exchanged worried glances, and I realized why in an instant.

"I know that Princess Roshia is not currently at the castle," I said airily, choosing to make it sound more like she was out for an errand rather than betraying Cirrus. "I'm referring to Princess Elisha and Princess Nambra. I barely got to speak with them at the feast, but would love the chance to do so now."

The men exhaled as one, and the fae Dee had taken a shine to nodded. "The sisters usually take breakfast together and are likely still enjoying their meal before they prepare for the tournament. I'll show you to them."

We followed the armored guards through the castle. I wasn't sure, but I thought we were going the same way we had when we'd traveled within the walls.

When Dee tugged at my hair and whispered "Left" in my ear, I knew I was probably right.

Discreetly, I twisted left as we crossed hallways, and saw five soldiers standing outside a door, guarding a room the way Roshia had mentioned the Hall of Prophecies would be.

That has to be it.

If only I'd somehow finagled my way in before Cirrus relocated the information I needed. No point lamenting that now. I had to work with where we were at.

"They like to take in the ocean air in the morning," the guard told me, bringing me back to my current objective. "Or at least, they do when it's not scorching."

He opened a door, and fresh, salty air blasted me in the face. It was windy today.

"How refreshing," I said, trying to tame the hair that was already flying around my head, whipping the pixies in their faces.

"Sorry, girls," I muttered, wishing I had an elastic.

The princesses had worn their hair up, in simple, elegant, braided styles. Not a single strand appeared out of place. By contrast, I was an utter disaster.

The soldier escorted us down a path and then a narrow, rocky staircase, to a small beach. On the sand, the princesses dined alfresco, with six servants—all dressed in brilliant sapphire tunics dotted with lime green stones—at their beck and call.

Why were the stones different colors from the ones Cirrus put on his plate during breakfast? Did they indicate different stations?

The wind was so strong that the women didn't hear us coming. Though, once we got close enough, I saw that one of the princesses, or perhaps a servant, had placed a shield around their dining area. The area shimmered faintly when the sun hit it just right.

The moment we stepped inside their protective bubble, the winds stopped.

No wonder their hair isn't blowing about, updos or no.

"Thank the aether," Dee muttered. "Your hair was about to strangle me!"

"It has a mind of its own," I agreed.

The princesses turned toward us when we were steps away, and two pairs of eyebrows raised.

"Good morning, Princess Alice," greeted Princess Elisha, the elder of the two sisters. "To what do we owe the pleasure?"

"I thought it might be nice to get to know one another before the tournament starts. You know, in case I marry into your family."

It still rankled me that, as a woman, I had no say here if I wanted to marry the prince or not. The only way out for me was for another man to challenge the prince for my hand.

Even though Hatter and Jax were doing so only as part of our ruse, I didn't like that I couldn't stand up for myself and still get what I came for.

Well, I could . . .

My ability to force the prince to give me what I wanted had crossed my mind, but using that particular skillset of mine wasn't smart. I still had no idea what his powers were, and challenging him in such a way might not put only me in trouble, but Wonderland too.

Just because the Crystal Court had been isolationists for years didn't mean they wouldn't attack my land if I provoked their prince. For now, doing things this way was better, even if the whole situation was absurd and wasting my time.

My best hope was Hatter would kick Cirrus' ass. Jax succeeding would be fine, too, though he'd be much more vocal and annoying about the win.

"Would you like to take a seat?" Nambra invited, her violet eyes twinkling as she gestured to the spread of fruits and cheeses on the table in front of them. Amongst the food, light green gems and brilliant yellow ones sat, as if they were a garnish.

"I would," I said, noticing how the princesses dined very differently from Cirrus. He'd made a show of it, as he did practically everything.

It made me think he was either trying to impress me, or hide something.

I thanked the soldier who'd showed me the way. He left as I relaxed onto a chair brought to me by another servant. Dee and Dum took the armrests, their legs dangling off the end.

"I assume you're wondering where Roshia is?" Nambra asked after a moment.

"Actually, no. Prince Cirrus told me she is . . . indisposed. I'm happy you're here, though."

The sisters exchanged glances, and Nambra turned back to me.

"Roshia has always been the most fanciful. I suppose it comes with being the baby of the family." The princess took a sip of her drink, a juice of some sort. "She has certain ideas on how our kingdom should be run, and while I love my sister, I find her to be . . . misguided."

Well, that answered my question. They weren't in cahoots with their sister. As far as I could tell, Roshia was the only one on my side. I needed to be careful here.

It would be so much easier if I knew what I was being

careful to avoid—there was something happening in this kingdom that wasn't openly talked about.

"Sisters are precious, though," I said.

"Of course. You'd know that as well as us. Love for your sister is why you're here, after all," Nambra replied, her face softening.

I nodded. "You wouldn't happen to know how the fae from your court got through the Rift, would you?"

A heavy silence followed my question, and I even sensed the servants behind us tense, though I couldn't see them.

I was walking a line, but rescuing Elise was my priority. Everyone here was well aware of that, so it wouldn't do me a bit of good to pretend I was actually interested in their prince

For something to do, I leaned forward and plucked a grape from the bunch. When I popped it into my mouth, the juices exploded on my tongue.

My eyes flew open wide. That had to be the sweetest grape I'd ever eaten! Tangy too. It was almost unnatural—like so much about this island.

"We do not know how the individual who crossed the Rift did so," Elisha finally answered. "Only our brother is privy to that information. It—"

"Do not speak it," Nambra hissed, and the older fae's lips zipped. "He will kill us all."

I gaped. "I'm sorry, but *what*? Who will?"

Yet another of those loaded looks passed between the sisters, but I could not let this slide.

"Do you mean the prince?"

Nambra swallowed loudly, and turned to face the servants. "Privacy, please."

They each backed up ten more paces, and when the younger sister met my eyes again, tears shimmered in her violet eyes.

"He's not well, our brother." She drew in a long breath. "I'm sorry that you're caught up in this, but all I can say is keep your guard up. Cirrus is tricky . . . and neither of us will act against him."

"Because he's blood or because you're scared?"

"A bit of both," Elisha admitted.

I didn't reply right away. If they wouldn't act against Cirrus, they weren't going to give me any information that might let me escape.

I supposed I could understand their position. I'd spent most of my life under a vampire's thumb, after all.

But I wondered if their good breeding meant they would still act like gracious hosts.

Cirrus had shown me his kingdom. He'd wanted to show me off, like a prized pony. But I knew little of his *home*, which made me think that, at least in the palace, he wanted me to feel out of sorts.

I stood. "You know what? I'd love a tour of the Jewel of the Sea. Would you do me the honors of showing me the castle?"

Relief swept across the women's faces, and though they clearly weren't done with their meal, they stood as well.

"We'd be delighted," Nambra replied. "Follow me, Princess Alice."

They led the way back up the steps and into the palace.

"Shall we start with the solarium?" Elisha suggested.

If I was going to do this, it was best to get it over with.

"Actually, as I might be married to him soon," *over my dead body,* "I'd love to see where Cirrus stays. Get the feel for his style. I can't imagine that all this is to his taste." I waved at the crystal-work that filled every nook and cranny of the palace.

Nambra nodded. "Astute. His chambers are this way."

We hadn't gone far when we turned into the section of the royal wing that Cirrus called his own. A line of guards met us, but not a single one stopped us, which I took to mean that Cirrus had not informed them that I was interested in certain manuscripts.

"Here's his chamber." Elisha waved at a door that featured a single sapphire the size of my head set into the wood. "I believe he's inside preparing for the tournament, so we best not bother him. But as you can see, the hallway is plain. His quarters are too. Filled with crystals, but only those that correlate to his powers, few are decorative. His work station is in there too, but that's it." She smirked. "Our dear brother is not big on decorating. If you'd like to see something fabulous, I can show you my quarters."

I was getting the sense she actually would enjoy showing me around, which worked to my favor. It was better they thought I cared about the castle, when really, I'd gotten the information I needed.

I nodded to the princesses, and when they turned and continued down the corridor, I looked to the pixies.

"Remember this area, girls. We'll be back really soon."

CHAPTER 15

My dress swished and sighed around my legs, and beneath the skirts, I sweated.

Unfortunately, I couldn't complain. The dress itself was light enough, suitable to the climate, which was tropical—but I also wore pants and a top underneath.

All the better to allow freedom of movement when I snuck away from the tournament to break into Cirrus' chambers.

"Okay, is the whole kingdom going to watch this?!" I asked in disbelief and eyed the pixies sidelong. Still acting as my ladies, they never left my side.

I was accompanied by a few soldiers and the silver-winged commander who had taken me to be cleansed upon arrival. The same one, I was sure, whom Prince Cirrus had told to search Princess Roshia's room last night.

Already, we were closing in on the arena, which, from the outside, sort of reminded me of the Colosseum in Rome. But this one was made of a shining, opalescent stone, rather than plain rock, and around it, tropical plants rioted, vines climbing the smooth walls.

The arena had not been on my tour of the kingdom, and was far larger than I'd imagined. Judging by the noise coming from within, it was also filled to bursting with fae.

"Everyone on the island is invited," the commander answered in a tone that said I should have realized that would be the case. "Prince Cirrus wishes for his people to witness his prowess."

I pursed my lips. From everything I'd learned about the prince, it seemed like he was strong in magic. What his power was, I still was not sure. I had not seen him use it once, and no one spoke about his abilities, only cowered from him just enough for me to know they were terrified of him.

"This way," the commander said.

As we neared the stadium, fae from the city began to notice us. They even pointed and gawked, so I was glad when our escort led us through a side door rather than the busy main entrance.

"You're in the royal box with the princesses."

My jaw tightened, but I didn't argue. The commander probably trusted me as much as I trusted him —which wasn't at all. It would be best if I went along with this. Then, once I got the lay of the land, I'd devise a way to sneak out.

We wound through a hallway, passing only one other fae, a servant carrying a tray laden with empty goblets.

"Someone is already partying hard," I muttered to the girls.

"Hopefully in your box," Dee whispered back.

That was an idea. If I got those around me drunk, I could do as I wished. Intoxication also had the added benefit of loosening lips.

I'd take that into consideration.

We climbed a set of stairs, and the volume of shouting, cheering, and singing increased, telling us we'd soon find ourselves in the arena.

I was proven right only seconds later when the commander stopped on a landing to stand before a door.

"This is the servants' entrance to the royal box," he explained, his hand on the knob. "Normally, you'd arrive in a more regal fashion, but too many fae are interested in you. We thought this would be better."

It was, for the reason he gave, though now, I wouldn't know my way through the main arena when I snuck out. I hoped it was well-marked.

The commander opened the door, and the smell of dirt came at me hard and fast, likely billowing up from the pit of the arena. We had to be at least two stories up. That I smelled it indicated that, below, something was already happening.

I stepped inside, studying the space quickly. The space was larger than I expected, able to seat twenty arranged in four shallow tiers, though only the two princesses were seated there currently.

They were dressed in lavish gowns of sapphire blue adorned with the same green and yellow stones I'd seen earlier. Nambra's gown was more modest, while Elisha's neckline plunged to her navel. Each dress was absolutely gorgeous, albeit out of place, considering most others in the stadium were dressed in tunics and loose-fitting pants.

Though I too wore a gown—teal, as befit my house— I was plain next to the sisters'.

A half-dozen soldiers stood at the edges of the royal box, swords at their hips and eyes watchful. Two servants were present as well, each with a jug of liquid in hand. I suspected they contained wine or some other alcoholic drink.

Banners featuring the crest of the Laval family hung behind the royal seats. Unlike those of most royal families, theirs did not feature an animal, but a ring of multi-colored crystals.

Considering the island and the strange fae living here, the design fit, but it was still an odd choice.

"Princess Alice." Nambra didn't bother to stand from the middle seat she occupied in the front row.

I approached the seats. "Has Princess Roshia returned?"

Nambra's lips tightened. "No. This is for you." She gestured to the empty seat next to her, which I took.

The pixies floated down to perch on the armrests. Nambra arched her eyebrows at that, but said nothing. It might not be usual here for ladies-in-waiting to sit with the royals, but I didn't see any tiny chairs provided for the twins. Where else were they going to sit?

"I take it Prince Cirrus is below?" I craned to see.

"Preparing for the tournament," Elisha replied, her eyes alight with excitement.

"What are they going to do exactly?" I asked.

"Fight!"

"With weapons?"

"That or magic. They can choose."

"They must also defeat beasts," Nambra said. "That is how the first round is decided."

"What do you mean?" I pressed.

"In this type of situation, there is usually only one challenger. However, there are guidelines in place if two or more wish to impede on a royal's right to his betrothed."

I bristled at the word 'right,' but said nothing.

"The males you arrived with will have to fight off monsters. The first to defeat his monster, by drawing blood, wins."

My mouth went dry. "What kind of monsters are we talking about here?"

"Only the High Councilor and those who brought the creature here knows." Nambra leaned forward over the railing, as if hoping to glimpse the beast.

I peered around the arena too. The open-air seating allowed me to view everything. Thousands of fae stood in the stands. I thought of the rocs we'd encountered on our way here. What if the creature the High Councilor chose could fly?

"What about your subjects? If the beast has wings, won't they be hurt?"

"Protections are in place." Nambra reached out and flicked an invisible barrier that crackled with electricity.

"All around the arena?"

"Of course. No harm will come to anyone. Except perhaps to my brother's challengers."

I gulped. "You said whoever draws blood or kills the creature first wins. What if the creature draws their blood? And what are they winning? Clearly not me, since Prince Cirrus isn't even involved yet."

"They fight until they draw blood, no matter how badly they're injured in the meantime. And if they win, they get to go second in fighting our brother," Elisha answered. "Once the true fight is over, the one against my brother, for both males challenged *him*, Cirrus will then fight the remaining contestant. Whether he wins of loses, he has two fights today."

"What if he loses one?"

"Then whomever beat him wins." Elisha did not look at all worried that would happen.

Hatter and Jax were both strong. I had to hope one would win so we could not only get what we came for, but avoid creating drama between courts.

In Faerie, drama could lead to utter disaster. Even though his court had been isolationists for years, I wouldn't put it past Cirrus to start a war if he felt slighted. And as I had not officially refuted my possession of the throne, the fae of Wonderland still relied on me to keep them safe. I'd do my best to see to it that their trust wasn't misguided.

On a more personal level, I already had so much to make up for in my life, I wasn't looking to add 'caused a war' to that list.

A horn blared, grabbing my attention, and from one corner of the arena, a tall, muscular fae appeared. Though he was far away, he looked dirty, and his skin red—like he'd been wrestling with something. A second later, another giant of a fae appeared, and then another. Ropes of steel trailed all three males, and I gasped as a creature of myth appeared last, following his handlers.

"Is that what they're fighting?!" I demanded as the crowd around me went wild, leaping from their seats and shouting unintelligibly at the monsters below.

"Looks like it!" Elisha squealed as a second beast appeared. "It usually takes five full-grown male fae to make a minotaur submit! This will be so exciting!"

I squinted at the pair of half-man, half-bull hybrids. The creatures were at least twice Hatter's height, and stacked with muscle.

But being big didn't make them unbeatable. My Cheshire Cat had taken down a queen kraken. Every creature had a weakness, it was simply a matter of finding it.

"Are they fast?" I asked, taking in the minotaurs' cloven hooves.

"Very! And their skin is resistant to magic," Elisha said.

"Not that magic can be used in this round," Nambra reminded us. "That would be unfair."

I sputtered. "U-unfair?! Those things are enormous!"

I barely stopped myself from adding that if they really wanted to make things fair, Prince Cirrus would be down there, taking on a third beast.

"True. It will be quite the show!" Elisha smiled at me, violet eyes flashing with glee, as if she thought I was enjoying this.

She might look beautiful and sweet, but she wasn't fooling me anymore. The girl was a psycho.

"Attention! Attention please," a magically amplified voice called.

I directed my focus to the pit of the arena, where High Councilor Larrel had appeared and was waiting for the crowd to fall silent. The roars, cheers, and jeers of the fae diminished, and for the first time since I'd arrived at the stadium, the air seemed to still.

"Welcome, good fae of the Crystal Court!" Larrel waved at the stands. "Today, we witness a tournament of strength, magic, and will between our brave Prince Cirrus, and two outsiders who dare to challenge him for the hand of his intended, Prince Alice White of the Wonderland Court!"

"Boooo!"

"Drown the invaders!"

"Hurl those dirty scoundrels off a cliff!"

A hundred other threats toward Hatter and Jax filled the air, making my fists clench. The din quieted only when Larrel called for silence once more.

"Justice will be seen today," he assured us. "It's in the *lapil*'s hands. Prepare for battle!"

Again, roars of joy came from those wanting to see their prince emerge victorious.

"What's *lapil*?" I hissed when the onlookers, princesses included, bowed their heads.

"The sacred crystals," Elisha replied. "Where we draw magic from."

This place was so unlike the rest of Faerie. A part of me wished I could stay and learn about these *lapils*. I wanted to see how the magic here worked and see all the different variations. But the larger part of me, the part connected to the men being ushered side-by-side into the arena at that very moment, just wanted to get the hell out of here.

Good luck, Henri. And Jax, I thought as the pair marched toward the minotaurs. The beasts were already posturing, pawing at the dirt with their hooves, kicking it up in the faces of the fae who held them.

Determination that hadn't been there seconds ago lined the monsters' faces. Did the minotaurs get something for this fight? Were they subjects of this court? Fae could look odd sometimes, though I'd never seen any that looked like those two.

"What if the minotaurs win?" I asked, knowing that would mean the worst, but needing the rest of the answer.

"If they kill the challengers, you mean?" Nambra asked, not sounding at all saddened by the prospect.

"Yes," I gritted out.

"They are freed."

"They're prisoners?"

"Slaves. They work in fighting pits."

I ceased asking questions, instead choosing to watch as the minotaurs' handlers ushered them fifty paces from Henri and Jax.

The handlers stood behind the beasts, and the fae holding spare swords for my friends—their only lifelines in this screwed-up tournament—tossed them ten feet in front of the guys, so the metal hit the dirt with a *clang*.

High Councilor Larrel had made his way to the edge of the pit and now stood, holding his arms up. "On my mark!" he yelled.

Dropping his arms, he bellowed, "Let the match begin!"

The fae holding on to each minotaur's chains released them, and one held up a crystal. The chains vanished, making me blink.

"How—"

"Crystal Spellsmith," Nambra answered before I

could even get the words out. "You'll learn all about our gemstones and what they can do for us, when you join our family."

"Who knows, maybe you'll be inclined in the way of the crystals yourself," Elisha added, not bothering to look at me, her attention so fixed on the unfolding scene.

Below, Henri and Jax had separated, and one minotaur charged each. I wasn't sure if there were rules, like each minotaur was set to fight only one of the guys, or if they could work together. But I figured I didn't want to know. If there were rules, they wouldn't have been made to benefit my side.

Instead, I watched the men battle the monsters, my attention ping-ponging between them so fast that, at times, my vision blurred.

I'd only just switched back to Henri, when my heart stopped. The beast he fought had managed to get too close, slashing his claws at my man.

Everything around me seemed to slow as the claws cut through Henri's shoulder. Blood spurted. Fae roared with pleasure, and my own cry of horror mixed with their gleeful ones.

"*Hatter!*" I shouted as Henri spun and ran, putting a safe distance between him and the monster. The sleeve of his shirt had torn open, and even from here, I could see the livid gash on his skin. "Run!"

The minotaur chased Hatter, and inside me, my aether magic begged to be released, to save him. Though it took everything I had, I fought it back down.

Fighting for the guys would not be acceptable. It might even put them in more danger. I had to trust that they could survive this. I *had* to . . .

"Alice? Are you unwell?" A hand landed on mine. I turned to find Elisha watching me with concern. "You're shaking."

I looked down at my arm. So I was.

"I-I-"

"Perhaps you should pull yourself together in private," Nambra suggested, her tone cooler than before. "My brother has eyes everywhere, Princess Alice. You do not want anyone to suggest that you were pining for the opposition."

How deluded was she? I'd arrived here *with* Hatter and Jax. She expected me not to care about them?

Or was this all for show? Were these guards only loyal to Cirrus and would report the sisters' actions?

That had to be it.

The princesses were scared of their brother. Why, I wasn't entirely sure, but I understood he was off-kilter. For them to be putting on a show was the only thing that made sense.

"If you will, Princess Alice," another voice came from behind, and I twisted to find a female guard standing there. "I can escort you to the privy. You might contain your emotions there."

A part of me wanted to stay, to make sure my friends survived. But another part recognized this as a golden opportunity. I needed to sneak out of this box, then out of the arena.

At least one of those would be easy.

"Yes please." I stood, and on either side of me, the pixies lifted into the air, ready to act as my ladies-in-waiting. "I'll return when I feel more composed."

Elisha resumed watching Henri and Jax run from the beasts chasing them. Nambra hadn't even bothered to look away at all.

When another roar of pleasure came from the crowd, I swallowed and gestured for the soldier to lead.

She did, but to my frustration, another soldier, also female, slipped out of the box with us.

Dee shot me a look, and I knew exactly what she was thinking. Two guards would make things doubly difficult.

Of course, if I had to fight and incapacitate two, I could. It would be messier, perhaps even draw attention, but I was Alice the Dagger back home. I'd faced difficult opponents before.

They escorted me down a hallway that presumably led to the areas where the public could mingle. However, before we even got close to where the masses would mingle, one of the soldiers inched closer.

"Alice, it's Roshia," she whispered.

The pixies let out surprised cries, but I kept it together, narrowing my eyes. The woman looked nothing like Roshia. She had dark brown hair and eyes, and darker skin, more olive than fair.

I studied her. "Prove it. How did you get into my rooms?"

"A secret passage in the walls. Good on you for checking."

I believed her. There was no way those passages were common knowledge. If they were, I would not have been given that room.

"How did you . . .?" I gestured to her face. "There are no aether-blessed fae on this island."

"We have other means of disguise," Roshia said. Her voice had changed from when we were in the royal box. It sounded familiar now. "This is my . . . accomplice."

I got the distinct sense the other woman was more than an accomplice, but didn't push. I also didn't ask her name. Partially because I was sure she wouldn't tell me, but also because, if we got caught, it would be better for the guard if I didn't know who she was.

"Why are you here?"

"To help you get into Cirrus' quarters, of course." Roshia arched an eyebrow. "That is your plan, isn't it?"

"How'd you know?"

"Did you see me spying?" Dee interjected, her tone worried. I could tell she really didn't want to be the one to have screwed it up.

"No one told me of a pixie running wild," Roshia assured her. "But I have eyes and ears in the castle who are loyal to me. Servants who want what I want. They mentioned that my sisters took you on a tour and you wanted to see where Cirrus' rooms were. I assume it's not because you're already *so* in love with my brother?"

The princess' blonde companion snorted and rolled her brilliant blue eyes. I liked her already.

"No," I spat. "He moved the tomes I need from the Hall of Prophecy into his chambers." I paused. "Ransacked your room too."

"He's such a swine." Roshia's lips curled up in disgust. "What do you say we pay him in kind?"

CHAPTER 16

We stopped at the privy so that I could glamour my face and, most importantly, my telltale hair, darkening it to an unassuming, brown shade. I also shed the gown I wore and, to be safe, threw on Roshia's companion's cloak.

"There are pockets on the inside for your small friends. They'd give us away if they flew with you." She gestured to the pixies, and I opened the cloak.

The girls soared into the bucket pockets.

"All set!" Dum grinned up at us, always the spot of levity in a tense situation.

"Thanks," I said to the soldier I'd internally named Barbie. That was kind of who she looked like.

"No problem," she replied and opened the door. "We must hurry."

I didn't need telling twice. I fell in line, content to follow since I had no idea where I was going.

Swiftly, Princess Roshia and Barbie led me out of the arena and along the streets of the city. I took in the area I found myself in. I hadn't gone this way before, and things seemed . . . rough. Buildings were dilapidated. The roads bore potholes. The animals tied up outside of homes looked too skinny to be healthy. It reminded me of the Heartstown neighborhood where rebel headquarters was located.

The route proved a good one, though, because no one was around, and in minutes, Jewel of the Sea Palace came into our sights.

"How long do you think it will take us to get to the castle and into Cirrus' rooms?" I asked.

"We'll be done before anyone comes looking for you. My sisters will be enthralled with the tournament for a while yet."

"And they probably really think she's crying," Barbie snorted. "They're so ridiculous. Anyone with eyes could see this one isn't a crier."

I glanced at her. Barbie was older than me by a few years, probably the same age as Hatter—around twenty-five or so. That was, *if* what I was seeing was real. Was she disguised, like Roshia? And who was she that she thought she could speak about the princesses that way? Or me?

Not that she was wrong. I wasn't a crier. But still, I got an odd vibe from this fae.

Keeping my impression to myself, I remained quiet as we raced toward the palace. Once we were close enough to see a cluster of guards standing at the entrance gate, Roshia swore and took a hard left.

"This way!"

"There a problem?" I asked, thankful I was quick on my feet and able to accommodate her sudden change of course.

She shrugged. "I thought there'd be fewer guards, but don't worry. I can get us in."

As if I'd doubt her. The young woman knew about a tunnel in the walls, and she'd managed to slip out of the palace so others were none-the-wiser. I trusted that she could take me where I needed to go.

We reached a wall of bushes, and the disguised princess stopped our mad dash and plunged her arm into the shrubbery.

"Where is that—*aha*! There you are!"

A squeal of hinges announced she'd found a door, and Roshia gestured for the other woman to go in. "Check the other side."

Barbie did as she was told, and I glanced around.

Minutes ticked by, and with them, images of Henri and Jax fighting the minotaurs were starting to torture me. Not that I could do anything about their current predicament, but I did want to make sure they were safe. Or at least that things hadn't gotten worse. Could that even happen?

The dueling desire to find the information I needed *and* watch over the guys was frustrating.

Apparently, the worry was showing on my face, because Roshia arched a brow at me.

"How long do you think we've been gone?" I asked impatiently.

"Five minutes. No more. *Really,* you'll be *fine*," she assured me. "We're fast, and I took the quickest route. The commander took you the long way because he didn't want you to see the poor parts of the city."

"I noticed that."

"I'm not surprised you did."

"All clear!" Barbie shouted, her voice muffled by the thick barrier of bushes.

I filed through, the leaves brushing my skin as I went. Once on the other side, the palace loomed beyond a garden.

"His room is in this part of the castle," Roshia said once we were on the other side of the hedges. "Stick close. We'll travel by passageway."

"Is there one that goes into his room?" I asked.

"It leads to right outside it," Roshia said. "There's a possibility that we'll have to deal with a couple of his personal guards, but Cirrus might have taken them to the tournament. In that case, he'd simply lock his room. Too bad for him, I've known how to pick locks for *ages*."

This princess was my kind of woman. I'd been eight when I learned how to pick locks. Now, I could use aether —unless Cirrus had magic on the locks that prohibited it. Still, I liked the old-fashioned way too.

My heart pounded as Roshia led us to the castle's

outer wall. We were nearly there, when a soldier rounded the corner.

"Who goes there?" he barked.

"By the *lapil*," Barbie grumbled. "Can't he mind his own business?"

"Who are you? Identify yourself!" the guard yelled.

Roshia smirked, and Barbie shook her head as if the male was the most annoying fae on the planet. "Allow me."

She pulled an amber crystal from her pocket, muttered a word I didn't understand, and the man fell to the ground.

"Is he dead?" I asked, somewhat shocked by how fast it had happened.

"Asleep. He'll be out for about twelve hours."

"What if Cirrus hears of this when the man wakes?"

"Hears what? That there were three females standing by the palace? Not much else the guard can say."

"You're in guard attire," I pointed out.

"Maybe he won't remember." Roshia shrugged. "In any case, we have to move. If I hear him talking about three women later, I'll deal with him then."

I hoped that didn't mean she'd kill the guy. He'd only been trying to do his job.

Roshia approached the wall and placed her hand on it. There was a faint *click*, and the wall opened, revealing a tunnel. We entered, and she shut the door behind us before assuming the lead once again.

"How many secret passages are there?" I asked curiously as we strode deeper into the castle.

"A ton," she replied. "And Cirrus doesn't know about a single one of them."

"How is that possible?"

"He was a suck-up growing up. Always wanting to outdo the rest of us. Always wanting to prove to Father that he should rule. He was such a know-it-all that when I found the passages—which I think were used by servants back in the day—I didn't share their existence with him. I guess I wanted something to hold over him."

My eyebrows pinched together. I was surprised that he'd have to prove that, being the heir and all, but maybe things were slightly different here.

Roshia twisted and turned through the passages, and Barbie and I followed close behind. When she slowed and held up a hand, my breath tightened. We had to be close.

"It's on the opposite side of this hallway," Roshia whispered. "Let me go first. I'll see if there are guards."

Before anyone could say another word, the princess slipped out.

I tensed, waiting.

But no hiss of a sword filled the air. Nor questions from a guard. When the princess reappeared, I exhaled loudly.

"We're in luck. No guards. The door *is* locked, but . . ." She pulled two pins from her hair and handed them to me. "You want to do the honors? That would probably piss Cirrus off the most. Not that I'd tell him it was you, but I like to know that what I'm doing is what he'd like least."

"I got you."

I swept into the hallway, and stuck the pins into the lock. Tuning in to my sense of touch, I felt around within the mechanism a bit and then followed my gut.

Swift clicks followed, and I tried the knob. It turned.

"Wow," Dum breathed from where she nestled in my cloak. "Teach me!"

"When we get home."

I swung the door inward to reveal a room filled to bursting with crystals, mostly in shades of blue. One such gem was half my height and set in the direct line of the sun coming in through the window.

"Someone's got a favorite color," I murmured.

"He draws most of his power from sapphires," Barbie explained. "That big one is charging."

"How do you know?"

"I make it my business to know about the prince. Shouldn't you be looking for something?"

"Over here." Roshia swiftly directed us across the room, toward a desk partially hidden behind a privacy screen.

Piled on the desk were at least fifty books, but off to the side was a stack of three that appeared more weathered than the others. Smelled it too.

"Those have to be them," I said, nose wrinkling at the musty scent. How could he bear to have these in his chambers?!

"Agreed." Roshia grabbed the pile and handed one to me and one to the other guard. "Look for anything on the Rift or oracles who were in Wonderland in . . . What year were you born, Alice?"

I told her my birthday, almost eighteen years to the day, and we got to work.

The book I held detailed the historical feats of fae from the Crystal Court. The record was not long, and I was looking for only one word: 'Rift.'

I found it quickly, almost exactly in the middle. "Here!"

I pinned my finger on the passage and read the words around it, backtracking to make sense of the information. Dee and Dum read along with me.

Dum got to the end first, flitting to the opposite page and pointing. "He used an illumination crystal to get through the Rift! What's that?!"

"It's—" Roshia started.

"Do you hear something?" a deep voice in the hallway asked, and footsteps sounded, coming closer.

My chest tightened. We'd gotten lucky on the way in; it wouldn't go the same way on our exit.

"I have information on the oracle who visited the Wonderland Court!" Barbie hissed. "They were male, but he's not named . . ." She turned the page, and her face fell. "And there's *nothing* here on what he said."

I groaned. "Are you sure?"

"Positive. The passage goes on to describe his other travels in the Riverlands. It even gives the prophecies he made there before returning home. But there's nothing on your birth. It seems like—"

"What are you doing in there!" a male voice boomed, and Dee squealed from her hiding place in my pocket.

"Time to run, ladies." Roshia set her book down.

I followed suit. The tome couldn't come with me, as my possession of it would only implicate me in the crime we were committing. And whatever was still to come.

"Alice, want to give me an aether demonstration?" the princess asked.

"With pleasure."

We rushed the door, and I tapped into my aether magic. It whipped out of me, soaring toward the male fae and wrapping around their necks.

They hadn't attacked us yet—I suspected they were too taken aback at actually finding people in the prince's chambers—and now they wouldn't get the chance.

I tightened my hold on the guards, and slowly, their faces turned blue. Seconds later, one fell, then the other.

"I'd like to add the finishing touch!" Barbie flung magic at the men.

When nothing seemed to change, I furrowed my brows in confusion, but she only winked. "I can affect bodies and minds. Now they'll be passed out for hours."

"Can you make them forget we were here?" I asked, following Roshia through the door.

"No. If I could, I would have done it to the other guard," Barbie pointed out. "That's what the disguises are for."

True, but I still didn't feel totally protected. Would Prince Cirrus still suspect me? Should I have killed the guards?

The instant the last question formed in my mind, I cringed.

No. I was the new Alice, no longer an assassin. I wouldn't kill unless it was absolutely necessary, like in instances of self-defense. Or to save Elise.

Plus, if the prince was inclined to suspect me, that would be the case regardless of the condition of the guards.

"Come on!" Roshia opened the secret passageway outside the prince's quarters.

We slipped into the darkness and ran, slowing only when we arrived at the door leading to the outside.

Again, Roshia checked that the coast was clear, and then we walked more naturally across the palace grounds, trying not to draw attention. We saw only servants, and none of them questioned us, but I couldn't help but worry.

"How long have we been gone now?"

"Twenty minutes. Maybe thirty." Barbie looked me over. "You need to look worse."

"What do you mean?"

Suddenly, my face began to tingle, like a swarm of bees was stinging me all at once. "What are you doing?!"

"Making you swell up like you've been crying your little princess eyes out."

"How about a warning next time?!"

She chuckled. "As if there will be a next time. I must say, though, you're blowing up nicely."

How mortifying. I groaned inwardly, slipping through the bushes and the hidden door that led off the palace grounds and into the city.

Once on the other side, we broke into a dead sprint for the arena.

CHAPTER 17

"Princess Alice! We were starting to worry about you!" Elisha tossed a glance over her shoulder as I entered the royal box, my breathing barely under control.

Between sprinting back to the arena, having to change rapidly, and undoing my glamour, I was experiencing a new level of exertion. The pressure in my chest was so tight, I might burst at any second but I forced myself to act sad, like I'd just finished my epic sob-fest. Barbie slipped into place at the back of the royal box, once again wearing the cloak I'd borrowed, but Roshia remained at my side, corroborating the effect that I was barely keeping it together.

"You missed the rest of the first challenge!" Elisha added when I didn't reply.

My heart plummeted. "Are they in the second round? Who's fighting?"

Elisha didn't answer, only turned back to face the pit, her smile wide at the promise of spilt blood.

Nambra wasn't as flighty as her sister and stared at me openly, though she did not appear to have heard my question. Her nose wrinkled in disgust. "You look horrible."

Thanks to the stinging effect of Barbie's magic, and the tears I'd forced myself to shed, I was sure I looked like Hell warmed over. But at least the Lavals didn't seem to suspect I'd been dishonest with them.

"The princess was in quite a state," Roshia murmured as she guided me to my seat. I marveled at how her tone dipped into a voice so unrecognizable, even her sisters didn't know it was her. "Alas, she returned because she was desperate to see Prince Cirrus battle, and insisted she leave the privy. Just in time, too, it seems."

"Yes. He's doing quite well," Nambra replied, riveted on the arena. "But then, wizards aren't nearly as strong as fae, are they?"

So, Henri had beaten his minotaur before Jax. Had my ex been injured? Or had Henri simply drawn blood first? I peered over the balcony, and my mouth went dry. A dozen large, dark splotches marred the dirt below. *Is that blood?*

"Was anyone injured?" I asked. "Against the minotaurs?"

"Not really," Elisha appeared disappointed by that fact, but I couldn't help but exchange furious glances with the pixies.

Both Dee and Dum had done well staying quiet, as ladies-in-waiting would. Though, currently, they looked like they wanted to rip Her Royal Highness' face off.

"The fae competitor got a scrape after the wizard already lost, but that was about it," she added.

"Then why does the ground look like that?" I asked, as below us, Cirrus and Jax danced around one another. The latter was lithe, but the prince was something else. He moved like the wind made flesh, like nothing at all worried him or would touch him.

The wizard fired off a spell, which the fae prince avoided with a graceful twirl that sent his blue cape billowing. Sapphires ran the length of it, as if the prince thought this was a ball, not a tournament.

The crowd roared at his escape, and once he was no longer spinning, the prince sent a smile as cruel as a blade up at the stands. Females screeched, and my blood boiled.

Seriously, though, a cape in a fight!? That smarmy expression?! How pretentious and unnecessary.

I could really get on a roll with hating Cirrus' fashion choices, but at that moment, a bolt of light zinged out of the sky, stunning me so much that my inner monologue ceased.

Jax hurled himself out of the way in time for the lightning to hit the ground, and the dirt where it struck turned black.

Wait a minute . . .

The mark matched the other splotches. All those

places where I thought blood had been spilled, they'd really been hit by lightning?

My shoulders tensed. Cirrus wielded lightning!

"He's avoided being struck that many times?!" I breathed. There had to be at least a dozen marks on the ground.

Elisha grimaced. "Far more than most. Our brother is generally much better at aiming, but the wizard appears to have a sixth sense for this sort of thing. I suppose it's a way to make up for his lack of magical talent." Again, she looked put-out.

Lack of magical talent? Jax was a very strong wizard, but I didn't bother correcting her.

From that point forward, I could only worry about Jax. I might not love him anymore, but if he got fried because he'd come here with me, I'd feel awful.

Thankfully, what the princess said was true—Jax did seem to have a certain sense for Prince Cirrus' power. And with each miss, the prince lost his composure a touch more. His confident smirk dropped, and his face deepened to a livid crimson.

No longer caring how regal I appeared, I leaned forward and placed my palms on the hot, stone railing of the balcony. Beside me, the pixies stood on the balcony's edge, their mouths open wide, as Jax sent green magic at the prince, only to dodge a bolt of lightning the next second.

My fingers itched to work my own magic, to help, but that would be pointless. And, after breaking into the prince's chambers, it really was best to not draw attention to myself.

I shouldn't fight. Shouldn't cry out. I needed the guys to do their bit to lay out this pompous prick so we could leave Crystal Island without starting a courtly incident.

My reserve lasted precisely one second longer, until Jax was struck by lightning.

"Nooo!" I screamed as he fell to the ground, clouds of dirt flying up to obscure him.

The crowd went wild, and Prince Cirrus raised his arms. I took his gesture as a victorious one, but suddenly, the air in the royal box felt electric. I looked up in time to spot a nebula of crackling, deadly light coalescing over Jax.

Cirrus was going to strike again.

Over my dead body.

I thrust out my aether so hard that a hole formed in the shield protecting the onlookers. My power streaked toward Jax in my desperation to get to him before Cirrus could land another blow.

"Princess Alice! What are you doing?!" Nambra shrieked.

But she was nothing to me, easy to ignore as my magic tunneled through the electrified air.

It slammed to a stop over Jax, forming a shield as another bolt of lightning lanced toward him with so much power that my aether shield shuddered. No doubt that assault would have killed Jax.

Cirrus spun, locking eyes with me.

"You won!" I shouted. "He doesn't have to die."

Pure silence rang. It was almost like no one in the arena dared to breathe. Thousands of eyes were on me, but I only took notice of one person: the prince who'd tried to play dirty.

Finally, his lips curled up in a grin. "As you wish, my love." His voice boomed, filling the stadium with his presence and false charm. "I will spare *him*."

His intent hung in the air.

The other may not be so lucky.

"Remove the wizard and bring in the other challenger!" Prince Cirrus demanded.

The doors to the arena pit flung open, and out ran two armored fae. As if they'd done so a million times before, they picked Jax up by his feet and hands. Dread drenched me as his body swayed between them, limp.

Was he okay? If he needed medical attention, would he get it?

I wasn't holding my breath, and as the fae darted back into the innards of the stadium, I felt the urge to follow them.

But then Henri was pushed into the pit, and my feet rooted me in place. I couldn't leave. I had to hope the other fae had more humanity than their prince.

"Sit!" Nambra said, her tone more commanding than usual.

Again, I ignored her . . . which was more than could be said for Dee, who straight up spun and scowled at the princess.

I wanted to fist-bump her, but refrained. I needed to be alert for the next fight. If the prince did the same to Henri as he had done to Jax, *I'd* be the one who went feral.

I studied Hatter as he strode toward Cirrus. His gait was slightly off, giving away that he was tired, which, considering he'd taken on a minotaur not long ago, wasn't a surprise. But when he stumbled over nothing, a more malicious thought seeded in my mind.

I'd been assured the guys were being taken care of. Fed. Given water. Basically, treated well.

Was that true?

"Dee," I said her name, careful to keep my voice low. "When you saw Henri and Jax, did they look okay?"

"Yeah," she whispered back. "But that was the night after the feast."

True. It wasn't like the guys would starve over the course of a night, or even the two days that we'd been here. But being deprived of food for that long would be enough to weaken a person.

Henri stopped a few dozen paces away from the prince, one hand on his loaner sword. I prayed to the old gods I was wrong about his condition and that he'd kick Cirrus' ass.

As the fight began, my confidence rose. Henri might be tired, but now that the competition was underway, he wasn't letting it show. He rushed the prince, aggressively striking with his blade, drawing blood.

I gasped. "Is that it?!"

"What?" Elisha snapped, annoyance in her eyes.

She'd seemed so scared of her brother the other day. Why did she care if he won?

Maybe if he doesn't, he'll make his sisters' lives more difficult?

If that were the case, that sucked, but I wasn't willing to risk Henri, or even Jax, for the princesses' comfort.

"Henri drew blood," I pressed. "Is it over?"

It didn't seem like it. Cirrus had drawn his sword and was retaliating. But I wouldn't put it past the prince to continue fighting even if it was over; he was insane and clearly desperate for a bride. Plus, he'd already tried to zap Jax in the most cowardly manner. "Of course it isn't *over*," Nambra replied. "The drawing of blood was only for the minotaurs. In these rounds, contestants fight until one surrenders, loses consciousness, or dies."

"Ugh," I huffed.

Henri was doing reasonably well. He had gotten close to the prince with his blade, alternating blows with earth magic to shake the ground beneath Cirrus, throwing the prince off balance many times.

But even without being unsteady on his feet, Cirrus was hesitant to use his lightning in close proximity. Perhaps his aim wasn't entirely accurate?

Come on, Hatter, I urged as he slashed with his sword again.

The blade whistled by the prince, nearly cutting into his arm, but Cirrus had a trick up his sleeve. As he twirled, he dipped, and when he rose again, he hurled a fistful of dirt into Henri's eyes.

My guy staggered back and called upon air, retaliating in kind. Vicious clouds of dust blew at Cirrus, but he used his cape to block it, and once the gusts ceased, Cirrus glared at Henri, who still hadn't recovered.

In that instant, I knew the prince was seeing red.

Again, the air in the arena electrified, but before I could locate the lightning, it exploded from the sky, slamming into Henri.

He collapsed to the ground, twitching. The princesses leapt up and cheered exuberantly, but I remained frozen in place. Watching him, my fingers dug into the stone of the balcony. *Get up. Get up. Get. Up!*

But no matter how desperately I urged him to move, Hatter didn't stand. In fact, his jerky motions slowed, and he soon stilled. My pulse began to pound in my throat. He couldn't be dead. Could he?

Suddenly, everything else disappeared, and my breathing thinned dangerously. I gasped, desperate for air, for something to right me. To make this reality cease to exist. Before I could hyperventilate to the point of passing out, however, someone came up behind me, their soft hands landing on my shoulders.

"Alice," Barbie whispered in my ear. "He's not dead. Pull yourself together."

Not dead. Not dead. Not dead. But how did she know?

"I read bodies," she reminded me when I very clearly did not calm down.

I gasped, recalling that from earlier, and air flooded my lungs. Henri wasn't dead. Barbie had no reason to lie about that. Henri was alive, passed out, but alive. My shoulders softened, and I nodded so Barbie knew I'd returned to myself. I felt when she distanced herself, and resumed watching the arena below just in time to see the prince lift his arms in victory.

All around the rest of the arena, fae were cheering, screaming Cirrus' name, celebrating his triumph, some literally crying with happiness. Dum couldn't take it any longer and burst into silent tears.

"Well, it looks like you're part of the family now, Princess Alice," Elisha chirped. "We'll have to go dress shopping before the wedding ceremony."

I was saved from making what would surely be a waspish reply by Prince Cirrus calling for silence. He'd been regaling the stadium, but now he turned to face me.

He bowed. "My love. The challengers have been defeated. Now, by the law of my land, we may wed."

I stood frozen, unable to speak, unable to even think.

"She's so grateful, she has no words!" Prince Cirrus simpered, a hand on his heart. "Save them for tomorrow, my love. For that is the day our two hearts become one."

Whispers rushed through the crowd, but none of them faster than the racing of my heart. He'd set the wedding for *tomorrow*?! What happened to an appropriate courting period?!

"Now," Prince Cirrus looked to the edges of the stadium, where soldiers likely waited for his command, "if someone could get this fae out of here? Take him to prison with the other one. I have an engagement ball and a wedding to prepare for."

CHAPTER 18

I sat on the edge of my bed, vibrating with anger. Barely an hour before, Hatter and Jax had been taken to the prison. Guards had swiftly escorted me and the other two princesses back to Jewel of the Sea, and I'd been locked in my room, where I was to stay until the ball that night. A celebration of my upcoming nuptials.

In the streets, fae sang and danced. I did not share their sentiment, and had no freaking idea what to do.

At this point, I had the knowledge of what I needed to cross the Rift, but no illumination crystal to actually do so. Plus, even if I knew how to sneak off this island, I couldn't leave without Henri and Jax.

Then there was the real kicker: Prince Cirrus had set our wedding for *tomorrow morning*. I definitely had to find a way out of that.

There was too much to do and not enough time. My power might be strong, but I couldn't take on an army—

which was exactly what was at the palace. Plus, I'd seen firsthand that fae here had formidable magic. I'd never fought someone who could wield lightning.

"We're so screwed," I whispered.

"Don't say that!" Dee retorted.

Dum, the more sensitive of the twins, sniffled. She'd been crying since Hatter fell, and her tears had only come harder after Cirrus threw the guys in prison.

"Well, do you have any ideas on how we're going to get out of this?" I challenged her sister. "Aside from killing?"

I was no stranger to death, but I'd recently been given a choice: remain a killing machine, or turn over a new leaf and become the version of myself I might have been, had I never met the vampire assassin lord Xavier Doru. I wanted the latter.

Of course, to save Elise, I'd probably have to spill some blood, but we weren't there yet. Currently, people were locked up, but no one was in mortal danger.

"We'll sneak out of course," Dee scoffed.

"There's a small army outside our room," I pointed to the door. "And before we leave, we still need an illumination crystal. Otherwise, how the heck are we going to get through the Rift?"

"Maybe you can ask one of the princesses to come and talk about the crystal," Dum suggested with a sniffle. "Then we'd know where they're kept."

"I'm not so sure they'd want to talk," I said. "I could try approaching them at the ball, but . . . I have a feeling they won't be as warm toward me as they have been."

My actions at the tournament had not gone unnoticed. We might have been able to convince them I'd been crying for Cirrus in the privy, but after that, thanks to my aether shield and my temper, they'd seen how concerned I was for the other guys.

"They're horrible anyway. I think it's best if we try to leave *before* the ball." Dee soared over to the windowsill. "Could you climb out this window?"

It wouldn't be the first time I'd escaped a building by leaving out a window, so I joined her to assess that route. One glance told me it would be possible. We all had wings and there were plenty of outcroppings to hide us–at least for a while.

"Once we're on the ground, we still have the issue of all those soldiers," I reminded her. "They're everywhere."

"You're a warrior princess!"

"I am, but—"

"Alice doesn't want to shed more blood, Dee," Dum sighed.

"Not unless I have to," I admitted.

Dee pursed her lips and furrowed her brow in thought, and my gaze went to the passageway in the wall. That was an option, but would it take us anywhere useful? Ideally, the prison?

Even traipsing through it glamoured screamed risky. The palace was on lockdown since Cirrus had learned that *someone* had broken into his chambers. And the prince might get it in his head to come see me—his beloved. *Blech!*

We certainly hadn't made escape easy for ourselves . . . Still, we had to do what we could.

"Maybe we should search the tunnels for an exit?" I posed.

Before either pixie could respond, a soft knock came at the door.

Was the prince already here to gloat?

"Princess Alice? Are you decent?"

The voice was feminine and familiar. I went to the door, heart beating quickly, and opened it to find Roshia. Her face was still disguised as it had been in the arena.

"Tea, Princess?" she held out a tray, and only then did I notice that she'd changed her attire from that of a guard to a servant. "It'll settle the nerves."

"Of course, come in."

"Ask me to clean," she whispered, stepping past me.

"Uh, can you make the bed and . . ."

"I'd be happy to assist. Perhaps straighten this closet too?"

"Definitely."

"Close the door," Roshia called to the soldiers still waiting on the other side of the threshold. "No one shall see the princess' undergarments except our dear prince."

One of the soldiers' faces turned red and he quickly shut us in. For good measure, I placed an aether lock on the door.

"You're insane," I hissed. "What if someone notices

you were a guard not long ago?"

"Those guards are with my sisters so they won't notice a thing. Not that it would matter. Most male fae pay a pittance notice to female fae in uniform."

"That's annoying."

"Yes, and if my brother rules, the misogyny will only become worse. As it stands, many male fae think females are only good for select things—and defending our home is not one. They'll learn better soon."

I had no idea what that meant. Largely, her motive was a mystery to me, and it would have to remain that way. We didn't have too much time before others would try to force me into marriage.

"We were discussing how I was going to get out of here without causing a courtly incident or shedding blood," I told her. "Any ideas?"

"Yes. We can talk as we go." She gestured to the bed. "I actually have to leave your room clean. They'll check. How about you help me?"

I rounded the mattress to do as she asked, and looked at her expectantly.

"I'll come back at midnight," Roshia said, tucking in the sheet. I mirrored her movements while listening. "Be prepared to fight and run."

"I still have to get an illumination crystal. And it's not like I can ask Cirrus for one."

"No," Roshia said. "Then he'd know who broke into his rooms. He might even bring in a marriage officiant then and there."

I swallowed. It sucked enough that I was unwillingly engaged—I would not marry anyone by force. I'd rather die.

"We'll stop by where the crown jewels are kept first. Then the prison." Roshia exhaled. "Those areas are not physically close to one another, but . . . we have no other choice."

"Can you get the crystal without me?"

"I could if I appeared as myself, but I must remain in disguise. And I'll need help."

"What about the other female who was with you?"

"She can't be here."

The way she said that made me question her motives even more. What was her end game? She'd made it plain that she wouldn't tell me, but I couldn't stop wondering.

"I'm with you." I plumped a cushion, and she moved on to the armoire. But instead of hanging the clothes that had been taken from their hangers and draped over a chair, she simply plucked them up and shoved them inside the cabinet.

"That was half-assed cleaning if I ever saw it," I smirked.

"My business is done. And it's not my fault you're a slob." She arched her eyebrows. "Be ready at midnight. If you must, use an excuse to leave the ball early. I'll arrive via the passageways, and we'll follow them for as long as we can."

"I'll be waiting." I paused but couldn't contain my curiosity. "Roshia?"

Though she was halfway to the door, she turned. "Yes?"

"What's in this for you?" I asked finally.

The princess exhaled. "My brother should not be king. He does not deserve it, nor is it his birthright. But if he marries you, an aether-blessed fae, and provides an heir with your power, my father will be pleased.

"Our magic is different from the rest of the fae, and he's always coveted the aether. He'd undoubtedly pass the crown to Cirrus before I can put someone more worthy in my brother's place."

I had an idea she already had that *someone* in mind, but just nodded.

To her, this wasn't about me saving Elise, but the future of her kingdom. And I was sure she'd fight for that future tooth and nail. I could depend on her.

"I'll be ready for you at midnight."

***

A knock on the door summoned me.

"Princess Alice," a voice called. "The ball has begun. It is time to make your entrance."

I rose, already dressed in a sapphire blue gown I suspected might make Cirrus happy. Or at the very least, less suspicious of me. I was planning to do some shady shit tonight, so it was in my best interest to soften his defenses.

"The prince awaits," the commander said as I opened

the door. He held out his arm, which I took with a barely repressed shudder.

"Ladies?" I called, not about to experience this night alone. Even if Cirrus prevented my friends from being at my side the whole time, just the knowledge they were at the event would steady me.

Dee and Dum soared out of the room, dressed in gowns the same color as mine, but in miniature.

"You look lovely, Princess," the commander commented as we made our way down the hall.

"Thank you."

I should hope so. After all, I'd been ready and waiting for at least two hours, thinking that Cirrus would stop by to gloat. Or perhaps accuse me of breaking into his room.

But the prince either didn't suspect me, or he had more important matters on his mind. Perhaps he was basking in the glory of his wins. Or was he planning the wedding? Had he even told his father?

How would Cirrus play this? Surely, the monarch would need to be present at the real announcement of his son's engagement? The reason for this ball.

If he was, there was a chance I could tell the king what an asshole his son was. But then again, Cirrus could silence me by threatening my friends.

So many matters were up in the air. There was so much about Cirrus I couldn't predict. I had to make it through this night, take it one step at a time, and hope Roshia knew what she was doing.

The commander led me and the pixies to the ball.

Music, lyrical and happy, filled my ears before I laid eyes on the Hall. But when I did, the decor took my breath away.

As ever, crystals were a common motif, but whoever decorated had brought in floral arrangements that were as tall as me, an ice sculpture of an alicorn—presumably, an homage to Valia—and a brand-new throne. It was positioned to the right of Prince Cirrus' seat, which the prince himself currently occupied.

The backing of my throne was teal, a hint to my heritage. I didn't know why Cirrus cared to showcase that. Perhaps to remind the kingdom I was a royal from another part of Faerie, and hence, aether-blessed.

It was all about the potential I gave him and his line.

The commander ushered me into the ballroom, toward my intended, and heads turned. This time, they weren't taking me in as an oddity, but a soon-to-be-queen.

Heads bowed. Some younger females looked at me with envy plain on their faces. A few fae even whispered best wishes for my wedding.

It all made me want to barf. However, after years of training with a vampire, I knew better than to show my true feelings.

We might have a secret passageway out of my room, but Cirrus was insane. If he suspected *anything* was amiss, he might have soldiers stand *inside* my room that night. I couldn't risk it.

So I smiled smally and kept walking in the direction of the thrones.

Play the game, Alice, I reminded myself as Cirrus smirked down at me.

"There's my beloved," he purred when I stood right in front of him. "I was beginning to worry that the pressure of the crown had become too much for you and you'd run scared."

A crown is far less frightening than you.

"I've been waiting for you to call me," I replied, trying to sound coy and not like I wanted to punch his face.

Smoothly, I removed my arm from the commander's and gave a slight curtsey. The pixies did the same, though theirs were more exaggerated.

"Apologies. High Councilor Larrel and I were preparing for the big day." Cirrus' lips curled up. "I promise not to keep you here too late. We intend for the ceremony to begin at sunrise."

My pulse fluttered. I'd known that, but still, the morning was far too soon for my liking. Yes, Roshia would be at my room at midnight, but what if she was delayed? What if stealing the crystal and freeing my friends took hours?

"How romantic," I replied, my tone so steady, I shocked even myself.

Cirrus stood. "I realize that we got off to a rough start, but you'll soon learn I can be quite romantic, Princess Alice." He swept a palm out and gestured to the throne upholstered in teal. "Sit for me? Your ladies might position themselves behind. There are small chairs for them."

I climbed the stairs to stand level with him, and slowly lowered into the throne. Dee and Dum, shuttled themselves behind it, out of sight. I wished they could be with me.

In this position, it was impossible not to look out upon the fae of the Crystal Court. Those dancing, eating, gossiping. The hundreds who were now staring at me.

"They're admiring you," he crooned. "My prize. My intended, and tomorrow, my wife."

"I've done nothing to be admired," I said. As far as these people knew, that was the truth. I'd merely shown up and asked for information, then been entrapped.

"Soon, that will change. We will begin our efforts to create a child tomorrow night, Princess, and you will fulfill a cherished destiny."

My stomach churned as he showed his true colors for the first time. It wasn't just the soldiers who thought females were basically worthless. Apparently, to Cirrus, I was really only good for one thing. Breeding.

"I can't say that I'm prepared for motherhood," I replied, because he was watching me closely, very clearly expecting me to say something, and I couldn't bring myself to flat-out lie and say I wished I could have his kid tomorrow.

"You will be. When the time comes." He shrugged and held out a hand. "Dance with me, my love?"

The skin on the back of my neck tightened. He'd used

that term before, and I'd always thought it was for show, like so much else about the man. But as he puffed his chest up with pride, I was getting the sense that he actually meant it. Or at least, he thought he did.

Unbelievable.

He was forcing me into this! He'd imprisoned my friends and nearly killed them! How in the world had he deluded himself into thinking we were *beloved?*

How I could love anyone who'd done those horrible things was beyond me. But instead of laying into him like I wished, I played the damn game. I took his hand, and allowed the prince to lead me to the dancefloor.

Fae parted for us, giving us the center position—the spot where we could be best observed. And observe they did, as the prince swept me along in a slow, waltz-like dance.

I moved with the grace I'd crafted from dancing with daggers. With each twirl and graze of Cirrus' fingers, I hid my revulsion.

"You dance like a dream, darling. Have you been practicing?"

"Yes," I lied. Before, I'd claimed not to be a good dancer, but really, it had been a mix of not knowing the moves and not wanting to dance with *him*. "I had little else to do in my room."

"Soon, you will not be alone. Soon, we will have one another for company, always." He leaned in, and my heart began to thunder wildly.

Is he . . .? No way!

But yes, the prince pursed his lips. The idiot really was going to try and kiss me!

I wanted to slap the shit out of him, but I couldn't. That would undermine the façade I was going for, perhaps even make Cirrus suspicious. I needed him to be sure we'd get married tomorrow. I needed him to think this was in the bag.

And yet, as his lips came closer and my revulsion grew. I could not let him kiss me.

So, before he made contact, I turned my face to the side.

His lips, which were desperately in need of balm, landed on my cheek, and his eyes popped open. Anger flitted across his face before he concealed it.

He'd done that quickly—too quickly. Clearly, the prince was practiced in hiding his emotions.

"Not before the wedding," I said coyly. "I want that day to be one of firsts . . . on multiple levels."

His shoulders loosened. "I understand. Apologies for being so forward, my love."

"Not at all." I winked, and he twirled me again, allowing me to take the first full breath I'd had in minutes.

When I returned to face him, Cirrus appeared happy, like he did not have an inkling that I was lying.

My performance must have been Oscar-worthy, because in reality, I could think only one thing:

Midnight can't come soon enough.

CHAPTER 19

"Rest well, Princess Alice," said the silver-winged commander, once again my escort, as we stopped in front of my room.

Dee and Dum flew alongside me, chaperones to protect my honor—as Cirrus had now named them. Like the pixies could do anything against a fae soldier. And if he didn't trust the commander, why was the man leading the prince's army?

So much about Cirrus made so little sense that I'd concluded he must be insane.

Thank the old gods I'm getting away from him. Just thirty more minutes.

I was cutting it close, though not due to my own choices. The prince had initially claimed that I would leave early to rest, but he'd kept me dancing for hours, showing me off to anyone who would look our way.

"Thanks for seeing me safely here," I said, then in an

inspired attempt to buy us more time, added, "The ball lasted much longer than I thought it would. Is there any way you might ask Prince Cirrus to push back our nuptials?"

"Why would he do that?"

"I want to look my best for our big day. What if I have bags under my eyes?"

The commander tilted his head to the side, as if really giving it thought. "I'll bring it up. Perhaps he could spare an hour or two. Either way, expect a cohort of stylists at your door in the morning." He bowed. "Good evening, Princess Alice."

"Good evening."

He left, and I nodded to the six guards who would stand outside my door all night before letting myself into my chambers. There were more now than before. I didn't know if it was because I was 'officially' engaged to Cirrus. Or maybe he thought I was a flight risk.

The moment Dee, Dum, and I were on our own, I blasted the door with aether, locking it from the inside. Then I pressed my back to the door and slid down it, loosing the longest sigh of my life. "I am so glad that's over."

"Same!" Dum chirped.

She looked tired. So did Dee, and I was sure I did too. It had been one hell of a long day, but there would be no rest for us tonight. Roshia would arrive soon, and I had to be ready to rock and roll.

As such, I stood and proceeded to remove the gown I

wore, replacing it with loose pants and a tunic. I'd arrived in this court with weapons, but those had long since been taken from me, so once I got my boots on and slipped the map of Faerie I'd used to get us here into my pocket, I was ready.

I hoped Roshia would bring me some steel with which to defend myself. Aether and magic were great, but I had a soft spot for a good old-fashioned dagger.

In the last weeks, a lot in my life had changed, but I doubted that preference ever would.

Finally, the wall opened up and Roshia appeared, still physically altered to be an olive-skinned brunette. She wore all black with a leather vest over her long tunic, which I assumed was meant to be protective.

She spotted me and the girls—who'd also changed— waiting on the bed. "I was worried he'd keep you late."

"He did, actually. I wanted to be back hours ago."

"My brother is such good company?"

I rolled my eyes. "Hardly. Especially not when he's trying to put the moves on me."

Roshia wrinkled her nose. "No need to say more. I do not want to picture him kissing anyone—or doing anything else with them."

I snickered, then eyed her accessories. Daggers were sheathed on both of her curved hips, and one of them also boasted a sword.

"Want to share with the class?" I asked, nodding to her mini armory.

Her eyebrows pinched together, telling me that the

modern joke hadn't landed, but she didn't mention it, simply undoing one of the sheath belts and handing it to me. "Thought you might want one."

"Thanks." I strapped it to me. "I'm ready when you are."

Roshia entered the passageways again. "Stay close and quiet."

"We've done this a million times," Dee huffed.

I rolled my eyes. A million . . . or twice. Whatever.

Roshia snorted and shut the wall behind us, then we were off, following the princess through the hidden tunnels of her home.

We went much further than the twins and I had on our own. What felt like an age later, the princess slowed her pace and pressed her ear to a wall. When she turned to look at me, her expression was serious. "We're here. And as far as I can tell, there's only one guard on duty."

My stomach sank. "One is still enough to sound the alarm."

"Count your blessings. Usually, there are three, but I think Cirrus might have redistributed his forces to keep an eye on you."

"There was only half a dozen outside my door."

"And a dozen outside the tower you stayed in. Plus some posted in the hallway after you went to bed. You didn't know?"

"No. They weren't there when the commander escorted me back. It seemed like the prince had trusted me when we were at the ball, but . . . I guess not."

"My brother is quite good at making people believe what he wants them to. He was working to make you comfortable, to forget your friends."

As if that could ever happen, but I could see how someone like Cirrus—someone self-centered with an overinflated sense of importance—might think so.

"Didn't work. How do we want to dispose of the guard?"

"Ambush?" Roshia asked, adventure glinting in her eyes.

"I'd love to."

She flung open the wall, and we were in the hallway before the guard could even draw their sword. Though I would have loved a little dagger-play, I opted for aether. It had worked well before and not killed the soldiers outside Cirrus' room. Silence was a priority, and daggers were, unfortunately, messier.

My aether magic wrapped around the guard's neck, constricting his breathing. He fought, but Roshia was there in an instant, binding his hands with rope she had stored somewhere on her person.

The soldier's breath ran out, and he slumped against the princess, unconscious. She gently set him down the wall.

No bloodshed. Little fear—on our part, anyway. That was how it was done.

"Nice work," Roshia said.

"Too bad we don't have your friend. She could put him to sleep."

"She's helping elsewhere."

She didn't elaborate on where exactly Barbie was or how she was helping, and I didn't ask. We needed to focus on one step at a time.

The princess stared down at the man, who posed a problem even if he was presently unconscious. He wouldn't stay that way, and then he could make trouble for us.

"Let's take him inside," Roshia said.

I helped her carry the soldier into a room and then shut the door behind us. Only when we were no longer in the corridor, in danger of being spotted, did I chance a look around.

The chamber was like so many others in Jewel of the Sea Palace, in that it was full of crystals. Though, there was also gold, and statues made of precious metals and gemstones.

"This is where we keep the most valuable items," Roshia explained. "I usually wouldn't include illumination stones in that category, but I've seen such a gem here before. I didn't know *why* it was kept here at the time, but if it's the same crystal that helped a fae from this island cross the Rift, then I get it. Just its history alone would make it a *treasure*.

"Good to know, but we still have this issue." I gestured down to the guard. "We'll need to keep him disoriented and contained if he wakes up soon."

"Tear strips from your shirt," Dee suggested. "It's long, and you can use the pieces to blind and gag him."

"Good idea! I'll handle it." The princess ripped a scrap of her tunic off, wrapping the strip of fabric around the guard's head to blindfold him. Another piece of her shirt was gone a second later, balled up and stuck in the male's mouth.

"There. At least he won't be able to call for help. If we're lucky, no one will find him until the change of guard."

Luck was not usually on my side. Especially on this island.

"Let's find that crystal," I muttered, not willing to test whatever luck I did have.

I drank in the room. The space wasn't huge, but it was packed with stuff. Depending on the size of the crystal, and Roshia's ability to recognize it if we did come across it, this could take a while.

"What color is it?" I asked.

"They're usually yellow citrine, but really, they can be any color or type of stone. It's more about where they're harvested from." The princess' eyes narrowed in thought.

"What does that mean?"

"Illumination stones soak up the sun, but for reasons we can't explain, that happens in only one spot on the island." She spun on her heel, taking a quick glance around. "If they were out in the open, they'd be obvious, because they're like torches. As they're not currently lighting up the space, I expect that the illumination crystals are being stored in boxes."

"Will they blind us if we look at them?"

I really didn't know what to expect, but I needed my senses to be on point if we were going to escape tonight.

"They'll glow, but not as brightly as they would if charged by the sun. They would need an influx of power to cause that. For you, the effect could probably be recreated by using aether."

My eyebrows furrowed. The magic of this island was unique, but if the sun only charged the stones in one spot, and no one had aether magic, how did they use them efficiently?

I didn't ask, because what would be the point? All that mattered was getting my hands on the gems and learning how I could use them to get through the Rift.

"There are a few boxes over here!" Dee exclaimed. She and Dum had split up to soar around the room and scope things out.

"And here!" Dum shouted from the opposite side.

Roshia and I split wordlessly, and seconds later, I was at Dum's side. She'd found a pyramid of fifty boxes, all latched shut.

"Here." One by one, I pulled ten of the smallest, no larger than a child's jewelry box, off the top. "Open these."

"On it!"

She might be able to fit inside the boxes, but the latching mechanisms were dainty. Dum could handle it.

I sifted through the rest of the larger boxes, squinting as I opened them, in case the stone was inside and had more charge than anticipated. When I got to the bottom layer, a stream of light beamed through one of the lids.

My breath hitched and, ignoring the other containers, I picked up that box.

It was about five pounds and items rolled around inside. It didn't feel like too many, though. If they were crystals, they were probably only a few.

Slowly, I lifted the lid and was rewarded by an even brighter beam of light. I winced and shut my eyes until the lid was up. Once the lid was up, carefully, I opened my eyes. Among a grouping of blue gems, a yellow one stuck out. The light had dimmed, as if the energy that had been stored inside only needed to dissipate to render the crystal non-blinding.

I pulled out the crystal. "Is this what we're looking for?" I asked the princess, holding the gemstone aloft.

She glanced over and her eyes widened. "Yes! It's a large one, too. I've had no luck."

"This is my first," I said, studying the gem that was about the size of a softball. "Let me check the rest of the containers."

Quickly, I did so, and found nothing. "Dum, fly over the room and tell me if you find more boxes."

The pixie did so, yelling for her twin to do the same. The pair performed a circle, then two, and when finally, they returned with downturned lips. They'd found nothing.

"Not even one?"

Dee shook her head.

Roshia came over. "I found this small one." She handed me a quarter-sized, yellow gemstone that glowed brightly.

"Do you think this is enough?" I asked, sensing the answer. They were small and I needed to protect an army.

"Have you seen the Rift?"

"No."

"I've not either, but we have books depicting it." Roshia bit her lower lip. "It's vast. So to be honest, I'm not positive these stones are enough to help, but . . . it appears that's all we have."

"Do you think Cirrus moved the rest? Were there more?"

"Perhaps," Roshia looked at me sadly. "But if there were, I don't know where they went."

It was either we take the risk of looking for more—which probably meant searching the whole castle and potentially getting caught—or leaving with only these two.

"Where do you think—"

Shouting from the hallway hit my ears, and I stiffened.

"Someone on rounds must have noticed that our guard friend was not at his post." Roshia grabbed my hand. "We have to go. If you want to search more, fine, but we must hide first. Stuff those in your pockets, they'll give us away."

I did as she said, tucking the gems deep in my pockets,

but the light from the illumination stones was still faintly visible. For a second, I considered grabbing the box the larger one had come in, but the footsteps outside the door were growing ever closer and we were in the open.

"This way!" Roshia hissed, pulling me toward a giant gemstone as tall as I was and, luckily for us, black as night. It hid us from sight of the door.

If we could get into the hallway unnoticed, we could slip into the passageway.

At that very moment, two male figures appeared in the doorway. One pointed to the guard on the ground, who was still passed out. Thank the old gods we'd pulled him far enough away from the door to still make an exit.

"Grom!" one of the guards shouted.

"He's gagged, idiot." The larger guard stalked inside, his gaze running over the room. "See to him. *I'll* find whoever did this."

Whereas before, the packrat nature of the room had been an annoyance that made our job harder, now I was grateful for it. We were hidden amongst the many gemstones and other precious items the royals kept locked away.

The larger guard took the pathway I'd originally carved through the room, while the other remained kneeling next to Grom. Roshia cast me a glance.

"Can you . . .?" She mimed wrapping her hands around her throat and gagging.

In answer, I tossed out a rope of aether magic. It slithered around the guard's throat and tightened before he even looked up. When he did, his eyes widened, and a soft noise left his throat, but I clamped down harder.

Seconds trudged by as his face grew blue. Finally, he collapsed on top of the first guard.

"Quick!" Roshia whispered. "Before the other one notices."

We hurried out the door, slipping into the corridor. The only sound we made came seconds later, when we opened the wall. We rushed inside, closing it behind us, then we waited. Listened.

After a dozen tense heartbeats, Roshia exhaled. "He's still searching. We did it."

"Maybe we should go get the guys and leave before he finds the first two guards?" Dee asked, her tone tight. "Unless you really want to look for the other gems?"

I could tell by the look on her face she didn't want to, and honestly, I wasn't so sure I was down either. That had been too close for comfort, and when the penalty was to be dragged to an altar to marry Cirrus at that very moment, all I wanted to do was leave the island.

However, I did worry the stones wouldn't be enough.

I extracted the largest one from my pocket, examining it.

"That is a good size," Roshia said, as if she knew what I was thinking. "One of the largest I've seen. I hoped we could find more for you."

"Have you seen it used?"

"I have not," the princess admitted. "However, if a common fae from my court could use it, surely you can.

Aether is an excellent substitute for many of our magics. It's why my brother is so set on marrying you."

To potentially pass along my magic. The idea of being reduced to a breeding machine made me want to vomit.

"Yeah, well, he's not going to get the chance. I—"

A roar sounded from beyond the hidden passage. It was quickly followed by footsteps and a fae yelling furiously for someone to alert the castle to intruders and inform the prince.

Roshia's hand circled my wrist. "You have no more time to search. You need to leave now."

CHAPTER 20

We raced through the passageways of Jewel of the Sea, not bothering to stay as silent as we had before. Those within the palace knew something was afoot. And all someone had to do to know I was involved was break into my room. I had not locked it with aether this time, hadn't thought to do so. Breaking in against a regular lock would probably be all too easy.

As we went, my heart thundered. On the other side of the castle walls, shouts rang out and boots stomped along the ground. It was so loud, it sounded as if all of the Crystal Court's army had been mobilized.

"This way!" Roshia took a sharp right turn that I would have missed had I not been watching her. "The door to the outside is close."

"Outside? What about the prison?"

"We don't attach it to the castle. Our ancestors didn't

think that housing criminals and royals under one roof was proper. Good thing for us."

"How is that a good thing?"

"Because the outbuilding is guarded, but not as heavily as it would be if it were in the palace."

I wondered if she'd seen the place since Hatter and Jax had been locked away, but didn't ask. She knew her home better than I ever would.

She glanced back at me, then swore. "I wish you had a hood. Your hair is so white, it catches the light."

"I got this," I said, envisioning my hair a darker color and releasing my aether magic.

Once the tingling stopped, I twisted to face Dee. "Did it work?"

"You're a completely unremarkable dishwater brunette."

I stuck out my tongue. "I'm lots of things, but unremarkable is not one of them."

"Here!" Roshia gasped and skidded to a stop so fast, I nearly bowled her over. When she turned, her eyebrows arched in surprise. "Wow. That is a change. It could buy us seconds."

"Which we might need." I would not discount an advantage, no matter how slight.

"Dee, come here."

Roshia urged the red-haired pixie forward, which surprised me. Every other time we'd appeared from the tunnels, she'd stuck her own neck out first. That she was using a pixie told me she didn't want to open the wall very far to make sure we were in the clear.

"If I crack it, can you peek out? Then if we're good, we'll run."

Dee puffed her chest up. "You can count on me."

As quietly as she could, Roshia opened the hidden door. "There's ivy on the outside of this wall. It should hide you pretty well."

The pixie squished herself out of the crack. She was gone only a moment before popping back inside. "The coast is clear, but I hear people close by."

"We have to be fast!" Dum squealed, zipping to the door. "Let's go!"

Together, Roshia and I darted into the night. Arms and legs pumping, she led the way to the outbuilding where prisoners were kept, veering toward the gardens and plunging us into a maze of bushes. We zigged and zagged, and while the greenery hid us, I couldn't help but think it slowed us down too. We were talking so long.

Finally, though, we exited. When we did, I bit my bottom lip. A wall of hedges twenty feet high spread out before us.

"Uh . . ." I could find no offshoot to this wall. "Fly over?"

"Can't risk being seen in the air. But the foliage isn't thick and there are no walls hidden within. Trust me on this!" Roshia urged, running straight forward. "Blast through it!"

I pushed my legs, leaping a second after the princess

and diving through the thick wall of green. Twigs lodged in my hair, and my eyes squinted shut, but we had enough speed and momentum to burst through to the other side.

A building made of dark stone, and seemingly without lights, stood before us.

"That's where we keep prisoners," Roshia said. "Now, where is she . . ."

A light flared to life in a window.

"There she is!"

"What in the hell are you talking about?!" I hissed.

"You mentioned you wished that my friend was here. Well, she is." Roshia pointed to the window. "And she's busting your male companions out right now!"

The words were barely out of her mouth before the side of the dungeon wall exploded, hurling rocks and a burning stench toward us.

"Take cover!" Roshia yelled.

We leapt to the sides seconds before two huge rocks would have pummeled the heck out of us.

My shoulder took the impact of my dodge, and I rolled with a grunt. "More notice would have been nice!"

"You're telling me," Roshia said. "And she was *loud*. That's not her usual style. They must have run into trouble."

Before I could reply, Henri soared out of the jailhouse. He and Barbie held Jax between them.

I sucked in a breath. My ex looked bad—terrible, actually. Was that from the fight with Cirrus? Or had he gotten hit in the explosion?

"We need to fly," Roshia said, as shouts came from inside the dungeon. "They suspect it's you and your friends who are causing the ruckus. And it won't take many guesses to deduce where you're going. Follow my lead."

My wings snapped out, and I lifted into the air, Roshia and the pixies at my side.

When Henri got closer, I saw he was filthy and looked exhausted. That didn't bode well for the long journey ahead, let alone the fight we might endure to leave this island.

"Are you okay?" I asked him.

"Fine," Henri gritted out as he adjusted his grip on the wizard.

"What about Jax?"

"He's . . . recovering." Hatter looked at the wizard, the worry plain in his gaze, but there was nothing we could do until we were someplace safe.

"Let me know if you need help holding him," I offered.

We continued our flight but didn't make it far before the first attack fell upon us. Literally. I should have seen it coming, but since I'd been in Faerie, aerial assaults had been rare, so the fae who dropped on to me took me by surprise and knocked me off-course.

Dum screamed, and my heart rate kicked into overdrive.

"Alice!" Henri yelled.

"Keep going!" I shouted back, righting myself and locating the threat. "Don't stop!"

My assailant, the commander, grinned. His silver wings fluttered madly and caught the moonlight in a pretty way that didn't fit him in the slightest. "We wondered if you'd try anything stupid."

"Freedom is stupid now, huh?" I shot back. "Well, I think you coming at me takes the cake for stupid."

I prepared to hurl a stream of air at him, but suddenly, blood spurted from his mouth, and he dropped toward the ground. A blade stuck out of his back, the hilt glinting in the moonlight.

When I looked up again, Roshia was there, her face livid.

"He has mental magic," she spat. "You might have attacked, but he would have stopped you. There was only one way."

"Fine with me," I said, and we were off again.

It was easy to catch up with Henri and Barbie. Jax's weight slowed them.

"How much farther?" Henri asked when Roshia and I appeared.

"The stables are around this corner, the far side of the palace from where you lot were staying. Let's hope we got there fast enough."

I held my breath as we rounded a turret, but then it all left me in a violent whoosh.

We totally didn't get there fast enough.

"Nooooo," Dee moaned.

Dozens of soldiers stood outside the stables, weapons in hand, and magic lacing the air.

I looked at Jax. We weren't helpless, but wizard-power would be helpful right about now.

"Take him!" Barbie shouted. "I have this!"

She veered my way and practically ripped off Jax's arm handing him over. Though I wanted to help, once I had a hold of him, Jax's bulk hindered me.

As it turned out, I didn't need to do a damn thing. Barbie mowed down six soldiers with magic, and then moved on to the others who tried to run, but failed. They fell, one after the other, like dominos. No one could stand up to her—not in the slightest.

Whoa. She'd made a guard fall asleep before, but that had only been one. To affect this many people at once . . . Well, I couldn't even do it with my aether magic. Maybe in the future, after I trained up more, but not now.

We soared over the soldiers, and I glanced down at them, making sure that no one was going to hop back up. I stiffened. Were they even breathing?

Roshia landed, then Barbie, then me and Henri. The pixies remained fluttering, their chests heaving from having flown so fast.

I looked at Barbie. "Are they asleep?"

She shrugged. "If that's what you want to think."

I gulped. Seeing as I was an assassin, and she'd leveled them to *help* me, I felt like I had no leg to stand on, but her actions made me uncomfortable. I also really hoped they wouldn't come back to bite me in the ass.

The Crystal Court had been isolated for years, and I didn't want to be the person to bring them out of that. Nor did I want to bring war to Wonderland.

"This way," Roshia said. "I know where they're keeping your alicorn."

"Why not take one of these?" Henri asked, which I didn't like. I didn't want to leave Valia. But then again, I could also see his point. Getting out of here was the priority.

"Any mounts from our court will return to the island no matter what. It's trained into the beasts, so you can't take them. Not unless you wish to return tomorrow."

"No thanks," I said, horrified by the idea.

"I'll stay out here. Keep watch," Barbie said.

Together, Henri and I carried Jax as Roshia entered the stables and wove through the stalls. The reek of manure and animals filled the air, making my nose wrinkle. I couldn't wait to get out of this place, and hoped we'd do so unopposed.

As always, fate made an ass of me. We made it past only a few more stalls before we met our next opponents.

Three male fae bolted out of the animals' pens, nearly knocking me to the ground. I called on my air, sending a gale their way and bowling them over.

Two slammed into the wood of the stalls. A loud *crack* indicated the force with which I'd flung them had likely knocked them out.

The third soldier wasn't so lucky. He was tossed into a stall, and a gryphon reared up, trying to get away from the fae, but there wasn't enough room. A faint *splat* confirmed thousands of pounds of gryphon landed upon the soldier.

I cringed and didn't dare look in the stall, not even to calm the gryphon, who was still rearing back, eyes rolling and wild.

What a horrible way to die. We had to leave before any more deaths occurred.

"I found her! Your gryphons are right next to the alicorn!" Roshia called out, racing back to me.

"Where do we go? I asked.

"Straight to the back. Your mounts are being kept there. I'll go out front and hold them off."

"You could escape too!" Dee shouted, and my mouth fell open at the brilliance of the idea.

"I-I'd be so thankful," Roshia said, eyes shining. "But I can't leave my home. I need to be here to help my people."

"You've done so much." Voices, shouting, from outside made the hair on my arm stand up. "I'm grateful. Good luck."

"You too. I hope you save your sister."

Roshia hopped onto the spooked gryphon and kicked its sides. The creature spurred into motion and, moving in sync, Henri and I did too, scooping up Jax and sprinting to the back of the stables.

In the very last stall, I found Valia. On either side of her was a gryphon, two in all. Though they wore no saddle from the Wonderland Court, they had to be ours.

"I don't think we'll need the second," I said, gesturing to Jax.

"He'd slide right off," Henri replied.

"Tie him to me." I pointed to a rope hanging from the stall, which was likely used to lead creatures out into the open.

Henri scowled, but I didn't have time for a hissy fit.

"Unless you'd rather him ride with you?"

"Fine," Hatter grunted.

"You'll take the pixies and the crystals."

"What are these?" he asked as I handed him the stones, which glowed faintly in the dim light of the stables.

"It's how we're getting through the Rift. More on that later." I grabbed the rope and shoved it at him, because voices were nearing.

Valia stomped her hoof as if to say *'Hurry up, girl,'* and I hopped on her back. Henri then draped Jax behind me. I twisted, righting the wizard, who moaned.

"Her wings will help keep him on," I noted, relieved.

"We'll see," Henri said, cinching the rope around my waist and then beginning to weave it around Jax.

It was at that moment that Jax's eyes fluttered open to lock with mine. "Hey, Al. Lookin' hot."

Heat dashed across my cheeks, and, unsurprisingly, Henri stiffened.

"He's out of it, Hatter. Let it go. Come on!"

"Yeah, hurry, Henri!" Dee commanded from the back of one of the gryphons.

He made quick work of lashing me and Jax together. As he worked, I caught sight of something. Fae were upon us. We didn't have time to get to the front.

"Henri, there's a back door! Open it!"

Hatter moved out of the stall to do so, but suddenly, blood spurted from him, and he fell.

"Henriiii!" I tried to leap from the alicorn, who was shifting on her feet like she was about to rear back, but Jax was connected to me.

"End of the road for you," a voice called out.

I looked up to find none other than Prince Cirrus stalking toward me, his lips pressed together in a cruel line. Somehow, he'd snuck up on us. "I can see I'll have to keep better tabs on you, little wife."

"Like hell you will," a voice roared behind me, and Jax sprayed magic at the prince.

It took Cirrus by surprise, giving me time to use my wind to do what I should have done in the first place: blast open the door.

Throughout the stables, creatures neighed and cried out, but I couldn't worry about them. All my concern was for Henri.

I scooped him up using aether magic, laying him on the back of the gryphon, and then checked the ground to make sure that the crystals hadn't fallen out of his pocket.

When I was certain we were all ready, I looked to Dum. "Get out of here!"

The pixie needed no further instruction. She snapped

the reins she held in her hand. Though the effect was small, the beast was trained, and it charged out of its stall to the open doors.

"Go, Valia!" I yelled, and we barreled out too.

Behind us, Cirrus cursed, but Jax was spewing hate right back at him, and I didn't have to turn around to know that he was fighting off the prince.

"Jax, I—"

"Go, Al! I've got the asshole this time. Go!"

I had to trust him, so I focused on guiding Valia.

As she raced out of the stables and took flight right behind the gryphon holding my friends, my heart leapt. No one was in the sky! They must have been certain they'd stop us in the stables.

Or Roshia and Barbie are holding them off.

Either way, we were free, and heading right for the Rift.

CHAPTER 21

"Alice! Henri is slipping again!" Dee called out over a particularly robust gale of wind.

I groaned, but released the rein with one hand and directed aether magic toward the gryphon flying alongside Valia, Jax, and me.

"Has he woken since the last time?" I asked once Dee gave me a thumbs-up, telling me that Henri was secure once more. I re-gripped my rein, the position achingly familiar. I'd been sitting on the back of my alicorn for way too long.

"Twice," the pixie called back. "But only for a couple of seconds."

The stable master in Wonderland had not given the pixies their own gryphon because he hadn't thought they could handle it. He'd been wrong. For hours I'd had to rely on Dee and Dum keeping a careful watch on Hatter and controlling the creature they rode upon. They'd completed both tasks like champs.

"We didn't get fed or given water once you left, Al," Jax said. "I was used to it because . . . well, you know. I don't think Henri is quite so used to skipping meals. He's hurting for sure."

I understood, and he was probably right. Henri had grown up a rebel, and thanks to his marketable skills he always had food around. Not like me and Jax.

As part of their training, Xavier would often test his assassins under brutal conditions, sometimes depriving us of food and water for days. Because of this, Jax and I might be hungry and thirsty, but we could function well on minimal food and water.

Sleep, on the other hand, was a different story. And between using my magic to keep Henri on his gryphon, and flying all night and morning with Jax pressed against me, I was really dragging. Not to mention my back hurt like I was an old woman.

I shifted, and the pain spiraled outward again. A sigh left me.

I supposed I should be happy that we were no longer roped together. After Jax woke, he assured me that he could stay on the alicorn without any aid, and untied us. If he had still been bound to me, my aches would be even worse.

"I was hoping we'd spot another island to rest on. Even for just a few minutes," I said. "I could look him over there, but we missed those islands we stayed at earlier. Wonderland will be our next stop."

"It's close!" Dum piped up. "I can feel it in my bones."

"For a pixie, she's pretty witchy, you know?" Jax teased.

"Fae sense things differently in Faerie," I replied.

My own senses had changed here and, like Dum, I sensed that we were getting close. Like the land of my blood was calling me to it.

I just hoped it really was Wonderland and not some other place. I was so exhausted, I easily could have screwed up the navigation.

Thankfully, about an hour later, an island appeared on the horizon, and as we got closer, I became more certain that it was Wonderland.

"That's it?" Jax asked.

"The castle is the right color," I told him.

I'd started implementing changes on the inside of the palace, but the exterior of the castle was still the same. The red and white motif stuck out amongst the browns, tans, and ivory hues of the city.

We got closer to the island, and my certainty solidified. I was about to tell Jax, when a gryphon bearing a rider rose in the air.

I squinted against the strong sea breezes. "Does that look like—"

"Isadora!" Dee waved frantically, as if the brownie might miss us.

"Let's meet her halfway!" I called out, and pushed poor Valia to fly faster.

The pixies did the same, and by the time we reached Isadora, the sides of my alicorn heaved.

I patted her on the neck. "Sorry, girl. You'll get some rest and a treat soon."

"Princess! I'm so happy you're back!" Isadora called out. "I'm to take you to the army. Alran and Sansu said you discussed meeting at the Rift, but Queen Aquatia decided the Riverlands Court would be best. Apparently, there were setbacks with the original plan."

My stomach sank. "Do you know what happened?"

"Word came by letter, but it only mentioned that the troops were met with resistance and the Queen of the Riverlands convinced our leaders that taking refuge in her court for a time was in their best interest. I believe they were intentionally vague on the details, in case the letter was intercepted."

I huffed out a long breath. I'd been totally ready to follow my trusty map to the mainland of Faerie, but maybe this was better. Not only did I trust the Queen Aquatia's judgment, but after the journey I'd had, I would be happy to be in a castle for a few hours, rather than resting in a tent.

As much as I wanted to push on, I couldn't do so and be at my best—which was imperative if I didn't want to endanger my army.

"What about Hatter?" Dum asked, concerned for the fae still slumped over the gryphon.

"He's coming with us," I said, unable to push down my guilt because he was so poor off.

For many of the long hours spent flying, I'd been warring with myself over what to do. Stop in Wonderland and get Hatter help? We *were* a few days ahead of schedule after all. Or should we continue on?

"Are you sure?" Dum pressed. "He—"

Suddenly, Hatter began coughing up a storm and shot up from where he lay. The pixies squealed, trying to stay on the gryphon's back while the large fae was causing such a ruckus.

"Henri!" Dee shouted loudly to get through to him. "Are you okay?"

Her voice appeared to center him, and though he was still coughing and looking around—eyes wide because he probably hadn't expected to be flying—his shoulders loosened.

"It's okay, Hatter," I said, my tone intended to calm him. "You're safe."

"Water?" he asked.

I chewed on my bottom lip. I'd thought I'd done well, remembering to grab the map before we escaped the Crystal Court, but I'd been shortsighted. The rest of us had been dying of thirst for hours.

"I have some," Isadora offered. "I always keep a water skin handy when I'm running errands." She urged her gryphon closer to the other. "It's about half full, but you can have it all."

Hatter reached out and pulled the skin to his lips,

glugging it down. Once he was done, he looked more alert, and sat up slowly to straddle the gryphon. As he did so, the pixies lifted into the air, giving him space.

"We're home?" Henri asked. "I've been out a while."

"All night and day," I said. "With a couple of breaks of consciousness."

"The last thing I remember is getting ready to run. We were in the stables, and . . ." His dark eyebrows screwed together. "What happened?"

"Prince Cirrus zapped you like he did me." Jax's tone was filled with loathing. "Struck you in the back."

"He's a coward," Henri agreed, glancing about. "Are we landing in Heartstown? Has the army not left yet?"

"They have. We're on our way to the Riverlands Court. The heart of it." I looked at Isadora. "And, if everyone is ready now, I'd like to get on with that."

"It's a six-hour flight to the mainland," Isadora warned, her attention shifting to Henri. "Are you up for it?"

"Yes," he said, before anyone could question him further. "I'm with Alice. Let's continue."

I should have said no. I should have insisted that, at the very least, he land and rest, but the lure of discovering what had happened in my absence was too great, so I nodded. "Let's fly."

We'd just spotted land, when I got my first glimpse of what we were up against.

The Rift.

Even from miles away, the blotch on the horizon was vast and terrifying, like a storm of darkness crawling over the green grass of the Riverlands, devouring the countryside.

Was that what it was doing? Did it move?

The images I'd seen of the black cloud blighting the land had not done it justice. Not even close.

Suddenly, I was glad we were going to be delayed. I might have the illumination crystals in my pocket, but I clearly did not know enough about the Rift to take it on.

Then again, would we ever be ready?

A lump lodged in my throat and it didn't move as we soared over the grasslands and, finally, into the center of the Riverlands Court.

From above, this kingdom looked a lot like the Wonderland Court, save for the fact that there were no hearts, and everything was a striking verdant shade. If I had to take this land and plop it into the human world, it would fit in best in Ireland, all lush and green, brimming with life and flush with water.

Isadora led the way to the castle, and when we arrived, soldiers were already present, waving flags and directing us. They did so expertly, and we touched down in a field outside the palace grounds.

I'd no sooner dismounted Valia's back than the gates

opened and out walked Prince Halad, flanked by Sansu and Alran.

"You're early!" Sansu cried, waving at us as he drew closer. "I take it all went well?"

Hatter needed only to slip off his gryphon and collapse to the ground for them to know that was not the case.

I scowled and ran over to him. "You said you were okay!"

"Al! I'm not sure I can walk!" Jax called out. "Remember, I was hit by lightning?"

I rolled my eyes. He was such an attention whore.

"What!?" Sansu's eyes flared wide. "There was a storm while you flew?"

Oh, by the aether. This was going to take some explaining.

But first, Hatter.

"Did you lie to get here?" I pressed as I knelt by him. "Because that's going to piss me off. We've already pushed so hard. What if you've done irreparable damage to yourself?!"

"I'm honestly fine," Henri assured me, sitting up slowly. "I haven't moved in too many hours. I thought my legs were okay, but they're numb."

That seemed . . . possible, but I wasn't going to stop helicoptering yet.

Helping him stand, I gave the guy a once-over—and not in the fun, sexy way. "You sure? Walk carefully."

"What happened?" Halad asked, taking everything in with worry.

"All was not well in the Crystal Court. We had to make a quick exit and didn't find anywhere to stop on the way back."

Of course, no one was going to let me end it like that, so I relayed the details of our trip then and there.

Once I was finished, Alran and Sansu stared at me with their mouths hanging open. Halad appeared disgusted, and Isadora was sobbing.

It was the brownie's emotions that made me the most uncomfortable. I'd grown leaps and bounds since arriving in Faerie, but dealing with the sadness of others was still hard for me. If I was being honest, it was yet another reason why taking the crown did not appeal to me.

"I can't believe he was basically forcing you to marry him," Halad spat venomously. "That's despicable."

"That court is all sorts of messed up," I said, thinking of Roshia and Barbie and how they'd worked against Cirrus. "I always got the sense there was more I wasn't seeing, too. Something sinister."

The prince gave a single nod. "I'll keep that in mind in case he tries to wed any of my female cousins."

"Do you guys think maybe we can go inside?" I asked. "I want to hear about what happened at the Rift, but a cushy chair would be amazing right now."

"Ditto," Jax said, and the others agreed.

We'd been sitting for hours, but horseback—or gryphonback—was an active sort of sitting. My muscles ached like I'd run a marathon. I was sure the others felt the same.

"Water would be good too," Dee added.

"And food," Dum chimed in.

"Of course," Halad said. "I'll show you to my family's parlor and send for food. An early supper, if you will. There's much to tell. We've had to tweak the battle plan, but we believe we have a good substitute in place." He looked behind him and waved over two waiting guards.

"Prince Halad?" One soldier bowed.

"Take their mounts to the stables. They look like they've been through the ringer," the prince said. When he received nods from both soldiers he smiled and turned to us. "Follow me."

We trailed the prince into his palace. Though I was dead tired, I drank in my surroundings with interest. Like the rest of the kingdom's lands, this castle would fit in well in Ireland. It was made of gray stone, with dominant hues of green provided by the ivy crawling the walls. The windows bore gorgeous stained glass, and plants were a common feature in the corridors. One chandelier we passed was positively dripping with some sort of luscious moss, making it look ethereal.

"Here we are." Halad stopped before a set of double doors, beyond which, I could hear voices.

He opened the doors, and Queen Aquatia and another woman, dressed in a splendid light gold gown, turned our way.

The other female was regal, even without the crown

of gold and diamonds on her head. Her blonde hair was even longer than mine, hanging well past her butt, and her ice-blue eyes shone with such intensity, it felt like she was x-raying each and every one of us. The only thing on the woman that was out of place was the fur stole she wore around her shoulders.

"Queen Tially," Queen Aquatia rose from the settee she'd perched on, "might I introduce Princess Alice White of the Wonderland Court?"

Swallowing, I stepped forward.

I looked like hell and was in no state to meet someone new, but I wouldn't ask to delay the introduction. In Faerie, power was everything. I needed to appear ready for anything when meeting other royals.

"Princess Alice, Queen Tially graces us from the Snowcap Court, my kingdom's northern neighbor."

The visiting queen and I stood in front of each other now. She inclined her head, and I performed the smallest of curtseys, which drew a smile from the fae.

"I was friends with your mother and was ever so glad to hear that Sela had been defeated."

"Not yet," I corrected. "She escaped and has taken refuge in the Dark Court. I need to get to her before she flees again—and rescue my sister."

Tially nodded. "I am here to help. Shall we sit?"

Nothing had ever sounded better. I practically collapsed into the wingback armchair set next to the roaring fire.

As I settled in, a groan slipped out of me, earning me a concerned look from Queen Aquatia.

"Should we do this later?" she asked, not unkindly.

"No." We were already here, and I was dying to know why they'd pulled the Wonderland forces from the Rift. "I want to know what happened."

"First," Queen Tially inserted, "you must understand that we believe Dark Court Shadows not only guard the Rift, but other beings live inside it too. Monstrous ones. Shadows can cross over from the court without issue as well. They always emerge unscathed and without aid from magic."

I shuddered, but I wasn't surprised. Having seen the Shadows once before, I recognized that they weren't normal fae. Most were so pale they probably hadn't seen the sun in years. And then there were the red eyes . . .

"Are they ghosts?" I asked.

Tially shook her head. "More like possessed fae. They have slipped so often into my lands, it's believed that the thinnest line of the Rift borders my kingdom."

The Queen of the Snowcap Court bristled. "You might have heard that the single soul who passed through the Rift also entered my lands. It was years ago, when my grandfather ruled, but he told me the tale."

"He did?" I leaned forward. "In the Crystal Court, I learned that the traveler used an illumination gem. We managed to find two of them and bring them with us. Do you know how he used such a stone?"

"I don't, but I do know of them," she replied. "He

gave us a bit of information in return for a bed and, eventually, a gryphon to fly him home. The crystal was his saving grace. A light in the dark. Apparently, the vile creatures of the Rift cannot tolerate light, and he had the magic to wield it."

My eyebrows furrowed together. "But I can make light with aether. A witch or wizard could do so too."

"Of course," Tially conceded, "but I mean *true* light. Natural. Harnessed from the sun. The origin of all light. That is what the illumination gems provide."

The crystals in my pocket warmed, as if they'd been set in the daylight that very moment. I thought about the giant blue gem in Cirrus' room. Roshia had said that one was charging, but these had been in a box and still gave off light.

"Like they charge in the sun? How long does it take? And will they last the duration of our march through the Rift?"

Tially shrugged. "I cannot know that, but if the gems you hold give off any light at all, I assume there is still energy in them and they'll work. With aether, you should be able to access it, to use and amplify the power of the stone."

It would be easy enough to test. Making it work properly might be another matter, but I'd surely know if I was doing it right.

"Are you here to suggest we enter the Rift from your lands?"

"Not at all. The mountains around my land are

perilous. They would slow you. However, I am offering soldiers and knowledge."

"It would do no good to veer north anyhow," Queen Aquatia chimed in. She folded her hands together on her knees, looking the very picture of queenly perfection, while I was over here looking like a dingy rat. "The Shadows are arriving on this side of the Rift already, ready to beat you back."

I sat up with a gasp. "No."

"Yes," Halad interjected. "And scouts claim they are even thicker in the mountains. That's why we pulled our own army back here. Why risk their lives so early when you weren't even around to infiltrate? And that's not even the worst part."

What could be worse than Shadows popping up all over the place? I swallowed. "What else is there? Is the Rift growing?"

"Thank the aether *no*!" Queen Aquatia shuddered. "But other vile creatures have emerged from it. Ones we have seen before, albeit briefly."

"You know how your aunt has a jabberwocky?" Halad asked.

Hatter swore beneath his breath as a pit formed in my gut. I could guess what was coming next . . .

"The Dark Court has dragons too, but theirs are . . . well, dark."

"Do you mean possessed?" Hatter asked.

I suspected he'd been trying to be respectful and quiet

in the face of the royals but could no longer do so. I was glad for it, because at that moment, I had no words.

"In a way." Halad paused. "Like the Shadows, their eyes are red. That is a sign of possession in your world, correct?" The prince looked to me, and I nodded.

"It's thought that," he continued, "while demons cannot venture here, they are somehow spreading their influence. So yes, the Shadows, and perhaps the dragons, could be controlled by demons. Or perhaps their essence has corrupted them in some way."

"How many are there?" I asked, my voice smaller than before.

"Only two that we saw."

"Are they large?"

I didn't know why I was digging for more bad news. It was like I couldn't stop myself.

"Massive. At least three times the size of the jabber-wocky." Halad twisted his lips. "To be fair, your aunt's dragon is rather small."

I snorted. "Oh yeah, so dainty."

At that, Jax roared with laughter. The pixies joined in, and even Hatter couldn't help himself.

The others in the room watched us as though we were delusional.

Maybe we were. There had to be a certain level of crazy involved to take on what we were about to do.

CHAPTER 22

As much as I'd have loved to save Elise right away, I wasn't an idiot. I needed to be as sharp as a dagger, so rest was crucial if we were to succeed.

After the meeting with the queens, I was shown to a bedchamber, and I commanded that once the doors to my room were shut, no one was to interrupt me.

And because I was very scary when I wanted to be, no one did.

When I woke the next morning, after a good twelve hours of sleep, I felt rejuvenated. Sore in body still, but mentally ready. Prepared to begin planning exactly how we were going to slip past an army of shadows and two dragons.

I opened the door to my chambers, found a guard standing outside, and waved awkwardly. "Is there a place to eat around here?"

After sleeping so long, food was a must. If I didn't eat soon, my stomach threatened to consume itself.

"Of course, Princess Alice. Your compatriots are enjoying their lunch with Prince Halad now."

"Do you know how long they've been up?"

"The wizard awoke quite early this morning."

That tracked. Jax had always been a morning person.

"I'm unsure when the fae male woke, but the pixies have not been up much longer than you. They attempted to make me wake you." He closed his eyes, and I got the sense the twins had probably been very persistent. Likely loud, too, knowing them. "They swore you wouldn't be mad, but I insisted they let you rest."

"Thanks," I said. "They'd have gotten away with it, but I needed my sleep."

"Pixies tend to get away with a lot." He gave me a smile that hinted he knew a tiny fae or two.

I chuckled. "For sure. Can you show me to lunch?"

He obliged, and within minutes, I walked into a room smelling of freshly baked bread, fruit, and . . .

"Is that mac and cheese?! Please tell me that I am not hallucinating!"

Jax wiggled his eyebrows. "I know what you like, Al." He cut a glance to Henri, who didn't notice because he was watching me approach the table "Taught the cooks to make it from scratch this morning. The cheese is different from ours, but they still mastered it pretty fast."

I brushed aside the innuendo that he knew me better than Hatter and thanked him, sitting down and spooning a monster scoop of mac and cheese onto a plate that a servant supplied.

I was glad they were allowing us to eat family-style. Oftentimes, servants wanted to baby royals, and the habit made me uncomfortable.

"What's the plan for today?" I asked, because I was sure there was one.

I hadn't known Halad long, but he wasn't one to let grass grow under his feet. Neither were Sansu and Alran. Now that both sides were rested and caught up on what had happened in the countryside of the Riverlands and in the Crystal Court, it was time for action.

"Well," Halad jumped in, not disappointing me. "How do you feel about riding again so soon after your travels? It's a full day's and night's journey to the Rift, and we'll have to sleep on the road for one night, but if we leave today, we can reach the boundary line by tomorrow afternoon."

Just the idea of sitting astride a horse or a gryphon— or anything, really—made the muscles of my inner thighs cry out in agony. "To be honest, I'd rather not." I scooped a gooey bite of mac and cheese into my mouth.

"Understandable, though it is the fastest way to cover ground." Halad also took a bite of mac, his first, and his eyes widened. "This is . . . wondrous."

I was observing a mac and cheese convert before my eyes.

"Yeah, it's my fave," I said as he took another three bites in rapid succession, as if he couldn't stuff enough pasta into his mouth. "I could fly," I proposed, hoping that wasn't against some bullshit royal rule.

The prince just shrugged, intent on his bowl. "That's possible. But it's a long way, so we'll still bring you a horse for when you tire."

"What about Valia?"

"I'm not sure you'll want to bring her, Princess," Alran interjected. "The Rift is . . . no place for creatures you've become attached to."

Meaning that my alicorn was likely to die. I swallowed. That didn't bode well for any of us.

"We might not even be able to get the horses into the Rift," Halad remarked. "They're well trained but they may run from it. Though, a lot of that depends on your use of the illumination crystals. I presume you have not had a chance to play with them yet?"

"Not at all."

"What if we brought a litter for you, Princess?" Sansu suggested.

I stiffened, and my fork stopped halfway to my mouth. "Do you mean one of those platforms that men sometimes use to help carry their royals?"

Alran snorted, catching my incredulous tone, but Sansu beamed. It was almost like he thought I appreciated the idea.

"Exactly!" the blue-haired dwarf replied.

I gaped. Did this guy know me at all?! There was no way I wanted to ride on a platform with an army streaming by. That was so pretentious!

"Actually, that's a great idea," Halad decided. "Alice could save her legs, and during the ride, she can learn how to use the crystals. It's that, or wait here until you figure it out." He narrowed his eyes, assessing me. "Which I'm assuming is out of the question?"

My annoyance over the litter vanished. "Absolutely. I've already wasted too much time. The longer Elise is in the Dark Court with my aunt, the more danger she's in."

Granted, she'd been held hostage in the most dangerous court of Faerie for years, but the arrival of Sela White posed a new, direct threat.

"We leave today," I declared, then shuddered. "And, yeah, I'll use the litter. But only so I can figure out how to work the crystals!"

"Of course," Halad said, but his lips twitched, and it wasn't lost on me that Jax was trying his best not to laugh. Even Henri looked amused by my adamance.

Jerks.

"I'll have one set up, and we can leave for the Rift this afternoon." The prince stood. "I'll prepare the forces now. Alran, Sansu? A hand?"

The elf and dwarf rose to assist, but the rest of us stayed, and the meal resumed. Wisely, no one mentioned the litter again.

I'd barely finished eating and cleaning up when I received word that we were ready to march. Halad moved freakishly fast.

Less than an hour later, I was loaded into an emerald green litter, basically a pretty box complete with gold curtains and cushy seats. It was large enough for four to sit in comfortably and gave us a lot of privacy. To my relief, no fae were carrying us, like humans had carried emperors in their day. Rather, four gryphons bore my weight.

The pixies were riding with me. As was Henri because though he claimed he was better, certain people thought it was best not to risk anything, and urged him to take it easy for another day.

Unfortunately, those same rules applied to Jax—who told anyone and everyone at court that he'd been struck by lightning. As he was usually more secretive about his struggles, I knew he was only doing it so someone would suggest he ride with me. Though his week of trying to win me back was dwindling away, he still hadn't given up hope that I could love him again.

Truth be told, my feelings toward the wizard *were* warmer. Oh, he still annoyed the crap out of me, and I'd never forgive him for what he'd done in the past, but I couldn't discount more recent events. Jax had shown that he cared. He'd risked his life participating in that stupid tournament—partially to prove his love, but also just to help me.

I no longer loved him like I once had, but I found I didn't totally hate his guts anymore either. Past Alice wouldn't have believed such a thing could be possible.

Plus, he really had been struck by Cirrus' lightning, and what did I know about lingering effects? Saying no to him riding in the litter would be a dick move.

Supposedly this was the largest conveyance of its type, but with three human-sized bodies and two pixie ones, the interior of the palanquin was cramped. It was a relief when we left the city and could open the windows to look out upon the countryside of the Riverlands.

As if he'd expected me to do such a thing, Prince Halad rode up next to us. He smiled at me, and from his other side, Sansu gave an amiable wave.

"How is it in there?" the prince asked. "It's my mother's litter!"

"Comfortable," I assured him, because as much as I didn't want to be on display in this manner, I wasn't about to diss Queen Aquatia's hospitality. She'd been nothing but kind to me.

"Have you started experimenting with the illumination crystal yet?"

In truth, each person in the litter had been too preoccupied with checking out the city as we marched by. There was a little conversation, but all of it was overly polite and weird.

Henri and Jax seemed to be caught in an odd limbo where they didn't hate one another any longer—but they weren't friends either. That left me and the pixies to buffer the conversation, and that wasn't a natural position for me.

"Not yet. I'll start." I fished the larger crystal out of my pocket and held it up for him to see. It glowed, though not very brightly.

"Good luck. I'm heading to the front of the line. Let

me know if you need anything." And then the prince dug his heels into the sides of his horse and was off.

The moment he left, I shut the curtain again and stared down at the stone in my hand. I'd have preferred to keep the drapes open, but I needed to be able to watch any shifts in the gem. To know for certain what I was doing was right or wrong.

"Maybe I could play around with the smaller one?" Jax asked suddenly.

I glanced up from the facets I'd been studying. The idea had occurred to me, but I'd horded the gems. Protected them, as I liked to think. "The princess told me the other fae used aether," I reminded him.

Jax shrugged. "I'm not fae, but maybe my magic can work with it too. We won't know unless we try."

"Having two people controlling the gems would be best. What if you get hurt and can't light it up?" Dum offered, clearly trying to keep the peace in the litter and make me see sense.

No argument there. I supposed it would have the added bonus of keeping Jax busy while I worked. And it wasn't like he would be able to harm the crystal. Or at least, I didn't think so. Maybe he really would be able to use it, too.

Relenting, I fished the smaller illumination stone from my pocket and handed it over, my skin brushing Jax's as I did. The wizard looked like he wanted to grab my hand, but he refrained, which I appreciated, because Henri was watching closely and he surely would have hated that.

"You just pour aether into it?" Henri asked once the larger, yellow crystal was in the center of my palm.

"That's what Queen Tially said. It sounds easy enough, so I'm going to start there."

"Has it always glowed so faintly?" Hatter asked, studying the gem.

"Yes. I actually set these in my window while I slept. I wanted them to absorb more sunlight." I'd gotten the idea from Cirrus, recalling the large gem he'd placed just in front of his window. The one that I now suspected harnessed electric power somehow. "They only had a few hours, but that's more than they've had in a long time."

I paused, turning the stone over in my palm. "When I opened the box they were in, it was intense. Now that they've had some charging it should be more so. You guys might want to close your eyes. Or shield them. If I do this right, the light could be blinding."

"Let's hope not." Jax arched his eyebrows. "I don't know how we're going to lead an army through the Rift with our eyes closed."

He had a point, so I just shrugged and dropped my attention to the gem.

It filled most of my palm, and had fewer facets than I thought was natural. I wondered why and wished I could have stayed at the Crystal Court and learned more about how their magics worked . . . And what Roshia was up to, because that princess was definitely shaking things up in her homeland.

But no. I was needed here, to save Elise.

Putting my game face on, I called my aether. The magic of the old gods wreathed my hands easily and, while I was not paying attention to them, my friends were watching. I could feel their eyes on me.

So do something, I chided myself, and without waiting another second, did as Queen Tially had said the other fae did, and pushed my aether into the illumination crystal.

Light pulsed within the facets, sparkling off one another, and then blasted upward to form a perfect circle on the ceiling of the litter.

I gasped.

"Whoa," Dee whispered, soaring up to touch the ceiling. The light played on her hand, remaining a solid, steady stream as I continued to supply the gem with magical energy that pushed stored sunlight from it.

Dum joined her sister, eyes wide. Then, she held out her fist. Dee reciprocated the fist-bump.

"Are you giving it a lot?" Henri asked.

"Not really, but . . ." I tried to press more magic into it and met with resistance. "I don't know if there are limits. It doesn't seem to want more."

"Maybe you just need to break it in?" Jax suggested.

"This isn't a new pair of boots," I shot back, even though he might very well be right. I released the power I was siphoning into the gem and a sense of defeat crept in. I beat it back. I didn't have time for that negative nonsense. "You try."

He smirked, as if he already had this in the bag.

Reacting to his cockiness, I folded my arms over my chest, a clear challenge.

The wizard cupped the crystal just as I had. Often-times, Jax's kind worked with spells, but there were types of magic that were instinctual, like the one many witches and wizards used when they fought battles. I suspected that was the type he would use now.

Everyone knew when Jax's power flared to life, because the energy in the litter shifted. The air circulated and heated, so within seconds, sweat trickled down my forehead.

My lips pressed together as he shot me a cocky grin. I was pretty sure he was doing this not just to make the crystal light up, but to impress us. Impress *me*.

Really, I found his showmanship ridiculous, but was saved from saying so when, the next second, the gem in his hand glowed brighter than before.

He sucked in a breath. "It worked."

"Oh, so you had doubts?" I niggled.

He rolled his eyes. "I'm a strong wizard, Al, but I've never used one of these."

"It's not a lot of light," Henri remarked, eyebrows pinched together skeptically. "Neither was yours, Alice. We'll need a lot more than those stones have to offer to get through the Rift."

I exhaled loudly through my nose. "Yeah, so I guess now that we know how to do it, we'd better start practicing."

Henri gave me a soft, encouraging smile. "Luckily, we have hours of travel ahead of us."

I looked down at the crystal that would lead to either my sister's salvation or my own doom, and set to mastering it.

CHAPTER 23

I hobbled out of the litter, my entire body exhausted after hours of channeling aether into the illumination stone. Though I'd scoffed at being carried that morning, now I was secretly glad it had been an option. If I'd had to practice with the crystal while riding a gryphon or horse, I'd be dead on my feet.

"You alright?" Hatter pressed his hand to the small of my back.

"I need to move around." I stretched my arms and made some wide circles with them, relishing in the extra space after being cramped up with four other people for hours. Two of the four might be teensy, but Dee and Dum took up more room than should be possible.

Halad appeared. He was no longer on horseback, and, somehow, looked full of energy. "Before the sun goes down, I need to have a word with a wild pixie swarm living in the area. Once it's dark, they're more difficult to find. Commander Verdan will oversee the meals."

My brow furrowed. "How do you know there are pixies here?"

We were on the edge of a nondescript wood. There were no pixies in sight.

"I've been here before, with your friend Odette and her allies, from your world."

I wouldn't have called Odette a friend per se. An ally, yes. Someone I respected, absolutely. But friend? We'd only met once. Though, if we met again, I would be glad to see her.

"The pixies kicked us out on my last visit," Halad continued, "but I'm fairly certain that's because we didn't request permission to camp here beforehand."

"Yes!" Dee piped up. "You have to ask! Otherwise, they get very upset."

"Truth be told, we didn't know they were here, but yes, we were lucky to escape without violence." The prince shook his head, eyes wide.

"Do you want me to come?" He was royal, but so was I—a fact I seemed to be coming to terms with more and more as I went through day-to-day life. Even speaking with two queens yesterday had felt normal.

So weird.

"Actually, I was hoping your pixie friends would." Halad looked at the twins. "Could you put in a good word for us? Assure them we're not trying to steal their land?"

"Of course!" Dum rose into the air.

Out of everyone who had ridden in the litter, the pixies were the most awake. They'd been able to fly about to stretch their wings and even napped for a few hours.

"Perfect. With me, then?" Halad gestured for them to follow, and the twins did, chatting his ear off as they went.

Under the eye of Halad's commander, the rest of us helped set up pots for supper. I'd just helped set up a table upon which pots of soup would be served in an hour or two, when someone came up behind me, wrapping their arm around my waist.

I spun, ready to bat the person away, when I found Henri grinning slyly at me.

"Hey," he said.

"Hey yourself. You almost got smacked." I lowered my hand to grip his.

"Thank the aether you have excellent reflexes." He dipped, surprising me when he pressed his lips to mine.

I wasn't too surprised to kiss him back. We'd been through so much with Jax's arrival and then traveling to, and being separated at, the Crystal Court, that I'd barely had any time with him at all.

When we broke apart, I smiled. "That was nice."

"*Nice?* I think I may need to work on my seduction skills."

"Oh, are you seducing me, Henri?" I trailed a finger along his jaw, then down his chest.

"If we get the go-ahead from the pixie swarm, we're camping here tonight," he replied. "But there aren't enough tents for people to have their own, so I was wondering . . . if you'd like to share?"

My heart leapt. In the Wonderland Court, Henri had always been proper; I was a princess, so he made sure to treat me as such. As a modern woman from Los Angeles, it equally charmed me and drove me crazy. But now, he had loosened up a bit.

"Naughty things could happen, Henri," I whispered.

"I'm aware."

"And you're okay with that?"

His Adam's apple bobbed. "When we were apart at the Crystal Court, you were all I could think of. Well, and making sure that you weren't married off to that monster."

"Always the gentleman."

"I don't know about that." He snorted. "I might have punched a wall or two when Jax made innuendos about your past."

I stiffened. "Whhhhhhy am I not surprised?"

"He was just doing it to get to me."

"That's right." I grabbed Henri by the front of his shirt, pulled his lips to mine again, and kissed him hungrily.

His mouth opened, urging mine to do the same, and Hatter took advantage, his tongue sweeping in, tasting me. His hands, so large compared to mine, slid lower, grazing the top of my buttocks.

I wished they'd go even lower. But though he might deny it, damn if he wasn't a gentleman.

And damn if I didn't get more turned on just by wanting him to do more.

I pressed myself into him harder, my hands roaming his chest, feeling the muscles there before moving to his back and touching his wings.

Hatter hissed, and I grinned.

So, fae wings are sensitive. I—

His fingers found my own wings, and I nearly died. Yes, our wings were sensitive when we were aroused. I'd never known, having routinely bound them until I came here, but the right touch was enough to make me want to rip his clothes off right there and then.

Which I *so* couldn't do. We were in the middle of a group of soldiers! Oh, good grief. How many were watching?

A modicum of sense slipping in, I broke away from him, gasping for breath. Hatter stared down at me as if his whole world had just been upended.

Mine had too.

"You're who I want, Henri," I assured him, in case the kiss hadn't made that clear. "It's been that way since I met you."

"And you're who I want. Forever, if you'll have me."

My breath hitched. Was that a proposal? Did those work the same here? I wasn't sure, but from the way he was looking at me, his gaze burning with desire and love, I wouldn't be surprised.

What should I say? Mere days ago, I'd been sure I was leaving. That I'd deny the crown and return to my world.

After what I'd been through at the Crystal Court, though, I'd started to see things differently.

Before, I'd believed the Wonderland Court was an anomaly, rivaled only by the Dark Court, its ally. But it wasn't. Not at all. There was far too much corruption in Faerie, and the more I learned about it, the more an obligation to erode it seeded within me. More than an obligation, actually—a *desire*.

Was I, Alice the Dagger, turning into a do-gooder?

The idea was almost enough to make me burst into laughter, but at that moment, someone called my name.

Breaking the connection between Henri and me with a squeeze of his hand. Hopefully, he wouldn't take that as a rejection. It certainly wasn't one.

"Alice! Over here!" the voice called again, and I turned to find Sansu waving madly.

"Looks like he needs you," Henri said behind me, his voice a deep, sexy rasp.

"Just a sec!" I called, and twisted back to Hatter. "I want you and no one else. I don't know what to say about forever. We're walking into a war, Henri. We—"

He pressed two fingers to my lips. "You don't have to commit now. It's enough to know that we're still in this together."

"That never changed." Even in my brief moments of insanity, when I thought that Jax was all that I deserved, I'd still wanted Henri more. "Let's go see Sansu."

We strode across the growing camp hand in hand. The feel of his skin against mine felt so good and natural, and a part of me hoped Jax would see, so he'd give up on his pursuit and slip away to build his own life.

The truth was, I no longer wanted to hurt the wizard. No longer wanted to see his heart crushed as he'd done to mine. Maybe it was a sign of my growth, I didn't know, but I had come to the realization that even though he annoyed me, his presence also brought closure that I hadn't gotten before. Like his appearance not only reopened my wound, but helped to heal it correctly.

However, when I finally spotted Jax in the camp, he wasn't even looking for me. In fact, my ex seemed very involved in a conversation with a purple-haired, female fae soldier whom I recognized as having brought us water during our long journey in the litter.

A smile tugged at my lips as Jax ran his hand through his curls and leaned against a tree. I recognized the look on his face. He was *totally* getting his flirt on.

Hmmm, maybe things will work out for everyone . . .

"Hey," I said when Henri and I got to Sansu. "What's up?"

The dwarf waved for me to follow, entering the grove, thick with trees. "You'll never guess what Dee and Dum have managed!"

I looked at Henri, who shrugged. Where the pixies were concerned, literally anything could happen. Had they taught a gnome to fist-bump? Wrangled a phoenix for their own personal ride? Convinced Halad to propose to one of them?

The last one had me snorting. Just imagining Dee or

Dum hovering in front of the prince, batting their eyelashes as he confessed his love, was too much. The girls would probably explode from excitement.

But as it turned out, it wasn't any of those things. Not even close.

When I caught sight of the twins, it was to find them in a large clearing, surrounded by hundreds, maybe thousands, of pixies. *Cheering* pixies.

"What in the world?" I muttered.

Halad was standing off to the side, like he was a nobody. I shot him a look, and his lips curled up in an amused smile as he came my way.

"What's going on?" I asked.

No one else could answer. The girls hadn't noticed us, Sansu seemed too gripped by glee to remember that he'd brought me here, and Henri was just as confused as me.

"Do you see this?" Halad gestured to the twins, still speaking to the crowd.

I cocked my head. Did they just mention . . . the Rift? What were they talking about!? "I do. What's going on?"

"Your friends just got us more soldiers."

I gasped. "No! You mean . . ."

"The whole swarm will be traveling with us tomorrow." Halad shook his head incredulously. "And they're letting us stay here. I must get back to camp and spread the word so the soldiers can set up their tents without worry."

The unforeseen turn of events eased some of the ever-present tension in my chest.

The swarm had quieted just enough for me to hear Dee shouting about the noble nature of our mission. About how we wanted to save not just Elise, but others from the Dark Court. I'd never outright said that, but I agreed.

"We'll come with you and leave the girls to their fan club," I told Halad.

Hand in hand with Henri, I followed the Prince of the Riverlands back to camp.

The sun had long since set. Supper had been served. And the soldiers from Wonderland, the Riverlands, the Snowcap Court, and the pixie swarm sat together, talking and laughing.

The sight warmed my heart.

Not long ago, the fae from Wonderland had never left their island. Watching them now, I wouldn't know it. They joked with fae from other courts as if they'd known one another all their lives.

"The soup was good," Dee declared from where she sat next to me. "Especially for only being on the fire for an hour!"

"Are you a chef now?" I teased. I'd never seen either of the pixies cook a single thing.

"I don't have to be a chef to appreciate good food, Alice. You know we've become accustomed to the finer things in life!"

I laughed, as did Henri, Jax, Sansu, and Alran, all of whom sat around the same fire as us.

Overall, the meal was surprisingly pleasant. Jax hadn't tried to flirt with me once. Instead, I'd caught him casting glances at the purple-haired fae he'd been speaking with earlier.

I was dying to ask about her, even if that was kind of weird, but I refrained. His week was almost up, and I didn't want him to think I was pushing him on another female. If Jax thought I was manipulating him in any way, he'd double down on trying to win me back. But if going after another fae was his idea . . . it was really just best to let him think that.

"Who's up for stories before bed?" Sansu asked out of the blue.

My eyebrows shot up. "Stories?"

"You do have those in the human world, don't you?" the dwarf teased. He'd had three ales, which was two more than normal, and clearly, he was feeling himself.

"Of course we do." I rolled my eyes. "Like, ghost stories?"

The dwarf shrugged. "Whatever you want. They can even be family tales. Or those from your life."

That was out. My life before Wonderland had been an utter disaster.

"Or made up," Sansu added. "It's just fun. To help us relax before we sleep."

"I don't think I need more relaxing," Jax said, yawning.

He was probably thinking the same thing as me: that no one wanted to hear about our past lives. Much of it was too violent. Too depressing.

"How about I start?" Sansu offered. "I can see that just the notion of telling a tale is straining your brains."

Damn! The blue-haired one was saucy tonight.

"Regale us!" I cheered, and we settled in as Sansu began to weave a story about a female fae, crazed by the death of the male she'd loved.

I listened, amused and delighted as the dwarf grew more animated by the minute. Slowly, I dropped my head to rest on Henri's shoulder, and relaxed into him.

I sighed, wanting this to be normal, if only for a moment. My eyes closed, and I breathed Henri in, taking in the night. The smoke in the air. The scent of horses and gryphons. The noises of soldiers putting away pots and pans or just talking.

We were going to war, so there was never really a moment of complete peace, but this was close.

"And that," the dwarf declared as he drew his tale to an end before an enthralled crowd, "was how the banshee devoured a whole town!" For flare, he clapped, sending sparks of magic into the air, and making Jax—who was once again staring at the female soldier across the camp —jump to his feet in surprise.

I laughed at his reaction, as did the others.

Jax's cheeks turned pink, but he just shrugged. "Got distracted."

"I'll bet." Alran arched his eyebrows. "She is quite distracting."

Jax shot me a look, but I glanced away. I didn't want him to think I was jealous or mad or . . . *anything*. We weren't together. My emotions regarding this shouldn't matter. He had to move on.

And so did I—to bed.

"I think I've had enough for tonight." I rose. Henri followed, and together, we waved the others goodnight.

I didn't even bother to glance at Jax to see how that affected him. I wouldn't outright try to push him toward the other female, but if he did it on his own, that was just fine with me.

Because all I wanted tonight was Henri. No interruptions. Tomorrow, we would enter the Rift, so we deserved that much.

And so much more.

But more was never promised, so I wouldn't pine after it.

We meandered to the tent, making small talk with others we passed. Henri, naturally, knew many of the soldiers from the Wonderland Court. I didn't, but most wanted to meet me. Even though I was tired, they'd come here for me, for Elise, so it was the least I could do to spend time talking with them.

Finally, we reached the tent we'd set up earlier and ducked inside. As a princess, I'd received one of the larger tents. I could even stand up inside of it, which was nice.

Slowly, I turned to Hatter, and though we'd been

together for the last several days, gazing upon him right now took my breath away.

He was as stunning as the day I'd met him. More so, even. Then, he'd been a handsome man and a leader, which I found attractive. But I knew him so much better now. Knew his heart, his soul.

"Alice?" he whispered, and the rasp in his tone made my heart stutter. "Are you alright?"

"Of course. It's just . . . I'm finally with you. Alone."

Once, I'd thought all I'd ever get from him was a kiss. But one kiss would never have been enough. I needed to know Henri as thoroughly as a person could know another. Needed to *feel* him.

Up until this point in my life, Jax had been my one lover, the man I'd given everything to.

Since then, I'd retrieved my heart, but now I found myself wanting to place it in Henri's gentle artist's hands. I wanted to feel how he'd touch me. How we'd love one another.

Even if I was being selfish and it couldn't last, I no longer had the strength to deny myself that pleasure.

His lips curled up. "Privacy does seem to be a bit of a rarity for us." Slowly, he lifted his hand, extended it to me. "Come here, Princess."

Swallowing, I padded toward him, my steps so light, they were almost silent. When only inches separated us, Henri slipped his hands around my waist, pulling me close.

"Are we sure about this?" he murmured.

"I am," I replied with no hesitation in my voice or my heart. "Are you?"

"I've been sure of you all my life."

"You had a crush as a boy?" I teased, winking playfully.

"I think . . . I think even then, I loved you. Just in a different way."

All the air seemed to leave the tent. I'd thought it before, and I thought it then: was Henri for real? Could a man be so perfect?

My answer came when he dipped his chin, and his lips grazed mine. The sweetness of his mouth, the sweep of his tongue, filled me with pleasure, made me want to burst with it.

Hatter's hands were still clasped around my waist, still proper, but I'd had about enough of that. My own were wrapped around his neck, hidden in his sheet of long, black hair, but they wouldn't be for long.

Taking the lead, I slid my hands along his face, down his chin, down his chest, *down*. When I stopped at his belt, Henri pulled back.

"Someone is impatient."

"Is that really a surprise?"

"No, but I want to savor it." His deft fingers went to my shirt, undoing the top buttons, and slowly, almost painfully so, pulling the fabric up over my head.

I stood before him in a bra from the other world, which judging by how his eyebrows nearly disappeared into his hairline and his lips parted softly he appreciated.

"You like?" I fingered the black lace.

"I—I do." His voice had thickened, his eyes glued to the delicate fabric.

I knew I'd worn this impractical garment for some reason.

"I bet you don't know how to take it off," I challenged.

"That *is* a problem."

"I'll teach you. But first, to make things fair . . . " I grabbed his shirt and slipped it up and off.

The hard planes of his chest nearly made me salivate. By the old gods, I was a freaking goner, for *sure*.

"You like?" he mimicked me, his tone suggestive as hell.

The proper Henri was quickly devolving.

"You know I do," I purred, dying a little because we weren't already on the mattress, my hands all over him, him inside me.

"Good. Now, where were we?" He inched closer, his hands fingering the back of my bra. But then he stopped and cocked his head. Finally, shocking the hell out of me, he scooped me up. "This lesson will surely be better given horizontally."

I laughed, not about to argue, as Henri laid me down on the ground and climbed on top of me.

CHAPTER 24

The next day, I awoke feeling like a new woman.

One in love.

It wasn't the best timing, but where love was concerned, I had never been great at that.

Should I tell him?

I rolled over, gazing upon Henri's face as he slept. He looked so peaceful, so happy. There should be no resistance in telling him, but my words might change him, might alter what he'd normally do in a fight. Might compromise him.

But then again, what if I died?

I hadn't allowed myself to think such thoughts before. Though I'd delivered death unto others many times, it had rarely brushed close to me. However, since arriving in Faerie, those occurrences had escalated somewhat.

Like when I'd been lost in the Enchanted Forest.

Or when I'd faced a kraken.

When I'd battled my aunt's army on the beach near Heart Castle.

Yeesh, I really need to rename the palace.

That was a good sign. I might fear death, but I had plans. Many places to rename in Wonderland. Perhaps even a future with the gorgeous male beside me. The fae who had shown me love since he'd met me, and who'd worshipped my body the night before.

I stared at him, and as if he sensed me watching, Henri's eyes fluttered open.

His lips curled up softly. "Good morning, Princess."

"Good morning, hot stuff."

He burst out laughing. "I usually don't get your human sayings, but I think I like that one."

I leaned in and claimed his lips in a sweet morning kiss. "How did you sleep?"

"Well. I was exhausted after so much exertion." He waggled his eyebrows, and it was my turn to crack up.

"Same, Henri. I—"

My stomach roared, so loud that a person walking outside our tent actually stopped.

"You okay in there?" the fae asked, which only made me devolve into laughter again.

"Fine!" Henri shouted back. "There's merely a very hungry princess in here."

"Ah." The person now sounded uncomfortable. "There's food being served."

The moment he mentioned it, I smelled the scent of

roasted meat in the air. My stomach growled again, slightly quieter this time, but still insistent.

"I guess we should go get food." Henri glanced down at my belly in mock horror. "Or you might eat me."

I laughed, but as he rose from the bedmat, I stopped him. I might be starving, but I sure as hell wasn't going to let that take priority over what I needed to say.

"Henri?" I sounded smaller than usual. Less confident.

No wonder. This was about as vulnerable as a person could get.

"Yeah?" His tone shifted from playful to concerned.

"I-I-" I swallowed, the words seeming lodged in my throat. "I—"

Suddenly, the confusion in Hatter's face vanished, and he knelt at my side, his hand gripping mine. "Alice, I love you too."

Air gusted out of me. "How'd you know that's what I was trying to say?"

"You've never been great at allowing others to get close and opening up." He pulled me into his broad chest, hugging me, and pressed his face into my hair.

When we pulled apart, I looked him dead in the eye. "I want to get better at that." I drew in a deep breath. "So, yes, I love you, Henri. I want you to know before . . . today."

"Before we meet the Rift." His eyes darkened. "Your love will see me through. Give me bravery."

"I hope so," I said and again, my stomach yowled, so

insistent that it broke the magic around us. "Not to ruin the moment, but I guess we should go eat? Seems like a lot of people are up."

He kissed me, and we rose and dressed. Once we were appropriate, we exited the tent.

A few people stopped and stared. A couple of guys looked like they wanted to give Henri a thumbs-up, but it was the pixies who managed to mortify me in less than three seconds after flying up to us.

"You two are a couple!" Dum shouted, soaring toward me, hands waving around with excitement. "We love it!"

"Did you do it?!" Dee asked, drawing sniggers from the soldiers.

"I'm going to pretend you didn't ask that." Still, as I pulled Henri away, Dum whispered to her sister, "They definitely did!"

Sometimes, the twins were just too much for words.

Henri and I joined the food line. A few soldiers gestured for me to cut to the front, but I wasn't having that. These people had marched all day yesterday while I rode in a litter. I might be starving, but they surely were too. I'd wait my turn.

When we had our food, bread and chunks of roasted meat—*pig?*—and an apple, I scouted for a place to sit. Before we could get comfortable, however, Hatter was summoned.

"Prince Halad would like a word, sir," the fae soldier who'd found him said respectfully.

"Want me to join you?" I asked.

"No. Eat. I'll come back." He kissed me on the cheek and rushed off to see what the prince wanted.

I settled onto a log at the edge of a wood, and dug in. Actually, it would be more honest to say I inhaled my food. By the time I'd finished the bread and meat, my stomach was feeling more settled, so I took my time with the apple. It was a fae apple, gold and juicy and crisp. Really delicious.

It was in those moments of alone time that I spotted Jax flirting with the same fae he'd seemed into yesterday.

I smirked. For someone who had come all this way for me, he really appeared interested in Purple Hair. Not that I blamed him, she was hot.

As if sensing my stare, he turned and locked eyes with me.

"Crap," I muttered when he broke away from the female and jogged over.

I didn't want Jax to ruin my magical morning. I wanted to revel in the glow of using the L-word with Henri.

No matter how much I wanted to bring up the topic of the girl Jax had been flirting with, it wouldn't do me any good. It would probably just make him defensive.

"Hey, Al," he said, coming to a stop before me and running his hands through his blond curls.

He looked well-rested, vibrant, happy. He hadn't looked like that since we'd reunited.

That fact only brought my guard up more.

"Hey," I replied. "What's up?"

"Can I talk to you?"

"Isn't that what you're doing?"

Without invitation, he sat next to me on the log. A few seconds of quiet passed between us.

"So, you and Hatter, huh?" he said finally.

"That isn't really your business, Jax."

"I know! I—" He cleared his throat. "That came out wrong. It's just . . . I guess I'm embarrassed."

That got me.

"Why?"

"Well, I came all this way for you. Into another realm. Followed you to a court full of insane fae who worship crystals, and now I'm in an army, heading toward . . . something freaky." He looked me dead in the eye. "And all this time, it's been so obvious that you love him. I thought I could change your mind, win you back, but I see now how stupid that was. You're head over heels."

I swallowed. "I don't know if it was love then. When you first came."

"Now it is, though, isn't it?"

"Yes," I admitted.

He sighed and leaned back, pressing his palms into the rough wood. "He's a good guy. Did you know we talked a few times when we were separated from you? Like, without wanting to fight one another." Jax snorted. "It's hard to say, but I like the guy."

"You . . . do?"

"Yeah. And I can see that you do too, so I'm going to

make this easy for you. I'm bowing out, gracefully, as a suitor."

My mouth fell open. "You are?"

"Rarely have you had so few words on a subject, Al."

He was right. Usually, I could hold my own in a conversation, but now, I was stunned.

"It's just—I . . . I didn't expect this. Even when you flirted with that female."

"Calia. She's pretty cool." His eyes had lit up at the mention of her. "Well, I just wanted to come over here and let you know that I won't interfere anymore. You love him, and I need to move on. I think I needed to come here to see that." He stood. "We good?"

I nodded, unable to form words.

"Then I'll catch you later."

Jax ran off, probably to find Calia. And I watched him go, unable to believe what had just happened.

I stared out the litter window, my dread mounting.

The Rift had been growing in size for hours. With each passing mile, I questioned my sanity more. Up close and personal, the swath of blackness was nothing like any description, faraway sighting, or image had led me to expect. It was so much bigger. Bolder. More devastating.

A blight on the land. An all-encompassing stain on a field of green. Death swirling before us, waiting for us to walk into its arms.

I looked down at the large illumination stone in my hand. Would it be enough? Even when combined with Jax's, would they work?

I'd ridden in the litter again, though this time, it was just me and Jax working with the stones. Henri hadn't loved the idea, but after our night together he felt more certain about where we stood and he wanted to discuss military tactics with the rest of the army. The pixies weren't there either. They thought it would be best to fly with the newly recruited swarm.

Seeing as Jax and I had made up that morning, our time together had been pretty pleasant. We'd passed the hours working magic, pushing power into the stones and receiving varying degrees of light. On one such push, a soldier outside the litter had told me that I'd encompassed at least five horses and riders in front and behind the litter.

Jax had done well too, better than Prince Halad, the only other aether-blessed fae we traveled with. For a while, there'd been debate as to whether Halad or Jax should carry the crystal, but the prince had conceded quickly when he saw that Jax could maintain a protective orb that was double the size of the one he had created himself.

But even with my and Jax's powers combined, it wasn't enough to keep an army—or, more accurately, three armies from different courts and a pixie swarm—safe from the unknown.

We marched with thousands of fae. I was sure we could only protect a handful with our light.

My stomach twisted. What were we going to do?

"Maybe we should get out and ride?" Jax suggested after peeking out the window for the hundredth time. Though he hadn't said as much, I knew his nerves were growing too.

He held up the illumination stone, which was still glowing strongly from his last influx of power. "We're probably as good as we're gonna get, so I think we need to pivot the plan."

Accepting that he was right, I opened the door. The gryphons carrying it continued to plod along at a slow pace, and I hopped out, Jax following.

We'd barely walked ten paces when Prince Halad appeared.

"Something wrong?"

"No," I said, though it wasn't the whole truth. I wished I felt more settled in the plan. "We're close, right?" I gestured to the top of the Rift, climbing skyward, touching the clouds. The monstrosity loomed just over a long, sloping hill ahead of us.

"We are. Let me retrieve horses for you."

Halad called out orders for spare horses to be brought, and they were there in an instant. Jax and I mounted the beasts and resumed the march with the rest of the forces.

"Twenty minutes, perhaps less, and we'll crest the hill," Halad said. "If I've led us the right way, you'll see a small home. A shack, really. And of course, the Rift. That monstrosity will stand behind it."

"How do you know there's a home? Why would someone live there?"

"I've been there before, with others from your world. We sought the fae who lived there. She's dead now."

I had a hunch he was referring to Odette and her friends again. From the look on his face, things hadn't gone well for them, but I didn't want to consider that. I needed to remain positive. Ingenious. Ready for action.

So we plodded along, following the column of soldiers as they climbed ever higher.

The first wave reached the top of the hill, then the second. They stopped.

I swallowed, wondering if that was normal. From the stiff set of their shoulders, it didn't seem so.

As if in answer, one of the soldiers whirled, and steered his mount to right, beyond the line of fae, before he raced down the incline. As he galloped down the army line, other soldiers' horses danced skittishly.

Beneath me, my own beast tensed and threw its head. This fae was clearly coming to deliver a message and judging by the fear on his face it wasn't a good one.

"Whoa, buddy," I leaned forward, patting its neck, calming the creature, though, I kept my wings at the ready too, just in case. If I needed to lift into the air when the beast bolted, and possibly caused a stampede, I would.

Thankfully, it didn't come to that. The horse was well trained and calmed, though its muscles remained taut.

The fae who'd peeled off from the forefront approached Halad, his gold eyes wild. "Prince. They've anticipated our arrival."

"We knew that," Halad reminded him.

"There are *more*. Many more than before, and they keep coming. They're assembling too, protecting the boundary."

Keep coming? My heart leapt into my throat. "How many?"

"If I had to guess, I'd say our forces are equal. They might even have a couple hundred more than us." The soldier looked like he hated each word coming out of his mouth.

"No," I whispered. "All Shadows?"

"All Shadows," the fae replied.

"I need to see this." I kicked my horse in the side. The creature picked up pace, galloping past the column of fae still climbing to the top of the hill. I thought I heard hooves beating the earth behind me, probably Halad following, but I didn't turn back. My focus was solely on the summit of the steep hill and when I got there all my breath left me.

"By the old gods." I whispered.

We were exactly where Halad had said we should be. A dilapidated shack—the deceased fae's home—stood in the distance. Before the shack, an army was gathering, already numbering in the thousands.

And honestly, the opposing army was my *second* worry. The Rift being the first. Though ghastly and vast from a distance, it was far more violent up close. A stain on an otherwise bountiful land, it reached to the skies. When I squinted, the blackness swirled and pulsed, like it was alive.

I patted the illumination crystal in my pocket. So small compared to what we faced. Would this really work?

I didn't even have time to debate the question, as Halad caught up. Jax, and Hatter appeared seconds later, the pixies sitting with Henri. Alran and Sansu were just behind, their chests heaving nearly as hard as their horses'. Everyone stared up at the darkness, as mesmerized and horrified as myself.

"Un-fucking-believable," Jax muttered. "I mean, we could see it on our way here, but . . . can you *feel* it now?"

"Feel it?" I asked.

"Be still. Attune to the energies."

Xavier had often told Jax to do the same. Training for a wizard was different from that of a fae, but I knew what the words meant, knew how to do it for myself, so I did.

The moment I felt what he was talking about, I recoiled. How I'd not sensed it before, I didn't know. The presence of the Rift wasn't just intimidating, but *vile*. Like the dark magic that had rolled off the demons in the Battle of Spellcasters.

"It wasn't like that the last time I was here," Halad whispered.

"Is it coming from the Shadows, then?" Hatter asked.

"There couldn't have been this many last time you were here."

Even as he spoke, more poured from the cloud of night. They held swords and shields and spears. A line of archers stood nearby, arrows in hand, ready to be nocked.

I doubted they needed any weapons. Each pair of eyes gleamed red, like a demon's would, and that magic was far stronger and more destructive than any steel.

"No," Halad confirmed. "Only a couple of hundred posted here when we first thought to assemble, and even that had been enough to make me hesitate . . ."

"You were right. The Dark Court has to have bound themselves to demons," I insisted. "It feels the same. This magic is the same as black magic in my world."

"I usually love being correct, but not in this matter." Halad shuddered.

As if in response to our horror, the opposing army loosed an animalistic roar.

"They're readying!" Halad cried, rounding his mount. "Prepare to fight! Commander Verdan, see to the archers!"

I twisted and was relieved to find nearly all of our forces had made their way up the hill. Why the Shadows hadn't engaged us from where they stood left me at a loss.

Unless they wanted to fight. Wanted the blood. The destruction. The war.

That had to be it. They had archers, just as we did; they could have shot us down while we were at the disadvantage, but they didn't. They'd stayed put, waiting for the bloodshed to come.

Halad rallied the army, but I couldn't stop staring at the Shadows and the Rift, assessing everything we were up against. How would I get an army through here?

My stomach pitted as the answer, tentative before, still allowing for a sliver of hope, became painfully obvious.

I wouldn't.

I'd learned to use the illumination stone, I couldn't encompass everyone I traveled with. Only a small group could continue on. The rest . . .

I turned to my friends. "We go in alone, no army. Jax, how many can you protect? Don't overestimate."

"Five?"

That number wasn't large enough. I might be able to protect more with my light. Perhaps ten. But I couldn't risk overestimating either.

"Gather them. I'll tell Halad. I—"

My words died on my lips as a shriek ripped through the air. No army could make that sound.

Slowly, I faced the Rift once more, just in time to watch two dragons, black as the expansive wasteland I was about to barrel into, erupt from the darkness.

CHAPTER 25

"Oh my God! Check out those teeth!" Jax hollered as the dragons circled in the air.

One opened its mouth, spraying a blast of fire into the sky. I swallowed. There was no need for the dragons to eat us, or even get close to us, to kill us.

"Looks like the teeth are the least of our worries." I whirled, looking for Halad.

A moment later, the prince appeared out of the crowd of soldiers, his emerald cloak billowing behind him. His army was dressed in that same green, the rest, silver, and —because we had not had time to change the Wonderland attire since the Red Queen had left—red. The pixie swarm was a rainbow of colors, hovering to our left.

Halad's face was stark, devoid of blood. "I'd hoped they'd returned to the Dark Court. You can see how they pose an issue."

"Two, actually," I said, watching the dragons curl

around the masses of Shadows. "Their eyes are red. Do you think they've undergone the same . . . change as the Shadows?"

"It seems that way," he replied. "I'll set archers on them. Their arrow tips are filled with aether. I had my cousin do it before we left."

He turned to give another soldier a command, but I stopped him.

"Halad."

"Yes?"

"There's no way the whole army is getting through," I confessed. "I wasn't sure how I'd do it even before this, but now . . . "

Who in the world would think it was possible?

Immediately, I felt like an idiot for thinking I could try. Was I suffering from a goddess complex?

"Alice," Henri whispered. "This is it."

"What?" I asked, as all around fae rallied, waiting for the word. The other side, too, seemed frozen in stasis, though I wasn't sure why.

"Your prophecy. It said you would bring Wonderland into darkness." He gestured forward. "This."

I sucked in a breath. "You think?"

"I do. But you can break it. You have to."

Henri was right, there was really no other choice. Not only did I not have great enough power over the illumination stone, but even if I did, the entirety of the armies we'd amassed would not be able to get through the Rift. Thinking I could see them safely through the veil of darkness to the other side was a fool's hope. Or maybe just something a horrible ruler would do. Someone like my aunt wouldn't balk at sending her army into the Rift. Not if it meant getting what she wanted.

"Halad," I said. "We're breaking off. Take care of the Wonderland soldiers. I—"

"Absolutely not," the prince drew himself up, his eyes still on the threat before us. In his armor and cloak, he looked every bit the knight from tales of old.

"This isn't your fight," I reminded him.

"It's my land. I will do as I wish."

"What about your people? They came here for me, though. So I could save Elise."

"With all due respect, Alice, they also came here for me and our home. We want this plague vanquished. We want to walk the countryside without fear. We want to see our family, free from the darkness." Halad's face had become as hard as the stone of his castle's walls. "So yes, I'm coming with you. Commander Verdan will control my forces. He's been doing it for far longer than I've been alive anyhow."

"You're the heir to the Riverlands," I pressed. "Your mother—"

"She will understand. I will do what I must for our people." He looked at me, eyes penetrating. "I was injured and unable to fight in the demon war of your world. Here, I am well and I am coming. That is final."

I wished more than anything that I could tell him no.

That I had power over him. Now, Halad would just be one more person I was determined to protect.

Relenting with a sigh, I nodded. "My friends and I are going in. Call a handful of soldiers you trust, will you? Jax and I can only handle about fifteen total."

The prince went to it, shouting into the army. Jax looked to me. "I want to bring someone."

"Sure," I said. "Just one."

He nodded and slipped away.

The tension in the air had mounted, and I was just thinking I still couldn't believe no one had made a move, when the first arrow flew from the other side. It soared aflame, and landed in the center of the field.

Suddenly, more fire burst from the land. I groaned. They'd doused the field with some sort of flammable substance, creating a wall of fire that we'd have to pass through.

"Alice!" Dum's voice filled my ear. "The pixie swarm can come with you!"

I considered that, shook my head. "I can't be certain pixies are subjects of the Dark Court. They weren't in the Crystal Court, and we needed as little attention drawn to us as possible. You and Dee can come, but it will be too hard to hide a swarm. They can fight here."

Dum zoomed over. "At least let the swarm fly above and protect you until you enter the Rift."

"Okay," I said, already worried about what I'd just agreed to.

I didn't have long to fret, though, because Halad and Jax appeared again, a mob of people at their backs.

"They're with us," the prince informed me.

Jax had brought the girl he'd been flirting with. I met my ex's gaze. Was this wise? But Jax wasn't an idiot. He clearly liked the fae, so he'd have considered the pros and cons of involving her. He knew what he was risking.

I had to trust him.

"We'll also require a vanguard to get across the field," Halad said. "I'll call one."

"Fae above too," Henri added. "More than the pixies."

For a moment, I didn't understand why. When I did, horror crashed over me. Hatter was talking about a meat shield from the dragons. Fae to take the flames that would surely come from above so we wouldn't have to. I hadn't thought about that but he was completely right. The stretch of land we needed to cross was as long as three football fields, placed end to end. To think that we would only be attacked on the ground was shortsighted.

"Unfortunately, yes," Halad agreed. "And we need to assemble quickly."

Halad straightened. "Water elementals! Ready!"

Normally, if there wasn't a wall of fire before us, we'd charge and leave the archers back to set on the dragons. But extinguishing those flames had to come first. They were small in comparison to the Rift, but still fifteen feet high. Many of our number could die without ever touching an enemy.

Henri stepped forward. He was a powerful water-worker, and though I hated that he'd be on our front line, I said nothing.

"Loose!" the prince bellowed, and water soared toward the wall of fire.

Some fae were clearly not as strong as others, as their attack made it only halfway, but others landed, so the fire sizzled, dying.

"Again!" Halad commanded.

The water elementals did as he said, and after three more dousings, the fire was mostly gone.

Halad nodded to Commander Verdan, handing control over to him.

A number of the fae in the group Halad had brought closed in. And more fluttered their wings and lifted off their horses to fly above us. Others would take their mounts to fight.

"Forward!" Commander Verdan cried, and the army charged.

Screams, horrible, high, and eerie, rang from our opposition as they charged as well.

It had begun.

"Let's move," I said, and my friends and the eight others who'd join us in the Rift surged forward.

I drew my sword and urged my horse into a trot that gained speed. My mount responded to my slightest touch, though surely it was as terrified as me. Its hooves pounded the grasslands as we closed in on our adversaries.

The fire now gone, I could easily see the Shadows.

Not that it was my first time doing so. I'd seen the creatures that had once been normal fae when they'd saved my aunt from her execution. But they hadn't fought then. They'd only been interested in saving Sela White.

This time was totally different.

They had the bodies of elves, faeries, dwarves, and other races of fae, but they were altered. Dark. Nearly demonic, but not quite demons. Almost like, if they tried hard enough, they could be saved.

Was that the case? Or just wishful thinking?

As our forces crashed into one another, as the first blood sprayed and bodies fell, I realized it didn't matter. We were here now. We were about to enter the Rift, about to save Elise—and hopefully bring down my aunt for good—and there was no going back.

Before I knew it, I was colliding with the opposing Shadows. The sword in my hand arched high, whining through the air.

It sliced off the head of a Shadow, and I moved on, not daring to look back.

My friends and I worked our way forward, inch by inch, step by step, foot by foot, fight by fight. The Shadows pressed us back, and we took the land again. With every pace gained, I waited for fire to rain from the sky. For the dragons to appear.

And then, they did. Heat bloomed in the air above me, as oppressing as when I sat on cement in L.A. in the thick of a summer afternoon. Worse, actually.

"Get on the ground!" someone, Halad, screamed, and I did, rolling off my horse.

I landed on my back, knocking the wind from me, but I kept my head and witnessed the instant Jax cast a shield over those with us.

It stretched out but wasn't fast enough—maybe it wasn't strong enough, either—to protect the fae flying above. They burned to nothing and the black beast soared onward, blasting fire at anyone who did not have gleaming red eyes.

Ash fell from the sky, sliding down the invisible shield, and shockingly, tears sprang into my eyes. I'd been through a lot. This wasn't my first battle, but this was different. Personal. In the land of my blood, the loss resonated deeply, forming a chasm within me.

"Up!" Jax shouted. "Shield is down!"

"Vanguard, fly!" Halad roared, and those fae who'd been in front of us, meant to take the first blows so we'd make it into the Rift, soared above to protect.

We didn't bother mounting the horses again, but pressed forward on foot. Every few steps, I got in another kill, more blood splattered.

Somehow, the pixie swarm had avoided being incinerated, and those tiny suckers were proving how vicious they could be. Together, they clouded around Shadows, their fangs sinking into skin.

"Almost as good as aether!" Halad noted appreciatively as Shadows fell to their knees, and the twins freaking fist-bumped mid-battle.

Of all the times! "Almost—crap!"

A Shadow, this one larger than most, leapt in front of me. He wielded an ax, and swung it down like I was nothing but a log that needed chopping in half.

I hurled my body out of the way, rolling on blood-drenched grass. By the time I sprang back up, I'd already recalculated my surroundings. I wasn't the only member of my group to be engaged in one-on-one combat. Everyone had an adversary.

For now, I was on my own.

I pulled my sword arm back as my foe approached, red eyes gleaming. There was no regard for life in them. They were just evil.

The ax came down again, and I retaliated, swinging my sword. It slashed into flesh, and the creature howled in pain. Before I could confirm if he was dead or not, I pushed onward, wheeling through Shadow after Shadow.

We'd come closer, within fifty feet of the Rift, when a familiar cry came from behind me. I whirled, and my heart dropped.

A Shadow's blade dripped with blood, and before the monster, Sansu sprawled on the ground, his neck open. Blood gushed from it, and though adrenaline rushed through me like a river, I found that I couldn't move.

For the first time in my life, I was frozen in a battle.

I thought of Circe, his beloved, who'd also died for her kingdom. Of Isadora, who loved the dwarf even though her daughter was no longer living. I thought of Sansu telling stories around the fire.

My throat closed. This wasn't right!

But before I could take a single step toward my friend, Alran was there, sword blazing. The Shadow's head fell to the dirt a moment later, and it took all that I had not to stomp on it.

"Alice! Move!" Halad yelled.

"But, Sansu!"

"He's gone, Al," Jax said, spinning and shooting magic at another adversary. "We're going to go the same way if we don't take our shot."

I twisted and his meaning became clear. One of the dragons had unintentionally burned part of their own army when they were attacking our people. Luckily for us, it was the very squad of Shadows that was standing between us and the Rift.

"It's coming back!" Dee shrieked from above.

"Go!" another fae above us yelled. "Run!"

Tears sprang into my eyes but I sprinted so hard that my legs burned. Fire blazed. I pushed harder. My friends were at my side, at my back, the pixies soaring just above. Shadows lunged, but we were fast in both blade and body, and they fell. The heat intensified, and though I didn't dare look up, I suspected we had only seconds of cover.

"Faster!" Henri roared as the dark mist of the Rift grew closer, so close I could smell the cold emanating off of it. "Have the crystals ready."

I ripped my illumination crystal from my pocket and looked up in time to see another blaze of fire, to watch the wind and water from the soldiers meet flames, the elements hissing on impact. Dee and Dum shot downward, their hands grabbing for my shoulders, my hair, any part of me, desperate to latch on.

The elemental attack was enough to save my friends and me, but not the guard above, and as I crossed into the Rift, ash rained down on my face.

CHAPTER 26

I'd wondered what it would be like to traverse the Rift, but I could never have imagined the eternal night of this hellscape. Where I stood, darkness surrounded me so thoroughly that I couldn't even see the tip of my nose. Cold rushed through my body, and a vile stench made me gag. It was almost bad enough for me to turn and run.

It felt so wrong in here. Evil. Hopeless.

Light flared from Jax at my side.

"Al! The crystal!"

I jolted and followed his lead. Light bloomed from the stone in my palm, and from where she perched on my shoulder, Dum shielded her eyes at the brightness of it. Dee, on the other hand, didn't seem to notice. She stared backward, the way we'd come, where the swarm was still fighting. Hopefully, still alive. Guilt and despair flooded me and trying to stave it off, I swallowed and looked at the gem. My power poured into it and the glow it gave was strong. Combined with Jax's illumination, we safely encompassed fifteen souls.

We'd come with the intention of crossing the Rift with an army, and that had been pared down to this.

Just getting into the Rift, we'd lost many lives. Sansu among them. My throat tightened at the memory of his fall.

"We need to go deeper," Halad said. "What's to stop the dragon from coming in?"

He was right. Although I wanted to run back into the battle to grab Sansu's cold hand and pull him with us—to make sure he remained untouched by Shadows, his body whole—I refrained.

My heart hated it, but there wouldn't be a point. Corpses wouldn't help us on this quest.

"Alice," Henri whispered.

I turned to him toward the fae I loved. Behind him, everyone else was waiting, watching me, ready to venture deeper into the inkwell that was our reality.

The prophecy had said I'd lead Wonderland into darkness. Perhaps I'd subverted that fortune, left it broken and useless, but that didn't really bring me complete peace. Not now, anyway. My friends were here with me, and though we didn't know what to expect, we were clearly in danger. I couldn't lose them. Not even one. I may not survive it.

"Stay close." I held the illumination crystal overhead to give us a large barrier of light.

We took our first steps, then our first dozen. Goose-bumps ravaged my arms, and beneath my feet, something cracked or shattered every few steps. I envisioned bones, but didn't dare look down to check. How wide was the Rift?

"Anyone feel anything yet?" Alran asked, his voice raspy. Tears streaked the elf's face. Out of those in our group, he had been closest to Sansu.

Pain for the dwarf we'd lost to the aether washed over me anew.

Don't let his death be in vain.

"It's cold," Jax answered. "And the energies feel off."

"Like we're being stalked by something really vile," I said in agreement. "Like when Doru would hunt us during training."

"Yup." Jax closed his eyes and shuddered.

Since we'd made up, I had no reservations about pulling him into a side hug, so I moved to do just that, but the next moment, Calia was there, her bloodied hand on Jax's shoulder, lending him strength.

I smiled, hoping more was blooming between them than a flirtation or a fling.

"Do you think more dragons are after us? Or maybe the ones from the battle have already entered the Rift? Would we hear them in here with us?" Henri's green eyes scanned the darkness ahead.

I doubted he could see beyond our illumination bubble, but I did the same because we had to look somewhere.

"I'm certain we'd hear them," Halad said. "They were loud in the battle, wanted to announce their presence. And I can hear wind, or something like it, so the Rift isn't devoid of sound."

A soldier in Riverlands green nodded his agreement. He walked on the edge of the illumination, the darkness wafting into our light faintly, as if it wanted to caress his shoulder. "From what I know of dragons, that's normal. I hope—"

A hiss cut through the eerie quiet, and the male fae screamed as black tentacles that looked like smoke wrapped around him and sucked him into the never-ending night. Immediately, we lost sight of him.

Acting on instinct, we bolted, scattering away from one another, weapons drawn as if this was some foe of blood and bone and breath, and not . . . whatever it was.

Big mistake.

More ribbons shot out, taking a female soldier from Wonderland. Then another male from the Riverlands.

"Stand together!" Henri shouted.

Like oil in water, we coalesced, pressed so tightly, I could feel Alran and Calia shaking at my sides. I shot a look at Jax, who gave a terse nod, and together, we pushed our magic into the crystals.

Three more feet of illumination expanded on all sides, and though tiny fingers of blackness tried to encroach again, to pick off a susceptible figure, they couldn't. They would only venture into the very edges of our light, furthest away from the crystal.

I exhaled. The crystal was working, and against all odds, Jax and I were torches in this horrible night. We just had to keep it up long enough to get the hell out of here.

"Hold hands," I ordered, extending only one of mine, since I needed to keep the illumination crystal in the other. "And whatever you do, don't let go."

Henri grabbed my hand, his other going to Halad's.

One by one, our party formed a chain and wrapped into an open circle. Once we were as safe as we'd get, we prowled forward.

I wasn't sure how far we'd gone, but a sense of security had begun to hover tentatively over me. We'd figured it out. Not soon enough to keep everyone safe, but I'd have to dwell on the lives lost *after* we left the Dark Court. Doing so now might cost more souls.

"Anyone see that smoke again?" Calia asked warily.

"None," I replied. "I think—"

I cut off as my eyes began to water. I blinked, thinking it was dust from the ground, which was dry beneath my feet. Blinking did nothing, however, and a minute later, the pain had grown exponentially. My eyes were still watering, and the discomfort had spread down to my throat. It itched like the devil.

From where she and Dee flew above, Dum coughed and drooped. I wanted to reach up to make sure she didn't fall, but didn't dare let go of Hatter.

But then the twins' wings stopped fluttering, and like flies that had flown into a toxic cloud, the pixies fell to the ground.

"Stop!" I screamed, not wanting anyone to step on them.

Halting abruptly, others shot me confused glances. I pointed down as dread crept through me, my heart thundering so hard I could hear it in my ears. Though I wanted to move, to give them CPR or something —*anything* to save them—I couldn't move. No matter how much I wanted to, fear gripped me too tightly. Thankfully, others had more control over themselves and Alran carefully broke the chain and scooped them up.

Their bodies were limp. Their chests still, not even a hint of a movement indicating that they drew breath.

"Are they—" My question died on my lips as one of the Snowcap soldiers, a short and petite female, fell to her knees, gasping for air.

Realization struck like a match being lit. Whatever was making my throat itch was toxic. It was probably affecting all of us, but the smallest ones were suffering the most. They were the canaries in the coal mine, so to speak.

As if in confirmation, my next inhales came harder than normal, tighter.

"Guys," I whispered. "Is anyone else itching and finding it hard to breathe?"

Everyone nodded and I swallowed thickly.

"There's poison in the air, we have to run! Alran, can you help her?" I pointed to the Snowcap soldier. She looked like she might topple over at any second.

"Take the twins," the large elf ordered, handing Dee and Dum to Halad.

"In here." Halad stepped forward, opening his cloak to reveal large inner pockets.

Gently, the prince settled them in his pockets, and Alran scooped up the short fae, draping her over his shoulder, fireman style.

"Get in the center," I told Alran. As there was no way he could be a part of the chain, he needed protection.

"Everyone else, stay in position," Halad reminded us.

Then, we ran.

Perhaps the fact that we were having to breathe more exacerbated the toll the poison was taking on us. Each inhale burned like fire, and my eyes watered as if I'd burst from the depths of a lake.

How much further?

It was impossible to tell. No one knew exactly how wide the Rift was here. Then, an even worse thought crashed over me. What if we hadn't cut a direct course?

"Have we been moving forward in a straight line? Does anyone know?"

No one spoke, and I felt even worse. Clearly, none of us had been thinking about that. We'd been on edge since the second we entered the Rift and it had begun to kill us off.

"Straight," I said, wheezing slightly now, but determined to take on the power of positive thinking. "Keep going straight. I think we are."

"Yeah!" Jax urged, as if also trying to convince

himself by sheer force of effort. "We're on the right track."

Our legs ate up the ground, and my muscles began to burn as hot as my throat and eyes. It was hard to guess how far we'd gone, but if I had to estimate by the pain brought on from running, I'd say a mile or so.

"Hey! Who hears that?" Alran was panting. On his shoulder bounced the other soldier, now completely passed out. "The voices!"

"What are you talking abo—"

The words died on my tongue, because at that moment, three voices—belonging to Hatter, Dee, and Dum—spoke in my head. More accurately, they were *screaming*, begging for help, for *me*.

The hairs on my arms stood up, but since my friends were with me, it took me only a second to realize that their cries weren't real.

Like in the Enchanted Forest, I thought as yet another of the soldiers we'd asked to accompany us broke away.

"Trisi!" she screamed and twisted into the darkness.

I spun and transfixed on her blonde braid, as fingers of black wrapped around the fae and pulled her into the inky night.

Just like that, another soldier was gone.

I feared she wouldn't be the last. Halad, too, seemed to be engrossed by whomever he heard in the expanse of the Rift, and broke the chain. He jerked left and leapt for the blackness. As one, Henri and I severed our connection to catch him and pull him back.

"No! *Father! Mother!*"

"Halad! It's not real!" I shouted, trying to overpower the voices in his head, those of the Queen and King of the Riverlands, begging for help. The effort made my throat burn harder. I swallowed. The air still burned dipping into my lungs. We needed to run, to get out of here before the combined psychological and physical torture killed us all.

"I have an idea!" Jax called out. Unlike the others, he looked pained, but not tempted.

I understood why. He had few he loved. In that way, we were so similar.

A spell slipped off his lips, and all sounds ceased. I looked at him, and the wizard pointed with the illumination crystal, straight ahead, as if to say, *keep going*.

I wouldn't be able to hear him or the others as long as the spell was in place. This was good against the sounds that were screwing with us, but bad if someone got injured. Still, it was the best we could do, so we trudged forward, throats and eyes burning.

With each step, I prayed harder that this was the right way. That we hadn't screwed it up. That I hadn't led these people to their doom.

When the light came, it was instantaneous and blinding. One moment, we were in the pitch-black of the Rift, the next, I was closing my eyes against natural sunlight, reclaiming my hand from Henri's to shield my vision. Frantically, I gulped down the cool, pure air and my desperate lungs filled. A cry of relief ripped from my raw throat, but I couldn't hear it—or anything else—thanks to Jax's charm.

So when I opened my eyes and found three fae, I jumped. A male, a female, and a young boy, all with various shades of red wings and dressed in rags, stood before a backdrop of dead forest and watched us with wide eyes.

We hadn't entered the city, which was probably for the best, but this wasn't ideal either. Already, we'd been spotted, and the fae looked at us like we were mutants.

The male held a blade in his trembling hands. His lips, chapped and bleeding, moved, but no sound hit my ears.

I twirled, found Jax, and shook him. Reluctantly, he opened his eyes to the brightness, and I pointed to my ears. With a snap of his fingers, the charm lifted.

"Who are you?! Tell us! Tell us *now!*" the male fae was shouting, his voice deep but shaky.

I turned back to them, dropping the crystal to the ground to show I meant them no harm. Only then did I notice ash from the Rift, floating down around us and fluttering to the ground, a macabre kind of snow.

"We're here to save a prisoner," I told the man, knowing that a story wouldn't work here. I had to tell the truth. If it backfired, we'd deal with these people then. By the old gods, I hoped it wouldn't come to that. "To take her home from this court, back where she belongs."

The tall male, so thin I could probably break him in half with my bare hands, looked to the female, then to the youngling. The boy couldn't be more than nine years old, and trembled like a leaf in the wind.

The male fae stepped forward. "If we help you, will you take us too?"

Hope shone in their eyes, and suddenly, I realized how this must look: a group of well-fed, muscular, healthy people had walked out of the nightmare that shielded the Dark Court. Their home, their prison.

"Yes," I said firmly.

The female choked out a sob, while the male closed his eyes, as if fighting back tears. The child simply looked lost. He'd been born here, raised here. He knew nothing else.

Though our circumstances were different, I understood. I'd been raised by a vampire lord and known nothing else until Herald the pooka arrived in California.

It only took one person to change a life.

Halad spun to face me. "Alice, it's too dangerous. We've lost many. And the battle, what if it's still raging when we return?"

"I can't leave them."

"You can't take the entire kingdom with you." In his cloak pocket something stirred, distracting him. Quickly, he pulled out Dee and Dum. They were still unconscious, but breathing deeper. They'd wake soon. I hoped.

Watching the pixies, pain lanced through me, as sharp as though it had been dealt by a sword. We'd almost lost them, which led me to only one conclusion: Halad was right.

There was no possible way I could bring so many back. Not without obliterating the Rift first, and though I thought pretty highly of myself at times, destroying the inky stain wasn't within my scope.

Could anyone do such a thing?

Maybe the old gods . . . but not me. No aether-blessed fae is strong enough to take that on.

"I know," I said finally, "but we can help these people. And that *matters*. Tell me you don't agree."

The prince didn't respond, and I knew he was thinking of his own subjects, of what he'd risk to save them.

Those of the Dark Court weren't so far from being Riverland or Wonderland fae. Only a thin line of night-mares and a bit of ocean separated us.

"They're coming," Henri agreed, stepping forward with an easy smile.

The female stopped sobbing. Catching Hatter's motion, she pulled her son closer.

Henri stopped. "We won't hurt you, but we could use your help. Do you know where the castle is? And even better, how to get in?"

"We do," she said hesitantly. "We supply Shadowveil Castle with fruit, so we cart our produce there often."

My brow furrowed. Fruit? The trees I could see were dead. I doubted a single leaf would be able to grow on a branch. How would fruit thrive?

"Our farm is close by, though you're correct in your thinkin'," the male said, clearly noticing my confusion.

"Our orchard takes much tending and earth magic. It often drains me and my mate. Though we still take it as a blessing that our magic even works."

"I see," I said. "Well, we need to get into the palace as soon as we can. Is it close?"

"Beyond this grove and through the city wall." The male chewed his lip, as if debating something. "I'm set to take a wagon of apples today. You could ride among the fruit, hide in it."

"Your wagon is that large?" Halad asked.

"The crown only allows a few families to produce fruit. As such, we must supply the city with much food, and require wagons that would carry thirty men—or a dozen fae and many apples. So yes, it's large enough to hide you."

I looked to my friends, to the pixies, still limp in Halad's large hands. Was the infiltration scheme ideal? Probably not. It risked innocents and relied on guards being sloppy. But it *would* save us a ton of time trying to figure out how to get through the city gates and sneak into a castle that we knew nothing about.

"That works for us," I told the ragged family. "If you need help loading up, we're here to assist."

CHAPTER 27

The father and mother were Daga and Latzi. Theg, their son, was clearly their pride and joy. Their home was a two-room shack, most of which had been taken over by crates of apples they'd harvested so they wouldn't starve to death.

Apparently, food was expensive here, so most farmers survived on what they grew or caught. However, the woods weren't rife with prey like in the Riverlands, so meat was a treat.

It all made me furious.

I didn't know why the leader of the Dark Court had imprisoned his people in this hellhole, or how. But I knew one thing: if I got the chance to end him when I went looking for my aunt and Elise, I would. He deserved nothing less than a long, tortuous death, though whether that be by dagger or magic, I didn't care.

"What is your king's name?" I asked Latzi as she poured another box of apples into the cart.

The conveyance was larger than I'd expected, and it shocked me that their twiggy horses could pull it.

"King Icul. His son and only heir is Prince Mionis. They're cut from the same cloth."

I tipped the contents of my crate in after hers, and then we turned around, going back for more. My friends did the same, with Daga and Theg in their midst.

The pixies, now back to normal, flew above, too small to lift boxes of their own, but even the short soldier from the Snowcap court helped. She'd regained consciousness before we arrived at the farm, and so far, there seemed to be no lasting effects from the Rift's attack. The same was true of the twins, thank the old gods.

When we entered the storage shed, I eyed the diminishing mountain of apples. Only a few more crates' worth, and we'd be ready to go.

"Have you ever seen my sister? Princess Elise." I asked as Latzi began double-checking the crates of apples for bad ones. I'd offered to help before, but she'd declined. She didn't want to risk anyone of my friends letting a bad apple slide and angering the castle. Even if they planned to escape, they were fearful of the palace's wrath. So instead of diving into the crate with her, I leaned against a wall and let her do her job. "Maybe she was walking the city or something?"

We'd filled them in on our mission on the way back to

their home. Now they knew who Elise was, who I was. And they'd accepted the story and our aim.

Latzi averted her gaze, the gesture so sad, weak, that it hit me in the gut.

There was so much good I could do here. I looked the fae over, took in her drooping wings. Once, they'd probably shone a brilliant red, but now the color was dull. I'd never seen that on a faerie before. The city was a short ride away, and in it lived more fae like Latzi.

So many people to help.

"I saw her once," she said. "From afar."

"How did she look?"

"Beautiful."

That wasn't really what I'd meant, but then again, perhaps it was. If Elise was considered beautiful, she probably was not malnourished or beaten. She was likely healthy.

"She radiates. Even here, among death and destruction," Latzi added, tossing a piece of bruised fruit out of the crate with a frown. "I think they treat her well." She sighed. "If only the king cared as much for his people. Did you know your sister is only about ten years my junior? I look much older."

Yes, she did. Latzi was only twenty-four, but, though fae were a race that retained their youth for a long time, she looked at least thirty-five. The hard life of this court had aged her. Probably Daga, too. But Theg . . .

"How old is your son?"

"Nine. I had him very young. That is common here." Her eyes softened. "Children are one of our only joys."

I couldn't imagine having a child at fifteen, having to care for it on my own. I would have been so lost.

This talk of her life was starting to depress me, so I exhaled and changed the subject. "Were you in the city when the jabberwocky arrived?"

She shook her head vehemently. "I have not seen the Queen of Wonderland. Nor her beast. I only heard gossip that she was here, having fled her lands."

"Ex-queen," I reminded her, swatting at a spider that descended from the rafters.

"Yes, of course. Though, she doesn't call herself that. At first, I thought she'd arrived for the ceremony rather than to seek refuge."

Ceremony? That hadn't been mentioned. If an event was taking place, it would be good to know.

"What's happening in the city?"

Latzi stopped sorting out the bad apples and gave me a curious look. "Princess Elise is to marry Prince Mionis at sunset."

"Sunset *today*?!"

"Of course. When you mentioned rescuing her, I'd guessed that you had planned it that way."

"No, but thank goodness we arrived in time! Nobody knows anything of what goes on in this court. Does news travel here?"

I'd always assumed their isolation went both ways, but King Icul had to have a way to receive information. Spies.

Otherwise, how would Shadows have known to show up at my aunt's execution. Seeing as the spies couldn't be Shadows—they stood out too much—I wondered how long they'd been in other kingdoms. Did they get through the Rift the way we had? Or did they do so under the protection of Shadows, like my aunt had apparently done?

"We are kept in the dark." She gestured in the direction the Rift loomed, not far away, "In a way, literally."

"Do you know how wide the Rift is?" I asked, completely aware how random the question was, but this information would be useful when we fled.

"It's said that the fastest Shadows can run through the darkness in twelve minutes."

I'd seen the Shadows move. They were freakishly fast. I was in excellent shape myself and could bust out a five-and-a-half-minute mile if I needed to. It would not surprise me if the Shadows regularly sustained six-minute miles.

Taking that into account, I guessed the Rift was about two miles wide.

"And the width of where we exited?"

"I cannot say," Latzi grunted, hefting a crate of apples onto her shoulder. "I've never been on the other side." She gestured to the other box of fruit she'd been rifling through. "These are pristine. Take one."

"Can you run through the Rift then?" I asked, grabbing my own crate. "We will have to leave quickly. Perhaps a mad dash to escape."

"We do not run often. Have to save our energy for work."

I didn't ask anything else, sensing I'd gotten as much out of her as she knew, and just hauled my apples to the wagon.

Once we'd deposited the fruit and the others followed, it was full.

Latzi beamed at the load. "It usually takes much longer to fill. Many hands make light work."

She reached out for my empty crate, which I gave to her, and she returned it to the shed. As she walked, I couldn't help but notice how her arms trembled.

It had been a lot of work, even spread thin. How did this family of three usually handle it themselves?

Henri appeared at my side. "I wish we could take more fae away from this place."

"Me too. But Halad is right. The more we take, the more dangerous it gets. For everyone." I twisted, catching sight of the blight again. I doubted there was a single place in this kingdom where it wasn't visible. "And when we get back to the Riverlands, they would find themselves involved in a battle. There's no way they are strong enough to fight."

Hatter pulled me close. "We're doing the best we can."

I nodded and rested into him, and once Latzi returned, her and her husband rearranged the apples, making spaces for us.

They didn't trust anyone else to do it, fearing that

doing so might cause damage to their merchandise. Even though it took more time, leaving the task solely to them, I understood and waited.

Finally, ten human-sized pits formed in the vast pile of apples. Daga looked us over. "The disguises are already in the wagon, so we were ready. Those with wings, will you please assist those without? Put them in a hole—preferably without bruising the flesh of the fruit."

I turned and found Jax standing behind me. He shrugged sheepishly and lifted his arms. "No spell for this."

I laughed. Not having to worry about him trying to win me back was really a weight lifted off my shoulders. "We've got you."

With the help of Calia, who I'd shared a few words with since arriving at Daga's and Latzi's orchard, I lifted Jax into a hole. Soon enough, everyone else was nestled in too.

The pixies shared my hole, and once we were all ready, the farmers covered us with apples. The sweet scent of the fruit engulfed me, and I inhaled deeply.

A hand wormed its way through the fruit from the hole nearest mine and brushed my arm. "Alice."

"Henri," I whispered. "You, okay?"

"Don't move!" Daga called out. "Not until we're in the palace and tell you the coast is clear. There are many apples above you, but one shift in your bodies, and you might uncover your heads."

Alran, easily the tallest and most built of our group,

probably only had a clearance of about a foot of the fruit above him.

"We're putting the covering on the wagon now, so it will get dark," Latzi warned softly. "But be assured guards will check on the produce before we get to the palace. We'll pull the cover back before that to make sure you're not visible. If you are, there may be a bit of a scramble to get you situated again."

"Is it time to say goodbye to our home, Mother?" Theg asked, his tone wobbly.

Earlier, they'd taken him aside to explain what was going to happen. He'd seemed confused, but how could he be any other way? Daga and Latzi had never even left this court, so Theg certainly hadn't. He had no idea what to expect, but at least his parents had had more time to hear tales of the outside.

"It is, Son. Say it from here and be grateful. Soon, we'll be free." A strap of leather cracked against the horses' rumps, and suddenly, we were inching forward.

I swallowed, and closed my eyes. I felt so raw for these people, like I was responsible for them. I hoped to all the old gods that I could deliver them to safety and a better life.

The wagon jostled, and I wondered how long we'd been going. It felt like forever, but probably hadn't been more than an hour. Not thinking about the canvas covering us, eliminating a view of the sun in the sky, I glanced up and an apple bonked me in the eye. A soft stream of curses rang from my lips.

"Alice?" Henri whispered.

"I'm fine," I assured him. "Just antsy."

The cart made enough noise as it rolled over dirt roads and, eventually, the cobblestones in the city, that there'd been a fair amount of whispering during the ride. But from the noises outside, the talking, the yelling, the crying of children—and, most notably, the absence of laughter—I could tell that we were in the thick of civilization now. We had to be more careful about our communication.

"Should be there any minute, Theg!" Daga said loudly, as if his son was begging to know how much longer the ride would be, though Theg had asked no such question. It was our signal. "That's the gate, just up there."

My muscles tensed. This was it. The moment of truth. Once they got in line, Latzi would check that we were still covered. As long as the guards were lazy about their inspection, as Latzi said they usually were, we'd be fine.

But literally one hair in sight, and we were screwed.

"It's okay, Alice." Dum tried to soothe me from her position in the same apple hole as me, though she sounded pretty nervous herself.

"It has to be," I whispered back.

The wagon slowed, then stopped. I waited, wondering how many carts were ahead of ours, when Daga spoke.

"They'll get through these three merchants fast. Their carts are small."

I swallowed, taking in the information Daga was giving.

"Why don't you prepare the wagon for viewing, Latzi?" he continued. "Theg, help your mother."

Above, the canvas covering the apples, hiding them from sight of the hungry residents of the Dark Court, rustled, and light filtered through the layer of fruit weighing down on me. Latzi and her son balanced their small frames on the floorboards that wreathed the wagon, and then pulled the fabric back inch by inch.

"All done. Everything looks good. No bruises," she said, and I exhaled a breath.

We were still not visible. As long as the guards didn't dig for fruit, we'd be fine.

The wagon rolled forward once, twice, three times, and then we were there.

"Halt," a gruff voice called out. "What have you here?"

"Apples for the wedding," Latzi said sweetly.

"They ordered this many?" the guard sounded skeptical.

"Well, it is our dear prince's wedding day!" Daga boomed, as if he really cared that Prince Mionis was to be wed.

Preposterous. Why would anyone care about a monarch who treated them so poorly?

"True. The kitchens have been at work since dawn. Let me see . . ." The guard stepped closer, his boots scuffing the ground. "Maybe I should test one."

The wagon shifted as his weight landed on the right-hand floorboard. Though I couldn't see him, I swore I felt him peering in.

My heart began to race, and I fought the urge to curl in on myself and make my body smaller, more hidden beneath the fruit.

"This one's nice. Thanks."

"Pleasure," Latzi said, though she didn't sound like she meant it. "Might we go?"

"You know where to deposit the goods?"

"We do. We supply the palace with fruit often."

"On your way, then."

Again, we rolled forward. Everyone stayed quiet until the wagon stopped once more. Then, at the front, the family dropped to the ground.

"Theg, be a good lad and make sure no one is coming. Over there." Daga must have pointed some-where, because light, fast footsteps sounded and quickly faded.

"One at a time," Latzi instructed us from nearby. "Alice first."

I raised a hand, and Daga grabbed it, helping me out. Once I was free to fly, I did so, shaking the perfume of apple from me as I landed lightly. "The *Olizati* robes?"

We hadn't wanted to wear them when we'd been covered in fruit. It had been too hot in there for the extra layer. But we needed a disguise, and apparently, the *Olizati,* holy fae of this court, wore plain black robes when they traveled the Dark Court to help those in need. Which, in this place, was basically everyone. It was a simple cover, and I knew from experience those were often best.

"Under the seat," Latzi said, grabbing another hand —Halad's—and pulling him up from the pit of fruit.

I retrieved the disguises the family had procured for us, garments that, Theg had let slip, had cost them what meager savings they had—the money that was supposed to buy them food for the next week.

I cradled the rough-spun and scratchy robes as, one by one, my friends emerged from the wagon. They came to me, and I handed out the burlap-feeling garments.

"Where will you be?" I asked our hosts when everyone was cloaked and Dee and Dum were hiding in the inner pockets of my robe.

Pockets which Latzi had hand-sewn hours ago because, while pixies lived in this kingdom, we couldn't be sure how common they were at Court.

"Around this area," Latzi said. She pointed to the right. "The kitchens are through that door. The palace's methods of bringing in food lack structure, so we are often here for hours, waiting to be relieved of our wares and paid."

"What a waste of time!" I said, indignant on their behalf.

"Nothing is easy here," she agreed. Then she pivoted so that she faced the kitchen doors. "I've been inside once. If you enter through there, you'll be on the lower levels. Take the first staircase up, and that will lead you into the castle proper, into a foyer of sorts—I'm not sure what it's really called. From there, your guess is as good as mine as to where your sister's quarters are."

"You're sure she's there, though?"

She nodded. "It's tradition for a bride's maids and ladies to indulge her all day in her chambers. For most in the Dark Court, such a luxury is impossible—a relic of when times were better here."

Her lips compressed, her eyes going to Theg before she continued, "Most fae have no 'chambers' to speak of. But your sister will have her own space. She will be there until the ceremony begins."

So we had to find Elise's rooms, glamour her, then extract her and return here. After that, we'd escape the city.

Then, the real work would begin.

"Thank you," I said. "We'll return soon."

I could only hope I was telling the truth.

CHAPTER 28

Though I wished Latzi or Daga could show us the way through the palace, there was absolutely no way I'd ask them to risk their lives.

Even in the itchy cloaks that hid much of our figures, our group stood out. None of us were starved.

Everyone tried to mimic an injury as we entered the kitchen, but I wasn't sure we were at all convincing. Henri's back was too straight and confident. Jax walked with a swagger that he couldn't seem to quit, and Alran was a beast of an elf, radiating power no matter what he did.

Can elves even get that large here, when food is so scarce?

Our new friends had mentioned that most fae here had been struck in anger by the Crown at least once. Most did not survive it unchanged, and that change was something that couldn't be faked.

It was obvious we were unbroken in that way. Unbowed.

Perhaps it would have been better to procure guard uniforms?

To hear Daga tell it, they were at least better fed than the rest of the fae in the Dark Court.

But as our group of ten, plus two concealed pixies, entered the kitchens, eyes simply shifted to us, then back to what they were doing. Each worker wore a limp, gray smock, even the males.

Cheaper to produce only one outfit, no doubt.

The worktops gleamed, but the ovens looked old and worn—the floor was scuffed, cracking in places. A sharp lemon scent hung heavy in the air, as if the workers were constantly cleaning every nook and cranny to make sure everything was up to standards. This was no deluxe kitchen, though surely the staff and servants did their best to mimic the quality of one.

We'd interrupted what was clearly a busy time, so most barely looked at us. However, one fae did approach. The old female limped aggressively, but even so, she had the air of a person with a shred of authority. She must be the head of the kitchen.

"What are *Olizati* doing in here?" she demanded.

"We were called in to help today, to bring refreshments to Princess Elise," Alran grunted, looming over the female.

These people were downtrodden, but we weren't above using intimidation if necessary. We were on a mission, after all.

"Why?" the woman arched an eyebrow.

"She's been in her quarters all day and is famished."

Inside the deep pocket of my cloak, one of the pixie twins shifted. The motion caught the old fae's attention.

"Can you help us?" I asked, trying to stop her from staring at the spot on my cloak.

"Why not send one of her ladies?" The kitchen worker's eyes narrowed. "That's their job, is it not?"

"Of course it is, normally—but this is no normal day," Calia interjected. "The princess also requested that we dispense food to others along the way. A tithing to the people, if you will."

The old female's shoulders softened, and the annoyance left her face. "That does sound like the princess. Here, then, I'll give you extra. But if anyone running the castle asks . . ."

"We will not mention it," Calia assured her.

I blinked as the old fae turned her back to us to gather rations. Calia twisted, catching my eye, and I nodded my thanks.

One hurdle down and no bloodshed.

I hoped we could get through the rest of the castle without hurting anyone. After all, it wasn't their fault they lived under the rule of a tyrant, nor that they worked here.

Still, I wasn't holding my breath. If I had to use my magic or the dagger slung around my waist to get to Elise, I would. Too many had already laid their lives on the line for this mission. Failure was not an option.

And if I crossed paths with my aunt, violence was certainly in my future.

A stream of cooks and bakers and children who looked far too young to be working approached next, weighing our arms down with trays. Platters were filled with fruits, cured meats, breads, and other delicacies I couldn't place. It rankled that the king could have all this and not care if fae died from starvation outside his walls.

"Which do you suggest we feed the people from?" Calia asked the woman in charge. "I would not like to give them any of Princess Elise's favorites."

A smart way of asking what was valued most in this kingdom. What would draw the most attention—even from a crowd of hungry citizens—if we gave it away as a distraction.

"She's partial to the berries and cream," the old fae replied. "Not so much the bread. But as you can see, there are many loaves. Bread fills bellies." She gave a small smile. I got the sense that she was tough because she had to be, but really, she'd do what she could for her people too.

"Someone get the door for them!" the old fae yelled then. "Their hands are full."

In another stroke of luck, we were directed out the proper door, and as the kitchens were located at the end of a passage, we went the only way available to us.

As soon as we were far enough away, Calia, who walked in front of me, turned.

"Thank you," I whispered. "You probably saved us."

"It's what Queen Aquatia would do," she replied. "I try to emulate her."

I, too, admired the queen. "She is full of goodness. Definitely someone to look up to."

Calia eyed me with interest. "You are too, you know."

I swallowed. Few had ever called me good. Or a role model.

I didn't respond, just let the words settle over me as we neared the end of the hall and reached the stairs.

"They said up," Jax murmured loud enough for everyone in our group to hear. "Once we get to the main floors, then what? Did you work something out, Al?"

I'd been dreading this moment, but to get what we needed and raise as little suspicion as possible, there was only one thing to do.

"I'll create a distraction that draws lots of fae. From there, Henri and Alran will take a servant hostage and question them. Once we have the information we need, I'll make them pass out."

No blood. Hopefully. But innocent people were going to get hurt no matter what I tried to do.

I prayed the distraction wouldn't raise my aunt's attention before we got to Elise. It said a lot that I was more worried about her than the King and Prince of the Dark Court.

"You gonna steal their air to distract?" Jax asked.

"Yup."

It was the easiest way, untraceable too. The small matter holding me back was that only strong air elementals could pull air from another's lungs. I was incredibly strong with air, but how many others in the kingdom shared that magic? To hear Latzi tell it, most fae magic here was weak—they needed all their energy to survive. Her family was an exception, having strong earth magic, which is why they were given the job of tending orchards.

Really, they were more like slaves, using their powers so that the kingdom—the royals in particular—would have fruit to delight their tongues.

Among the other exceptions of this magical weakness were the royals and the soldiers. Perhaps nobles too, and they'd be in the palace. But were any good with air specifically? I couldn't be sure and that might give us away. Should the Red Queen hear of what happened, would she suspect I'd come? Or would she think of me only after we snatched Elise from her room?

Then again, my aunt might be proud enough to believe I'd never get through the Rift. Without Roshia's help in the Crystal Court, she would have been right about that. But Sela might also realize that we were of the same blood, and some things crossed over. As much as I hated her, the Red Queen was as determined as me.

"How about I use a sleeping spell on the one giving us info?" Jax offered. "That way, only one loses their air. Less chance your power will raise suspicion."

"Good idea." I smiled at him. "I'm glad you're here, Jax."

The words were out of my mouth before I could stop

them. But I found that I didn't want to anyway. His arrival had been unwelcomed, his declaration of wanting me back even more so, but now things were good between us.

I'd needed the closure, the assurance that I didn't still love him, even more than I'd thought. I'd also needed him to know how badly he'd hurt me. And now, we needed his magic, powers that were not common in this world, to save my sister.

Jax might have come into my world like a wrecking ball, but in the end, he was helping piece it back together.

If we lived through this, that was . . .

"We've got this, Al," Jax said. "We're survivors. Always have been."

I jerked my chin up in agreement. "Let's go. Jax and me in the front. Hatter and Alran, be ready to snag a servant and question them. Everyone else, just don't drop your food or the cover."

If this didn't work, we'd have to entice a starving servant with the grub. That sounded more peaceful, but also repugnant. I didn't want to use food, something these fae needed to *live*, to get what I needed. I'd rather take the information and then pass out the food with no strings attached.

As a group, we climbed the steps. Though I'd fashioned an image of the Dark Court castle in my mind, the reality was so different that, at the top landing, I stopped.

From where they'd been tucked neatly and quietly in

my robes Dee and Dum let out a squeal, and Halad slammed into my back, almost bowling me over.

"What are you doing!?" the prince hissed. "I nearly dropped the bread."

"Sorry," I whispered back. "Didn't expect . . . *this* . . .
"

This room—an entryway, or something like it— gleamed black and red. Statues of fae on the sides of the cavernous space were adorned with garnets in their eyes, making the hairs on my arms raise. They looked like the Shadows. Evil. Not like other fae at all.

While the kitchen had been old and dingy, in the main levels of Shadowveil Castle, everything was immaculate and dark as hell. Busy too. Fae walked to and fro. This was clearly an area where paths crossed; if not close to the front doors, then at least a point where wings of the castle met.

"The name is Shadowveil. What did you expect?" Halad scoffed, annoyance in his tone. "We fae are rarely overly creative with our decor. In that respect, we follow nature."

He had a point. The Riverlands was largely green, but a massive river did run beneath the castle, audible from almost every room.

"Take your pick of a target," Jax whispered to me. "Ten o'clock. Far end of the room. He looks promising."

I climbed the last step, trying to appear like what I was seeing did not shock the hell out of me, and searched for the fae Jax directed me to.

He'd chosen well. The man was well-dressed and the only fat fae I'd seen since we entered this court. His physical state could be natural cause for shortness of breath, which added a layer of protection against my influence being discovered, but more than that, it made me *want* to target him. Whoever this fae was, he was important, and gluttonous while others starved.

"On it," I replied. "The rest of you, get ready. This will draw a crowd for sure."

I struck out with my air magic, and slowly began to tease the oxygen from the fae's lungs. It took only seconds before the plump lord, whoever he was, stumbled. His hand went to his heart, his eyes wide as he caught himself.

That he didn't look around in suspicion that someone was attacking him was a victory, but I didn't slow in either my step or my attack. More air left him, and after a dozen heartbeats, the fae stopped walking altogether.

Around us, others noticed his pause, their eyes going to him. When he fell to his knees with a *crack* a moment later, at least twenty servants were already rushing over to the male, calling Lord Stavel's name with worry.

"Now!" I hissed to Henri and Alran.

"Target in sight," Alran replied. "Take this," he murmured to someone.

A tray shuffled to other hands behind me, but I pretended not to notice. Instead, our crowd had stopped to take in Lord Stavel in mock-horror. All the while, I continued depriving him of oxygen—and would for as long as it took my friends to work.

Thankfully, the pair were on it. From the corner of my eye, I caught them approaching another fae who was on his way to check on Stavel. The servant appeared harassed when they stopped him, determined to get to the lord and assist. But Henri and Alran were like mountains, unmovable.

Their size and their trustworthiness were why I'd given them this job. I could count on them. A point that was proven when the servant tried to run past Henri, and my man grabbed him by the arm, wrenching him back.

The servant's eyes were wide with fear, though not for himself . . . for the lord dying a few feet away.

Like Stavel would even bat an eye if you were dying in the street, man.

It infuriated me that people like the fat fae got so much respect here when they were abusing their power.

"*Olizati! Olizati!* We need a blessing!" someone called from the crowd gathering around the lord.

Jax swore. "I guess this is what the holy fae do."

Frustration that I hadn't foreseen this cut through me.

"One moment!" I called back to the one that had summoned us. Then I lowered my voice. "Jax, take care of the servant. The rest of you, stay back and be ready. The moment the lord wakes, we leave."

"You got it." My ex turned and swept toward Hatter.

Though I couldn't see it, I could tell by the way the servant calmed that the wizard had seen fit to use a spell on him. Whatever he'd done, I hoped it wouldn't draw suspicion.

"Olizati!"

"I'm coming!" I handed my tray of food to one of the warriors who'd joined us, and dashed over.

The crowd parted for me, desperation lining every face.

Lord Stavel's face had taken on a distinct blue hue. Though I probably should have been more worried about killing him, I found I was not. He was a lord, someone who probably groveled at the dark king's feet to better his standing. I didn't have a lot of sympathy for him.

"What's wrong with him?" I asked, falling to my knees. "Are you sure he's dead?"

"Not yet, but look how blue he is!" a servant cried in panic, probably drawing more attention.

Well, we had wanted a distraction. I only hoped everyone else was watching us and not Henri, Alran, and Jax.

"He choked on something!" another person yelled, fear riddling their voice.

Would something happen to these people if they were around when a lord died? Would they be held account-able somehow? I hadn't considered such a thing before, but the idea had merit.

Dammit.

I eased up on my power, allowing the lord to draw a shallow breath, then pointed.

"He's not dying! Perhaps he overexerted himself." I looked around and beckoned four servants, because we'd need as many to carry this huge fae. "You should take him to a healer."

The crowd paused, seemingly shocked before someone flew into motion when I allowed the lord to take another breath, this one deeper and more obvious. The urge to help cascaded and the four I'd singled out did as they were told, hefting the fae with effort. As I'd hoped, others went with them, clearing the way.

Everyone else watched them go, gossip running through the cavernous room, but I turned toward my friends.

Henri was watching me and gave a nod. The fae they'd accosted was nowhere in sight. I suspected that Alran, who was now climbing the stairs with Jax right behind, had deposited the fae safely at the bottom of the steps. He'd be better hidden there than in this cavernous foyer.

Time to move. I went to gather my tray.

"Follow me," Henri said when I joined the group. "I know where to go."

A chill went up my spine. I liked it when he sounded like that, all authoritative and hot.

With our trays still in hand, we rushed through the palace. News of Lord Stavel's predicament had obviously spread, because more servants had arrived and now whispered in corners.

Thankfully, no one cared about the group of robed holy fae who tiptoed toward a decorative corridor that screamed *royal quarters.*

"This one." Henri pointed to a statue of a woman with three faces, six eyes burning red as rubies. "She'll be at the end, on the right."

He led the way down the corridor, but when we reached the door that would open to Elise, he paused and looked to Halad. "Riverland fae should be at the front. There might be ladies and guards inside. The rest at the sides. Be ready for anything, hands on weapons, but not visible."

Halad nodded his acceptance of Henri's strategy. I, however, withered as Calia and two others did as he said, positioning themselves in front of me. "But I want to see her first."

"Of course," Henri said softly, "but what if your aunt is in there too? It is Elise's wedding day. Sela's presence would not be so odd. If she is there, you can use the benefit of being hidden to strike before Sela realizes she's in danger."

He was right, and I hadn't glamoured any of us yet. I wasn't sure how long I could simultaneously maintain this many illusions and was saving my strength for the escape. Or for whenever we really needed it.

"I get it." I shuffled to the back of our formation, heart pounding hard in my chest.

I was about to meet my sister—well, re-meet. I didn't want to delay it for another second. "Go on."

Calia knocked, her fist heavy on the door.

"I said I'd like to be alone!" a feminine tone, commanding yet also sweet, called out from the other side. "A moment to reflect, if you will. There are wards on my door. I'm perfectly safe."

"We . . . brought sustenance."

A long pause filled the air, until it was broken by heavy footsteps on cobblestone, and a muttered, "I guess if I must be interrupted, food is a good reason."

The door opened, and a girl of fifteen stood before us, smiling. Then her smile dropped. "I didn't expect *Olizati*. My blessings have already been done."

"Of course, they have, Princess," Calia said, pushing her way inside. "We're here to give you another type of blessing."

"And food," I added, and felt like a total idiot.

I had not seen my sister in over a decade, and that was the first thing I'd said!? I wished I'd kept my lips shut.

"Oh, alright. I suppose so," Elise relented, but didn't sound convinced. "Come in."

The rest of us filed in, and I tried not to look at her, tried not to spill my guts until the door closed. The second it did, I could wait no longer.

I turned to my sister, throwing the hood off my robe. "Elise, it's me, your sister Alice. We're here to save you."

Taking a step forward, I neared her. In truth, I longed to hug her, but refrained. We were rushing a reunion as it was, and I didn't want to freak her out.

Showing I was right to be somewhat reserved, Elise took a step back, clasping her hands in front of her loosely.

She looked so innocent, her light brown hair curled

loosely, a pale blue robe tied around her thin waist. She looked more like a princess than I'd ever be.

"Pardon me?" she replied.

"I'm Alice, your sister. We're here to—"

"I heard you," Elise interrupted, light brown eyebrows knitting together. "But there's been a mistake. I don't require saving."

CHAPTER 29

My lips parted in surprise and, for reasons I couldn't explain, I looked to the others, even the soldiers I didn't know well for answers. They appeared shocked by the turn of events too so I locked eyes with my sister again. "Are you saying that you don't want to be saved?"

The sister I'd thought about daily since learning that she existed inched her hand toward the doorknob. "I wish to marry Prince Mionis."

"Th-that can't be true," I breathed, even as her hand hit the metal handle. "Henri!"

Earth magic shot out of him. The metal inside the lock clicked violently into place, shutting us inside with a damsel who, it turned out, was not in distress and did not want our help in the slightest.

That pissed me off.

"Do you know what we risked to come here, Elise?

How many died for me to get to you?" Somehow, my tone remained level, the volume natural, even though I was seconds from exploding.

"That has nothing to do with me," Elise retorted, her thin arms crossed over her chest, and green eyes narrowed.

Our coloring was different, but in that moment, she looked so much like me when I was being stubborn.

She really didn't want us here. Unthinkingly, I extrapolated that she didn't want *me*.

"How so?" Hatter asked Elise when I didn't reply. "Saving you was our aim."

"And that has everything to do with Alice," Elise replied, her eyes on me. "Our aunt told me you had a bit of a savior complex, sister. Now I believe it."

"Our—She—You believe *her*!?" I roared, unable to hold it back. "I'll tell you right now that she's a horrible person. Vile. Violent. A murderer."

"From what I've heard, those words can apply to you as well." She said this, but her tone was softer, like she didn't quite want to injure me.

But she did.

I staggered back and ran into a soldier from the Snowcap Court, my heart stopping as the fae bolstered me. What was happening? She couldn't be like this, could she?

Halad stepped forward, stopping me from losing my head entirely. "Might I introduce myself?"

"No need," Elise said. "I know who you are, Prince Halad Vapos of Riverlands Court."

The prince's eyes widened. "I must admit, I'm shocked you know that. We're—"

"Under the impression everyone here is an idiot?" Elise snapped. "Well, we're not. *I'm* not. And a few others make it their business to know what is occurring in other kingdoms."

"If you know what happened in Wonderland, how can you support Sela?" I barked.

"I don't support her, Alice!" Elise shouted so loudly, I hoped her rooms were soundproofed. It was already a miracle that we'd caught her in here alone, without her ladies or maids, but if they heard her, they'd certainly come running.

"I do know what she's done, though," she added, gentler this time. "How else would I get revenge?"

I drew in a long breath. Okay, now *that* was a solid point on which we could stand.

"I want revenge on her too," I said. "She was sentenced to death by a jury in the Wonderland Court. But what I don't get is why you trust her opinion of me."

"It's all I have to go on." Elise shrugged thin shoulders. "You and I are sisters, but I've been here a long time. I've made connections. Acquired loved ones that I cannot leave. You're a stranger to me, Alice."

It felt like someone had punched me in the stomach, and suddenly, tears filled my eyes. "I—I didn't mean to leave you here. I didn't know. Didn't remember." I studied my sister. "But you did. No one gave you the mercy of erasing your past, did they? No trauma made you forget it? You've been here all along, with a monster of a king and his horrible son."

"Do not speak of Prince Mionis that way," Elise snarled. "His father is cruel and horrible, but my prince is not the same. He was merely brought up in the image of his father and cannot fight it. King Icul is too powerful. No one stands up to him."

She swallowed, as if forcing down a deep, painful emotion. "But I love Prince Mionis, and I will not leave him here."

So, that was it. Somehow, my sister had truly fallen in love with the Prince of the Dark Court, and she would not leave him behind.

As someone who had once been left behind and used as a pawn by our aunt, I could understand her resolve. But the fact remained that we needed to get her out. Needed to leave. Too many lives depended on our rapid escape.

"Then we'll take him too," I blurted. "If he really is who you say, Prince Mionis can seek refuge in Wonderland. But please, Elise, join us. I can't leave you here again."

My sister looked me over in a way that made me think she knew that I, alone among the fae, could lie. Thanks to Doru, I retained that ability for a few more days.

But I wasn't lying to her, I *wouldn't*.

"Are you serious?" she asked. "You'd take him, even if

it meant endangering your court? You'd take him, even though no one will trust him? Do you know what he is?"

"I don't," I admitted. "But if he means so much to you, then yes. He will come. But we have to hurry."

"What of Sela?" Elise asked. "You didn't just come here to save me, I'm sure. She must have wounded you by escaping as she did."

She spoke the truth. And a part of me had hoped to run into my aunt once we got Elise, but now that I had my sister, I could forgo that. I wanted everyone out of this hellhole of a court and safe. Sela could be dealt with later—preferably, on ground I controlled.

"If I see her, she'll get what's coming to her," I finally replied. "If I don't, she lives another day. Until then, we retrieve your prince and escape."

"And the farmers," Henri added.

"Farmers?" Elise asked.

"Your sister made a deal with farmers from this court. They told us where the castle was and got us inside, and in exchange, she promised we'd whisk them out of here." Henri smiled. "It's only a family of three, a small number to help, but it's what we can manage."

A tear streaked down Elise's cheek as her gaze came back to me. "You did that?"

"I did," I said. "I would save more, but . . ." I pulled the illumination crystal from where it was tucked safely in my pocket. "We only have two of these to get us through the Rift. They emit light that staves off the darkness. Jax," I gestured to the wizard because, besides Halad, she had not gotten introductions, "is a wizard and the only other person, so far, who can use one too. So, we're limited in the number of people we can take."

Elise stared down at the stone. "I wondered how you'd gotten in. That was clever, sister, but now that we're here, I have another way."

My eyes widened. "You do?"

"King Icul travels the Rift. Of course, he is possessed, but I am not and I have gone too."

She shuddered. "He thought it would make me feel safe, to know that such protection surrounded me. In reality, it only drove home how much of a monster he is. But during our travels in the Rift, I was untouched. No light assisted us. No possession marred us."

"How?!" I gaped.

"You saw the dragons?" Elise asked, though in a tone that hinted she already knew the answer.

I nodded grimly. "They're on the other side of the Rift."

"Attacking a whole swarm of our kind!" Dee shouted from inside my cloak. "That's not right!"

The girls had been so quiet, I'd almost forgotten they rode with me.

Elise eyed me, confusion plain in the feminine purse of her lips. I opened my cloak to reveal the pixie sisters tucked in the deep inner pockets.

Exposed, they soared out, wings humming in the otherwise silent room.

"Oh, Alice! She looks like you!" Dum cooed.

"Twins! Like us!" Dee held out her fist, and Dum bumped it.

Elise's eyes widened, but she must have decided to pretend the twins didn't have the worst timing in the world, because she turned back to me. "Once we get to Mionis, his dragon won't be on the other side of the Rift for long. We can escape on the beast."

"I . . . I don't get it," I admitted.

"There are two dragons and they travel the Rift without issue. They are born of the power my intended wields which is the same as the Rift."

She cleared her throat, as if about to impart delicate knowledge. "Mionis, you see, is not full fae. He is part demon, and the Rift is born of a darkness that does not belong in this world."

"How is this possible?" Halad whispered.

Demons did not live in Faerie. They could never cross over. So that meant . . .

"The king went to the human world and mated with a demon?" I asked.

"Not just the human world," Elise admitted. "Hell. Mionis is a son of the Furies. He was born in Hell, then brought here. From his blood, the Rift was created, as well as all the darkness you see in this land." She swallowed as she revealed this secret. One that had baffled fae for a long time. One that directly implicated a male she loved.

"No one out there knows that," Halad said, astonished. "There are many theories as to how the Rift came to be, but they're just that—theories."

"Well, this is the truth. However, it was done against Mionis' will. I swear to the old gods that my prince is *good*. That he wants to end his father. That—"

"If you trust him, then I do too," I interjected. "But this is no time to explain. We have to find your prince, have him call his dragon, and leave."

"Very well." Elise looked down at the silk robe she wore. "I must change."

"Do that," I nodded. "Do you have a cloak? Or a plainer robe, like the ones we wear?"

"I have a dark navy cloak."

"Put that on. I'll glamour your face."

Elise looked taken aback. "You can do that?"

"You probably can too. Right, Henri?"

"Both of your parents could use aether," he affirmed. "It's almost a certainty that you can."

"I've not been taught," Elise mused. "Fine. You may do that, but keep my eyes the same. Mionis will need some way to recognize me. He does not trust easily."

"You know best. Now change," I urged her. "We'll wait."

My sister scurried off behind a screen, and quickly, the luxurious robe she wore when she answered the door was flung over the top. Seconds later, the sound of fabric rustling came.

"Not a dress . . ." I heard her mutter. "That won't do . . ."

"Pants," I hissed. "If you have them."

"Don't be ridiculous! This court might be backward, but some things are just sensible. I wear them for riding around the city."

Even after all that I'd learned, it shocked me that she knew how to ride. Though Elise was a prisoner here, she had been treated well. I wondered how much of that was down to Mionis going to bat for her.

The Furies are his mothers . . .

Revulsion sparked inside me. I'd seen the triple goddess at the Battle of Spellcasters. The Furies were rumored to be separate but also the same. They were demonesses of such extreme beauty that they could have whomever they wanted.

They were also exactly as horrible as one would expect Princesses of Hell to be, and they'd survived the demon war and were still on the loose in the human world.

Would they seek a way to enter Faerie? This court, at least, would grant them entry and a place to hide. They had a child here, after all.

I hoped it wasn't a huge mistake to trust Mionis, but I had to believe Elise would know it was okay to do so. Plus, as someone who'd spent many years as an assassin, I knew firsthand that sometimes all someone needed was a chance to prove they were good.

The prince wouldn't get that chance here. I didn't know his father well, but I could guess that much. So, he'd come with us and get it. When his father retaliated, because surely he would, Mionis could show the world what he really wanted. If Elise loved him I had to believe that what Mionis desired wasn't the nightmare landscape his father had created.

"How's this?" Elise rounded the dressing screen.

She wore dark, loose pants and a tunic that looked well-made. Probably a bit too well-made, but I highly doubted that my princess sister had rags she could throw on.

"The cloak?" I asked.

"Oh right." Elise reached behind the screen and grabbed the dark navy garment.

"That will do. Put it on and come here."

She did as I said and came to stand before me. I studied her face, still astonished that, though her hair was darker and her eyes were green, we looked almost like twins. If we were the same age, the similarities would be even more pronounced.

"Close your eyes," I murmured.

Her eyelids shuttered closed, and I got to work, tweaking the shape of her mouth, the fullness of her lashes, and, at Dum's insistence, adding more oomph to her cheeks to make them plumper. I changed Elise's hair, too, darkening it to black, but, as she requested, kept her eyes green. I also changed the shade of her robe to better match ours.

She'd stand out, but only if someone looked closely enough.

"Done," I said.

Elise went to her mirror and gasped. "You're good."

"I am. Now let's go. Show us to the prince, and then we leave."

"If he can call the dragon to where the farmers drop off produce, outside the kitchen, that would be best," Hatter added.

"Great idea," I said. That way, we wouldn't have to fly around on what was probably a vicious dragon, to get to the family who'd helped us.

"He can do that," Elise assured us and went to her door. "Unlock this, please."

Henri released his earth magic, and I secured the pixies in my pockets before our group slipped out of the room.

Elise led the way through the palace. It seemed like an awfully long way to our destination, but I guessed that the king thought it prudent to keep his son away from the princess. Maybe he cared about preserving her virtue.

As we went, we stopped occasionally to offer the trays of food to the servants, usually at the behest of the princess. They lapped it up, and I hoped the charity would keep them from looking at us too deeply. Sela might have spies in this court, and if she did, they'd surely know what I looked like.

Finally, Elise turned a corner. "He's in this wing, at the end."

We rushed down the hall, and she stopped before a door.

"No guards?" I asked warily.

"Mionis needs none," she said, knocking on the door. "He has powers that others here can only dream of."

Footsteps sounded on the other side, and the door opened. A male fae appeared, as tall as Henri but not as thick in the chest and arms. He had blond curls that resembled the Furies' tresses, and dark eyes tinged with red.

Yes, there was no doubt that this prince was part demon, and of the Furies particularly. He radiated seduction, and though he was doing nothing to attract a person, a sensual nature rolled off of him.

How his lineage had been kept secret for so long was the only shock.

"My love, it's me," my sister whispered.

"Elise?" The prince stepped back, clearly recognizing her, but confused. "What's wrong with your face?"

Wrong!? I took offense to that. She still looked good, and my glamour was top-notch, if I did say so myself.

"I'm glamoured," Elise told him. "Let us in. I'll explain."

He looked unsure, but opened the door anyway. We all rushed inside.

To say that the prince's rooms surprised me was an understatement. Elise's chambers had been grand, but these were plain. Understated. Dimly lit, and spare.

"What's going on?" he asked. "Who are these people?"

Elise pointed to me. "That one is my sister, Queen Alice of Wonderland."

I wanted to correct her, to say that I had not accepted the crown, but she said it with such pride that I found I couldn't. Plus, I had to admit that, for the first time, I didn't hate the title.

"She's here to save me," Elise continued. "*Us.* We're leaving today, Mionis. You'll no longer be under your father's thumb. Call your dragon, we can leave together!"

His mouth fell open. "You're sure? You trust her? Them?"

"I do," Elise said firmly, eyes meeting mine for the briefest of seconds before locking with the prince's again. "This is our chance. Perhaps the only one we'll ever get."

Mionis stared at my sister, his gaze so intent I was sure he'd refuse. But then he nodded, the gesture tight, riddled with tension.

The prince eyed me then. "You and Elise look very much alike."

"I know." I stood steady under his gaze.

What he saw in me must have convinced him, because he said, "If I call Urzwar, my father will know. He's connected to the other dragon and can see through its eyes. He might attack my dragon with his own."

I swallowed. "Then we'll have to be fast. Are you coming?"

In answer, he closed his eyes. When he opened them again, he stared at me once more. "It's done. Urzwar, my loyal companion, is on his way. Unfortunately, my father will be alerted within seconds. Whether he will call his dragon from the battle across the Rift, I cannot say. Father is watching the progress of the fight."

That wasn't creepy at all.

"Tell the dragon to meet you where the farmers distribute food to the kitchens," I said, trying to keep my head in the game. "Also tell him not to harm anyone if he gets there first. We have people coming with us who we owe a favor to."

He closed his eyes again, briefly. "Urzwar knows. He will be here in minutes."

"Then grab a cloak. We need to run for it."

CHAPTER 30

s we hurried through Shadowveil Castle, Jax and
I positioned ourselves at the front of the group,
just behind Elise, who led the way to make
sure we took the fastest route.

As a thin cover, many in our group still held trays of
food. Not Jax and I, though. He used his free hands to
cast various spells that would dissuade those we passed
from paying attention, or urge them to look the other way.
I was less careful, using my power to rip air from some
fae's lungs, knocking them out.

We were leaving a trail, but we had to weigh the bene-
fits of being discreet with getting the hell out of there. We
had minutes, maybe seconds before an army would be
upon us. And maybe even the king's dragon.

With the original plan, that amount of time wouldn't
have been enough. Now, though, I had hope. We only

had to get to Mionis' dragon, not run through the city and cross the Rift.

"This way," Elise hissed, as Jax nearly skidded past the hallway she'd turned down.

Stairs came next, and someone behind us cursed as plates shattered. They'd dropped their tray.

"Leave it," I said loudly. "Jax, a little help!"

He twisted, taking aim with his hand. "*Vanesca.*"

"Whoa!" Halad called out as the mess disappeared. "Neat trick."

Wizarding magic *was* handy. Especially when the witch or wizard in question knew the correct spell by heart.

"Makes cleaning up after parties a breeze," Jax quipped as we reached the bottom of the stairs.

"If only you could have done the same with the people," Hatter muttered.

No one liked that we were leaving unconscious fae in our wake, but it was what it was. We had more important things to worry about, and as Elise led us into the same cavernous lobby where I'd attacked Lord Stavel, our urgency multiplied.

The Red Queen stood in the center of the vast space, smirking self-righteously, a battalion of red-eyed soldiers —Shadows—at her back. Behind her was the stairwell leading to the kitchen.

We were so close, but our streak of luck had finally run out.

"So, you made it here, Alice. I'd ask how, but I find

that I don't really care." She flicked an invisible piece of lint off her shoulder, as if to emphasize her lack of emotion. "I do care, however, that you're trying to abduct my ally's son. He's busy trying to wrangle a dragon into submission, so I promised I'd take care of you."

She snapped her fingers. "Seize them."

"Elise! Get behind me!" I wasn't sure my sister had been trained in any sort of battle tactics. From the terrified look on her face, I was guessing no.

She did as I said, leaping behind me.

"Jax, demon spells! Halad, aether!"

The others would be able to use their elements against the Shadows, but witchy magic and aether seemed by far the most effective.

"On it!" the Riverlands' prince yelled, and as if we'd planned it, aether blasted simultaneously from Halad and me, bowling over a handful of Sela's soldiers.

"*Nex*," Jax shouted, again and again, taking aim at one Shadow after the other.

Each one fell down dead, but it wasn't enough. My aunt had gathered at least three dozen soldiers, and even with aether and witching spells flowing from my group like water from a burst dam, the guards kept coming, the distance between us narrowing.

Though I couldn't see her behind them, Sela White laughed, the sound cruel.

"There are more where that came from, niece!" She clapped her hands, and smoke billowed from above.

I gaped as a dozen more Shadows materialized, falling upon us from out of nowhere.

What sort of magic was this?!

"Does she have a demon stone?" I asked. It was the only thing that made sense.

Demon stones were gifts from royal demons that bestowed dark magic on the recipient of the stone. As demons did not exist in Faerie, they weren't usually used in this realm. Then again, I had to remember the Dark Court wasn't like any other court. Did demons live here? Were they trying to cross over as the royal demons recently had into the human world? Or was it just demonic power that could exist in this realm?

"Let me handle this." Mionis stepped to the front of the group, and suddenly, inky black smoke formed around me. It billowed forward, plowing through the Shadows, obscuring my vision.

"What are you—"

I didn't even get to finish my sentence before the smoke vanished, leaving behind a sea of dead soldiers.

"Whoa," I whispered.

My aunt stood beyond them, a white light glowing around her. An aether shield that the prince's power could apparently not penetrate.

Mionis exhaled, and only then did I get a good look at him. His face was wan, pale.

"Are you okay, my love?" Elise asked. "Is it too much?"

"Fine. Yes, using my power . . . it drains me."

That much was obvious.

"Could you do it again?" I pressed. Elise might worry but I was not blinded by love and we needed to get the hell out of this place.

My aunt was staring at us with murder in her eyes. I suspected we had only seconds before another attack came.

The prince grimaced. "Not like that."

"Can you use the smoke to trap her, then?" Halad asked. "She made a shield, so she knows what it is and she's wary. But we need to get to that stairwell behind her."

"Brilliant!" I exclaimed. "I knew there was a reason we brought you."

Halad snorted, but didn't retort, his eyes firmly on the Prince of the Dark Court.

"I think I can manage that," Mionis said finally.

"It's the only way," Elise urged. "Now that your father knows we're trying to leave, we cannot stay. He'll kill me."

My throat closed up. *Over my dead body.*

Mionis was clearly on the same train of thought, because smoke poured from him again.

My aunt hadn't brought down her shield, perhaps anticipating such an attack. Sure enough, at sight of the smoke, the barrier pulsed, strengthening.

This is going to work, I assured myself. It had to.

The smoke curled and licked at the shield, covering the outside of it completely, and once Sela was firmly ensconced, we ran for it.

Servants had been watching from the sidelines, terrified but also intrigued. Now that we were on the move, they scurried away, not wanting to be anywhere near Sela White when she broke free. When she found that we were gone.

Our group had reached the stairs, when Mionis stumbled. Henri caught him before the prince could faceplant on the stone ground.

"Help," Hatter grunted. "He's heavier than he looks."

The prince wasn't a small guy, so to me, he already looked pretty freaking heavy.

Alran stepped forward and assisted Hatter. "He's passed out."

"He has lots of raw magic, but doesn't have a lot of stamina when using his powers," Elise explained. Then she gasped and pointed. "Look."

The gas around the aether shield protecting my aunt was already disappearing. Mionis' attack would be short-lived.

I groaned, then yelled, "Run!"

We raced down the stairs and through the corridor that led to the kitchens, but before we got to the end of the passage, a roar of fury left the Red Queen.

"Jabberwocky!" she bellowed, and my stomach cratered.

She was calling her creature. If Mionis' dragon showed up, we might have an easier time escaping, but what if Mionis' dragon wouldn't cooperate without the prince issuing commands? He was passed the hell out. What if the dragon thought we had done that?

"Hurry!" I pressed, my own arms and legs pumping. "And can someone wake the prince up? We need him to talk to the dragon."

Henri began murmuring to Mionis. I couldn't hear his words over the sounds of my own steps, but knowing Hatter, it was the right thing to say.

The door to the kitchen had just come into sight, when a blaze of fire shot right over my head. The Red Queen was right behind us.

"She's coming!" one of the soldiers at the back of the group shouted. "We'll distract her!"

I wanted to say no, that I didn't want anyone else dying for us. We were so close, there was no need.

But then another wall of flame shot our way, the heat on my back unmistakable. I heard the sizzle of water, thrown by one of our soldiers, as it hit the fire, dousing it, but not before a shout of pain wrenched out of Calia.

Jax twisted, his eyes wide, and for a moment, I thought he'd turn around and go after her. Thankfully, he wasn't an idiot, and instead hurled a spell back at the Red Queen.

"Nice one!" Calia yelled, confirming she was alive.

"Deflected, though," another soldier reported. "She —*arrrrgh!*"

I craned my neck around in time to see flames devouring three soldiers from behind. Tears pricked my eyes, but there was nothing to be done. The fire my aunt wielded was unnaturally strong, blue and hot. My allies' bodies were already ash, and we were mere steps away from the kitchen door.

I burst through, Jax right behind me, and the rest followed. The fae within seemed to have known we were coming, as a few held up knives in defense. The older one in charge of the kitchen used her earth magic to shoot a metal pan at us. I deflected it, snarling.

"You lied!" she screamed. "He'll kill us all for this!"

My mouth dried up, but the next instant, my sympathy dimmed as she hurled a knife at me and it impaled my shoulder.

I screamed, ripped it out, and flung it to the ground before grabbing my arm to stanch the bleeding.

What the hell?! I had not dodged my aunt's attacks just to be taken down by this woman.

Apparently, Henri felt the same, because he hurled the fae's metal pan back at her. The skillet hit her in the face, and she fell.

The remaining kitchen fae cowered, and we made it the rest of the way through without incident, rushing through the door to the outside.

Daga, Latzi, and Theg were still waiting for us, the wagon half-emptied of fruit. When they caught my eye, saw the terror there, Latzi's hands went to her mouth.

She pulled them away the next instant to shoo her son. "Into the wagon!"

"No time!" I shouted. "We're using a dragon!"

"*What?!*" Daga looked at me like I had lost my mind in the Rift.

"A dragon, Prince Mionis'—Oh no . . ."

The jabberwocky soared over the castle wall, into the courtyard, talons extended as it approached the family's backs.

"Watch out!" I screamed, pointing and hissing as my shoulder screamed out in pain.

Daga and Latzi turned. The latter pushed Theg to the ground, but in that act, she didn't have time to save herself before the jabberwocky snatched her and her husband up.

Screams filled the air. Theg's. Latzi's. Daga's. The monster roared, as if laughing, and soared ever higher.

I knew what was going to happen seconds before it did, so when the dragon released them, I was ready. Falling back on my most natural element, air burst from my palms.

If I could get it under them, I could cushion their fall, save them.

But then a wall of aether flung up from my aunt, who still pursued us, blocking my air magic.

Behind us, Sela laughed, and everyone watched in horror as the pair went *splat* on the cobbles. Blood instantly pooled around their broken forms, sending waves of fury through me.

"Papa! Mama!" Theg screamed.

The boy ran toward them, but they were gone, and I wasn't about to let him go the same way—or see his parents in such a state, smashed on the ground like they were nothing.

"Someone get him!" I commanded.

Calia ran forward, grabbing the boy, who kicked and screamed and cried.

"Alice! Let us out!" a faint voice hit my ears.

It took a second for me to recognize it as coming from the pixies. Who knew how long they'd been screaming for me.

I opened my robe, and they flew out, looking disheveled but fine.

"We can help!" Dum shouted.

"How?"

Anxiety was building inside me. The jabberwocky was circling back, my aunt apparently having called the creature.

Really, it was a miracle that she hadn't attacked us yet. Or maybe she was relishing in her most recent kill; both seemed like viable options.

We weren't prepared, anyway. Mionis was out cold, and Calia was wrestling the small fae boy into submission. We needed fighters, and what could the twins do against a jabberwocky and an aether-blessed fae set on murdering us all?

"The prince!" Dum replied once she'd oriented herself to the courtyard. "We can wake him!"

Okay, now I was confused, but as several apples lifted from the cart into the air, I knew we were also out of time. My aunt had caught up to us.

As if to confirm, the fruit soared our way at the speed of bullets.

"Henri!" I yelled.

Alran took all of Mionis' weight, and together, Henri and I used earth and aether power to fight back the fruit. It flew farther away, dropping harmlessly to the ground.

"Our venom!" Dum shouted, as if she still needed to explain herself. "It can kill, but it can also wake in the right doses. Like adrenaline—it can do both!"

"What are you waiting for?! Do it."

Mionis might be pissed I let the pixies bite him, but we needed him awake when his dragon showed up. I simply could not take the chance that Urzwar wouldn't recognize us as friends. And battling two dragons? Yeah, no way.

One was plenty for now. I needed to focus on Sela and the jabberwocky, because this might be my last chance to deliver the justice the Wonderland Court had dispensed. Justice the Red Queen had evaded.

Once, I let her live. But today, it was either my aunt or me—and I'd beaten her before. I'd do so again.

The pixies went to work on Mionis, as the jabberwocky made its second approach. Fire blazed in its mouth, and Jax threw up an overhead shield to protect us all, seconds before it laughed and expelled its load.

Even with the shield, the heat was dangerous. If Jax had been a weaker wizard, we'd be toast. As it was, we were sweating bullets when the beast finished and soared away.

The jabberwocky landed next to my aunt, consequently kicking up dust from the ground into her face.

It was now or never. Blocking out the pain of my injury, I pivoted to focus on my powers. Aether spooled from me, forming a hundred daggers.

However, Sela was watching even through the dust, and her smile only grew as the daggers got closer. With a wave of her hand, she dispensed her own aether power, and the weapons fell to the ground, harmless.

My jaw clenched. "So, what? We're going to keep parrying back and forth? We're both aether-blessed, Sela. Both strong."

"One of us is stronger," the Red Queen replied, and suddenly, she was levitating over the jabberwocky, then seated on it. "And one of us knows how best to use her magic."

She kicked the beast's sides, and it soared high above. My stomach plummeted to my knees as the creature glared down at us, its prey.

There was only one thing to do. Fly up to it, fight it in the air. Separate myself from the others to keep them out of the jabberwocky's reach.

"Everyone, take cover," I shouted, but my voice was drowned out by a roar.

Though this time, it wasn't from the jabberwocky. Another dragon, black as night and with glowing red eyes, flew over the castle walls, spewing fire from its mouth.

I couldn't see Sela's face, but from the way the jabberwocky veered, she had to be terrified. To be honest, I was too. The jabberwocky was no pet, but the black dragon looked far more dangerous, more *demonic*. Like it wouldn't think twice about killing everyone in the city.

I prayed this was Urzwar and not King Icul's dragon.

Somewhere behind me, Theg screamed in terror.

"Dee! Dum! How's Mionis?" I shouted, watching the dragon's progress. By the old gods, he looked *piiiiiiiissed* as he soared our way.

"He's waking up!" Dee replied. "One more bite shoul—oh!"

"Oooowwww!"

I spun and exhaled all the breath in my lungs. Mionis had awoken.

Elise was there beside him, reassuring him. And while that was all nice and dandy, we had bigger issues to deal with than royal confusion.

"Mionis! That had better be your dragon!" I waved frantically to get his attention. "Tell him we're not harming you!"

The prince's eyes widened and latched onto his dragon. He stood, straightening, and threw up a hand. "Urzwar! They're with me."

Thank the old gods! It *was* his.

Though I was no expert on dragon expressions, I swore Urzwar's shifted. His narrowed eyes grew less slanted. The number of teeth he showed lessened, and he slowed a bit as he got closer to landing.

"Thank the aether," Calia whispered, and pressed a trembling Theg into her side.

The boy wasn't even looking at the dragon anymore. He had his face buried in the fae soldier's armor.

I swallowed. I was determined to save this kid, but damn would he be screwed up after this.

"Everyone, on his back," Mionis instructed, as Urzwar landed and knelt.

No one moved. I wasn't sure that anyone besides Mionis and Elise had ever ridden a dragon.

Finally, the couple took the initiative, moving toward Urzwar, who lowered his head helpfully. Once there, Mionis turned and held out a hand. "The boy will ride behind me, in front of Elise."

My eyes narrowed, but before I could say anything, Mionis added, "He's one of my court. I must protect him."

Fine.

His logic was fair. I'd have done the same. Plus, the jabberwocky had come closer again, and I needed to buy the others time.

"Go," I told them. "Get on. You all came here for me, for my sister. But now I have work to do. Alone."

Jax looked at me, the set of his jaw told me that he was clearly about to argue, but I shook my head. "You can't fly. Plus, the others need you. And the stone."

Mionis said we'd be able to cross the Rift on the back of his dragon, but I wasn't so sure about that yet. Nor was I sure about the prince who gave me the willies. I trusted him, but only to a point. The illuminator gem was insurance that I clung to.

"But I can fly," Henri spoke up. "I'll go with you."

I'd really rather him not. More than anything, I did not want to see Hatter harmed. If I didn't live through this, Wonderland needed him. Their once-rebel leader would slip into the role of Kingdom Councilor with ease, and he'd help the island flourish.

But there was a glint in his eyes that told me it was pointless to argue, so I didn't.

"We'll tag team the jabberwocky," I said. "I need to kill my aunt before we leave."

"No argument there," Hatter nodded. "We'll help in flight," Mionis said.

"Stay safe. That's your priority." With that, I shrugged off my cloak and launched into the air.

Gripping my dagger in one hand, I kept the other free so I could use my magic. Below, the others scurried over to the dragon. They grew smaller and smaller, only Henri staying his normal size, as he thrust skyward too.

The moment we leveled with the jabberwocky, my aunt shook her head.

"You, girl, are either incredibly brave or incredibly stupid. To take a dragon on in flight?"

Instead of doing the banal back and forth that my villainous aunt so loved, I attacked with my aether.

Her face was priceless, outraged and shocked, her mouth falling open almost comically. As if she couldn't believe that I'd *dared*. But didn't she see that she'd talked enough? That I was done with her nonsense? That Faerie was done with her?

The jabberwocky turned so my assault struck it in the side, and Henri took his shot, sending a stream of water to surge up its nose.

The jabberwocky bucked, nearly throwing my aunt from its back. Unsurprisingly, that pissed her off, and once she regained her balance, she conjured a stream of aether arrows and sent them racing toward me.

I dipped, leaving Henri unguarded.

Worst mistake of my life.

He too avoided the arrows—but not the sword my aunt threw at him. The blade ran through the right side of his chest, and all my air left me as my love screamed out in pain.

"Henri!" For a moment, I lost all drive to kill my aunt. How could I spare her a single thought when he was there? When he was injured? All I could think about was saving Henri.

"Focus Alice!" Jax bellowed, and the intensity in his voice broke my climbing anxiety for long enough to get through to me.

I spun in time to see Urzwar, loaded down with my team, surging up beneath me. Wings flapping, I soared to the side, and the black dragon caught Henri before he could fall further.

"Move, Al!" Jax screamed. "Get your aunt! We've got him!"

Alran secured Hatter, and I watched in shock and awe as Mionis' dragon snapped at the jabberwocky, which had foolishly taken the opportunity to attack. The timing was not to the jabberwocky's advantage and Urzwar's teeth sank into flesh. The creature my aunt was so bonded to bucked and let out a roar that could probably be heard on the other side of the Rift.

Sela clung on for dear life, unable to control the beast, and sure that Henri was safe, I seized the moment.

I soared higher, barely noticing the pain in my shoulder from where the knife cut in. As quickly as possible, I positioned myself above the jabberwocky still writhing in pain. Somehow, Sela had stayed on its back, so I dropped and landed right behind her.

"It's over, Sela," I growled.

She turned, clearly not having felt me land. Her eyes narrowed, and her lips parted, a snide remark surely on the tip of her tongue.

Before she could voice it, I became Alice the Dagger one last time and drew my blade across her throat, shutting her up forever.

Blood poured. The life drained from her before my eyes.

I launched into the air, away from the jabberwocky, and watched as Sela White slipped off of her beast's back and fell to the courtyard below.

CHAPTER 31

I veered away from Urzwar as he angled for yet another chomp of faltering jabberwocky. He got it, too, his teeth sinking into the thing's stomach.

I saw the moment the beast slipped across the veil, its eyes dimming. It fell to the ground seconds later, its massive body landing right on top of my aunt.

I exhaled. *It's finally over.*

"Al!" Jax yelled. "We gotta run! Mionis says his dad called his dragon. We have to get to the Rift. He says no one over here will follow us through it!"

It was tempting to laugh. Who knew the Rift and a dragon would be what saved our butts?

I flew over to my friends. Once Alran scooted back a bit, I settled onto Urzwar, right behind Henri.

"He's alive," the elf assured me. "The sword missed anything vital."

"Thank you," I said, wrapping my arm around the

male brave enough to take on an aether-blessed fae and a jabberwocky with me. With his body pressed against me, it dulled the pain in my shoulder a bit. The moment we were safe, I'd have to get it looked at. But for now, compartmentalization would have to do. Luckily, I'd been trained to tune out minor injuries for long periods of time. The moment I was sure I had Henri safely in place, I grabbed the illumination stone from my pocket.

Mionis caught the gesture. "You won't need that."

"Just in case."

The prince shrugged and patted the side of Urzwar's head. "Fly, across the Rift."

"Wait!" I cried out, and the Dark Court prince stopped the dragon before it could surge forward. "What if the war is still brewing?"

Mionis smiled, and though he was on my side, allegedly, the sight was slightly terrifying.

This male was . . . eerie, even if he wasn't trying to be. I wasn't sure I'd ever entirely get used to him

"Then we'll settle the score," he growled. "I owe it to many to right the wrongs of my father. Will you allow it, Queen Alice?"

I swallowed, and everyone on the back of the dragon stilled, awaiting my answer.

This felt weighted, like I really was taking on a responsibility that I'd been shirking.

One that I'd grown more comfortable with by the day.

One that I suddenly realized I wanted.

After all my doubts, my denials, my insistence that I was to return to the human world and live normally there —albeit on my own terms— I found that wasn't what I wanted. Not at all.

I wanted *this*: Adventure. Family. Love. The ability to help others.

To bring glory to my family's court and name.

All of that, including a new legacy for the White family, would begin today. It would start by bringing home the lost Princess Elise, and helping to weaken the Dark Court.

"Only attack the Shadows," I said to Mionis. "Try not to harm anyone else."

He grinned. "I'm one of the two fae in this realm uniquely suited to that task. Now hold on."

We took off like a shot, and I clung hard to Henri as we soared over the Dark Court.

For the first time, I was able to glimpse the city. In a way, I wished that I hadn't. Below was a place of grime. Of desperation. Of sadness and poverty.

I swallowed, glad that I was liberating Elise from here, but sorry for those left behind. I hoped that King Icul, wherever the hell he was, wouldn't take his fury out on his citizens when he learned his son and royal prisoner were gone.

The Rift drew closer, and though it was hard not to think about the devastation below, I wrenched my focus to the foreboding curtain of blackness we were about to enter. Urzwar flapped his wings, seemingly unfazed. The prince looked similarly unaffected.

Why, though? How could the prince be so sure that we'd be fine?

Before more doubts could plague me, we pierced the darkness and, once again, the Rift swallowed me whole.

My breath ceased to come as I waited for the horrors within to crash over us, to take us from this life. For an unseen monster to rip us off Urzwar, one by one.

But it never happened. The dragon simply raced forward, his large body undulating beneath me, his torso heaving with the effort it took to fly as fast as the wind.

How long had we been here? Ten seconds? Thirty? Two minutes? How fast was the dragon flying? Certainly faster than any of us ever could. His powerful wings beat at the air, and there was no fear in his movement. No hesitation.

And then, as suddenly as we'd entered the Rift, we burst out of it.

Light flooded my vision, and I covered my eyes with the hand holding the crystal, crying out in pain.

"By the aether . . . Look!" Alran shouted, and though I didn't feel ready to, I opened my eyes.

In the hours we'd been gone, the battle continued to rage. Shadows swarmed. Their forces had diminished by half, but still, the dark side had prevailed. They had beaten our side back, away from the Rift, all the way down the steep hill we'd climbed to reach the flat grassland.

Though we were far too high above the killing grounds, I swore I could smell blood on the air. Dead fae lay everywhere.

Sansu's death came back to mind, and a lump rose in my throat. *No more.* We had to stop this.

"Mionis!" I yelled over the howling wind. "What are you going to do? There are so many!"

"And they've put your forces at a disadvantage." The prince studied the landscape. "Just like they were taught to do. Good."

Good?!

Was I about to be proven right? Should we never have brought him?

"Urzwar, light them up," Mionis commanded.

"Light them up!? What are you talking about?!" I screamed and lunged, only to be stopped by hands holding me back.

For one terrifying moment, I was sure that Mionis meant our side. But when the dragon swerved and dipped toward the line of Shadows aiming arrows and balls of fire at our army, safe down the hill, I exhaled.

I'd misjudged.

Below me, the dragon rumbled, and warmth radiated from its body. Everyone except Mionis and Elise looked at each other, alarmed.

"Hold on!" the prince warned from the front.

The dragon dove, and a scream ripped from my throat before I could pull it back, hide it. What if the Shadows attacked us? Was that possible?

I worried about that until the dragon loosed his first blast of flame. It was red-hot, mixed with black swirls.

I gasped. That was not normal fire. It was not even enchanted fae fire, but something far darker.

Not one single Shadow even saw it coming. The blaze struck, and then they were all burning before our eyes. Each possessed fae turned into ash, and the army fell as Urzwar made one pass, then two, then a third. On the fourth, no enemies remained.

Mionis twisted and caught my eye. "Should we land?"

I took a breath, my first full one in far too long. "Yes. We have to search for the injured and gather our dead."

"You'll have to explain my presence."

"I've done far more difficult things. But just one thing before we descend." I held up a finger to the prince and sought my ex. "Jax!"

I caught the wizard's eye. "What's up, Al?"

"Do you have that potion on you? The one you tried to bribe me with?"

He snorted. "Like it was hard. Of course, I do."

"Do me a favor and . . ." I nodded to the ground.

His amber eyes widened. "You sure?"

Before I'd been terrified that without the potion that allowed me to lie, others would learn what I'd done and hate me for it. Perhaps they still would, but after what we'd been through, I found that I no longer wanted to hide myself—the good and the bad—any longer. I was who I was. I'd made my mistakes, but I'd also changed. People would either accept that, or not.

"I don't need it," I assured him.

Jax fished the vial from his pocket and with one last glance at me tossed it into the air. The glass glinted and soon, I couldn't see it any longer. The potion I'd been so desperate for was gone.

"I'm ready now," I said to Mionis.

"Hold on tight." The prince grinned and urged his dragon downward. As we descended, my hand landed on the back of Hatter's head. He was still passed out. When he woke, it would be to a world turned on its head.

We'd done it. We'd retrieved my sister and passed through the Rift—*twice!*—and defeated an army of Shadows.

However, the cost had been high.

Looking upon the dead, regret swelled inside me. I had so much to make up for. I would, in time. But for now, it was time to heal and rebuild.

CHAPTER 32

Three days after escaping the Dark Court, I strode down the corridors of Heart Castle, which would soon officially be renamed White Rose Palace. I just had to sign a couple of documents.

Later.

Though I had not laid eyes on them yet, the voices coming from the meeting room down the corridor were loud. My friends had gathered and wasted no time waiting for me; they were already discussing what we could do next to make Wonderland better.

When I turned the corner, I found that I truly was the last one to arrive. Like the gentleman he was, Henri tried to stand when I entered, but he still wasn't fully healed from his injury, so I motioned for him to stay seated.

"Sorry," I told those assembled. "Chester popped in to give me a few updates about the island."

I'd had my Cheshire Cat working since we returned

home. As he was bound to the island, he hadn't been able to help in the battle, but now he was spreading the word of a new reign far and wide, and taking accounts from our subjects, seeing what they wanted and needed to live their best lives.

"I have a list." I held up a page filled with requests and details of the lives of fae in Wonderland.

"Then we should get to it," Henri replied, a soft smile on his lips.

The meeting began in earnest, starting with smaller, but no less important, matters of the villages. Funds and resources were distributed to those who had seen little help in the past years.

Once that was done, we shifted to the task of compensating those who had lost family members in the Battle of the Rift. There were many, and it would take much more time to bring home all the bodies of the fallen, but we were doing what we could.

Queen Aquatia, Prince Halad, and those of the Riverlands Court were helping too. They brought the injured and dead back home. Their healers cared for those who couldn't be moved right away. I was lucky to count the Riverlands as allies, and they considered themselves lucky that their border lands were safe.

At least, for now.

"Prince Mionis, how are you finding your new home?" I asked, moving along to the final item on the agenda.

The Prince of the Dark Court sat next to my sister,

their fingers entwined, as they usually were. Though I still hadn't gotten used to his creepy appearance, I had to admit they were cute together. And it was plain that he made Elise happy.

"It's lovely. There's so much color," he said, as if he could barely believe it. Considering where he was from, I supposed he couldn't. Almost nothing about the Dark Court was colorful. "Are we prepared to speak of my father?"

"Hell yes," Jax replied.

The wizard had been dying to talk about the Dark Court for days, but there had been other things to deal with first. It wasn't like a kingdom that had been in isolation for years was going to come out of it in a few days and attack. Particularly not when they'd lost many of their forces.

"As I said before, my father knows the Furies." He looked sheepish at the understatement, but no one pushed him on it. It wasn't like he had any power in who had birthed him. "They gifted my father power, nearly as much as I was born with." Mionis released my sister and leaned forward, ready to lay it all out for us.

"He controls his dragon, which was probably on its way through the Rift to find us when we arrived on the other side—or he might have no longer been able to control his beast by that point. It fought for a long time, and that takes much of my father's energy."

He pursed his lips thoughtfully. "I expect that is why he didn't show his face when we encountered your aunt.

He also controls the Shadows, through use of a very powerful demon stone."

"Those are vile," Jax shuddered.

"Yeah," I nodded.

It had recently been revealed in the human world just how pervasive those stones were and how many people were in league with the royal demons.

"They are," the prince agreed. "But I'm sort of a living demon stone. One with a mind of its own that, hopefully, is not entirely evil. A Prince of Hell and Faerie."

Elise took his hand, assuring him that though we all had concerns over demon stones, we did not put him in the same camp as objects. Even if he was part demon, Mionis had a will of his own.

"When do you think your father will be able to replenish his army?" I asked. "Does he have to control them at all times?"

Would the King of the Dark Court always sit behind walls of death? Or would he fight, too, one day?

"I cannot say how long it will take," Mionis replied. "But you would do best to prepare Wonderland, the Riverlands, and the Snowcap Court as quickly as possible. The war is not over. And yes, he controls the Shadows. Maintaining control of an army of them is more difficult. He'll be exhausted for days, maybe weeks after that battle. But if he only wants to puppeteer one Shadow, he can see through its eyes."

I shuddered, wondering if, at any point when I'd looked upon a Shadow, I'd been staring at the king.

"I'm sorry I cannot give you more," Mionis said softly.

It was true, that wasn't the precise answer I'd hoped for, but it was along the lines of what I'd expected. King Icul was not a peaceful man. He hadn't been for years, and now we'd riled him, stolen his heir.

While Faerie had always been dangerous, now the King of the Dark Court would be out for blood.

"It's okay. This is new to everyone," I assured him. "And your input is helpful, even if there is uncertainty."

Elise gave me a grateful smile, and I smoothly pivoted the topic away from King Icul.

Instead, we discussed other topics, like how to introduce Mionis to the greater population, how to best prepare for an attack, and how to warn those in the human realm about what was happening.

Jax had volunteered for the last job, and though he wasn't a fae subject of mine, I gave it to him. The position suited him, and I trusted him with it. Our relationship had healed.

Finally, we had covered everything on our agenda. I was about to call the meeting to an end, when Henri turned to me.

"There's only one more thing."

"Oh? What's that?" I cocked my head.

"The matter of your coronation. That is what you wish for now, isn't it, Alice?"

I sucked in a breath. This had been the topic on my mind for days—no, *weeks*. Before, I'd been adamantly against taking the crown, but since the Battle of the Rift, I'd changed my stance.

So many had fought for me, died for me. Many had done the same for my aunt, but that had been against their will. I wanted to make up for her cruelty, to show them that the White family could truly give them a better life.

Even with a probable war on the horizon.

Actually, *especially* with that. I'd fight to keep the violence away from my shores.

And then there was the matter of leaving the ones I loved, if I did not accept my position. After all these years, Elise and I were learning about one another. The pixies had grown into sisters of mine, too. Alran was like a brother, and Henri . . .

Henri was unlike any man I'd ever known. One I'd never be able to find again in a million years. I loved him, and I could not leave him.

Nor my title, my responsibilities, my birthright.

"I accept the Crown of Wonderland," I declared.

The pixies burst into tears, and I couldn't help but chuckle.

"Schedule the ceremony for as soon as possible," I added. "I wish to take the crown and begin making this kingdom wondrous once more."

CHAPTER 33

My chest tightened as I walked down the teal carpet bisecting the throne room of the White Rose Palace. Crowds of fae, from my kingdom and others, lined the runner. Every eye was on me and for once I found that I didn't mind in the slightest.

The citizens of Wonderland had all been invited, no matter who they were or what they did for a living, and as I'd instructed, the door did not close behind me.

If someone showed up late, that was fine. This was not to be a private affair. Not an event just for nobles. It was for *everyone*, and the faces in the crowd reflected the varied walks of life.

The audience we had assembled made me proud, and as I beamed at those I walked past, I thought they might feel the same. Each and every person was smiling at me. Though some cried too.

Today was my coronation day. Today, I took my place among the fae for good.

It was a lot to absorb, but after everything I'd been through, I was ready.

Before, I'd equated becoming queen with giving up my freedom—which I'd never had to begin with. I thought that others would hold my past against me, that they'd never be able to see beyond it because I had a difficult time doing so. Now, I knew better.

I'd still be beholden to others, just as they would be to me, but my connection to this land and these fae made a difference. Even the ones I didn't know very well yet, like Mionis. If he could live with his past and upbringing, then I could deal with what I'd been dealt too.

Finally, I got to the end of the aisle. I glanced to the right, and my sister, Mionis, Hatter, and some of my friends were there, grinning at me. My heart swelled and, unable to help myself, I threw them a wave, before climbing the three steps up to Isadora.

At the top, my surrogate mother held my crown in shaking hands. The piece was stunning, crafted of gold, with three points in the front, pinnacled with diamonds the size of my pinkie nail. Aqua stones lined the base, and a large gold rose stared back at me from the center.

It wasn't something to wear on the daily, but I couldn't wait to get that thing on my head.

"Princess Alice," Isadora whispered. "Are you ready?"

"I am."

She nodded, and I knelt.

Some had claimed that Isadora, a rebel and a merchant, wasn't fit to perform a coronation. I'd retorted that they were idiots.

I didn't want some holy fae, who I didn't even know, crowning me. It needed to come from someone I loved, someone of the people. By those criteria, Isadora was the obvious choice.

She moved closer now, eyes shining with tears as she looked down at me. On this level, I was a foot shorter than her.

"Today, we gather to witness Princess Alice White swear her duty to the Kingdom of Wonderland and take the crown."

The crowd cheered, and more than a few people broke out into sobs.

"Princess Alice, do you swear to always uphold the laws of the Wonderland Court?"

"By the aether, the old gods, and this land we love, I do," I spoke the traditional fae reply.

"Do you promise to protect our borders?"

"By the aether, the old gods, and this land we love, I do."

"And do you swear to care for its subjects and rule justly, fairly, and with compassion in your heart?"

That line made me wonder if my aunt had ever taken this vow. It was more likely she had slipped the crown on her own head and proclaimed her right to lead. Either way, she hadn't cared at all for those she ruled. I would be different.

"By the aether, the old gods, and this land we love, I do."

Isadora swallowed thickly. "Then by the power of the people, I now pronounce you Queen Alice White of the Wonderland Court."

The crown settled on my head, heavy, but also natural. A weight I'd been fated to bear.

"Rise," the brownie instructed.

I stood, but bent once more at the knee, and held out my arms. Isadora folded into them, her tears unstoppable.

After we broke apart, I turned to the crowd. "I'll do my best to make you proud and prosperous. To secure alliances and friendships across all of Faerie. And to protect you when enemies knock at our door."

Those gathered clapped and cheered. In the crowd, Henri, Elise, and Mionis smiled up at me. Alran, Jax, Calia, Halad, and Queen Aquatia were on the left bank, also beaming my way.

Each of them looked so proud. It felt amazing to have this sort of support. Friends and family that I could really count on.

Wait . . . where are the girls?

A moment later, I spotted them. The pixies fluttered near the back, among a swarm of their race that had traveled from the Riverlands. The same pixies who'd battled at the Rift with us. By some miracle, most of the swarm had survived.

The twins waved, and though I couldn't be sure,

because they were so far away, I'd bet my crown that Dum was wailing her heart out and Dee was trying to hide her tears.

I held up a hand for silence, and the chamber hushed. "Now that the official ceremony is over, what do you all say we have a party?"

On cue, castle guards opened the side doors to reveal a feast in the next room. The scents of fruits and other delectable sweets wafted in and filled the throne room.

"Well, what are you waiting for?" I locked eyes with a trio of children who looked about ready to soar over the heads of everyone else to dig into some cake. "Go celebrate!"

With more cheering and laughter, rivers of fae surged toward the refreshments. Isadora squeezed my hand and went to join them, so I stood in place alone, accepting congratulations and well wishes.

When the throne room was mostly empty, only those I loved the most stared back at me. The pixies. My sister and her betrothed. Hatter.

Alran, Jax, and Calia had moved into the party space. I twisted and caught sight of them already by the refreshment tables, laughing. My heart swelled at seeing them looking so carefree, Jax's arm around Calia's waist, and Alran grinning widely.

Halad and his mother were not far from them. Their own guards stood back, giving them space, as the royals conversed with subjects of my kingdom. Halad, of course, was fending off female fae at every turn.

"What a day, huh?" Dee's voice was pinched, as if she were holding back emotion.

"Totally," I agreed.

"Alice," Dum soared up, smiling through the track lines of tears on her face. "Dee and I have something to tell you."

"What's that?" I asked.

"We met males! Handsome ones, who think we're the best thing since aether!"

I laughed. These two were as boy-crazy as it came. "That's great. Where are they?"

"In the swarm from the Riverlands," Dum replied. "But if it works out, they'll move here. They like the island, and they fought for our side. Will you meet them later?"

"Of course!"

I spotted the pixie swarm and the two males hovering apart from the group, watching us. They looked worried, tense.

I snorted. "I'll need to thank them for helping, but for now, maybe you should get them a drink so they loosen up?"

Dee cast a glance that way. "Oh boy. Let's go, Dum. Congratulations, Alice! You're going to be the best queen!"

Dum kissed my cheek, and with that, the sisters were off to join the party.

As the twins neared the male pixies, the faces of the latter lit up, and the couples hugged.

No kissing yet, but maybe later . . .

"Alice?"

My sister's voice brought me back to the trio standing before me.

I gave her a smile. "What's up?"

She blinked, and I recalled that she'd never stepped foot in the human world, so some of my sayings and terms were odd to her. Apparently, this was one of them.

"Well, Mionis and I . . ." Elise's cheeks flooded with color. "We're engaged."

My lips curled up slightly. "Weren't you already?"

"Yes," the prince admitted, "but that was by my father's order. This time, I proposed of my own will. Last night, in fact."

"We didn't want to tell you before the coronation," my sister rushed to explain. "You had so much to do, but I couldn't wait any longer!"

She was only fifteen, nearly sixteen, but here, that was not unusual. I was the odd one out in thinking that she should wait to make such a commitment.

"Are you in a hurry to wed?" I asked, unable to stop myself.

"No, we want to take our time with this," Elisa said. "A year at least. Have a second chance to decide our own future. Do we have your blessing?"

Oh, right. As queen, I'd be expected to bestow blessings upon those who sought them.

So weird to have that control over someone else's life.

"Of course," I said, because while I didn't know the

prince well, Elise did. She trusted him. Loved him. If he proved to be unworthy, *then* my sister and I would talk, but for now, who was I to stand in the way of love? "Mionis, I'll be happy to welcome you into our family."

He broke into a grin that made his face look almost normal in its joy. Elise turned, kissing him on the cheek, and the pale prince colored.

"You two should go celebrate," I added, pointing to the party already in full swing. "I'll be right there."

Mionis bowed, and Elise curtsied, then they did as I asked, leaving me alone with Hatter.

Finally.

I took his hands. "Hi."

He smiled. "Your Majesty."

Then he closed the narrow gap between us, taking his lips in mine. Inside my shoes, my toes curled. We had an audience, so the kiss was chaste, but full of simmering heat. I took it as a promise of more to come later.

"Your sister and Mionis beat me to a proposal. Are you upset by that?" Henri studied my face.

"Not at all," I said truthfully. "I've just gotten Elise back and become queen. There's a lot to do and learn. I love you, but I'm in no rush to be married."

"I completely understand." Henri pulled me closer, his hands landing an inch above my rear. "Just know, it's in my thoughts."

"You'd be stupid to let this queen get away." I winked, "And you're not stupid."

He laughed. "Glad you think so."

"What do you say we join everyone?" I asked. "If you whisk me away, rumors will start."

"Is that a bad thing?"

It was my turn to laugh. "Not really, but since I'm staying, we have all the time in the world to start rumors."

"Thank the aether for that," Hatter teased, turning toward the party.

Smiling and walking hand in hand, we went to celebrate with the fae of Wonderland.

Also by Ashley McLeo

<u>Coven of Shadows and Secrets</u>

Seeker of Secrets

Hunted by Darkness

History of Witches

Marked by Fate

<u>Spellcasters Spy Academy Series (Magic of Arcana Universe)</u>

A Legacy Witch: Year One

A Marked Witch: Internship

A Rebel Witch: Year Two

A Crucible Witch: Year Three

The Complete Spellcasters Spy Academy Boxset

<u>The Wonderland Court Series (Magic of Arcana Universe)</u>

Alice the Dagger

Alice the Torch

<u>Standalone Novels </u>(Magic of Arcana Universe)

Stealing Maid Marian's Heart

The Alchemist of Silver Hollow

<u>Fanged Fae Series - A Bonegates sister series</u>

Blood Moon Magic

Faerie Blood

The Bonegate Series - A Fanged Fae sister series

Hawk Witch

Assassin Witch

Traitor Witch

Illuminator Witch

The Royal Quest Series

Dragon Prince

Dragon Magic

Dragon Mate

Dragon Betrayal

Dragon Crown

Dragon War

The Starseed Universe

Prophecy of Three

Souls of Three

Rising of Three

A LEGACY WITCH, SPELLCASTERS SPY ACADEMY SERIES

e're not in L.A. anymore, Toto," I said as Maine's summer greenery whipped by the window.

"No, honey, we're not." Mom's tone was quieter than normal. "Are you having second thoughts?"

"No." Irritation that I normally didn't feel toward my parents flared at the question. We'd been over this at least thirty times. "I don't understand why you're so against me going to Spellcasters. You always said I could be whatever I wanted. Do you think I can't hack it?"

Dad grasped Mom's hand as his gaze caught mine in the rearview mirror, his hazel eyes understanding. "We're just worried, little pea. And believe me, we *know* you can do anything you put your mind to. Would we have flown across the country, driven from New York to Maine, *and* stayed overnight in Portland to drop you off on orientation day if we thought otherwise?" Hesitation flickered across his face, which was just beginning to show lines that came with age. "It's just that becoming a spy isn't easy. Even if you can use magic."

"And working in Hollywood is a cakewalk?"

"By comparison, yes," Mom replied. "And *much* safer. Besides, you love theater. You know we can help get you started. As a dancer you'd be a double threat."

"Honey . . ." Dad squeezed Mom's hand, and she shook her head, resigned.

I rolled my eyes, and we fell into silence.

I didn't have the desire to argue that following in their footsteps was a good thing. Sure, working in Hollywood would have been glamorous and fun, but espionage had always interested me more. The choices made by Spellcasters graduates rippled out into the rest of the world on a large scale. Even if I was never known publicly for it, making a positive difference meant a lot to me.

I'd always thought it mattered to my parents, too. They'd attended Spellcasters, spied for the U.S. government, and even patronized the academy after they quit espionage. It was because of their history that I'd expected them to laud my choice.

Their resistance to my enrollment was baffling and frustrating in equal measure.

Unfortunately for my parents, I was eighteen and an academy legacy. I didn't need their permission. Spellcasters had accepted me the moment I'd written the headmistress and expressed interest. There had been no stopping me after that. Dad recognized my drive, but Mom was still holding out.

The terrain beneath the wheels changed dramatically, and my suitcases rattled in the trunk. I glanced out the window. Smooth pavement was still flashing by even though it felt like we were traveling down a dirt road. My eyebrows furrowed.

"That's the signal. We're almost there." Mom twisted her long, brown hair and laid it over her shoulder—an anxious tic.

"They haven't changed the first marker after all these years," Dad noted with a shake of his head.

Mom snorted. "They *will* change it. And soon."

I was about to ask what she meant, when a sign came into view that sent chills up my spine. I could just make out the words.

'Saint Albert's Academy for High-Risk Boys and Girls.'

My heart rate sped up, and I pressed my nose against the glass in anticipation.

Barbed wire flashed by in the spaces between trees. It looked menacing, and from what I'd read about Spellcasters before I applied, the precautions were even more dangerous than they appeared. The fences would not only keep out curious humans, but fae and demons trying to sneak in from Faerie or Hell.

Spellcasters was one of the most secure places I'd ever seen. That was saying something, considering my parents had warded every nook and cranny of our Beverly Hills home.

Dad slowed the car to a crawl as we neared the sign. He whispered a word under his breath, and the silver prophetess seal of Spellcasters split and the academy gates opened. A shimmering blue cloud engulfed the car, seeped in through the closed windows, and caressed my skin. A laugh tipped my tongue. It tickled.

Then, just as suddenly as it materialized, the cloud disappeared.

I was about to ask my parents what the magic had been detecting, but something else caught my attention first. The letters on the sign had begun to rearrange themselves, morphing into new words. My heart thumped hard when the letters stopped.

'*Spellcasters Spy Academy.*'

I held my breath as we drove through the gates, barely able to contain my excitement.

Woodlands dominated the grounds, although I was sure I'd spotted a lake and a golf course peeking through the dense trees. As the drive narrowed, long branches started to bow inward, creating the effect of a stunning green tunnel.

My legs shook as if I'd just chugged three espressos. When the trees broke, and the school emerged, I squealed out loud.

"It's like a mix of Neuschwanstein and Westminster Abbey," I whispered.

The white facade and green-topped towers mimicked the German fairytale castle, while the stained-glass windows above massive front doors, and gargoyles resting at various intervals on ledges and windowsills reminded me of the famed abbey.

Dad laughed for the first time since we'd left Portland, Maine. "I suppose it is. In my day, we coined it 'Gothic-cheery,' but your description is more precise." He shot Mom a smile she didn't return.

Dad parked in front of the double doors, which looked like they belonged on an old Spanish cathedral. I shot out of the car and straightened my dress and the long leather jacket that gave me the perfect spy-in-training air. Spellcasters would eventually provide me with a job after graduation and I wanted to look the part. Plus, what if I met my spouse here, like Mom and Dad had found each other? First impressions were important, I didn't want to mess this one up.

I took a big breath of piney air, soaking in the fresh scents of summer.

"Where do we go?" I asked once I felt grounded.

"Someone will be here in just a second." Mom waved her hand.

"How do you know? Did you call ahead?"

"They always send someone, pea," Dad said, his tone more gentle than Mom's.

As if on cue, the doors burst open, and a tall, thin woman about my mom's age strode outside. Her chocolate brown hair was pulled back in a heavy bun that coiled at her nape. She was smiling, a tight, thin affair that didn't reach her appraising eyes.

"Pris Wake!" I blinked as the corners of Mom's

mouth quirked upward for the first time in hours. "This is a surprise. Usually, they send a junior spymaster, not the headmistress."

Wake. I knew that name. I had studied her lineage after receiving an acceptance letter bearing her signature. She was a descendant of a famed spy from World War II —Nancy Wake, also known as the White Mouse, one of the Gestapo's top five most-wanted Allied spies.

A thrill ran through me. This woman could teach me a thing or two about changing the world for the better.

"It's not every day our most esteemed donors drop off their only daughter." Headmistress Wake's eyes drifted from Mom to me and looked me up and down. "Odette Dane, I presume?"

My hand shot out. "Yes. It's nice to meet you, Headmistress Wake. I've heard a lot about you and your escapades."

She cocked a pencil-thin eyebrow.

"The ones that are public," I amended, not wanting her to assume my parents had shared secrets about her spy days. That would have broken protocol, and my parents *so* did not do that. They never even talked about *their* spy days, or why they had quit. Probably because they didn't believe I could live up to their reputations.

I planned on proving them wrong.

"I suppose there are a few of those," the headmistress said and turned back to my parents. "Will you be staying a while? As benefactors, I'd love to lunch with you in my chambers."

"We're not leaving Odette until we have to, right after the orientation dinner."

Mom had been so dour on the ride upstate, but now her tone was light as she gazed wistfully at the academy grounds. It seemed that, although she hadn't wanted me to come here, returning to her alma mater was lifting her spirits.

"Wonderful." Headmistress Wake glanced at her watch. "My daughter should arrive at any minute."

Once again, the front doors to the school flung open. A statuesque, attractive girl appeared and made her way over to us. Her pin-straight, blonde hair was so thick and heavy that it barely moved against her shoulders as she walked.

It's like they time these things.

The girl stopped to stand next to the headmistress.

"Odette Dane, this is my daughter Diana Wake. You're both first years—or as we call your class at Spellcasters, initiates. If you're amenable to parting with your parents, she'll show you to your rooms."

"Hi! And totally!" I beamed at the girl who returned my exuberance with a tight smile similar to her mother's. "Should I grab my bags?"

The headmistress shook her head. "Just what you'll want right away. The rest will arrive shortly."

I snapped up my backpack and waved at my parents. Mom's face fell, the bit of joy that had made an appearance since arriving on the school grounds, gone in a second.

"See you at the orientation dinner." I turned around quickly so I didn't have to dwell on Mom's anxiety.

She'll be fine. She's just nervous about her baby girl leaving home and playing with the big boys. Once I start killing it in classes, she won't worry so much.

With those reassurances in mind, I followed Diana into the hallowed halls of Spellcasters Spy Academy.

Read more in **A Legacy Witch**, Spellcasters Spy Academy book one. Also available in audiobook format.

About the Author

Ashley lives in Portland with her husband, Kurt, their dog, Flicka, and the house ghost that sometimes makes appearances in her charming, old home.

When she's not writing urban fantasy and portal fantasy novels she enjoys traveling the world, reading, kicking butt at board games (she recommends Splendor and Dominion), and frequenting taquerias.

For all the latest releases and updates, subscribe to Ashley's newsletter, The Coven, today. You can also find her Facebook group, Ashley's Reader Coven.